FIGHT BACK

Anna Smith was a journalist for over twenty years and is a former chief reporter for the *Daily Record* in Glasgow. She has covered wars across the world as well as major investigations and news stories from Dunblane to Kosovo to 9/11. Anna spends her time between Lanarkshire and Dingle in the west of Ireland, as well as in Spain to escape the British weather.

Also by Anna Smith

The Dead Won't Sleep
To Tell The Truth
Screams in the Dark
Betrayed
A Cold Killing
Rough Cut
Kill Me Twice
Death Trap
The Hit
Blood Feud
Fight Back

FIGHT BACK

ANNA SMITH

Quercus

First published in Great Britain in 2019 by Quercus

This paperback edition published in 2019 by

Quercus Editions Ltd
Carmelite House
50 Victoria Embankment
London EC4Y 0DZ

An Hachette UK company

A CIP catalogue record for this book is available from the British Library

PB ISBN 978 1 78747 392 8

10 9 8 7 6 5 4 3 2 1

Typeset by Jouve (UK), Milton Keynes

Printed and bound in Great Britain by Clays Ltd, Elcograf S.p.A.

For Katrina – for all that you are.

'The stars shine only in darkness'

PROLOGUE

They had heard nothing since John O'Driscoll went missing six weeks before. It could only mean one thing. And every day that passed with no news made Kerry's heart sink further. Maybe she shouldn't have sent him to Spain to oversee everything after the attempted robbery. Even though she knew it was pointless to blame herself, it troubled her that perhaps she could have done things differently. But Kerry Casey was the head of the Casey family now. There was no going back. From the moment she took revenge for the murder of her brother, Mickey, and the slaying of her mother at his funeral, her life hadn't been the same. This was who she was now, dealing with the scum of the earth, people she would have crossed the road to avoid just a few months ago. And if that wasn't enough, she was sitting on a three-million-pound stash of cocaine that every gangster from Glasgow to Dublin was trying take from her. It was well hidden, but the Caseys hadn't even been able to move it on because right now it was too dangerous. Drugs were a filthy, stinking business, and she'd promised herself that she'd be out of them from the day she took over the family. She was one deal away from the start of her dream to make her gangland empire legit. One deal. And none of the hyenas waiting for the Caseys to keel over and die were going to stop her.

She'd jumped on a plane and come to the Costa del Sol, where Sharon Potter – who'd become her partner in crime – had been holding the fort for the last few weeks after the attempted break-in at the apartments where the coke was hidden. There were two men down already and the body count was rising. Sharon had been the last person to speak to O'Driscoll before he was taken.

'You're looking very pale, Kerry,' Sharon said as Kerry slumped onto the chair. 'Are you all right?'

'Yeah,' Kerry nodded wearily. She put her hands behind her head and sat back. 'Just tired.'

Kerry had been throwing up most of the morning but wasn't about to admit that. This was no time to be weak.

She could hear approaching footsteps on the marble floor from the hall, and looked as the door opened. She was glad to see her uncle Danny and Jack Reilly, and especially glad to see Jake Cahill among the group of men who entered. They all looked grim as they filed in and sat around the table. Danny came across before he sat and gave her a hug.

'So what do we know?' Kerry asked. 'Anything new?'

Danny looked at one of the other men, a wiry little guy with a shaven head.

'Paul?' he said to him. 'You fill us in. You've been here longer.'

Paul cleared his throat and sat forward.

'Okay. Word on the ground is that the Irish fucker, Durkin, is even more heavily involved with the Colombians than we thought. But he's not getting much of a say and is being shoved around like Pepe Rodriguez's bitch. That Colombian bastard is the main man down here, part of the cartel from back in his home, as you know. He's just steamrolling his way through other dealers and set-ups. I don't know if people are making deals with him, or standing back, or just shit scared. But he's getting everything all his own way. He's bringing stuff in and he wants to be the only guy anyone deals with all over the place. I mean that's never going to happen, as there are plenty of big shots who won't buy it. But he's an evil bastard. The stories about him in Colombia are legend.'

Kerry and the others listened.

'So there have been no phone calls?' she asked. 'Nothing to tell us what they want – if it's them who've got O'Driscoll? That's unusual, is it not?'

'A bit,' Danny said. 'I thought we'd have heard by now.'

'Okay. Should I contact him or Durkin or Billy Hill?'

'We should maybe think about it. O'Driscoll would have got in touch by now if he could.'

The room fell silent. Kerry knew they had to move on for the moment. She turned to Sharon, who had been tight lipped and looked tired. The last time she'd seen her was as she was leaving with her son Tony to spend the next few months in Spain to run the construction of the massive hotel complex.

'How are things with the plans?' Kerry asked.

'Well, that's one thing that's moving in the right direction,' Sharon said, fiddling with a pen and some papers. 'The lawyer here is getting good vibes from the town hall down in Marbella. We should be able to start work in the next few weeks.'

'Good. Well that's something,' Kerry said.

Everyone looked up when there was a gentle knock on the door. Jack got up, crossed the room and opened the door.

'*Señor*, there is a man at the gate with a delivery. He say it is for Miss Casey. Should I send him away?'

They all looked at each other. Danny and two of their henchmen stood up.

'What the fuck is this?' Danny said. 'Only a handful of people even know where we are, and most of them are around this table.' He turned to the man at the door. 'Is there a car? A delivery?'

'Is in a taxi. Only the taxi driver.'

Danny, Jake Cahill and Jack moved towards the door.

'We'll go and check this out, Kerry,' Jack said. 'It might

be some kind of trap. We've got guards outside all over the place. But I don't like the sound of this.'

Kerry nodded and looked at Sharon. She felt nauseated. She shouldn't be this sick with stress, but it had been hanging on her for days.

They came back to the room, carrying a large box wrapped in plastic.

'We talked to the taxi driver, but he said it was delivered to his office in another taxi,' Jack said. 'He didn't know who sent it. It's quite heavy.'

'What if it's a bomb?' Kerry said. 'I'm not sure we should open it. Can we get someone in?'

'Christ! I don't know who,' Danny said.

'It won't be a bomb,' Cahill said, gingerly turning the box a few times. 'Or if it is, then it's a crude-looking effort.' He crossed the room and clicked open his black attaché case as the others looked on. Then he clipped together some kind of gadget and brought it back to the table. 'This will detect if there are any explosives in the package,' he said. He pushed a button and scanned the box. The gauge didn't flash or make any warning noise. 'It's not a bomb.'

'Will we open it?' Jack asked.

'Yes. Go ahead.'

Jack took out a penknife and carefully took the plastic wrapping apart. Underneath, there was bubble wrap and then a heavy cardboard box, dark blue in colour.

'What is it?'

Jack shrugged as he slid his knife under and prised the lid open a little. He gave one more tug, and they all stepped back when the lid came off. The stench nearly knocked them off their feet. Kerry was on the verge of throwing up again, even before her eyes fell on the contents of the blue box. She covered her mouth and nose and peered inside, gasping as the recognition dawned on her. It was the bloodied face of John O'Driscoll. There were fleshy, gaping holes where his eyes had been torn out. But it was definitely him.

CHAPTER ONE

Kerry had woken up in a sweat from a fearsome nightmare where she could hear the agonised screams of O'Driscoll as they gouged out his eyes. She'd been crying, and even when she drifted back to sleep the nightmare chased her, until she finally got out of bed at six a.m., a wave of nausea making her bolt to the bathroom, where she promptly threw up. Christ! This was the third day running she'd been sick. For a fleeting, terrifying moment, it occurred to her that she might be pregnant. No way. Don't even go there, she told herself, pushing away the image of DI Vinny Burns as she stepped into the shower. She had to get ready to meet Danny and her crew here to work out their next move.

They hadn't called in the police yesterday when O'Driscoll's head had been delivered in a box. The grisly message had Rodriguez's fingerprints all over it, and the last thing they wanted to do was call in the Spanish cops. Even though some of Kerry's people on the ground here had good contacts inside the Guardia Civil, it was best to keep the police out of it. Executing O'Driscoll in the way that Rodriguez had was like marking his territory, that this was what was facing the Caseys if they took him on. Kerry was sure he didn't think they would come after him. But he was wrong. O'Driscoll had been family to her. People like him and Danny and Jack were all she had now.

Danny came into the room first and Kerry could tell by the look on his face that he had more bad news. She motioned everyone to the terrace and they stepped out of the wide patio doors and sat around the huge glass-top table. The old Spanish lady who had worked in the house for a generation came out with orange juice in jugs and the smell of percolating coffee filled the air from the kitchen. In another life, this would have been a pleasant morning, where the assembled friends could be planning a round of golf. But that was another world. Danny reached across for a jug of orange and poured the juice into glasses, passing them across to people. He sighed and shook his head.

Kerry looked at Danny and glanced at the others as all eyes turned to him, his eyes baggy from lack of sleep. He looked as though he'd aged ten years in recent weeks.

'I don't know if any of you have seen the news this morning. But there's been a headless corpse found in a suitcase in the boot of a car at Málaga airport.'

'Christ almighty!' Kerry sank back and looked at Danny. 'What are they saying?'

'Officially, not much,' he replied. 'But I've got one of our guys to make a call. It's O'Driscoll all right. Bastards left his credit cards and wallet in his jeans so we'd be left in no doubt.'

'Jesus!' Sharon said. 'Cops will have to put that out to the media soon. A Brit butchered on the Costa, it will be all over the front pages tomorrow.'

'I know.' Kerry nodded. 'Police will be contacting his family, so we'd better get that done first. I don't want them getting a knock on the door without being prepared.' She turned to Danny. 'Danny. Have you got John's wife's phone number?'

'Ex-wife, Alice,' Danny said. 'They split about two years ago. She's a bit flaky. But they have two lovely kids – ten and thirteen. Boy and a girl. They're great kids and Johnny adored them.' He shook his head. 'Fuck! They'll be in bits, poor bastards.'

Nobody spoke for a few moments as Kerry tried to think of how the hell she was going to break this to his family.

'I'd better phone Alice. What is she likely to do?' Kerry asked. 'Will she phone the cops or what?'

Kerry hated herself for even thinking this way. She didn't want the Scottish cops involved at all and sniffing around her doorstep, but she knew it was inevitable. But she wanted to get to Alice first and make sure she kept quiet. She hated herself for that thought too.

'She's all right. I think so anyway. Part of her problem is she didn't like O'Driscoll working and keeping late hours, as he did sometimes. To be honest, with Johnny though, it wasn't all work, if you know what I mean. He liked the ladies.' Danny paused, but nobody said anything. He rubbed his face. 'Anyway, I think she'll be okay. I mean she's not going to go shooting her mouth off to the papers. We'll look after her. And the kids.' He shook his head.

Kerry was thinking she should fly home and talk to them after making the initial phone call. But there was such a lot going on here, she had to wait to see what was happening. She didn't even know the kids, but she could only imagine the desolation they would feel knowing that they would never see their father again. She'd known that agonising pain – she hadn't been much older than that when she lost her own father. When the dreadful details of O'Driscoll's murder reached the press, as it inevitably would, she would have to find a way to help them through this.

'Okay,' she said. 'I'll make the phone call to Alice once we finish up here. But let's work out how we hit back for this.' She looked at Jake Cahill who had been sitting, taking it all in, saying nothing.

The room was silent for a long moment, then Danny spoke.

'I think the quicker we hit back the better. Rodriguez can't be everywhere. We already know some of his movements from the Guardia Civil contacts who are on detail to keep tabs on him.'

'Are you saying we should hit *him*?' Sharon asked, frowning at Danny.

'No,' Danny said. 'Not a direct hit at him. But he has several places along the coast here where he does business. Bars that are basically just money-laundering places where he has one or two Colombians to run them. Hitting a couple of them would be one thing we could do. Short and sharp.'

Kerry thought about this for a moment.

'What about his drugs? Stuff he is moving in and out of the country? Can we hit them?'

'Probably a bit more difficult. But we could, once we get more intelligence. I think we should look at that too, so that we can hit him again and again.'

Kerry felt perplexed.

'But he's going to come back every time we hit him. That's for sure.'

Danny nodded, and again the table was silent.

'Well, that's how it goes, Kerry.'

Christ! The last thing she wanted was another bloodbath on her hands with innocents caught in the crossfire, the way her mother had been at Mickey's funeral.

'What about these bastards Billy Hill and Pat Durkin?' Sharon asked. 'I take it they've not been in touch yet.'

'No,' Kerry said. 'But they will be. That fat little bastard

Durkin will be standing by admiring how the Colombians do business. But I don't think Durkin has really got the stomach for getting his hands dirty. What do you think?'

'I think any message or talk that Rodriguez wants to make will now come through Durkin. Maybe he'll be sent like the lapdog he is to ask for a meeting,' Danny said. 'I'll be surprised if he isn't on the phone before the day's out, to offer his condolences.' He paused, looked at Jake Cahill. 'We could certainly take out a couple of Durkin's money-earners down here – bars and two flop-house hotels he owns in Fuengirola and one in Torremolinos. That would hurt the Irish prick – and in turn would get the message back to Rodriguez. We know they're hand in hand now.'

Jake nodded but he still didn't speak.

'Okay,' Kerry said. 'Let's look at that. We can meet back here this evening for dinner. By that time I'll have spoken to Alice. But I'm thinking I should go back to Glasgow in the next day or so. I don't want to be so far away from everything we have there to find it in ruins by the time we get back. There's enough vultures over there to think if we're getting hit, they might just steam in and get something for themselves. I don't want that to happen.'

'I've left some good men in charge, Kerry,' Danny said. 'Big Pete's running the show and he's got a few reliable guys with him. Also, those wee guys – Cal and the Kurdish guy. I think we should look at putting them to good use.'

'What do you mean?'

'Maybe they could be over here, on the ground. They're the right age to be working in bars gathering intel and stuff. Getting close to people. That's something we should look at for the future. I think they're shaping up to be good hands.'

Kerry listened. The thought of putting her lifelong friend Maria Ahern's boy Cal in the frontline sent a shiver through her, as an image of O'Driscoll's severed head flashed up. She couldn't take the chance of something happening to Cal. He was a good lad, who'd only ended up working for them because Maria had come to her destitute and in hock to loan sharks. Kerry had given Maria a job with the firm, put her and Cal in a flat the Caseys owned in Hyndland, and given him work to do on the fringes. But she hadn't thought of turning him into a serious criminal.

'Let me think about it,' she said. Then she looked around the table. 'Are there any thoughts or information on how the hell they knew where to send the delivery yesterday? I thought nobody knew we were here.'

'I just don't know for sure,' Danny looked at her. 'But I'll tell you this. I got some word on the grapevine from back home yesterday that Frankie Martin was in Spain. Nobody here has seen or heard of the cunt. But it came from a good source. Knowing that treacherous fucker, he could be worming his way in with the Colombians. He'd be useful to them with his background knowledge.'

The thought of Frankie back from the dead, trying to bring them all down after everything that was done for him as a kid, brought an angry flush to Kerry's cheeks.

'I need to know more on that, Danny. As much as you can, as quick as you can. If Frankie is out there trying to damage this family, then we take him right out of the game.'

'I'd be up for that on a personal level, since the slimy bastard was leading me to my execution by my late and less than loving husband,' Sharon piped up, almost bringing a smile to the faces of everyone around the table.

One by one they filed out of the room, until Kerry was alone. She sat gazing out at the hills to her left and the blue of the ocean in the distance. Winter was still trying its hardest on the Costa del Sol, but a watery sun was breaking through the greyness, and by midday it would be pleasant and warm even though it was January. It was so beautiful and peaceful here, she thought. The kind of perfect hideaway where she would make her base as she flitted from Glasgow to Spain, making sure she was hands-on in the new hotel and property business. Perhaps, eventually, she would even settle here, like a lot of the old hoods did once they had made their money and turned legit. She half smiled to herself at the idea of her being one of those relaxed, suntanned gangsters she used to see on the Costa del Sol, wealthy, but without any obvious means of income. She'd met many of them – associates and friends of her father – while she lived there as a teenager. She'd never really given much thought to how they all got there, rich and respected. Until over the years she listened to them tell their stories of robbery and drugs and wheeling and dealing. She had never judged them, because she knew her father had been a crook and that her family had made their money from crime. Although she had been a corporate lawyer for most of her life and far removed from how her family operated, she had always had a sneaking admiration for their philosophy that if you get dealt a shitty hand from the day you're born into poverty, then you have to go out and get what you can. Even if it wasn't all legal.

They would tell her that, at the end of the day, they were all gangsters – the lawyers who kept them out of jail, the crooked accountants who laundered their money, the politicians at local and national level who took bungs to make things happen, and worst of all the bankers. The suits who moved your money around didn't give a toss where it came from, as long as they could get their cut. Meanwhile the rest of the punters, toiling away in their nine to fives and weekend shifts, got shat upon from a great height. By everyone.

And so, many of them had come to the Costa del Sol, to capitalise on the proceeds of crime, just like her – even though her route here had been one of private schools and university degrees. She was here nonetheless, among them. And now she was planning on how the Caseys were going to hit back to avenge the execution of John O'Driscoll, one of her most trusted lieutenants. John had served and protected her father and their family since as far back as she could remember, and now he had paid for it with his life. She had to be ready for this fight.

CHAPTER TWO

Marty Kane watched his little grandson Finbar, relishing the moment. Days like this, relaxing in a café with his wife, and delighting in the chatter of the three-year-old boy were all too rare. And he'd promised himself and Elizabeth that things would be different in the future.

The most sought-after criminal defence lawyer in the country was rarely in court these days. He was winding down. The bulk of his legal firm was run by his son Joe, a chip off the old block, making a name for himself as a more than able brief. Now Marty's main work was with Kerry Casey, steering her empire out of the swamp of drugs and bloodshed, and turning it into a legitimate and enviable property kingdom here and abroad. Such was Kerry's dream, and so it had been for her father, his old friend Tim Casey, a very long time ago. But it was proving to be a difficult task. And the body count was already piling up. The news from Spain last night about Johnny O'Driscoll being executed by the Colombians had turned his stomach. Marty remembered Johnny's father, and the swashbuckling character he'd been back in the day when Tim Casey and his gang were building up a name for themselves in Glasgow and beyond. They were hard men, lawless men who carved a massive niche for themselves in the underworld. But they didn't gouge out the eyes of their enemies. It took a certain kind of pond life to do that.

'You're miles away, Marty,' Elizabeth said, picking up her handbag from the floor.

Marty shook himself back and looked at her.

'Just thinking how pleasant this is,' he lied.

Marty knew that Elizabeth could read him like a book, but he also knew she would never ask too many questions about his work.

'Sweetheart,' Elizabeth finished her coffee and placed the cup down, 'I'm nipping across there. See if the sales are up to much.' She stood up, pointing to the big designer clothes shop in the mall opposite the café. 'You stay here and keep an eye on Fin.'

'I want to go with you, Gran,' Finbar piped up from blowing bubbles with a straw into his chocolate milkshake.

'Darling,' she touched his cheek, 'you stay here with Grandad. I'll only be ten minutes.'

'Okay.' Finbar turned to Marty.

'That's my boy.' Marty ruffled his shock of blond hair as Elizabeth walked off.

They'd only been sitting a few minutes when Fin slid himself out of his seat and took his hand.

'We go to the toy shop, Grandad?'

Marty drained his coffee, left some notes on the table beside the bill, and got up. They walked two shops down, Fin eagerly pulling his hand, leading him towards the big, bright toy store.

'Look, Grandad. Zillions of toys.'

They stepped inside amid the garish balloons and toys piled high on shelves: every kind of motorised car and dolls and soft toys lining the aisles. Other children ambled up and down, some with parents, some alone. Finbar let go of Marty's hand.

'I go up here, Grandad.' He skipped off without waiting for an answer.

Marty watched as his grandson stopped at several displays, pushing buttons, lifting toys off the shelves and onto the floor and trying them out. Then he went up and around the corner into the next aisle, as Marty crossed from the bottom to where he could watch him play. Then Marty's mobile pinged with a message. Automatically, he opened it and scrolled down to read. It was from Kerry – there was more grief from Spain – O'Driscoll's headless corpse had been found in a suitcase in the boot of a car at Málaga airport. Bad news was coming thick and fast – only five days before another of their boys had been shot dead outside a bar in Fuengirola on the Costa del Sol. The papers were saying it was mistaken identity, as that's what Kerry had made sure was drip-fed to the press. He was about to text her back, but he decided it could wait. He looked up from his phone, but suddenly Finbar was no longer in the aisle. He crossed to the next aisle expecting to see him. He wasn't there either. An explosion went off in Marty's chest as he went to the last aisle, this time his steps quickening to his thumping heartbeat. Nothing. Blind panic swept through him. He hurried back along the aisles calling for Fin, his legs heavy with every step. But no sign of the boy. Then Marty rushed towards the young man on the till.

'A little blond-haired boy? Three years old. My grandson, Finbar. I came in with him. He was in that aisle, just a second ago, but he's not there now. Did you see him go out?' Marty blurted.

'No, sir. Place is quite busy. But I didn't see a kid wandering out by himself. Mind you, I've been tied up on the till.' The boy called to another staff member on the floor, 'You see a little blond boy leave?' The boy shook his head and shrugged.

Marty rushed out on weak legs, his eyes scanning the length and breadth of the shopping mall on the first floor where they were, and down the escalators to the ground. A sea of weekend shoppers. He looked across to the clothes shop Elizabeth had gone into to see her coming towards him. Christ! She was alone. When she saw his anxious expression and she realised he too was alone, Elizabeth went white. Marty opened his mouth to speak but nothing came out.

'Marty! Where's Fin?'

He heard the question somewhere in the distance as the place swam in front of him. He gripped the handrail of the escalator.

'He . . . He was here, in that shop just one minute ago. But . . . he's vanished. Oh Christ, Elizabeth! I can't find him.'

'Marty, don't say that! Finbar! Finbar!' She began running up and down the mall, screaming, 'Finbar!'

But Marty knew Fin was gone. He knew even before his mobile rang with the caller identity hidden from his screen.

'Marty Kane. We've got your boy,' the voice said in a strong Glasgow accent.

The line went dead before he could draw breath.

Within minutes the mall was crawling with police and security, as Marty and Elizabeth were escorted to an office on the ground floor. Marty's whole body was trembling and he could barely make it to the chair, slumping down, his head in his hands as his wife, flushed and crying, pleaded with everyone, 'Please. You have to find him. He must be here somewhere . . .'

Marty put his arm around her as her voice trailed off and she buried her head in his shoulder. He swallowed hard and tried to square his shoulders a little to pull himself together. He looked up at the big uniformed police Inspector standing over him, legs apart, his walkie-talkie crackling on his jacket.

'Mr Kane?' the man said. 'I'm chief Inspector Richard Marsh. I know it's hard, sir. Try to stay calm. We need a description. As much as you can tell us right now – what was Finbar wearing, for instance?'

Marty's mind was suddenly blank. He tried to think back, watching Fin's little legs swinging on the chair. But he couldn't remember anything else.

'I . . . I . . . Christ! I can't remember what he was wearing . . . Oh! Brown boots! You know. Like the ones kids wear. Suede, I think.' He turned to Elizabeth, who tried to sit up straight.

'A dark blue jacket,' she managed to say. 'One of those little bomber college type things, with a striped collar. He had beige trousers on. And a red jumper. He has thick blond hair . . .' Her voice began to catch. 'And blue eyes. Beautiful big blue eyes.' She broke down. 'Oh, Inspector. Please hurry. Fin wouldn't run off. He's not that kind of boy. He's a good wee boy. Kind. He . . . I know he wouldn't run off.'

Marty's eyes darted from the inspector to the PC standing behind him, her lips pulled back in a sympathetic grimace. He knew what she was thinking. Some pervert had lifted the boy. That was the fear of everyone these days. But Marty sat there, knowing that he knew differently, but unable to admit that. If his wife knew what he was hiding she would completely lose it. But he didn't dare do anything. He would have to phone Kerry. He stood up.

'Excuse me. I need to go to the bathroom.' He went outside, his head still light and slightly dizzy, and rushed to the toilets nearby. He punched in Kerry's number.

'Marty,' she answered after two rings.

'Kerry. I've only got a minute.'

'What's wrong?'

'Kerry.' Marty could feel his voice quiver. 'Someone's taken our Finbar. My wee Finbar. We were in the shopping mall in Princes Square. With Elizabeth – she went into a shop and left me with him. I was with Fin in a toy shop. I looked at my phone to see your text, and when I looked up he was gone. Christ, Kerry. My boy. Then within two minutes I got a phone call. No name. Just a voice. It said we've got your boy.' He paused to stop himself crying. 'It must be Rodriguez's men, Kerry. Who else could it be!'

'Jesus Christ, Marty! I'm so sorry. Listen. I know you're terrified, but we'll find him. Are the cops there?'

'Yes. It was sheer panic. We had to call them immediately. The whole place is turned out. But obviously they don't know about the phone call.'

'You did the right thing. The police will be all over it. But I need to get started here. If it's Rodriguez or any of his mob, then they'll get in touch.' She paused. 'Marty. They won't harm your grandson. He's only a little child. They won't hurt him.'

'I wish I could believe that.' His voice trailed off.

'I'm coming home from Spain. I'll be in Glasgow in the morning. Stay strong.'

Marty hung up and put his phone back into his pocket. He walked quickly back to the office where his wife was being comforted by a young female officer. Elizabeth looked up at him through tears.

'Why Fin? Why our Fin?'

Marty looked her in the eye, but he didn't answer. He couldn't. Because this was down to him, down to being part of the Casey family. And because of that his own family, the one he had lovingly created and which was the centre of his universe, was now faced with the most unimaginable nightmare.

CHAPTER THREE

Frankie Martin wanted to punch Pat Durkin out for the way he was salivating over the job the Colombians did on Johnny O'Driscoll. Fair enough – O'Driscoll had never been his bosom buddy when he was growing up with the Caseys. And once or twice when Frankie was in his teens and O'Driscoll was early thirties their dislike for each other had come to blows. But the way the Colombians had mutilated the poor bastard was just fucking ridiculous. O'Driscoll didn't deserve that. And he'd made that clear to Durkin when they spoke on the phone this morning, before they arranged this lunch down in Puerto Banus.

'What the fuck is wrong with you, Frankie?' Durkin looked a bit incredulous at Frankie's anger. 'It was you who fingered the bastard for us. Now you're going all queasy on it. Get a fucking grip, man.' Durkin lifted the sweating glass of lager to his mouth and took a long drink.

'That's not the fucking point, Pat. I mean, gouging the

bastard's eyes out. What the fuck is that all about? That's just shit, man. No need for that.' He shook his head, and leaned forward, lowering his voice. 'Sure, I set the fucker up. I've no regrets about that. Business is business, and I'm sure O'Driscoll would have had no qualms about putting a bullet in me. But that's all that was required to send a message back to Kerry Casey. Sending him in a body bag would have been enough, but a fucking head in a box? And that shit with his body at Málaga airport in the boot? Fuck me, man. That's pure psycho stuff. And I'm no fairy when it comes to dealing out some shit to people. But this. I mean it's just fucking wrong.'

'Ah, give your head peace, you fucking nancy boy. It's no worse than what some of our boys have done down in Limerick to grasses.'

'Well I'm not happy with it, and there's no point in me saying otherwise.' Frankie folded his arms, sulking. 'Where is this Rodriguez cunt anyway? I'm starving.'

Durkin looked beyond Frankie at the black Land Rover gliding along the quayside just a few yards from where they were sitting. He raised his eyebrows in acknowledgement as the car slowly went past.

'Here he is now,' he said. 'Driver is doing a recce to make sure there's no snipers lying in wait.'

Frankie could see that Durkin was visibly excited that Rodriguez was joining them, and he'd seen that from the first time he'd hooked up with Durkin when he arrived in

Marbella. Frankie had lain low for a few days when he'd arrived, keeping his head down in case any of the Casey crew down here were looking for him, which they no doubt would be. But he knew enough of them to make sure he kept away from the usual haunts. It was only when he contacted Durkin that he decided it might be safe enough to put his head above the parapet. When Durkin had filled him in on the deal he and the Colombians were trying to do with Kerry and how she was seriously fucking it up with her attitude, Frankie realised he could be useful in this. He didn't know Pepe Rodriguez, except by reputation, but had heard Durkin talking about him recently, almost like he had a schoolboy crush on the bastard. When Durkin had told him about the deal they were trying to cut with Kerry – about buying the stash of coke that fucker Sharon Potter stole from Knuckles Boyle – Frankie could see how useful he could be if he threw in his lot with them. And from where he was sitting after having done a runner from Glasgow and the Caseys, it wasn't as though he had a lot of options right now. So here he was, ready to break bread with Rodriguez, who was clearly a complete fucking nutjob. Frankie wasn't scared. He knew that if he didn't like what he saw here, then he had enough money to go far enough away that nobody could find him. He could reinvent himself. But the lure of having a bigger part to play, and of taking down Kerry Casey – who was in the fucking job that he should have – was the biggest attraction on his horizon at the moment.

He braced himself as the tall, well-dressed figure in khaki trousers and pale blue polo shirt, topped with mirrored Ray-Bans, came striding towards their table. Behind him were no fewer than three bulked up bodyguards whose eyes were all over the port. Durkin was on his feet by the time he reached the table.

'Pepe!' He gestured, one of his arms out as though imitating the way the elaborate Mediterraneans greeted each other. '*Amigo! Que tal?*'

Christ! He's going to hug the fucker, Frankie thought.

'*Buenos!*' Pepe made the slightest bow of his head as he stuck out a hand. '*Buenos, amigo!*'

He glanced down at Frankie, no doubt clocking that he wasn't on his feet like the fucking little arse-licking Durkin. He only stood up when Durkin turned to him, and led the introduction.

'Pepe, this is Frankie Martin. He knows more about the Casey mob than they know themselves.'

Frankie reached out and shook Pepe's hand, as the Colombian casually took off his Ray-Bans and looked straight at him with the darkest, blackest eyes he had ever seen. Frankie locked eyes with him and made sure his handshake was so firm that the handsome bastard would remember it.

'How are you, Frankie Martin? I hear good things about

you.' Rodriguez paused, pulling out a chair. 'And thank you for your assistance in pointing out where to find this . . .' he turned to Durkin, snapping his fingers, 'wha' is the name of the *coño* again in our message to Casey?'

'O'Driscoll,' Durkin said, quickly.

'Johnny O'Driscoll,' Frankie said, deadpan. Then before he could stop himself, he gave Rodriguez a sullen look. 'Glad to be of help, Pepe. But I have to say, I think it was a bit over the top to take his eyes.' He shrugged and looked away. He'd made his point. Whether Rodriguez liked it or not, Frankie was determined to establish who he was here.

The Colombian looked at him and gave a kind of snort and shrug.

'Oh. You think maybe we were too harsh?' He drew back his lips back in a sardonic smile.

It sent a shiver through Frankie. This cunt is a fucking nutter, he thought.

'Yeah. I do, actually.' He might as well dig a fucking grave for himself here, as that's where this kind of talk would get him, but he couldn't stop. It wasn't in his nature to back down. 'Not that I have any regrets in pointing him out to you, Pepe. Of course not. Business is business, and fair enough to deal with it. All I'm saying is that, well, where I come from we don't gouge cunts' eyes out.' He spread his hands. 'Call me old-fashioned, but it's not how we do things.'

Pepe nodded slowly. And Frankie could see that he was

concealing his irritation quite well, but he wouldn't be used to anyone talking to him like this.

'Okay. I respect that, Frankie.' He gave him a long look. 'But where you come from doesn't matter any more, does it? Because you are here now. And if you want to stay, then you will have to understand that how we do things is different. More effective, we believe.'

Frankie said nothing. He should quit if he wanted to get through lunch without getting a knife in his chest. The waiter arrived in a timely interruption. Frankie's appetite had somewhat vanished. But he would eat, and this fucker sitting opposite him giving him the black eye was not going to unnerve him.

'Good,' the Colombian said. 'Let us eat and celebrate. And let us plan our next move.' He looked at Frankie and this time he did show him his five-grand smile. 'Welcome, Frankie.'

They ordered a lunch of clams followed by a mixed platter of fish which the three of them shared, washed down with crisp white wine. Frankie could feel the atmosphere starting to warm by the time Pepe ordered the second bottle. Durkin was regaling the Colombian with tales of Dublin and Limerick, and how his father had established himself as the biggest importer of cocaine to Ireland and the UK in history. Since his father's sudden death from a heart attack last year, Durkin was saying that he was now heading up the family, and he would make it bigger and better. Frankie listened, nodding in all the right places, as Durkin described their gun-running enterprise in cahoots with Billy Hill's family in London and how it was well known across the UK who was in charge of drugs and trafficking. But he was still ambitious. He wanted more. He began to talk about the Caseys, and how Mickey Casey, the brother of Kerry, had been a loudmouth who had upset too many people. And he told how Boyle's mob took him out – giving Frankie a nod saying that this was with his help – but that the plans to make Frankie the head of the Casey family were thrown into chaos, once Kerry Casey decided she was now in charge.

Pepe listened intently, taking everything in, and shooting glances at Frankie, who'd said nothing so far. Then the Colombian turned to him.

'So, Frankie. Tell me more about this Kerry lady. You grew up, I believe, with this family. You are close to her – or were.' He paused, swirled some wine in his mouth and swallowed it. 'Tell me. Did you fuck her? She is very beautiful.'

Frankie was a little stunned by the question, and felt he would have had more respect from this bastard if he was able to say he had fucked Kerry Casey sideways for years. But that wouldn't be true. So he smiled and tried to look nonchalant.

'Sadly, *amigo*, no,' he said, feeling confident. Then he held the phone up to his face as though taking a selfie and added,

'Which is surprising, that she was able to resist a charming bastard like me.' He grinned. 'But maybe one day.'

Pepe laughed. 'Yes. One day perhaps.' He winked. 'But only after me.'

Frankie and Durkin both laughed, but Frankie could feel a little stinging rage inside his gut, as he vowed: over my dead body, you spick cunt.

They had been in the restaurant almost two hours, and as they sat drinking brandy, Pepe lit a cigar. He leaned back in his chair as the late afternoon wintry pall fell over the harbour. He rubbed his face with his manicured hand and Frankie clocked the chunky diamond ring that must be worth at least twenty grand.

'So, *amigos*, here is what I think we should do.' He looked from one to the other. 'You don't know this, but we have also sent another message to Kerry Casey.' He turned to Durkin. 'I didn't want to tell you about it until it was done. It wasn't up for negotiation. But it is something that I think will strike at the Casey heart.'

Frankie and Durkin exchanged glances but their faces showed nothing.

'We have taken a little boy – the grandson of the Casey lawyer.'

Frankie's stomach dropped and he tried desperately not to show his shock as Pepe continued.

'So now, we have a big bargaining chip in our hands.'

Frankie cleared his throat, suddenly sobering up.

'You've kidnapped Marty Kane's grandson? Wee Finbar? He's only three years old.' Frankie didn't care if this sounded full of indignation. He couldn't believe what he was hearing. He'd never even seen the boy, as Marty kept his family completely separate from business, but Frankie knew this would have sliced Marty in two. And also Kerry.

Pepe gave a slight shrug but looked directly at Frankie as though to let him know he shouldn't question it.

'Yes. We have the boy. Finbar. He's okay. Don't worry.' He looked at both of them as Durkin remained impassive. 'We are not going to harm him. We just took him because we could, and because kidnap is a powerful tool. I think we will find that Kerry Casey will be much more, how you say, amenable, with us now because we have this boy.'

Nobody spoke and they sat for a long moment in silence, Frankie trying to imagine the darkness that would have fallen over everyone in the Casey family. He was beginning to think he was out of his depth throwing his lot in with this mob.

Eventually, the Colombian spoke again. 'Obviously the police will be looking everywhere for the boy. But he will come to no harm, as long as Kerry Casey realises she has nowhere to go in this. So, what I think is that we go to her with our proposal.' He spoke slowly, precisely, glancing from one to the other. 'We tell her we want not just a stake in the hotel and the property business . . .' he paused for effect, 'but we tell her that now we are taking it all. Everything. Simple as that.'

Again there was silence. Frankie was stunned. Then Pepe looked at him.

'And Frankie,' he said, 'I think the proposal should be put to Kerry by you.' There was a smugness about him. 'After all, you know them well enough to be able to work out how you tell them and what you do to make this happen.'

Frankie suddenly felt suffocated, but he managed to take a drink of water from the table, and was glad the glass wasn't shaking in his hand when he picked it up. He knew Pepe would be watching for that. He looked at Durkin, who was wearing what could only be described as a look of sheer admiration for the ingenuity of this malicious fucker. But Frankie was indeed trapped. This was it now. He either ran like fuck as far away as he could, or he was in.

He took a breath and let it out slowly.

'I can do that,' he said, sounding resolute.

Pepe nodded his approval, like the local fucking bishop who was enjoying a performance from his favourite primary school's annual nativity play. Holy fucking fuck, Frankie said to himself as Pepe raised a glass and clinked from him to Durkin.

CHAPTER FOUR

Kerry was almost drifting off to sleep by the time the plane was ready to take off. She felt more exhausted than she'd been in a long time. The last six weeks had been more than hectic, and she'd barely taken time to grieve over the loss of her mother. Every time a thought or image of her mother came to her, there was an immediate flashback to the bloodbath of Mickey's funeral, when she had held her bloodied, lifeless body in her arms. She wondered if she'd ever be able to think of her mother the way she had been, the way she was all those years ago, from the early, impoverished days, to the woman she'd become, strong, determined and smart. Kerry had been promising herself that one of these nights she'd take time to dig out some old photographs and just sit there and have a good weep over them as she remembered. But all that was before the bombshells began to fall all over the place. She'd been prepared for a battle to follow her dream, but nowhere in her wildest imagination did she think that she would ever see what she saw in that box sent by the Colombians. And now, she was about to witness the agony of Marty Kane and his family as they waited for news of their lost little boy. She pushed the thought away for the moment as she recalled the conversation with Sharon before she left.

They'd been having breakfast in the kitchen of the villa, but Kerry was more or less pushing the food around the plate. The nausea was becoming frightening now, and Kerry was worried that she might be sinking into a depression with all the stress. She had to be made of stronger stuff than this, she'd chided herself as she'd thrown up just before Sharon came in. As they sat at the table, Sharon was eating a bowl of yoghurt and fruit, while Kerry nibbled at a piece of toast and sipped green tea. She was conscious that Sharon was watching her.

'You want to look after yourself, Kerry,' Sharon said, eyeing her. 'You've been like death warmed up for days now. And, by the way, I heard you being sick as I came in the front door.'

Kerry said nothing, just sighed.

'How long has that been going on for, girl?'

Kerry knew what she was getting at, and she tried her best not to look away. But Sharon kept on.

'Tell you what, love,' she said. 'You want to check that this throwing up lark isn't about to take feet. Know what I mean?'

Kerry looked at her, unable to escape her worst fears. She said nothing.

'Look, I'm not wanting to pry or anything, love,' Sharon said. 'But could you be pregnant? I know you and the big copper fella . . . Well, I could see that a mile away.'

Kerry managed a smile, but immediately blinked away the image of Vinny's handsome face. Eventually she answered. 'Well. Yes. That's what I'm scared of, Sharon, if I'm honest. I'm privately panicking that I'm pregnant. Imagine throwing that into the mix right now.'

Sharon let out a sigh.

'Well, these things have a habit of happening when you least expect it. So my advice to you is, if there's a chance you could be pregnant then get a bloody kit and do a test. As soon as you go back to Glasgow. Then you'll know, and you'll be in a position to think straight. Because right now, you're looking tired and emotional. The lads won't see that because, well, they're lads. But I've been there, so I can see it.'

'I know,' Kerry said, sheepish. 'I'll get a test when I get home.' She sighed. 'Dreading it though.'

'You'll be fine. You're a tough cookie, despite what you might think. You'll do whatever is right for you.'

Eddie, the Casey chauffeur, was standing outside the black Merc waiting for Kerry as she came through the automatic doors at Glasgow airport arrivals. Just seeing him and being back on home soil in the midst of all the misery she was feeling sent a wave of emotion through her, and she more or less threw her arms around him, feeling the choking ache in her throat. When he released her, he scanned her face.

'You okay, sweetheart?'

She nodded, not trusting herself to speak. It was only when she got into the car and sat in the front seat that she turned to him.

'What about Marty, Eddie? How is he? Have you seen him?'

'No,' he replied, easing the car onto the motorway. 'It's been all over the TV news though, and press were camped outside his son's house and Marty's office. But I don't think he's left Elizabeth's side since it happened.' He shook his head. 'It's an awful business, Kerry. I mean, what kind of bastard kidnaps a kid of three? The wee guy will be distraught. Doesn't even bear thinking about.'

'I know,' Kerry said softly. 'I can't stop thinking about it – the kid, Marty and his family. Christ, Eddie! I don't even know what I'm going to say to him. But I need to see him today.'

'Probably best if you can get him to your own house then, I'd say, rather than go to his home. The press might be there and you don't want to attract any attention. Plus, if his wife has any inkling that this is anything to do with us, then she won't want to see you.'

Kerry nodded, gazing out of the window, saying nothing. Elizabeth Kane was a lovely, warm woman, still with her Irish brogue even though she'd been away from Dublin since she met Marty almost fifty years ago. She was a clever woman, but chose to be the homemaker, the mother, the centre of the family. Marty was the high-profile criminal lawyer who would pop up on TV news now and again, on the steps of the courts, standing next to yet another hoodlum who was walking free because Marty had convinced a jury his client was innocent – even though most times they weren't. Yet between them they'd managed to make their marriage last, and all of that despite the fact that Elizabeth must have known the crucial role he played in the shady Casey empire. She never asked, probably because she didn't want to know. But this was different.

As Eddie left the motorway and drove up through the city to the north side, Kerry looked out at the tenements in Maryhill in the steady drizzle, and remembered the early days going to school playing in the street, times when they had nothing. Whatever had been going on back then in her own father's murky world, she was miles away from it, and happy. It felt like a more innocent time, though it probably wasn't, given that her father was a crook. Part of her wished she could go back there and start again. How different she would make things, but it was a pointless thought and she snapped out of it as Eddie pushed the remote of the big steel gates and they drove into the courtyard of her shuttered, protected, tall sandstone villa that somehow looked forlorn in the rain. A couple of security men in waxed jackets were on the door and in the grounds and in the secure gatehouse. One of them opened the front door for her and she went in to the smell of the wooden polished floors and the aroma of Elsa's cooking in the kitchen. She went straight upstairs to phone Marty. She had to make the call before she took the pregnancy test she'd just purchased in the Boots at the airport. In the study she punched in his number and he answered immediately.

'Marty. I'm back.' She didn't want to ask how things were.

'Hello, Kerry.'

She heard him take a breath and let it out slowly, and she pictured his face.

'Can you talk, Marty?'

'Hold on. Let me go through to the kitchen.' She heard footsteps and a door open and close softly.

'Yes, I can talk. Have you heard anything?'

Kerry felt choked.

'No, Marty, sorry. Not a thing. But we will. I'm sure. Before the day's out. Has there been nothing more from whoever phoned you when it happened? The voice?'

'Nothing.' He sounded almost distant.

'Can you come over? I don't want to come to the house.'

He waited a moment before he answered. 'Yes. You don't want to come here. It's like . . . Oh, Kerry. It's awful. My son Joe and his wife, and little Johnny, Finbar's big brother.

He's only five. Doesn't really know what's going on. Place has been buzzing with police, Serious Crime Squad, the lot. I feel as if I'm watching it in someone else's life. Best if you don't come here.' He paused. 'In fact, it'll do me good to get out for a while.'

'Good. Just come when you can.'

'I'll be there within an hour. I've got things to talk to Elizabeth and Joe about here first. The police are talking about a press conference. But I'm not keen on that.'

'Okay. We'll talk when I see you.'

An hour later, Kerry saw the big steel gates open and Marty's black Merc come through. She watched as he got out of the car, and was struck by how he looked as though he'd aged overnight. Even his movements were slower, his shoulders slumped as he came towards the door. She made her way to the study where she'd asked Elsa to make them some coffee. She stood waiting for him, and heard the bodyguard's soft voice greeting him with a 'Mr Kane', then the sound of his footsteps. He knocked and came into the room, closing the door behind him. Kerry stood for a moment, not quite knowing what to say. Normally it was Marty who was in charge, who would come to greet her, who had taken her in his arms the day her mother was killed and held her while she'd wept. But now he looked uprooted, lost, an old man whose heart had been torn out.

'Oh, Marty.' Kerry went towards him and opened her

arms. 'Jesus! This is so awful. I . . . I . . . There are no words I can say.'

She could feel him hold her tight for a long moment, and she was afraid to let go in case he would buckle. But he didn't. He released her, and looked into her eyes.

'Oh, Kerry.' His eyes were moist. 'How does it come to this? How in the name of Jesus would anyone take a little boy? He'll be terrified.' He swallowed. 'Fin is such a gentle little thing. Not like his brother Johnny at all, who's wild. Christ! Wee lad won't know what's going on.' He shook his head, to stop himself rambling.

'Come and sit down, Marty,' Kerry ushered him to the table. 'We'll find a way through this. I refuse to believe anything else.'

Marty took his coat off and sat down. Kerry poured coffee into two mugs and sat down. She leaned across and touched Marty's hand.

'Marty, listen,' she said, looking into his pale grey eyes, lined at the edges and with puffy eyelids, probably from crying. 'Whatever it takes to get Fin back, we'll do it. The call will come. I'm sure it's this Rodriguez mob. He's done this for maximum effect. But whatever he asks, we'll pay it.' She squeezed his hand. 'No matter what the price. I want you to understand that.'

Marty nodded, swallowed hard.

'Thanks, Kerry.'

For a few seconds they said nothing, and Kerry knew

that she had to talk about a strategy here, despite the agony. They had to be ready.

'So.' She looked at him. 'Tell me everything that's happened since the moment he disappeared. The cops et cetera. What are they doing? Just in your own time.'

Marty nodded. 'It happened in a flash. I was watching him in the aisle of the toy shop one moment, and the next I looked at my phone for a few seconds, and when I looked up he was gone. I knew straight away. I just knew that he'd been taken. But it must have been so organised. There must have been a team of at least two or three, anyway.'

He sipped his coffee, and Kerry was glad to see that he was thinking more about how it had happened rather than just feeling helpless. He put the mug down and continued to talk.

'I couldn't work out how they got out of that shop without passing me. Then, when the police came, and once they started taping the place off and going through the shop, they saw that there is an aisle that leads to toilets and the storeroom, and that must have been where they took him. They said the door at the end of the storeroom was open, and that it goes to an outside metal staircase. So they must have taken him that way. It's a fire escape. I can't understand why Fin wasn't screaming for dear life. Maybe they told him they were taking him to show him some toys, and that I was just along the corridor a bit waiting for him? Something like that? They must have had a car down on the street below. But how the hell did they know I was going to go to the toy shop? I didn't even know that until Fin asked me to take him. How did they know?'

Kerry shook her head. 'I don't know. They must have been following you for a week or so, watching your movements. They must have been planning this. It's possible that they were able to find out that Finbar is with his grandparents on a Saturday morning while Johnny is at football, or something like that.'

'I suppose if they were watching us they could know that.'

'Whatever they planned it must have been quick. Maybe they had the O'Driscoll murder planned for the whole time he was missing, and wanted to hit us twice – one after the other – where it would hurt the most. I honestly can't get to grips with it. But they must have known something. All it would take is a word in the wrong place from someone so they can find out where you go. And they waited their chance.' She paused. 'What about the police? What are they doing? I haven't had a chance to see the TV news yet.'

'Well they immediately put it out to the media so it was all over the afternoon news and the evening news, and the papers the next day. It's been the number-one item – top criminal lawyer's son kidnapped – and of course going into the history of me and my career. The police know I've been the Casey family lawyer for decades, so they will be looking into everything. I'm surprised you haven't had a call yet.'

'I'll get that, no doubt. Probably before the day's out. But they don't know about O'Driscoll. Not even that he's missing. I have to talk to his ex-wife Alice to break the news to her.' She looked at her watch. 'In fact, I'll have to do it today, before she gets a knock on the door from the Glasgow cops to tell her they suspect they've found her husband's body parts in the boot of a car at Málaga airport. Once the Spanish cops put it out it will be everywhere. Christ!' She shook her head. 'I don't know what the hell I'm going to say to her.'

Marty sighed. 'Poor Johnny. He was a good man. His father was so close to your dad and Danny, he would have done anything for them. What a horrible death to get. But that's the kind of people we are dealing with here.'

Kerry looked at him.

'So the police don't know about the phone call you got. Are they asking for your mobile or anything?'

'No. Not yet. I don't want to involve them. It's so delicate, Kerry. They'd blow a fuse if they knew that I'm withholding information from them – so would my wife and my son. But I've got no way out of that. I feel like I'm drowning here.'

'I know. But I really think you're right in not telling the police yet. I'm sure they'll come here and start asking questions – particularly after it comes out about O'Driscoll. If the Serious Crime Squad have been to see you, they'll already be looking at other ways. You might have been followed here.'

'Not that I could see. But it's possible. They might even be tapping our phones.'

Kerry was feeling the stress in her stomach at the rate that this was going, and with every moment that passed there was even more worry that Finbar was in serious danger. She had to believe that they wouldn't harm a child, particularly one who was such a bargaining chip, but she was really trying to convince herself. It was all beginning to overwhelm her and she had to take a slow breath to try to control herself. She wished Uncle Danny had come back over with her to be at her side. But she needed to stay strong, because Marty, the man who had been like an uncle to her all her life, was crumbling in front of her, and she had to take the lead to keep it all together.

'Listen, Marty: whoever has Finbar – and I'm sure it's all connected and to get back at us – then they have to get in touch. They won't hang about on that. They'll either get to you, or to me. I'm sure of that. But we've already got people working for us – I mean guys who can keep their ear to the ground and pick up information. There's bound to be a leak somewhere, especially in something as big as kidnapping a kid. The bastards who did this might think they've got this sewn up, but they haven't. This is Glasgow. And anything that moves, we'll get to hear about it. I really believe that.'

Marty looked as though he wanted to believe her, that he had to believe what she was saying. He glanced at his watch and stood up.

'I know, Kerry. You're right. But because it's about my own little grandson, I feel a bit unhinged by it, like I'm not thinking straight. I'm trying to keep it together so I can think it through. I'm trying with every fibre, but it's so hard.' He paused. 'I'd better get back. I think if the police are doing a press conference they'll have to do it without Joe. He's in pieces and his wife is worse. I might have to do it myself. Just keep it to a statement I can read out. No questions from media.'

Kerry nodded.

'Maybe if you do, then things will start moving and they'll get in touch – if they don't before then.' She walked Marty to the door, and gave him a long hug. 'Let me know if you're doing the press conference, and I'll keep you informed of every single thing happening here. But, Marty – this will be over in a couple of days. As I told you. Whatever it costs, it will be over.'

As soon as she saw Marty's car drive through the open gates, Kerry went upstairs to the bathroom with the pregnancy kit. A couple of minutes later she waited, watching the line in the little window, her heart in her mouth. Then a second line appeared and a little explosion went off inside her. Pregnant.

CHAPTER FIVE

Sharon Potter didn't feel safe. Not that she ever had, not in the way most people define safety, as in the safety of family and home and comfort. She'd grown up in fear, in grinding poverty with a drunk for a mum, then abandonment to the childcare system, which brought with it fear every single day. To feel safe was the only thing in those days that she longed for, and everything she had done from the moment the system turned her out into the street as a skinny teenager was in search of that security. To look for a home and a family and the comfort she wanted. She'd had all those trappings, especially in the last fifteen years with Knuckles Boyle, living off the wealth he'd amassed through his heroin and cocaine empire. But even then she was never really safe – always just keeping ahead of the law, always waiting for it all to come tumbling down in a hail of bullets from some of Knuckles' enemies. And safe was the last thing she felt once she'd realised Knuckles had grown tired of her and was planning to bump her off. But she'd sorted that out all right, even though she still woke up with the image of Knuckles' face as he lay dying from a bullet to the head. She'd made that happen, and she had no regrets. Coming to Spain, joining with Kerry Casey's crew: she was starting a new life on her own terms with her son, Tony. But once again it was all beginning to feel shaky under her feet. She should have bloody known.

The move to Spain in recent weeks had been going so well, despite the problems the Caseys were having with the Colombians who had tried to steal their stash of coke, which was to be the last criminal deal Kerry's clan would do. Kerry and her men were dealing with the fallout, while Sharon was overseeing the work towards the luxury hotel that would soon be under way. The Spanish town hall planners were onside, and taking bungs in the way she'd been told they would, and she envisaged the building work beginning soon. But then O'Driscoll. The brutality. Christ almighty! Sent shivers through her. And now the kidnapping of Marty Kane's little grandson. Sharon didn't know Marty well, only to talk to around the table with Kerry and close associates. But she could feel his pain. The thought of anything happening to her boy Tony would destroy her. And for the first time since she'd arrived in Spain, she began to ask herself if she'd have been better taking the money she had, and reinventing herself far away from here along with her son. But Tony was so happy, thriving in his new school, and as she'd dropped him off at the gates this morning in the sunshine, she felt a little lump in her throat at his delight, linking up with his new mates as they disappeared into the yard, and him turning to wave to her. Of course, she could never tell Kerry Casey of her fears, because Kerry had given her a lifeline when Knuckles' men were hunting her down. She would get through this, and she'd do it with the Casey family. They were all she had now apart from Tony. But nobody with any sense had ever taken on the Colombians. There had to be a first time for that, Sharon decided as she turned the car back down the twisting road towards her villa in Mijas Costa.

Sharon had never ventured out socially since she'd arrived on the Costa del Sol, for fear of running into some of Knuckles' old cohorts, or anyone who may have had a grudge against them over the years. Now she drove on the dual carriageway, past all her old haunts, recalling good times down here among the Costa set – and bad times too, as her life with Knuckles had begun to unravel. Her mobile rang on the passenger seat and she glanced over at it, but there was no name. She probably shouldn't answer it, because anyone who had her number here would be named on screen. But curiosity got the better of her. She touched the hands-free button on her steering wheel.

'Hello!' Her voice was sharp.

'Sharon Potter. Well, well, well,' the caller said, in a voice that she recognised instantly.

'Who's this?' She pretended she didn't know.

'Ah, come on now, Sharon.'

She didn't answer. And her finger hovered over the button to cut him off, but somehow she couldn't. She could feel her heart race. Vic Paterson had her phone number. Christ alfuckingmighty! She steadied her car as it swerved over the white lines and the car behind honked, then quickly took the slip road off the carriageway.

'What the fuck, Vic?'

'That's better, darlin'.' She could almost see the smile spread across his handsome face. She pulled into the side of the road.

'I have to say, Shaz,' he said, 'I hoped for a better reception.'

'What the fuck's going on? I thought you were inside?' Sharon wondered if she'd lost track of the years: she was sure he got fifteen years only nine years ago. He should still be in jail.

'Not any more.'

'Are you on the run?'

She heard him give a soft chortle.

'No, sweetheart. Parole. I'm a changed man, apparently.'

'Parole?' she exclaimed. The last she'd heard of Vic he had put two prison guards in hospital who were trying to restrain him from kicking the shit out of a paedo beast who'd been sent down for raping a ten-year-old girl. That was seven years ago, and he must have got extra jail time for that. But no. Here he was, paroled.

'Where did you get my number, Vic?'

'Don't ask daft questions, Sharon. You know better than that.'

'Where are you?' she asked, knowing what he was going to say.

'On the Costa, love. Looking to meet you for a drink, and a chat.'

Sharon let the silence hang. She could hear his breathing, and suddenly she could see him as though all the shit that had happened between them was yesterday. She'd made a mistake there. She should never have gone anywhere near him. She knew he was trouble, and she was with Knuckles. But it had happened. It caught fire, fierce and briefly, before she extinguished it once and for all. The last thing she'd needed back then, with a little boy of three, was for Knuckles to find out she was shagging one of his enemies. Nice one, Sharon. She'd spent the past ten years living it down, forgetting about it, trying to pretend it never happened. She took a breath.

'Vic. Look. I'm glad to hear you've been paroled, and good luck to you. But I can't see you.' She paused. 'I'm living a very different life now. I've got my son at school here. I'm in the middle of a big business venture, and I've moved on from everything – from Knuckles, from Manchester. Everything. Please understand that, will you?'

Again the silence.

'Well, Sharon. That's not the way I hear it.' He paused,

waiting for an answer, but she said nothing. 'Way I hear it is that you and the Casey mob are up to your arse in shit with the Colombians. They will fuck up every single dream you ever had, believe me.'

Sharon still said nothing. How in the name of Christ did he even know this?

'That little fat Irish cunt – Pat Durkin,' Vic went on. 'He's like a puppet on a string for that Colombian fucker. Trust me. You and the Caseys are getting wasted – one and all. You need to meet me.'

Sharon held her breath for a moment, her mind racing at how much he knew. How was this even possible?

'Why do I need to meet you, Vic? I hear what you're saying. But what the Christ has any of this got to do with you?'

Again, for a long moment there was nothing, and Sharon couldn't help herself trying to picture what Vic Paterson looked like now, and most of all what brought him here.

'You need my help, Sharon. That's why I'm here.'

Sharon swallowed as she looked out of the windscreen along the rows of cafés, half expecting to see him sitting at a table.

'Where are you?' she asked.

'Fuengirola. On the promenade.'

'Okay. I'll come and meet you.'

Sharon heard herself say it, even though she couldn't

quite believe it. But she knew Vic Paterson well enough to know that if he was this well informed, then he must have an inside track on the Colombians. But what if he was working for them, and fishing for information? Only one way to find out, she decided. Sharon turned her car around and went back on the dual carriageway, heading towards Fuengirola.

As she drove, the thoughts and memories came flooding back. Vic Paterson had been close to Knuckles Boyle for years as they grew up. They'd worked for one of the bigger gangland families, armed robberies and enforcers, but Vic had been given his own turf in Salford and the surrounding area. He ran several gangs and was known for being smarter than your average toerag on the street. But once his neck of the woods was doing better than Knuckles', Knuckles couldn't take it. There had been occasional dinners and nights out, and that's when Sharon met him – before it had all gone pear-shaped between him and Knuckles. Paterson had been hard as nails, charming, and dangerous. He was also ruthless. He had no qualms about taking anyone out of the game who trod on his toes or those of his mates. Sharon had met him over a dinner and he'd bombarded her with calls over the following days. It was a time when she'd felt vulnerable, when Knuckles was spending nights out of the house and she knew he was with other women, and felt even back then that he was going off her. She'd ended up in bed with Vic, and it had been the best sex she'd ever had. But she liked him as a person too, and for the next few months their secret affair had been explosive. There had been a little fleeting moment once when she was talking to Knuckles that she got the feeling that he had an idea that she'd been with Vic. So she stopped it. She didn't see him again. Not once. And not long after that, a deal with him fell through, and Knuckles became Vic's sworn enemy, bumping off a couple of his gang members who had tried to sell and move stuff on his turf. They never spoke again, and operated completely separately. Then Vic got jailed for possession with intent to sell, caught red-handed with a huge haul of coke in a warehouse. The word was that Knuckles had made sure he was grassed up and had set him up, but he had always been appalled at that suggestion. Privately, Sharon thought it might be true, but she had a young son and a life with Knuckles, and she wasn't about to do anything that could ruin that. She wasn't in love with Vic – nothing like that. It was a stupid thing to have done when she'd been feeling angry and hurt, and the truth was she had barely given him a thought all these years.

Now, as she drove along the promenade, her phone rang again and it was Vic, to say where he was. She parked the car at the harbour and walked across the road to the café. The sun was coming out and the Brits were beginning to filter into the pie and mash cafés and UK flag-wearing bars. The bar they were meeting in was just off the promenade, further down than most people ventured. Two streets back from the main road in Fuengirola was all Spanish bars and it was almost like walking between two different countries. And there he was, sitting in the corner watching her as she came through the door. He stood up.

'Sharon.'

He opened his arms and Sharon found herself walking into them. It had been a long time since she'd felt the strong arms of a man around her and she enjoyed it, despite how brief it was. She stood back and looked at him. How did the bastard manage not to age, all chiselled features and suntanned skin, topped off by close-cropped hair that made him look like ex military?

'By the look of your tan,' Sharon said, 'you've not been in Salford for a while.' She knew he'd expect her to be chirpy and with plenty of attitude.

'Fuck all that for a game of soldiers,' he said. 'As soon as they opened the prison doors, I was out of there and on a plane to Tenerife the next day. No more of that UK shit for me.'

Sharon sat down.

'When did you get out? I never heard anything.'

'I kind of slipped out below the radar – or maybe you were too busy keeping an eye on Knuckles to be interested on what was going on outside.'

Sharon glared at him, irritated.

'I have a thirteen-year-old son, who has kept me busy.'

He didn't answer, noticing her irritation. The waiter

came and he ordered another coffee and Sharon asked for the same.

'And how is your boy? Tony, isn't it?'

'Yeah. He's great. Settled. New school here. He's very happy.' She looked straight at him. 'I'm very happy too, Vic. Life is very different.'

He looked at her for a long moment, and Sharon was conscious that her face would have shown the signs of stress and agony of recent months and sleepless nights – even though things had picked up since she left for Spain. The stress had been beginning to leave her face, but she knew it was still there.

'Really? That different, Sharon?' Vic said. 'I hear you've thrown your lot in with this Kerry Casey bird. From what I hear on the grapevine, you guys are struggling.'

Sharon said nothing as the waiter came over and placed the cups on the table. She lifted hers to her mouth and sipped it. Then she took a breath and sighed.

Vic leaned across the table a little closer. 'I heard about this O'Driscoll guy. Fucking hell. Cut his head off? That's bang out of order, that is.'

Sharon nodded. She didn't really want to sit here discussing all of this, and so far Vic hadn't mentioned that Marty Kane's grandson had been kidnapped. If he was that well informed, he would know that. She spread her hands.

'So, Vic. It's good to see you doing well, and I'm glad life is back on the right track for you. But tell you what, mate.

I came here because I'm curious. Not desperate or anything like that. You said you could help us – not that we need any help right now. But I'm curious. Number one: how do you know anything about what's going on here? And two, what are you trying to do?' She kept her face straight. The last thing she needed was someone who was effectively just an old flame, coming over here and trying to dig up what she was doing. She didn't even know if he was anyone she could trust. He was obviously informed but that could mean he was in with the enemy. She leaned closer to him and gave an exaggerated look at her watch. 'So why don't you start talking. Forget all this small talk and cryptic shit as I don't have the time. I have to pick up my son in a few hours and I've got stuff to do.' She raised her eyebrows, waiting.

A smile spread across his face.

'Fucking sexy as ever, Sharon. Love that edge about you. Like you've got a gun below the table aimed at my bollocks.'

'I might well have.' She couldn't help but smile. 'Come on, for Christ's sake, Vic. Stop pissing around.'

'Okay,' he said, sitting back. 'Here's the sketch. I was inside with a Paddy called Shaun Dylan who knows the Irish set-up well. He talked to me a couple of weeks ago and said that Pat Durkin is in with the Colombians. Dylan's been out now for months and still mad that Durkin tried to do him over, so he's out for revenge. He's been asked back into the fold as he's a top bank fraudster. They need him. He's the best. Passports, credit cards – all that stuff. So he's working for them, but will fuck Durkin at the drop of a hat, he says. He can give me inside stuff if I wanted to use it against him. Like with someone like you or this Kerry bird.'

'So why would you want to help us, or offer your services to the Casey family?'

He rubbed his fingers together. 'Same as you, Shaz. Money. I'm moving on. I need big money. But I can get things done for you. I can go places that you can't go. Shaun has introduced me to Durkin already. And I've met this Colombian fucker.'

This was a lot to take in. Like someone who could help just dropping out of the sky. But still the niggle was there – what if she couldn't trust him? What if it was a trap? What would Kerry and the troops think of this complete stranger walking into the fray?

He lifted his coffee up.

'Let me tell you how well informed I am, by the way. These bastards have kidnapped some kid related to a lawyer who works for the Caseys. They're holding the kid. That's the kind of fuckers you're up against here. And believe me, if you want to get back at them, you're gonna need my help. Frankie Martin is in with them.'

Sharon hoped her face didn't show that her insides were going like an engine. She had to talk to Kerry.

CHAPTER SIX

When Kerry saw Vinny Burns' name come up as her mobile rang, she ignored it – for the second time in the last two hours. If he, or anyone else in Glasgow police, had wanted to speak to her officially about the kidnapping of Marty Kane's grandson then he would have been knocking on her door. She was surprised that the police hadn't come calling yet. If they were looking at all aspects of the kidnapping, as she'd seen a DCI say to a TV reporter on the news, then they would have to be looking at the Caseys. Marty had been the family lawyer for a generation, and while he may have made plenty of enemies in his life as a criminal lawyer, they would be wondering if his work for the Caseys was any reason for the kidnapping. But the cops hadn't come yet. So if Vinny was phoning her mobile, then he wanted to pick her brains. She was a little irritated that he might be using their relationship to see what he could dig out, but she couldn't blame him. She'd do the same thing.

But the last person she wanted to talk to right now was Vinny. She'd been keeping herself busy since she took the pregnancy test, because right now there was no room in her head to even think about it. And yet, she couldn't stop the thoughts flooding her brain, and the constant nagging question – what the hell was she going to do?

After the test had come up positive, Kerry had sat back down on the toilet seat, staring at the two pink lines, closing her eyes for a second, then opening them just in case she'd been wrong. She even took another test an hour later, and it was the same. She was pregnant. She had to accept it. But there were so many thoughts in her head – shock at first, then finally the tears came. She thought of the miscarriage she'd had over a year ago and the pain of losing a child she really wanted when she had a life to give it and a proper partner. But since then, she'd grown to accept that she may never be a mother, and she was trying to adjust to that. Now this. There wasn't a worse time in her life to get pregnant than now. And then there was Vinny. How could she possibly tell him she was pregnant with his child after a couple of nights of rekindling an old love in a situation that probably should never have happened? Despite what Vinny had told her when she broke the news to him that they could go no further with the relationship, this changed everything. He had told her he had real feelings for her and that he had never stopped loving her. It had been like some old movie scene, but once the heat died down, she was sure he'd accepted that there was no future for them. He was a career cop. She was the head of a notorious gangster family. It just couldn't work. Then the niggling thought came that he had a right to know. Sharon had said to her that if she found out she was pregnant, then she'd know what to do next. But for Kerry, there was not a single thought of doing anything other than going on with this pregnancy. She was in trouble, no doubt about it. And there was trouble around her, but this pregnancy was *her* trouble, and she would have to deal with it. She wished she had someone to talk to. She called Maria and invited her over for dinner at the house. As she was about to go along to the kitchen and ask Elsa to prepare something for them tonight, her mobile rang. No number. But as soon as he spoke, she knew.

'Kerry. It's me. It's Frankie.'

Her blood ran cold. She had to be calm. She wanted to scream at him, but she had to think rationally. Frankie Martin. Back from the dead. He wasn't calling her to wish her well. She waited.

'Kerry. You need to listen to me. It's about Marty's boy. I have a message for you. From Pepe Rodriguez.'

Kerry held her breath. The treacherous bastard was in with the Colombians, just as they'd suspected.

'So, you're Pepe Rodriguez's message boy now, Frankie. And we thought you were dead.' Her voice was deadpan.

'Kerry. There's no time for this shit, if Marty wants to see his boy again.'

Kerry bit back tears of rage.

'Frankie, you're a message boy. Don't try to monster me, you slimy bastard. Where is Finbar? You harm a fucking hair on that boy's head–'

'He's safe,' he cut her off. 'He's all right.'

'He's not fucking all right. He's three years old, Frankie. He'll be wanting his mummy and daddy. What kind of evil bastards have you got yourself in tow with?'

'Kerry. Calm down.'

'Tell me what this Rodriguez bastard wants.'

'He wants to meet you.'

'Get Finbar out of there and back to his family first.'

'That's the deal. Think about it. The boy gets released when you meet Rodriguez. You're fucked, Kerry. The Casey family is fucked, and you have yourself to thank for that.'

'Frankie,' Kerry could feel panic coursing through her, 'what does Rodriguez want? Is it money?'

'He wants everything. The hotel, all your businesses – taxi companies, restaurants, bars, estate agents in Spain. The lot.'

The line went dead.

'Frankie! Frankie!' But she knew he was gone.

She sat down, her legs shaky. She phoned Danny in Spain.

'Danny. It's me. That bastard Frankie Martin has been on the phone. Jesus, Danny, I can't believe this. I nearly died when I heard his voice. He's in with Rodriguez and Durkin right enough. The bastards sent Frankie with the ransom demand.'

'What?' Danny's voice went up an octave. 'That fucker Frankie. I'd hoped he was dead. He will be when I get my hands on him. What did he say?'

'He said he was giving a message from Pepe Rodriguez. The Colombian wants to meet me. They've got the boy all right. They said he was okay, but I wanted to strangle Frankie through the phone. Smug bastard.'

'Never mind that, Kerry. We'll deal with Frankie in due course. What did you say?'

'He hung up too quickly. He was just making contact. Asking for a meet. I asked what Rodriguez wants.'

'What did he say?'

'He said he wants the lot. Everything we have – including the hotel.'

'Bastard!'

'What do we do now, Danny?'

There was a pause.

'We wait for the next call. You'll need to meet him though. Jack and me will get a plane tonight. We need to work things out. By the way, have the cops been at you yet?'

'No. Just Vinny. He's been calling my mobile. But I patched it. He'll be wanting to pick my brains.'

'For sure.'

'Oh Danny, I can't stop thinking about poor wee Finbar.

That's a day and a night he's been gone. Poor wee kid will never get over this.'

'He will, Kerry. We just need to get him back safe. We'll work it out,' he said again, then paused. 'You'd better tell Marty.'

'I feel for Marty too, Danny. He hasn't even told his family about the call he got when the kid was taken, and now this. He's keeping secrets and they would go berserk if they knew what he was holding back.'

'I know. But this is about keeping Finbar safe. We can't fuck anything up here that might just jolt that Colombian bastard into doing something bad. You'll get another call tonight, I'm sure. I think you should call Marty and keep him informed.'

He hung up.

Kerry poured Maria a glass of red wine, but took only water for herself, as they sat at her kitchen table. Elsa had cooked lasagne, and Kerry was glad that her appetite had returned as she enjoyed every bite. Just sitting here with Maria, the way they used to sit in her bedroom as teenagers, gossiping when they should have been studying. How differently their lives had turned out, Kerry thought, as she saw how well Maria now looked compared to the waif with dark shadows under her eyes she had been that day they'd been reunited at her mother's funeral. So much had happened in their lives, but there was something precious that had brought them to this day when they could sit and enjoy each other's company. Before Maria arrived, Kerry wasn't sure how much she knew about Marty's grandson's kidnapping, but she would have seen it on the news. But the fact that they weren't discussing it here felt like the elephant in the room. Kerry knew she could trust Maria, and more than anything right now she needed to talk to someone about it.

'Maria,' Kerry said, 'you'll have seen and heard about Marty's grandson, Finbar.'

Maria nodded. 'I didn't want to mention it, Kerry, because it's not my place to pry, but I can't get it out of my mind.' She shook her head. 'That poor wee boy. And Marty, and of course the boy's parents will be beside themselves. Marty was so kind to my Cal that time when he got arrested. My heart bleeds for the man.'

Kerry knew that Maria would be wondering if the kidnapping was something to do with the Casey family, but she wouldn't want to ask. For a moment they said nothing, then Kerry spoke.

'I feel so responsible. It's enemies of the Casey family who have taken him. I'll never forgive myself.'

Maria didn't look surprised, but for a few beats she said nothing, and Kerry wondered if she was disgusted with her. Then she said, 'It crossed my mind that it must be something like that, or someone who wanted to hit back at Marty over a court case. Kidnapping a child is beyond evil.'

She took a sip of her wine. 'But, Kerry, I know what you mean. You are head of this family, and I know a little of what goes on here, but I'm doing the job I do and not asking questions.' She looked at her friend. 'I will always be grateful for what you have done for me, for Cal and for my Jenny. I will never judge you for how it came to this, that someone can use a child as a bargaining tool. So, I don't know what the answer is, but there has to be some way to get this boy back.' She paused. 'And I want you to know that whatever I can do to help in any way at all, I will. Whatever you are planning or discussing – I know I am not involved like that with your business – but if you need someone to help in any way, then I'll be there.'

Kerry looked at her, not quite sure what she meant. Maria was talking as though she wanted to be on the frontline.

'What I mean is,' Maria said, 'well, I suppose you must be looking at a way to get him back.'

'We don't even know where the boy is being held,' Kerry said.

'But you have so many people working for you, Kerry – eyes and ears everywhere – I can see that even in these few weeks doing my own job. There must be someone who can shed some light on where the boy is.'

'Of course. We are working on it. But then what?' Kerry asked. She knew Maria was the last person to have any insight on how to hunt down the Colombian and his cohorts, but she was interested in what she was saying.

'Then you find a way to get in there. To tear down their walls and get wee Finbar.'

Kerry found herself almost smiling at Maria's bold thoughts.

'You're talking like a military leader, Maria,' she said. 'I'm not knocking it, and once we find out where Finbar is we will be trying to find a way to tear down those walls – and keep him safe at the same time. I'm just surprised to hear this talk coming from you.'

Maria half smiled. 'I know what you mean. Easier said than done. I was just thinking back to stories my Al told me when he was home from Iraq. He'd been involved in rescuing those hostages that were on TV, where they smashed their way into the insurgent house and brought them out alive. I remember seeing it on telly, but never thinking for a moment Al was involved. He never told me himself about it when he came back. But one of his mates did, and when I asked him, he told me a little about it, and that people had died in the process – two insurgent teenagers in the house. He never spoke about it again. But these things can be achieved in hostage situations if the right people go in.' She pushed her wine away. 'I'm probably just talking rubbish, but I would feel pretty helpless right now and I'm sure you do, not being able to kick down doors and do something.'

'Exactly. But we have to wait and see,' Kerry said. 'But every hour that ticks by is another hour that Finbar will be getting more and more anxious and bewildered. What if he thinks his family have just abandoned him?' She felt choked.

'I know. But kids are amazingly resilient. You have to believe that.' She studied Kerry's face for a moment. 'Kerry. Are you all right in yourself? You look a bit peaky.'

The silence fell between them, the Kerry heard herself speak.

'I'm pregnant, Maria.'

Maria looked shocked.

'Jesus! Oh, Kerry! When did you find out? I noticed you weren't drinking wine, but I thought you were just tired from the trip and all the stress.'

'This afternoon. When I got back from Spain. Been throwing up for days, yet I didn't really seriously consider I might be pregnant. Stupid really.'

Maria looked at her. 'Is it Vinny?' she ventured. 'Sorry to ask, but you told me you'd seen him a couple of times.'

Kerry nodded. 'Yeah,' she replied. 'But that's it, Maria. Only a couple of times. It's not as if we were in a relationship.' She rubbed her face with her hands. 'What a bloody mess.'

'Does he know? Are you going to tell him?'

'Jesus no. Well, I don't know. Not yet anyway. He's phoned me a couple of times today, probably to ask about Marty and probably to fish if I know anything. But I patched his calls. I can't face him right now.'

Maria was quiet, then she spoke. 'You must be just about off your head with the shock and worry in the middle of everything else.'

'Yes. Couldn't be a worse time for this to happen. I have no room for a baby in my life right now. Because right now, it's Marty's grandson that overshadows everything. That's really all I can think about.'

'I understand. I'm sure you'll do what's best for you in due course.'

'I'm keeping the baby,' Kerry said quickly. 'I . . . I couldn't bear the thought of not keeping it. Especially with my miscarriage last year. But that was in totally different circumstances. I'm pregnant now in the middle of the biggest crisis in my life.'

'You'll find a way, Kerry. It's only a baby. You'll find a way through it. And I'll be there for you any time of the day or night.'

'Thanks, Maria.'

CHAPTER SEVEN

It was the lying as much as the cold fear that made Marty Kane feel sick inside. Every time he looked at his wife or his son, he felt a sense of betrayal. He had lied to his family in the very depths of their despair. Their little boy had been taken, and Marty was withholding information that they would surely believe could be crucial in finding him and getting him back. He felt helpless and responsible. But deep down he had to believe he was doing the right thing. Not telling police that the kidnappers had made contact with Kerry Casey was the biggest gamble of his life. He was trusting criminals over the police. The depth of that dishonesty was not lost on him and had kept him awake for the last two nights. But his gut feeling was not to come clean to the police yet. He watched his mobile every hour, waiting for another call. Kerry had told him that the weasel Frankie Martin had made a call to her, to deliver a message from the Colombian that they had Fin. Kerry told him the message was that they wanted everything the Caseys had. But she asked Marty to hold fire and keep this to himself. Whoever was holding Fin wanted his life to be something they could bargain over. And Marty was standing by allowing it to happen. He would never forgive himself for what he was doing. But he had to believe it was the right thing.

From the window of his study, Marty saw the unmarked police car pull into his driveway, and he watched as two officers got out. One of them he recognised as Vinny Burns, the DI that Kerry had made the deal with during the battle with Joe 'Knuckles' Boyle. He thought Kerry had taken a bit of a flier in that one – bringing in police so that Boyle would be caught red-handed with a container load of smuggled cocaine. But it had worked. He had never spoken to Burns, but through the grapevine he'd learned that Kerry had some kind of romance or fling going on with him – a rekindling from when they were teenagers. If Kerry had asked him his opinion of that at the time, he would have told her that he thought it was not prudent for someone in her position to be involved with a detective in the middle of an operation. But she hadn't asked him, so he respected that. Marty had always been more than just the family lawyer, and he loved Kerry as though she was a favourite niece, but it was not his place to go meddling in her private life. Now, as the detectives rang his doorbell, he wondered what role Vinny Burns was playing in Kerry's life at the moment, and what was bringing him here. There had been a succession of police and detectives to the house over the last forty-eight hours, including the senior DCI who was running the investigation. He hadn't seen Vinny Burns around at all, and had thought he was involved in the Drug Enforcement Agency, not kidnapping. Marty could hear the door being opened, and voices, so he came out of his study and walked down the hall where his wife was greeting the officers, her face so tired and aged overnight it broke his heart.

'Mr Kane?' Vinny stepped forward and reached out a hand. 'DI Vincent Burns. We met briefly before.'

Marty shook his hand, recalling the detective coming to question Kerry after the funeral to fish for information.

'Yes,' he said, glad that he hadn't mentioned the Casey family meeting in front of Elizabeth. 'I remember. Come in.'

'This is DS William Johnson,' Burns said gesturing to his sidekick as they came into the hall. 'We wanted have a chat with you, if that's possible.'

'I thought DCI Marsh was in charge of the operation? He was here this morning.'

'Yes. I know,' Burns said. 'I'm part of the team on it too now.' He glanced at Elizabeth then back at Marty. 'Is there somewhere we can have a chat?'

Marty looked at Elizabeth and was glad she looked weary enough not to want to be involved.

'My son Joe and his wife are not here at the moment,'

Marty said, leading them down towards his study. 'But we can have a chat, of course. Unless you want me to call him?'

'No,' Burns said, quickly. 'That's fine.'

They walked down to the study and went inside. Marty closed the door softly, bracing himself for awkward questions.

He motioned the two policemen to chairs opposite the fireplace, but stayed on his feet. They declined his offer of tea, and he stood waiting for the first question.

'Mr Kane,' Burns began, 'I'm sure that time we met at the Casey house, that I mentioned I am working with the Drug Enforcement Agency?'

'Yes,' Marty replied. 'I think I recall that.'

'Well, I may or may not have told you that I was seconded up here from London to work on the wider aspect of organised crime through the international drugs trade as we work hand in hand with agencies across the world.'

'I do recall that,' Marty said, wondering when he was going to get to the point of his visit.

A mobile rang, and the DS went into his pocket and fished it out. He nodded to Burns.

'I have to take this call. I'll go back to the car. It could take a few minutes.'

Burns acknowledged it and waited until he left the room. Then he spoke.

'Mr Kane,' he began. 'Look. I know this is the most difficult time in your life. I can only begin to imagine the agony for you and your family, but we are working very hard on this operation, and we feel sure that we will get Finbar back to you safe and sound.'

Marty took a breath. He had heard this before over the last two days, but it was just platitudes, because as far as he could gather, the police didn't really know where to start in all of this. And he knew that one of the reasons for that was because he was withholding information. He kept his face straight.

'I can only hope you're right, Inspector.'

Burns let the silence hang in the air for a long moment, and Marty waited.

'Look, Mr Kane,' he said. 'I'm going to be really straight with you here. I know you are the family lawyer for the Caseys and have been friends and close associates with them for at least a generation.'

Marty nodded. 'It's common knowledge, yes, that they are my clients. And indeed, I'm sure you may have read somewhere that I was very close to the late Tim Casey.' He cleared his throat. 'I am still the family lawyer, if that is what you are asking.'

'Then you must know of the problems the Caseys are having with the Colombian gangsters. One particular nasty individual named Pepe Rodriguez, to be precise.'

Marty said nothing, but his gut jolted a little just hearing the name. He managed to remain poker-faced.

'On a personal level,' Burns continued, 'I know of this

individual – I worked undercover in Colombia for over two years, so I know who some of the main players are. I know, for example, that Rodriguez is moving in big time across the Costa del Sol and that he and his henchmen are muscling in on all the turf of the various criminals down there.' He paused for effect. 'And I know because, Mr Kane, we have contacts and snitches in places that would surprise you – even within the Colombian organisation – that Rodriguez has expressed an interest in going into the hotel and property business down there.'

Marty kept silent, afraid that anything he would say might blow up in his face.

'Now,' Burns went on, shoving his hands in his trouser pockets, looking very much in command. 'I know personally that Kerry Casey wants take the family into the hotel business and property and that she has a particular hotel interest on the Costa del Sol that is currently under planning and that she hopes will be under construction very soon. And I know that Rodriguez and the Irish mob he's involved with – one Pat Durkin – are determined they will get that from her.'

Marty took a breath and let it out slowly.

'Inspector, I hear what you're saying. But what do you want me to do here? I'm not really sure why you are here.'

'I wanted to make personal contact with you, Mr Kane. Because I want you to know that perhaps we know more than Kerry Casey thinks we do.'

'So are you saying that you think these people may be behind the kidnapping of my grandson?' Marty felt bad at his own duplicity.

Burns stood up, so that he was at eye level with Marty.

'I'm saying it's a possibility. Perhaps even likely. But we are very surprised that there has been no contact yet from the kidnappers – no ransom demand – yet it is almost forty-eight hours now since Finbar was taken.'

'How do you know he was taken by criminals like this? How do you know it isn't just some random person who is behind it – that's our main worry; that it may be some kind of . . .' Marty wanted to say warped paedophile, but he knew this wasn't true, and felt he'd said enough.

'I know what you mean, Mr Kane. But we think the Colombian and Irish mobsters – who are working together – have him.' He paused. 'So I am here to make a connection with you, to say that if there has been contact with you or Kerry Casey then please, I urge you, don't leave this to anyone but the police. Please, if they have contacted you or the Caseys, don't let the Caseys deal with it. They are criminals.'

Marty let that stand for a moment.

'Are you seriously saying that you think Kerry Casey, who I have known since she was six years old, would actually use my grandson as a bargaining chip to help her build some luxury hotel in Spain? Are you saying that? Because I don't believe that. I *can't* believe that.'

'No, I'm not saying that, Mr Kane. I'm saying that of

course Kerry Casey and her associates would have your grandson's safety at their hearts. But my worry is that they and their criminal gangs and contacts believe they can take on the Colombians and come out of this without anyone being harmed. That is my fear. And that is the only reason I came here today. To tell you this. To make you aware of this, and to impress upon you the need for police at your back, and not criminals.'

'Have you spoken to Kerry Casey? Has anyone?'

'I have tried to contact her. But I haven't spoken to her as yet. But I will do. Today.'

Marty nodded. Burns buttoned his jacket. He had delivered the message, and it came over loud and clear to Marty. What if he was right? What if they couldn't just leave it to the Caseys?

'Thanks for your advice, Inspector.'

Marty nodded as he walked him to the door of the study. As he opened it to go out, Burns turned to him.

'And please, I hope you will understand that our only goal here is to bring Finbar home. Whatever criminal activity these people want to engage in, they will do it long after your grandson is back, and they will fight among themselves over turf the way they have always done. But a little boy's safety is at stake here. That is all we want to think about at the moment.'

'I understand,' Marty said. 'Thanks for coming. I'll see you out.'

They walked to the front door in silence, and Marty opened it and let him out. He glimpsed the DS in the car who didn't look as though he was doing anything other than giving his boss a wide berth so that he could get his message across. Marty closed the door and stood for a moment with his back to it. He glanced along the hall to the kitchen, where he could see his wife standing at the cooker. She was staring at him as though she could see into his soul, and he could barely look her in the eye.

CHAPTER EIGHT

Donna Williams knew there was something well dodgy about the way her man was behaving. As cokeheads went, Lenny Wilson was jittery at the best of times, but for the past two days he could hardly sit down for fully five minutes. She watched him as she sipped from a mug of tea at the kitchen table of their council flat in Glasgow's rough Calton housing scheme. He was up and down like a yoyo, going from the window to the bedroom, checking his mobile constantly. She knew better than to ask what was going on. The bruise on her cheek was still yellow from last week's slapping when she insisted he tell her where he'd been all night. She suspected he was shagging some bird who owed him money for coke but needed another few grams to give her the self-belief she needed to go shoplifting up the town. She knew what that felt like. She'd once been that bird, and that's how she had ended up here with Lenny in this pigsty. She promised herself that one of these days she'd walk out the door and never come back. She would go to her mum where her two little kids lived and start a new life. She promised her mother every time she went to see her children that she would quit the coke and get her life together. For the sake of the kids, who she could see were becoming more distant from her every time she visited. They were settled and happy with her mum now, since she had marched into the hovel Donna lived in nearly two years ago and told her she was taking them away from the shitty existence she was giving them. Donna was ashamed that she didn't even have the will to fight for them. The coke had become so important that there was no room for anything else. She was glad when she met Lenny Wilson, and could see that he had taken a shine to her. As one of the bigger dealers in the East End, Lenny would be able to feed her habit and she wouldn't have to hock her skinny mutton at the escort agency any longer. It had been good while it lasted. But not any more. Lenny had become violent, beating her up, jumping into irrational rages about the smallest thing, then begging forgiveness when he saw her bruises. She'd just kept taking more coke and as long as she did, she was his prisoner here. But now she was trying to find a way out. He disgusted her with how he lived and was content to live, and she was managing to cut down her coke use to a minimum without him noticing. She'd secretly been going to drug rehab meetings in the city centre where nobody would recognise her. Perhaps that's why she'd become more tuned in to the nervy way he was these past few days.

The television was on low in the background, and Donna glanced up as the BBC news came on. She was vaguely listening to it, then she heard the story about the kidnapping of some lawyer's three-year-old grandson. She'd seen that two days ago when it just happened and it was the first item on all the news. They were working round the clock, the cops were saying. They were still trying to find the boy, and were determined they would get him back safe. They had no idea who had him, they admitted. Probably some paedo, Donna thought, and felt a shiver run through her thinking of her own little Tommy, and how it would kill her if anything like that happened. Any time you watched the news and a kid went missing, you knew it would end with them finding the body, and she couldn't help herself thinking about the kid.

'Put that shite off.'

She heard Lenny's irritated voice from the doorway, but she ignored it and continued to watch. Then he marched across and snatched the remote control from the table.

'I said get that shite off. You fucking deaf?'

He glared at her, eyes wild with anger that seemed to come from nowhere.

'Christ's sake, Lenny,' she huffed. 'I was watching that! Poor wee guy. What the fuck's wrong with you these days? You're jumpy as fuck, man.'

He gave her a look that said watch your step or you'll get a sore face. She looked down at the table, feeling suddenly hurt and angry at the same time. She wanted to confront him, ask if he wanted her out, but she didn't have the courage in case he told her to go. She wasn't ready to go back to her mum yet. She needed a bit more time. Lenny's mobile rang and he turned and left the kitchen. She could hear him talking softly. She waited until she heard the bedroom door closing tightly, then she padded down the hallway quietly. As she stood at the door, she strained her ears. From his tone, it didn't sound like he was sweet-talking some bird. He was edgy.

'Fuck's sake, man,' he hissed down the phone. 'No' again. I was told all I had to do was drive the motor that one time. I was only supposed to drive him from the fucking shopping mall to the drop-off place, and that was it. I mean, that was fucking scary enough. But keeping moving the wean about now? That's fucking asking for trouble.'

Donna felt her blood run cold. She must be hearing things. Surely to Christ he wasn't involved in kidnapping that wee guy? Surely to fuck not. She listened hard, but Lenny wasn't speaking, so she assumed the other person was talking to him. Then she heard him again.

'I've only been paid two grand, man. The agreement was two grand – one drop. That was all. But that's two nights now I've had to go and drive again and I haven't been paid another penny. It's fucking dangerous, man. What if I get stopped by the cops or something? It's all over the fucking news again. I just saw it on the telly.'

Donna had her hand on her mouth in disbelief. It was *him*. That wee boy. Holy Christ. This couldn't be happening. What kind of bastard was Lenny that he would play any part in kidnapping a wee wean? Only a monster would do that. She slipped back down the hall into the kitchen and poured the remains of her tea into the sink, then scrubbed the mug furiously.

Donna convinced her mate Shona to come along with her. She wasn't exactly her best mate, but they'd met at AA, and Shona was already eighteen months drug free. She had a job and a council flat in a decent enough area. But most importantly – she had a car. Donna hadn't told her what they were going to be doing, but promised her it wasn't anything illegal, they weren't on the rob, but she would get well paid in due course. Probably sooner rather than later, she'd told her. Depending on how it worked out. She'd been cryptic enough to whet Shona's curiosity, but the promise of money was what spurred her on, because Shona had become houseproud since she'd got her own gaff, and was saving up to get a new kitchen. Donna told her mate to be standing by for the night, that she would give her a ring to tell her when to come. Donna had to wait until Lenny went into the shower so she could sneak a look at the text message she'd heard pinging late afternoon. She read it quickly. It said simply 'Be at the address at seven pm.' There was no address, which made it a bit more tricky. That meant they'd have to follow him, running the risk of him clocking them. But Donna was fairly confident that Lenny was so wound up, he wouldn't even be looking in the rear-view mirror. Wherever he was going, she had to get there too. If he was doing what she suspected, this was dynamite. This could bring her in a fortune.

She'd taken the precaution of telling Lenny she was going over to her mum's to see the kids, so she would be out by the time he left the house. As soon as he came out of the shower and was throwing some clothes on, she left. It was already six twenty. So wherever he was going, it wasn't that far. She went down the stairs of the apartment block into the street and walked briskly up to the corner where she could see Shona's dark blue Ford Fiesta parked with the lights out. She glanced over her shoulder at the darkened street, then opened the door and got inside.

'You are freaking me out, Donna, with all this cloak and fucking dagger stuff,' Shona said as she planked herself onto the passenger seat. 'Are you sure we're not going to get arrested by the end of the night?'

She could smell Shona's perfume and noticed the fresh look she had, all smartly dressed, and she wished she could get to that stage where she would look respectable like her. She half smiled at Shona.

'Don't be daft,' she said. 'We're not breaking any laws. All we're doing is watching.' She looked over her shoulder down the street. 'We have to follow somebody – discreetly, obviously. We need to find out where they're going without them seeing us.' She looked at her. 'That's all. Then once we see where they are, we disappear.'

'What if they clock us following them? I mean, if this is some fucking dealer or something and they see us, we'll get our heads kicked in.'

'No,' Donna said. 'It's nothing like that. It's a kind of watching and following situation.'

'Like a private eye?'

'Yeah. Like a private eye.'

'Fuck me! Maybe we'll get our own TV show out of this!' Shona grinned. 'So what do we do now?'

'We sit here until I see someone going into their car. In my street.'

'In your street?' She rolled her eyes. 'Aw, don't tell me we're spying on your man to see if he's out shagging. Christ's sake!'

'Not shagging. That's not what we're doing.' She paused, trying to keep herself calm, but she was cold and shivery with nerves. 'I told you. It's something that can make us money. Listen. Don't ask questions. Just trust me.'

'Fair enough. But there better be a decent payola for me.'

'There will be. Not tonight. But soon.'

They sat in silence for a moment, Donna's eyes peering

at her block of flats, watching for the light going off upstairs. It was half six. She was beginning to wonder what was going on. Then suddenly, a black Jeep pulled up outside Lenny's flat, She watched as the lights went off in the flat. Lenny never drove as he was always hyped up on coke, so he must be paying someone to drive him.

'Get ready,' she said. 'Don't switch the engine on just yet. But be ready. Any second now.'

Seconds later, she saw Lenny come out of the building and climb into the car. Then the Jeep eased out of the space and drove down the street.

'That's it. Let's go. Keep well behind, but don't lose them.'

'Christ! I must be off my fucking head.' Shona switched on the engine and carefully came out down the long street that led out of the scheme.

They followed the car in silence, Donna's heart in her mouth. She hadn't really thought out the plan in any detail, but she had to see where Lenny was going. She was even asking herself what if she had got this totally wrong and it was perfectly innocent, but her gut told her it wasn't. He'd been totally wound out of his box in the last two days. He was up to something. They followed the car all the way into the city centre and across Jamaica Bridge, then onto the Kinning Park area that was mostly warehouses and old buildings. It was a creepy, dark street with not much traffic except people heading onto the M8 motorway. But it was busy enough with moving traffic for them to keep a few cars behind and still see the Jeep. Then they saw it park at the entrance to a warehouse. There were a few cars in the car park next to it and lights on inside. Donna thought the warehouse might still be open, and wondered what the hell was going on.

'Pull over there, Shona. So we can still see what's happening.'

'It's quiet down here, Donna. It's not the kind of place you can just sit in your car.'

Donna looked at her.

'You're wrong about that,' she said. 'If you were to stroll up this street and car parks and look into some of these cars, you'd find some punter getting humped in the back seat by one of the hookers. It's where the girls sometimes take their punters. Close enough to the city, but far enough away from the main drag.'

'Seriously? How do you know that?'

'Don't ask,' Donna said, staring out of the windscreen, trying to blot out the memory of giving blowjobs to men in suits who were probably on their way home to their wives.

'Oh,' Shona said. Then she gave Donna's arm a supportive squeeze. 'Sorry. But all that's in the past.'

'Too right,' Donna said.

They sat watching, quietly, the car lights turned off, and Donna straining her eyes peering at the building. She took a little camera out of her bag that one of the shoplifters had sold her a couple of years ago. It was a good Nikon but small. She'd learned how to work it and had taken cherished pictures of her kids on it. She switched it on.

'Fuck's sake. Pictures and everything. This is like the telly.'

Donna managed a smile but her mouth was dry with nerves. They sat for a few more minutes. Then a shaft of light from a side door hit the darkened car park. She could see figures coming out of the building, and luckily for her, their footsteps set off a security sensor lighting up the car park. She snapped a couple of pictures, but only captured Lenny and whoever was driving the Jeep. They went forward and opened the back door. She watched, snapping away like the paparazzi, glad her hands weren't trembling because she was shaking inside. She wound down the side window to see if she could hear anything, but there was nothing. They were too far away to be able to hear conversation. But there were muffled voices. Then out of the building came someone carrying something wrapped up in a blanket. She zoomed in. Her stomach dropped. It looked like the feet of a child dangling below the blanket. Then they heard the screams.

'Muuuuummyy! I want my muuummy!'

Donna's heart stopped. She turned to Shona.

'Oh, fuck!'

'Donna. What the fuck is this? That's a wean screaming.'

'Ssssh. Keep down.'

They both watched in horror as the little booted feet

kicked and the child screamed all the way to the car. Then the bundle was shoved into the back seat and the car sped off. Donna snapped again, getting the number plate.

'I'm not following that car,' Shona said. 'Whatever the fuck is going on there, I'm not following that.'

Donna nodded. 'It's okay. We don't need to.'

CHAPTER NINE

Kerry sat in the semi-darkness of the living room with only the glow of the fire and the small reading lamp to give some light. So much had happened in the last couple of days, and she had scarcely drawn breath, trying to get her head around the mess they were in. The hotel venture was now looking to be given the green light by Spanish planning officials. The hard work to take everyone involved in the Casey organisation to a different level should have been about to begin. Now it was dawning on her that it wasn't going to happen. The dream was over. It wasn't important any more. Only two things mattered to her right now: Marty's boy – getting him away from the monsters who took him; and the little life that was apparently now settling into her womb. She hadn't even taken time to think about that, barely acknowledged that she was actually having a baby, apart from the confirmation of the pregnancy test kit. Yet sitting here listening to the rain rattling on the windows, it occurred to her that there was more to fight for now. It wasn't just her own dream to take the Caseys out of the swamps in memory of her father. She had to build a future for the baby that would grow inside her in the coming months. It was worth fighting for. She'd been ready to hand everything over without a fight after the call from Frankie saying that the Colombian wanted it all. It was only money, she'd decided. She would survive and so would the Caseys – in some form. But again the thought kept coming back to her. Why should she give in so easily? There had to be a way to fight back. She was tired, but she knew there was no point in even going to bed.

Her mobile rang on the coffee table, and she could see it was Vinny's number. Marty had called her earlier to say the detective had visited his home and was fishing to see if he was telling the police everything. Marty had also said Vinny was remarkably well informed about the Colombians, and the problems Kerry was having with them. She sensed from Marty's voice that he was beginning to buckle and question if they were doing the right thing – trying to go this alone without the police. Forty-eight hours had now passed. Two nights out of the house for little Finbar. She let the phone ring four times then picked it up.

'Vinny.'

'Hello, Kerry.' There was a pause for a single beat. 'I called you a few times.'

'I know, I'm sorry.' She was surprised at how emotional she felt. 'I just wasn't able to talk to you. I . . . We're all in a mess over Marty's wee guy. It's awful. Can't stop thinking about it.'

Kerry waited in the silence. She knew he would have to get to the point soon.

'I know, Kerry. I'm on the case now too. Was asked to get involved.'

She didn't want to say she already knew that because Marty had phoned, so she said nothing.

'Kerry. I don't know if you talked to Marty since I did earlier today, but I need you to know that if this kidnapping is anything to do with the problems you are having with this Colombian mobster, then we should talk.'

Kerry couldn't trust herself to say anything. So after another moment's silence, Vinny continued.

'Look. These bastards don't play the game the way other criminals do. They will stop at nothing. I know this. I worked in the Colombian cartels and I've seen the brutality. It's beyond anything you could imagine. They've murdered innocent children asleep in bed with their mothers. Believe me, Kerry. They will have no qualms about harming wee Finbar, if it is them who have him. If they are holding him to ransom, you need to know that you cannot do this alone. Not the Caseys, not even the combined forces of every gangster family in the UK. You cannot beat these people.' He paused. 'Please listen to me. If you have had any contact with them and if you know or suspect they have Finbar, then you need to bring in the police. If you don't do that, the blood will be on your hands.'

His words cut through her like a knife.

'Christ's sake, Vinny!'

'I'm sorry. There's no easy way to get this point across. If it is nothing to do with your family, then I apologise. But if it is – please, please don't put this off. I've seen how these things pan out before. Bad things will start happening to this kid very soon if they don't get what they want.'

Kerry shivered. The truth of what he was saying was overwhelming, and she had no answers. They stayed that way on the phone, saying nothing, until she thought for a second he was gone.

'Kerry,' Vinny said softly, 'I've been thinking about you since I last saw you. I want you to know that.'

'Thanks,' Kerry said, choking back emotion. She was sitting here alone and terrified, and carrying Vinny's child, and he was the one person in the world she should be able to confide in for support. But she couldn't.

'Can I see you?'

'Oh, Vinny,' she said. 'My head is all over the place. I can't right now.'

'What about tomorrow?'

She took a breath. 'I don't know.' She couldn't do this any longer. She had to get off the phone. 'Look. I have to go just now. I . . . I have to go.'

'I'll call you tomorrow,' Vinny said.

'Okay,' Kerry said as the line went dead.

She stood up and walked across to the window where she could see the lights of the security gatehouse and a couple of guards inside. Then her mobile rang again. No name or number. Her stomach flipped. She pressed the answer key.

'Kerry.'

She thought she was going to explode with rage.

'You fucking traitor. What the fuck, Frankie? A whole day. And nothing from you or the fucking monsters pulling your strings. A whole day, Frankie!'

'I know,' Frankie said, deadpan. 'Calm down. Just take it easy, Kerry. There was some sorting out to do this end. I've been talking to Rodriguez.'

'Where is Finbar, Frankie? Where is that wee boy? Tell me that right now or I'll hang up.'

'You wouldn't be wise to hang up.'

'Fucking tell me, you evil bastard!' Kerry could hear her voice quiver. She tried to breathe slowly but couldn't catch her breath. 'Tell me!' Her voice was almost a scream.

'Kerry! Calm down, I said. Blowing a fucking gasket isn't going to get you anywhere. Not with me, and not with the people I'm dealing with. Listen. The wee guy is safe.'

'Where is he?' She had managed to climb off the edge of hysteria. 'Please, Frankie,' she pleaded. 'Just tell me that?'

'Look. I shouldn't be telling you anything, Kerry. But I

need you to calm down and listen. I can't tell you where he is, but all you need to know is that he's in Glasgow.'

'And where are you?'

She heard him give a wry snigger.

'Well. I'm not in Glasgow. That's for sure.'

'Probably just as well, for your sake.'

'Aye. We'll see about that. But this is no time for fucking around arguing. I told you Rodriguez wants a meet.'

'You told me that yesterday. I've been waiting for your call.'

'And I told you what he wants – everything.'

'I know you did.'

'So. Are you ready to make a deal? To have the meet? To give everything to him?'

'Frankie,' Kerry said, trying to be calm, 'I don't have any documents here. Everything is in Spain.'

'We don't need documents. Rodriguez's men will bring legal stuff. Look, I'm not involved in that. But I suppose you'll be asked to sign something – an affidavit or some shit.'

Kerry didn't reply, waited to see what he was going to say next.

'And,' Frankie said, 'if you do what he wants, then that's it.'

'Where is Rodriguez?'

'He's not in Glasgow either. But his people are. And he'll be there for the meet. You just say the word.' He paused. 'But if I were you, then I wouldn't hang about on this. I've met him, and he's not a patient man.'

Kerry bit her lip to suppress another furious outburst. There will come a time, she made a vow to herself, when this is over, and I will have my revenge on you, Frankie Martin. For everything you've done.

'Okay,' Kerry said. 'Organise the meet. But only if Finbar is going to be there to be handed over.'

Frankie hung up without replying.

If ever anyone was out of their depth right now, it was her, Kerry thought as she paced the floor. She didn't even know where to start. Vinny was right. A little boy's life was at stake here. The police had more resources at their fingertips than the Caseys could muster in the next twenty-four hours. But if the Colombians got wind that the police were involved it didn't bear thinking about. She was glad Danny was home in the morning, when they would have to make a serious decision. There was a knock on the door of the living room.

'Come in,' she said.

The door opened and one of the security guards stood there, his hair wet from the rain. He was holding an envelope in his hand.

'Sorry, Kerry. This was pushed through the door of the gatehouse. Don't know who did it, because the bell was rung and the person must have run away. But we'll be able to see them on CCTV. I've got the boys looking at it now.' He handed her the envelope, a little wet at the edges.

'Thanks, Jim.' She took it from him, and he turned and left.

Kerry went across to the table and ripped open the pale cream envelope which was addressed to her. She pulled out a sheet of writing paper and read the scrawl.

'I can help find the boy who has been kidnapped.'

That was all. No name. Just a mobile phone number. Kerry didn't know what to think, whether it was some kind of hoax, and why deliver the note to her address and not Marty or Joe Kane's? Before she could stop herself she was punching in the number. A woman's voice answered after three rings.

'Hello?' Kerry said.

No answer.

'This is Kerry Casey. This number was on a note pushed through my door. Who is this?'

Silence.

'Who is it? What's going on? If you can help us find out where Finbar is, speak to me, for Christ's sake!'

'I think I can help.' The voice was soft, sounded nervous.

'How?'

'I think I saw him being taken from a place last night. He was covered in a blanket.'

Kerry's gut was telling her this was some nutter.

'What makes you think that a boy in a blanket being carried is Finbar Kane?'

'Because I think I know someone who's involved.'

'Who?'

'My . . . My boyfriend. He doesn't know I saw this. I followed him. He'd kill me if he knew I was doing this.'

Kerry's mind was a blur. She had to keep this woman on the phone. She had to see her.

'Can I meet you? Any time? Tonight if you want? Now?'

'I don't want cops. If this is the kidnapped boy, then I could get murdered for doing this.'

'I'll protect you. If you have information that is solid we need to act now. Where are you? I'll come and meet you.'

'I'm scared now.'

Kerry had to keep her calm.

'Listen. You came here and put the note through my door. You obviously want to help. You must be as disgusted and shocked as we all are by this kidnapping.'

'I've got two weans. I'd die if something like this happened.'

'Why give the note to me?' Kerry asked. 'Why not Marty Kane's house, or office, or his son's address?'

'I was scared in case there were polis there. Maybe someone watching. I read in the paper yesterday some stuff that Marty Kane was the Casey family lawyer, and there was a hint that this might be connected. I didn't know what to do, so I contacted you.'

'You've done the right thing, er . . . What's your name?

'I can't tell you my name. I'm scared.'

'Can I see you now? Anywhere. Just say where.'

There was a long pause. Then the girl spoke. 'In the city centre. A fish and chip café. Top of Hope Street.'

'Are you there now?'

'No. But I will be in about twenty minutes. I'm on the bus.'

'Okay. I'll be there.'

Kerry hung up, her mind in a turmoil. She called downstairs to ask for Eddie the chauffeur to bring the car round, then phoned Jack, told him briefly what was going on, and asked him to come with her for backup, just in case this was a trap.

CHAPTER TEN

Kerry saw Jack come through the gate with his four-by-four and climb out into the rain. Big Joe Brady was with him. Joe was a six foot two ex-boxer, built like a tank and with a face that you couldn't mark with a pickaxe. There were tales that Brady was used for meting out beatings to people they needed to get fast answers from, and word was that he never failed. Jack knocked on the kitchen door and stepped inside, as Kerry was pulling on her coat.

'Brady?' she said, raising her eyebrows. 'Are you expecting trouble, Jack?'

'You never know, Kerry. From what you tell me, we need to be careful this isn't a trap. That's the first point. The next is, whatever information this girl gives us, we might have to act on it straight away. That might involve paying one or two people a visit and getting some answers. Brady's our man for that.' He held open the door for Kerry. 'But don't worry. He's not going to go into the café kicking tables over.'

Kerry walked past him out to the courtyard, and got into the front seat of the Jag, nodding to Brady who sat stony-faced in the back. He raised his chin in acknowledgement of her greeting, but stared straight ahead.

'Howsit going, Eddie?' she said to the chauffeur. 'We're going to Hope Street, a chip shop café place at the top of the street.'

'Blue Lagoon,' he said. 'Good fish in there. Legend. But I don't suppose we're going for a fish tea.'

'No,' Kerry half smiled, 'not tonight.'

Jack had done a quick walk past the café to make sure this woman who was supposed to be meeting Kerry was on her own. He came back to the car and told her he saw one girl, sitting at the back of the café. Kerry decided that must be her, and she got out of the car. As she walked through the door a blast of hot air and the smell of fried fish and chips hit her. An elderly couple sat eating at another table near the door. The staff looked up from the fryers, and Kerry glanced along the café to the back, where a young skinny girl was looking in her direction. She walked towards her.

'Are you the girl who left me the note?' she asked.

'Aye. Are you Kerry?'

'That's right.' She sat down.

The girl looked shifty, nervy. Kerry leaned forward, bringing the letter out of her pocket and laying it flat on the table.

'You want to tell me all about this? What's your name, anyway?'

She nodded. 'Aye. But I'm scared. And it's Donna.'

'Not as scared as wee Finbar Kane is,' Kerry said, 'if that is who you saw.'

'I'm sure it is,' she said. 'Well, as sure as I can be.'

'How can you be that sure?' Kerry asked.

They sat for a moment, and Kerry watched as the woman fiddled nervously with a ring on her finger, and noticed her chewed nails and inflamed skin around the cuticles.

'Right,' Donna said. 'I'm just going to tell you everything I know.' She paused, but Kerry looked her in the eye and didn't answer, so she went on. 'My boyfriend – well the guy I live with. He's a coke dealer. I'm leaving him. He did this.' She turned her face so Kerry could see the fading bruise. 'I'm getting out of there. Soon as I can. When I get enough money to get far away from him.'

Kerry was suspicious straight away, but she urged her to go on.

'So,' Donna said. 'Yesterday. I was watching the news and it came up about that wee boy, and Lenny – that's my boyfriend's name – took a flaky and made me switch it off. Then about ten minutes later I heard him talking on the phone in the other room. I listened hard and I could hear him saying he'd been paid two grand and he was only supposed to do a drive from the shopping mall. One drop, he said. But now he was being asked to drive to more places. He was bitching about it. And then I heard him saying that he'd just been watching it on the news. So it was then I decided that they must be talking about the same thing. The wee boy. I felt sick inside. I've got two weans. Imagine that I'm living with a fucker who could do that. For money.'

'So what did you do next?'

Kerry listened, watching Donna's face for any clues as she recounted going to the warehouse with her friend Shona, and watching as Lenny and this guy went in and then somebody came out with the kid and then they drove him away.

'I took photos,' she said.

Kerry's eyes nearly popped out of her head.

'You took photos?'

'Aye.' She reached into her pocket and took the small camera out, then started to bring pictures up. 'I took photos of everything I saw, then of the car driving away. I got the number plate in them.'

This was almost too good to be true. She looked at the pictures and sure enough it seemed to be little feet with boots on wrapped in a blanket.

'The kid was screaming, "I want my mummy!" It was terrible.'

'Would you be able to take us to this warehouse?'

'Aye,' she shrugged, 'I suppose so. It's in Kinning Park, just over the other side of the river. I thought it would be shut last night, but it wasn't. The lights were on and there were people in it, but the people carrying the wean came out a side door, so that might be separate.'

'Can you come with us now?'

She looked nervous, eyes down at the table.

'There's no time to waste on this, Donna. This information could be crucial, but we need to see what we can do about it.' She paused for a moment, scanning her face. 'Why didn't you go to the police with this?' Kerry knew the answer, but she wanted it to come from her.

Donna looked furtively around her and leaned forward.

'Moncy. I need money. To leave that bastard Lenny. To get back to my weans. I want to start again.'

'You a coke addict?'

'Was. I go to meetings now. I'm finished with that.'

It occurred to Kerry that this might be a set-up by a clever junkie to stage a few images and get some money. Not many junkies would have the nous to take a camera with them on a finding mission. But people watched a lot of television these days, and they were more clued up than before. Her gut instinct told her this was genuine, though, and she'd learned to trust her gut.

'I've got a car outside. I want you to come with us now.'

'Will I get sorted? I mean, money-wise?'

'You'll get sorted,' Kerry said firmly.

She stood up, and watched Donna get to her feet: skinny waist, thin coat and ripped jeans. She was waiflike, with a face that should be pretty, but was drawn and old beyond her years.

'Let's go,' Kerry said.

They were at the warehouse within ten minutes, and they sat while she pointed to exactly where she had seen the people coming out. On the way there, once Kerry showed Jack the camera shot of the car and its number plate, he made a call to someone and told them to get an address for the plate. Kerry knew there were several police contacts who enjoyed bungs from the Caseys and were more than willing to help with stuff like this. The call came back in a few minutes with an address. Jack made another call and instructed someone to go to the address and get the owner of the car. Kerry heard him telling them to take him to a scrapyard and hold him there until they arrived.

'Let's go inside and talk to the owner,' Jack said, more to Brady than to Kerry. 'It's a Pakistani cash-and-carry this place, so whoever owns it must know something.'

'You think they're about to tell you?' Kerry asked.

'Oh they'll tell us,' Jack said, as he and Brady got out of the car.

'I'll come with you,' Kerry said.

'Are you sure you want to?' Jack said.

'Yes,' Kerry said, not sure at all that she wanted to, but she felt she should. 'Donna, you stay here for a few minutes with Eddie. We'll be back shortly. Don't go anywhere.'

'I won't.'

Kerry kept a couple of steps behind Jack and Brady as they marched up to the warehouse main door and pushed in through the swing door. She followed them. Inside there were tall stacks of carpets, household goods, everything from beds to toiletries to small bits of furniture in aisles that seemed to go on for ever. It was freezing and damp and there were no shoppers in – only a few Pakistani men who seemed to be working, moving stuff from aisle to aisle in trolleys.

'Where's your boss?' Jack said curtly to a teenage boy loading a trolley.

'Up there. In his office.'

They looked along and could see a large window with a Venetian blind half up, and a heavy-set Pakistani man standing up and on the phone. Kerry tried to keep up as Jack and Brady strode towards the door. Then she stopped as they burst in the office and the Pakistani man dropped the phone. Jack went across to the desk and put the receiver back on the hook as Brady closed the blinds. Then Brady stepped forward and stood so close to the Pakistani man he was tight up against the wall.

'You better start talking, son,' Jack said.

'What? What is this? I have no money here. Look. No safe. Nothing.'

'We don't want your money,' Jack said as Brady grabbed him by the throat and squeezed.

Jack stood in front of him.

'You had the wee boy in here. Finbar Kane. The kidnapped boy.'

The man shook his head.

'Listen, son. You've got five seconds to tell me everything, names, the lot, or my friend here will cut your heart out and stuff it in your fucking mouth. Five . . . four . . .'

The man nodded furiously, and Brady released his grip, but pulled out a knife and held it to his throat, poking into his flesh.

'Please! I have a family,' he pleaded.

'Fuck your family! You won't have a family either if you don't talk.'

'Please. I tell you.'

'Who brought the kid here?'

'It was . . . It was . . . Sinc . . . Billy Sinclair. I . . . I owe him a lot of money. He told me he needs my back room for something. I didn't know it was a boy, a child. I promise. I didn't know until they came and brought the child. Please, I am a father and grandfather. I am shocked. I want to tell police, but Sinc says he will murder my whole family. It was only for one night, he promised.' He started to cry. 'Then I saw on the news, that a boy has been kidnapped and I am terrified. Because he is in my warehouse. I want to tell police, but I am afraid.'

'Is the boy hurt?' Jack asked.

'No. I see him only one time. They were with him all the time. But he is crying. He stayed only one overnight. They took him earlier on.' He sniffed. 'Please don't kill me.'

Jack turned to Kerry, then back to the man.

'If you tell anyone that we were here, then I will find out, and I will come back and shoot you. Do you understand? Are we clear?'

He nodded furiously. 'Nobody. I speak to nobody. I promise. The boy is gone now. I just want to go home to my family.'

'You do that, son. Go home now. Close this place for the night and go home.'

Brady took his knife from the man's throat and put it back in his jacket. Jack nodded to Kerry and they walked out of the office and down the aisle to the exit. As they got into the car, Jack turned to Kerry.

'Fucking hell. I wanted to kill the bastard.'

'Me too,' Kerry said. 'He must be in hock to this Sinc for a lot of money to have to agree to something like that. Who's Sinc?'

'He's a fucking polecat. But he'll be a dead polecat before the night is out.'

'Kerry. I want to get this place torched. You okay with that? Not right now, in case it raises any suspicions with the kidnappers. But as soon as this is over, we torch it.'

She pictured little Finbar Kane, sobbing and lonely and scared. That the warehouse was someone's livelihood, a family with children and needs, then flashed across Kerry's conscience.

'No, Jack.' She shook her head, pushing down the anger

she felt. 'We're better than that. We're not going to sink to their level.'

Jack's mobile rang when he got into the car and he answered it.

'Fine. We'll be there in fifteen.'

Kerry sat in the front, stunned into silence by what she had witnessed in the past minutes. She decided not even to ask where they were going next.

Kerry had no idea what this scrapyard was or even if they owned it, but as they drove through the potholes and puddles to the far end of the place she could see a Portakabin with a light on, and two cars outside it. Jack and Brady were opening the doors by the time the car drew to a halt. Kerry glanced at Eddie from the corner of her eye, who gave a shrug. Donna sat still, looking terrified. Then Kerry stepped out of the car, avoiding the huge puddle. Jack and Brady were already at the door and pushing it open by the time she was at the bottom of the small wooden stair of the Portakabin. Inside, she stopped in the doorway and stifled a gasp. A man with his face covered in blood was sat on a chair, his hands tied behind his back. Two burly shaven-head men stood over him, one of them with his knuckles bloodied. Kerry was certain she would have remembered these guys if she'd ever encountered them, but she hadn't. She stood as Jack went across and stood over him. The guy with the bloodied knuckles shook his head.

'Saying nothing. Won't even admit to driving the car.'

'What's the prick's name?'

'Rab Bolton. Says he deals a bit of coke but that's all.'

Jack nodded to the minder, and he punched the man's face again. It jerked back and blood spattered across the room. He looked as if he was going to pass out. His head slumped onto his chest. Jack went across and lifted his head up by the hair, glaring down at him.

'Rab. Listen to me. This is not going to end well for you.'

The man blinked away blood and sniffed, but shook his head.

'We have a picture of your car, Rab. Of you, driving the car earlier. It's just stupid to deny you were there. You're only making it worse for yourself. All you have to do is tell me where you took the boy, then you can go. The boys will even drop you at the hospital. Just tell us where.'

'I . . . I don't know what you're talking about.'

Jack leaned closer to him.

'Rab. These boys are going to kill you if you don't tell us.'

'Fuck off,' he blurted through the blood bubbling from his swollen lips. 'I'm a fucking dead man anyway.'

'Well you've nothing to lose then.' He paused. 'Tell me. Why the fuck did you get involved in this, Rab? You're a coke dealer. You don't need to be shifting weans for cunts who steal them. What the fuck, man! Have you no fucking shame?'

Silence, just the sound of bloodied sniffing and groaning.

'Tell me where you took him, Rab. You and Lenny

Wilson. We've got him too. You've no way out.' He gestured to the big guy to untie Rab's hands and place them on top of the desk, palms down. Then Jack turned away and took a couple of steps across to Kerry.

'Kerry. You might want to step outside for a moment.'

Kerry knew what he meant. She had seen more than enough. This ugly scene was also part of who she was these days, as much as the hotels and the property and the big houses and the wealth. This was also part of the deal. She should feel disgusted that this was what men paid by her family did to people when they wanted answers. But she wasn't.

'Whatever it takes,' she said to Jack, then turned and slipped out of the door.

By the time she had crossed the yard she could hear the blood-curdling screams, and the thud of something heavy coming down again and again, and something she'd never heard before but somehow by instinct knew was the sound of bones being hammered and crushed to a pulp.

CHAPTER ELEVEN

In another world, this would have been a perfect little afternoon, Sharon thought as she sat opposite Vic Paterson in the clifftop restaurant, watching the afternoon sun twinkling on the ocean. Vic could have been a guilty pleasure, one that she could have relished over an exotic lunch and a few glasses of fine wine, before losing themselves in an afternoon of unbridled passion. For a fleeting moment, she allowed herself the fantasy as she remembered their fiery but brief encounters a few years ago. Christ knows, she could be doing with a bit of risqué sex – it had been so long since she'd enjoyed the attention of a real man who desired her. But that was not on the cards today, or any other day, and she chided herself for even entertaining the notion.

'What's on your mind, Sharon?' Vic sat back, a mischievous smile playing on his lips. 'You look miles away, darlin.' He lifted his glass and leaned across a little and spoke softly. 'And if I may say so, you look every bit as bloody hot as you did when I fancied the pants right off you all those years ago.'

Sharon put her hand up and squared her shoulders.

'Enough, already.' She shot him a firm but friendly look. 'What's past is past, Vic. Let's not even go there, pet. Okay?' She could feel a little flush rise on her neck, and took a gulp of her Sauvignon Blanc. 'We've moved on from all of that. I was just thinking though, how lovely this is here, in this little spot, and how great it would be if we were just a couple of mates enjoying lunch. But we're not. So let's keep it simple.' She looked into his pale eyes, crinkled at the sides. Christ! Vic must be forty-one now and he was still as handsome as ever. 'Tell me, Vic. You said the Caseys would need your help. So I'm all ears.'

'Have you talked to Kerry Casey yet? Told her what I'm offering?'

Sharon had called Kerry straight after her first meeting with Vic to tell her how much he seemed to know, and that he would work with them, but that he would want big money. Kerry told Sharon that it was her call, and if she thought they could trust him, then to go ahead and bring him on.

'I have,' Sharon said. 'She doesn't know you – knows nothing about you, only what I told her. But she is trusting my judgement. And I'm putting a lot of trust in you right now. I seriously hope you would never betray that.'

Vic spread his hands.

'Shaz. Come on. It was me who came to you. I've been in the nick long enough to know that when you get out, you have to stand back and see where you are going to pick up. And that's what I did. There is nothing for me back in Manchester with all the fucking pricks fighting among themselves, and with Durkin and the Colombians gearing up to demolish the lot of them. I could see how I can be useful to them with my experience and stuff, but I don't like them. And even before I decided I didn't like them, when I was getting out of jail, I was hearing all the shit through the grapevine about Knuckles and you and what he was doing.' He paused, ran a hand through his hair. 'And, I'll be honest with you, I did think about you in all of this. I know this is just a meet and talk, but I did think about you. That's all.' He folded his napkin and tossed it on the table. 'Only natural. But I came to you because as I've said, you are going to need my help.'

Sharon nodded slowly, clasping her hands on the table. 'And of course the money, Vic.'

He shrugged. 'Of course. The money. You haven't got a problem with that, have you? Has Kerry?'

She shook her head. 'No. We will sort you out. No problem. But the problem at the moment, Vic, is time. The priority back in Glasgow is getting the boy back to his family. So we can't do anything out here just now. But as soon as he's back, then we want to be ready.'

'You know of course that the Colombian has said he wants everything from the Casey organisation. The lot. And from what I see in the brief time I'm here, he has plenty of bodies to do that. Plenty. I had dinner last night with that Frankie Martin prick, and he strikes me as a slippery fucker. I'll be watching my back every moment I'm around him, I'll tell you that. But I have to be with him, listen to his fucking bragging, and make sure I get bedded in.'

'I understand that,' Sharon said. 'So what can you tell me so far? We want to know locations and stuff, where they operate from over here. If we were looking for them, where would we find them? We have enough people here who can look at that discreetly, so we can be ready to give them it with both barrels when the time is right.'

'I know. Durkin will be easy. He swans around like the fucking coke king, and I'm surprised nobody from his own neck in Dublin has popped him yet. He'll be easy. But the Colombians have a huge network going here, all of them shit scared of Rodriguez. So if you want to stop them functioning, you have to cut off the head of the snake. Rodriguez. Oh, the snake will still think it can bite you as it thrashes around, but once you get the head, then it's all over. Everyone who works for him will run for cover. They will have to send someone else from Colombia, but they won't have the appetite for that. There are too many other powerful mobs down here now – the Russians, for example. They're as ruthless as the Colombians, and the Albanians.'

'I understand,' Sharon said. 'We've a long way to go.'

When they'd finished, Vic paid the bill and they walked out into the narrow street, and Sharon clocked his eyes doing a quick scan of the area. Then they stood for a little awkward moment, and Sharon could feel the electricity between them as she looked up at him, shading her eyes from the sun.

'I'm going to walk into the village and take a taxi back,' she said. 'I've got to give Kerry a ring and see how things are.'

Kerry was glad to see Danny when he arrived at the house with Jack. She hadn't slept much last night after getting a glimpse into how Jack went about the business of getting information. By the time she went to bed her mind was too busy with flashbacks and bloodied faces to get much sleep. She'd lain for a while in the darkness thinking how naive she'd been when she left the house last night, thinking she was going to meet this girl Donna who could help them find Marty's grandson. It had been a baptism of fire, witnessing how swiftly Jack had dealt with some of the people involved, and she'd been impressed how quickly they were able to locate the driver of this Lenny Wilson character. Jack had suggested she go back to the house after they left the scrapyard, and she did, while he and Brady hooked up with another car and two more heavies. They were going to dig out this Lenny Wilson, and Billy Sinclair; when Bolton finally broke his silence he had confirmed what the

Pakistani warehouse owner had said – that Sinclair was the only one he'd dealt with.

'Jack's been filling me in,' Danny said, as the three of them walked along the hall towards her study. 'Sounds like quite a night.'

They went inside and sat around the table. As Kerry poured tea into mugs, she noticed that Jack's left hand was bandaged.

'What happened to your hand?' she asked.

'That wee toerag Wilson had a go at me with a knife. Wee bastard. He didn't realise how dangerous that would be for him – was hyped up to fuck on coke.' He shook his head. 'Anyway, he knows now.'

'So,' Kerry said, 'where are we?' She flicked Danny a glance. 'I'm almost scared to ask. Please tell me we've made progress.'

'We have,' Jack said. 'But we've hit a bit of a wall. Sinclair told us Finbar has been moved from the place he took him to, and is now somewhere else. He says he doesn't know where. And that he won't get told until a couple of hours before they're due to move him again. He says that's how it's been working since the boy was taken – says he's not the only one involved, that there are others too.'

'Christ!' Kerry said. 'Is he being straight?'

'Prick like him couldn't lie straight in his bed. But put it this way, the only reason he's still alive is because he said he will get a call on this in the next day. That's when he'll get the address to move the kid.'

'Poor wee Finbar. Kid must be bewildered and terrified.' Kerry looked at Danny.

'That's why we need to get him out of there. If this bastard is telling us the truth, then we have to wait to see if he gets a call.'

'Where is he?' Kerry asked.

'We've got him tucked away. He gave us the information without any problem. He knows he has to play ball with us or he's a dead man.'

'He will be anyway,' Danny said, tight-lipped, 'when this is all over.'

'What about this Lenny Wilson?'

'We're holding him too,' Jack said. 'He's only a cog in it – a delivery boy. But we can't afford to turn him loose. I don't think he's got any connections higher up than Sinclair, but best if we keep him where he is. He's a coke-head too, so both of them are strung out to fuck.'

'Yeah,' Danny said. 'Keep Wilson too, until this is over.' He turned to Kerry. 'What about this Donna bird?'

'She's up in the Thistle Hotel. She's not going back to the flat. Says she can't. She wants money for her information. I told her we'll sort her when we get the boy back, but meantime she stays where we can watch her.'

'She's a piece of work, is she not, Kerry?' Danny asked. 'Anyone with a scrap of decency would have gone to the cops with their suspicions – not try to make money out of it. But having said that, she did us a turn.'

'I suppose that's right that she wanted to make money,' Jack agreed. 'But at least she came to us first, and that gives us a shot at trying to get him back before the cops go in all guns blazing and fuck it up.'

Kerry was silent for a moment, then she asked, 'But how do we know the cops would screw it up? I mean, we can't be sure of that, can we?'

She let the words hang in the air, knowing it would strike a chord with Danny and Jack who glanced at each other. It was them she had had to convince only a few weeks ago to let the cops in on the bid to bring Knuckles down. That had been successful, and Danny had still got his pound of flesh, being able to take Knuckles out with a bullet to the head in the middle of the operation with armed cops crawling all over it. Kerry hadn't given serious consideration to bringing police in to get Finbar back, but the clock was ticking. And Vinny's words were ringing in her ears. She wanted Finbar home, and she wanted revenge as much as Danny and Jack. What their enemies had done here was to strike at the very heart of them by kidnapping a child. There were no depths these bastards wouldn't sink to. Revenge was for another day, though. This was about the life of Finbar. She didn't want his blood on her hands.

'Kerry, you look as though you're considering other options here.' Danny looked at her, raised eyebrows. 'Has your friend Vinny been in touch?'

Kerry knew he wasn't having a dig at her, but she also knew that Danny would be suspicious that she was being influenced by Vinny, because of their relationship. If he knew that she was carrying his child, Kerry thought, she would lose a chunk of credibility when it came to decision making. But she wasn't about to admit anything like that.

'Vinny has been in touch,' she said to both of them. 'He's been to see Marty too, and from talking to Marty afterwards, I get the impression he's beginning to buckle a bit. I perfectly understand that. We're not in his shoes, and what he's going through must be horrendous – especially because he knows his grandson has been kidnapped to get back at us, and he has to hide all that from his family.'

'Did he say we should think about getting the cops in?' Jack asked.

'No,' Kerry said. 'But I feel he is thinking about it.' She paused. 'Vinny phoned me and we had a conversation and I can tell he has this gut feeling that Marty isn't telling him everything. Vinny's words to me were that if anything happens to this kid and we have failed to do everything possible to get him home – he means by not telling the police everything we know – then we will have blood on our hands.'

They sat in silence for a long moment, each of them knowing that Vinny was right. Eventually Danny took a long breath and sat back with his hands behind his head.

'Then, we have to think about it,' he said looking from Kerry to Jack. 'I take it Marty doesn't know about the latest developments – I mean what we did last night?'

'No,' Kerry said. 'I haven't told him. I'm not sure if I should tell him, because it's something else that he has to keep from his family – that's if we are going to go this alone.'

'You're right. Marty doesn't need to know what's going on at the moment. And if this bastard Sinc gets a call in the next few hours, then we might even be able to get his boy back quickly.'

Kerry looked from one to the other, but didn't say anything. From what she had seen of their operation last night, and also when they took Knuckles Boyle out, her men were more than capable of handling anything thrown at them. But her insides niggled. This was about a little boy's life. If something went wrong, it didn't bear thinking about.

CHAPTER TWELVE

Marty Kane knew his son was watching him closely for any signs that he was holding back. He had never consulted his son or kept him informed of any of the business he had with the Caseys. But Joe knew that his father was the Casey lawyer, and that he and old man Casey went back decades. So he would be smart enough to know all that entailed. Yet over the years, even once he became a lawyer himself and worked in his father's firm, Joe had never questioned his role with the Caseys. Marty respected his son for that. As a lawyer, Joe knew that often you had to defend the indefensible, and he would have done that himself many times in murder and robbery, even rape trials. But as the Caseys' brief, Marty knew he sailed very close to being a gangster himself. He was more than just their lawyer. He was as embedded in the Casey family as every gun-wielding henchman in the firm. That had never mattered to Joe before. Until now.

Marty had gone into his study to get away from the oppressive atmosphere in the kitchen, where he and his wife had sat at the table with Joe and his wife, and their older son Johnny, Finbar's big brother. He was only five, and the family had so far been trying to keep him away from any newspaper and television reports about Fin's kidnapping. But they had had to tell him that his little brother had been taken by some bad people, and the poor kid was finding it hard to understand that his father couldn't bring his brother home. Johnny had been quiet, despite his mother's attempts to get a conversation out of him. Everyone had sat around, picking at their food, making small talk, when the only thing on their minds was Fin. Marty could see the anguish on every one of their faces.

He was standing gazing out of the window in his study when Joe came in carrying a mug of tea. He closed the door behind him. Marty turned around to see him, then went back to looking outside.

'You all right, Dad?' Joe said. 'You look terrible.'

Marty shook his head but didn't turn around.

'Ach, I just feel sick, son. Looking at your Johnny's wee face, the bewilderment in it. I can't take that.' Marty felt his chest tight with emotion.

'I know,' Joe said. 'But we have to believe that we'll get Fin home. There's nothing else for it.'

Marty nodded his head and sighed, but said nothing. They stood in silence for a moment, and then Joe spoke.

'Dad,' he said, putting his mug down on the table, 'look. I haven't asked you this, but it's in my mind and I can't get it to go away.'

Marty looked at him and then back out of the window. He knew what was coming.

'Dad. Is . . . Is Fin's kidnapping anything to do with the Caseys? I mean is it something they're involved in, and you're their lawyer, so someone is trying to get to them through you?'

Marty had known from the moment Fin was taken that his son would have been suspicious that it was more to do with his father than anything else. But the only time it had been brought up was when they were both talking about court cases or criminals they'd been defending, and Joe had said perhaps the kidnapping was to do with work they had done. The police had also suggested that, but there had been no close questioning. Well, apart from the private chat that Marty had with Vinny the other day. Marty turned to face his son. The last thing he could do was to tell him the truth, and it tore at his heart.

'Look, son. We both know that we have dealt with a lot of bad people in our lives, and we've defended them in court – even if our consciences told us they were guilty as sin. That's our job. It's to defend, not judge. But by doing that, who knows who we've noised up over the years. Both of us – yes, especially me – have stood on the steps of the High Court when bad men have walked free because of our defence of them. Who knows how many people that may have affected – the victims of their crimes, the families of victims. You know that yourself. There must be as many people out there who despise us as respect us. That's the way it is.' Marty was aware he was making a speech as though he had a jury in front of him.

'I know that, Dad,' Joe said. 'And I know I have defended plenty of men who were probably guilty. But so have dozens of other defence lawyers. Why now take *my* son? Why, Dad? And why, even if you've been doing the job for a lifetime, why now take *your* grandson?' He paused. 'It's just . . . It's just not right. Something isn't right about it.' He walked across the room to stand beside his father. 'Dad. If you know something and you're not telling us, please, you know I trust your judgement in everything – always have. But please, don't keep me in the dark. This is my wee boy. My life. I need to know.'

Marty said nothing for a long moment, then he looked at Joe and shook his head.

'I know as much as you do, son,' he lied.

Marty's heart was breaking, seeing his son like this. It was bad enough that he had to watch his family in pieces over Fin, but he was now standing in front of his own boy, and looking him in the eye and lying. To deny him the truth was a betrayal of everything he had been as a father. But the consequences of telling him the truth could cause an explosion.

*

Frankie Martin was beginning to feel like he was going places. The big Colombian, Pepe Rodriguez, was as arrogant and menacing a fucker as he had ever come across. But he reckoned his new boss saw the potential of having someone as clued up and ruthless as him by his side. Frankie saw himself as a bit of a swashbuckler who could sidestep a killer blow, but could knife you in cold blood without batting an eye. He could tell straight away that the Colombian took to him after their first lunch, and in recent days there had been a couple of dinners where he listened to Rodriguez tell tales of growing up in the Colombian city Medellín, and bragging how he fought his way to the top of the cartel, eliminating his enemies along the way. Kindred spirits they were, Frankie decided.

And one evening, after they had drunk two bottles of wine and settled into brandies in a bar down in Puerto de la Duquesa, Rodriguez hinted to him that from what he'd gathered, he thought that it was Frankie who was behind Mickey Casey's murder. Frankie didn't flinch. He knew Rodriguez would have heard the tittle-tattle about Mickey's demise through Durkin and the like, but he sure as shit wasn't about to admit it. He had said nothing. Even when the Colombian gave him a wry smile, indicating that it was okay to dispose of your best friend, because, as he'd said, 'We are not in this business to make friends. We are in it to win. To be masters of the universe.' That all seemed a bit airy-fucking-fairy to Frankie, but he got the point.

Rodriguez rated him big time, and that was what counted. He could go all the way with this guy. Okay, he still baulked at how Rodriguez had butchered O'Driscoll, and kidnapping Marty's grandson was not something he would ever have considered, but if Frankie could move on from that then he could look to a big future. And now that Rodriguez was gearing up to take everything from the Caseys, Frankie wanted to be there to witness it. Christ. He'd even light a fucking big cigar when he saw Kerry Casey on the bones of her arse, along with the dumbfucks she had around her.

Rodriguez had told him to organise the meet with Kerry, and that he had drawn up papers with his Spanish lawyer to be given to her to sign. Only then would they be taken to where Marty Kane's grandson would be handed over. If there was one thing in all of this that should niggle Frankie it was that a little boy was being used as barter. He should feel something about that, he told himself. But the truth was, he didn't. Initially Frankie had been horrified that the boy had been kidnapped, but as he got to know Rodriguez a little more, he felt sure deep down that the Colombian wasn't going to send the boy back in a box, or minus a couple of fingers, so a few days of sniffling and crying for his mammy wouldn't do the boy any harm. It would toughen him up. He wished he could be in Glasgow for the meeting, but he knew going back there was risky because someone could eyeball him on the plane and the word could get back to the Caseys, and he'd be dead meat before he got out of the airport. No. He would orchestrate it from here. It was Frankie who had got the boys back in Glasgow to organise the moving of the kid in the past few days. So far that had gone well. Now it might only be a couple more days until this part of it was over. He hoped so, because the longer it went on, the bigger chance of some dickhead letting something slip, and it could all go tits up.

Frankie looked at his watch as he stood on the balcony of the apartment in Estepona looking out to the sun on the water. It would be almost midday back in Glasgow, probably raining and grey, but here he was, swanning around the Costa del Sol rubbing shoulders with the big players who pulled all the strings back home. Did he miss Glasgow, running the betting shops and doing Kerry Casey's bidding like an errand boy? Did he fuck! He punched in her number. He'd have to try his best not to gloat when he spoke to her. He heard her voice after three rings, and a surprising little flip lashed across his gut.

'Kerry. It's me. How's it going?'

'Frankie. Get to the bloody point.'

'Now, now, Kerry. Where are your manners, sweetheart? I'm trying to do you a turn here. Listen. If it wasn't for me—'

'Frankie,' the voice barked back, 'if it weren't for you, I would still have my mother by my side, and my brother – even though he was a scheming bastard, just like you. So don't give me your shit. Say what you've got to say, and get the fuck off the phone. What's the score? When is this meeting?'

Frankie could picture Kerry's eyes blazing with rage as she hit back at him, and for a fleeting second he fantasised about throwing her on the floor and fucking those brains right out of her. The thought made him smile, and just listening to her anger gave him a bit of a hard-on.

'Okay,' he said, trying to compose himself. 'Here's the situation. Rodriguez will be in Glasgow day after tomorrow to meet you. He will have papers from his Spanish lawyer that will basically mean you will sign everything over to him. But he's a generous bastard, is Pepe. So he's going to do you a turn. He could crush you in front of everyone, take all you have, make an example of you, but he's going to make you his partner.'

'Partner? Fuck off, Frankie. His partner? No way.'

'Yeah. That's the deal. The Caseys get forty per cent, and he gets sixty of everything you have. The hotel, the lot. But you work together.'

Frankie enjoyed the long silence at the other end of the phone and he knew she was trying to catch her breath, come up with some smart-arse remark. But he also knew she was well and truly fucked.

'I want to meet on my territory. At a place of my choosing. You tell him that, okay?'

'Aye, so you come in with the cops or all guns blazing.'

'Don't be so bloody stupid. There's a little boy's life at

stake here. That's the only reason I'm agreeing to this. We meet, we talk, I sign. We take the boy. That's it.'

'Where are you talking about meeting?'

Again, the long silence. Eventually she spoke.

'There's a restaurant just outside the city. The Three Magpies. You know it? It's an old place. Quiet. We can go there.'

'I know the place.'

'Fine. We meet there. At two in the afternoon. Just me and him, and Finbar.'

'Pepe never has a meet by himself. He will have a bodyguard obviously, and he'll be armed. So don't be stupid, eh?'

'Just organise it. And make sure you're not there.'

'No chance. I've had it with Glasgow. I live in the sun now.'

She didn't react, just replied, 'Arrange it and let me know when it's done.'

CHAPTER THIRTEEN

Kerry was in her study when Jack and Danny arrived. Her mind had been racing with all sorts of scenarios. Danny had phoned twenty minutes earlier to say that Sinc had received a message on his mobile with an address from where he had to pick up little Finbar tonight and where he had to take him. This was really happening. She was now faced with the biggest decision of her life. If she made the wrong call, Marty Kane might never see his grandson again. To add to her worries, Frankie Martin had called her again this morning to confirm that Pepe Rodriguez would meet her the day after tomorrow in the restaurant she suggested. As she'd watched Danny and Jack drive through the steel gates to the courtyard, Kerry felt, not for the first time, that she was seriously out of her depth. Now she listened closely as Danny explained the latest development.

'When Sinc got the text with the details, he told us he

would have to get back straight away and agree to do it. So we told him to do that.'

'Good,' Kerry said. 'So what kind of nick is Sinc in?' She assumed he'd been given a good kicking to get any kind of cooperation from him.

Jack shrugged. 'Actually he's fine, Kerry. Not a mark on him. Sinc is a low-life prick, but he's smart enough when he's in the company he's in at the moment to know that the only way for him to stay alive is to cooperate with us. He knows if he doesn't, he's a dead man.' He glanced at Danny. 'He's a dead man anyway once this is all over, but we've told him we'll make sure he gets far enough away from the heat and we'll pay him a wedge. Obviously we won't. But he's shitting his pants right now. So we haven't had to punch anything out of him. He'll go along with whatever we ask. He says he can carry it off.'

'Good,' Kerry said. 'So where are they holding Finbar and what's the plan?'

'At the moment he's being held in an old bungalow out on the Maryhill Road. We've got the address and have someone driving past to case it as we speak. But from the Google Earth pics, it's pretty run-down. We're finding out who owns it and if it's occupied. It could be some place that some scally has bought and they use it to stash drugs or stolen stuff. So we're not sure. But someone will be there with the boy twenty-four seven, and they'll be armed. Therefore I don't think it's a good idea to batter down the door there at this stage.'

Kerry nodded in agreement, but she was desperate to get the boy as soon as possible.

'And where is he being taken?'

'To another address close enough to the restaurant where you said you've arranged to meet the Colombian,' Jack said. 'Oh, and by the way, we've got someone all over that to examine the set-up and exactly who's who. We've got some plans for that to run past you and see what you think, but we'll come to that in a minute. The message for Sinc was to pick the kid up from the bungalow late tomorrow afternoon and drive him to the next address – it's a farmhouse about a mile and a half from the restaurant. Presumably, the bastards are taking him there so that when you sign the papers they'll hand the boy over to us.'

Kerry got up and walked across to the window and stood for a moment. She didn't like the sound of this. Everything hinged on Rodriguez keeping his word and handing over the kid. She turned to face them and stood folding her arms.

'I just have a bad feeling about this. We're relying on Rodriguez to turn up like this was a business deal, get me to sign papers, then hand over Finbar. We can't trust him to do that. He might come in guns blazing as soon as he sees me, or he might just get his men to start shooting once I sign the document. We can't trust him to keep his word.'

Danny and Jack exchanged glances and both nodded.

'Of course, Kerry, and that's why it's important that we do this properly.'

Kerry looked at him, waiting for more. She came back to the table and sat down.

'Okay, so talk to me about it.'

'Right,' Jack said. 'From what we know of the restaurant, there are two waiters on in the afternoon, and obviously a chef and stuff in the kitchen – and a duty manager. But in terms of staff, what we plan to do is the waiters will be phoned by the manager a little while before they arrive for their shift, and told to take the day off, that they'll get paid, but just to keep their mouths shut. Same goes for the duty manager. He'll disappear too.'

Kerry looked at them, incredulous.

'Seriously? How you going to do that?'

'Someone is paying the manager a visit at his home tonight, and he'll be told the sketch. He won't disagree,' Jack said, glancing at Danny. 'He'll know not to open his mouth to anyone about it. And he'll be well paid.'

'This sounds like it's going to get messy.'

Danny sat forward, rubbed his chin then looked at her.

'Well, yes. It will.' He glanced at Jack. 'We've been discussing this, Kerry, and a lot of it hinges on what you want to do. But the bottom line is we bump Rodriguez and every bastard who is with him right at the restaurant. Right at the table.'

'Christ!' Kerry said. An image flashed through her head

of the bloodbath at her mother's funeral, bodies everywhere. She imagined similar carnage in the restaurant and her sitting in the midst of it.

'Don't worry. You'll be totally covered. It'll happen so fast. There will be a distraction for Rodriguez and the minute he takes his eye off the ball, we'll be all over him. That's the plan.'

'So who's going to be in the restaurant – I mean in place of the waiters and the manager?'

'We've got three of our lads geared up for it, but wanted to talk to you about it.' Jack looked at Danny. 'And also, you'll be armed, just in case anything goes wrong. It's not as though you'll have to shoot your way out, because you'll be covered at all times. But better to be safe.'

The words hung in the air for a moment, and Kerry hoped her mouth hadn't dropped open. She'd only in the last couple of weeks been shown how to handle a gun after Jack suggested she take some lessons, and while she found she was quite adept at it, she'd only shot targets. Actually using it had never really entered her head. She wondered, if it came to it, could she actually fire a gun at another human being? She was reconciled to the fact that she was the head of a gangster family who right now made their money from drugs, from people-trafficking and money-laundering. She knew they killed people and dealt out punishment beatings. But other people did that. She didn't do the killing part. Then a thought flashed into her mind about Finbar, frightened, crying and lost and being used as a pawn in a ransom demand by that ruthless bastard Rodriguez and his cronies.

'Okay,' she said. 'But how are you going to get me armed? Won't they search me when I arrive?'

Jack nodded. 'They will. But you go in and when you sit down you put your jacket over the chair. Then just forget about it. A few minutes later, when the waiters are fussing around, one of them will slip the loaded and cocked handgun into your jacket pocket.'

'You're kidding. You think someone won't be watching for a stunt like that?'

'Leave that to us, Kerry. You just keep your eye on the barman. He'll give you the nod, so you know the gun is there, and then you'll get another nod that it's going to kick off. As soon as the shooting starts, you go into your pocket and get the gun, then you hit the floor and someone will grab you and get you out. If you need to use the gun, then you'll do it by instinct.'

Kerry almost felt her head swim. Instinct?

'But don't worry.' Danny seemed to see her concern. 'We'll have eyes on you at all times.'

Kerry pushed any worrying thoughts to the side and focused on what was needed.

'Rodriguez is a complete bastard,' she said. 'To put a little kid through this kind of agony. It's unforgivable.'

Danny nodded. 'I know,' he said. 'It's fucking beyond evil. But they'll pay for this, Kerry. Every single person who has had a filthy hand in this kidnapping will pay for it – trust me on that.'

Kerry knew exactly what that meant, and she would not be standing in the way of Danny or Jack when they dealt out justice for this. The boy's photograph and story of the kidnapping had been the number-one story on the news since it happened, so anyone involved in it knew exactly what they were doing when they became a part of it. Whether they were doing it for money, or because they had no option, didn't enter into Kerry's psyche right now. She was thinking and reacting like Danny and Jack. She wanted revenge for putting the kid and his family through this hell. Her only concern now was getting him back.

'So do we know anything about the farmhouse?' Kerry asked.

'Not much. Only the name of the owner, who lives in the north of Spain most of the time. I don't know him. Retired company director, but I've got some people checking him out. He's obviously involved with some dodgy people if they can suddenly pitch up and use his place.'

'Interesting,' Kerry said. 'I wonder who he is. He might not even know what's going on. He might have his farmhouse rented out or something.'

'Possibly,' Jack replied. 'But we'll have a look at him when this is all over. At the moment we're concentrating on how we carry out this operation. We can't afford to put a foot wrong. We need everything planned to the letter.'

Kerry nodded. 'Of course.'

Danny looked at Jack.

'We've got enough people to be able to execute this properly, Kerry,' Danny said. 'But I think we should get Jake Cahill back from Spain. He's great backup and an insurance for us in a lot of ways.'

'Sure,' she said, looking at her watch. 'Give him a call and ask him if he can get on a plane tonight.'

'And, Kerry,' Danny said. 'We're looking at bringing in the young lads too – Cal and Tahir. They've been doing really well and learning fast. Jack's boys have been training them up with weapons, and they're sharp as a tack and keen.'

Kerry thought about Cal's mum, Maria, who had come to her for help when she was at her lowest ebb, and she took her in. Maria's life had changed and everything was going so well, with her daughter Jen doing well in rehab and looking like she may get back on track. It didn't sit well with Kerry that Cal was now working for the organisation, and she hadn't asked too many questions of how Jack was using him and Tahir. She'd left it up to them. But anything could happen in an operation like this, and she wouldn't be able to face Maria if something happened to Cal. But she had to dismiss the thought. Cal had wanted to work for the Caseys and he'd slotted in as though he was family. That was who he was now – a foot soldier, like the others in her organisation. But she wanted to protect him on some level.

'Sure,' Kerry said. 'Whatever you think. They're young though. And I'll be honest with you, I don't want to have their blood on my hands, so be careful how you use them.'

'We will, Kerry. I haven't spoken to them yet. I wanted to clear it with you. I know the lads are young, but they're showing promise – and appetite. When I was their age, I had earned my stripes. They know what they're involved in. Both of them were already doing drug drops by the time they were fifteen, so they're no choirboys.'

Kerry couldn't disagree with that.

'Okay,' she said.

'Good.' Danny glanced at Jack. 'Right. We have to get cracking if we want to make sure we're set up for tomorrow and the pickup.'

'Fine. Just keep me informed,' Kerry said, as they stood up.

'We'll talk later,' Danny said as they headed for the door.

CHAPTER FOURTEEN

Cal and Tahir waited outside Jack Reilly's office at the taxi HQ, where they'd been summoned. They were both a little edgy, as Jack hadn't told Cal why he wanted to speak to both of them. Perhaps word had got back to Jack about the trouble they'd been in with the mob who ran the show up at the high flats in Saracen. They'd got into a punch-up with the thugs because one of the boys insulted Tahir's new girlfriend – a Kurdish refugee like him – who lived in the high flats where dozens of asylum-seeker families from all over the world had been housed in recent years. The boy had called the girl a whore, saying she was just like the rest of them and it was well known that anyone who wanted a shag could go up there. Tahir went berserk and Cal had had to drag him off the thug and they had had to fight their way out of the bar, with their girlfriends screaming, terrified. Tahir had pulled a knife on another guy and cut him. They both knew that there would be a payback for that and had been watching their backs for the past couple of weeks. Now, they were worried that word had got back to Jack, who had warned them that they worked for the Casey organisation now and if they kept their noses clean they could go places. And it had been great in the last few weeks. Both of them seemed to grow in stature in Jack's eyes after they'd disposed of the traffickers who had taken Tahir's money and left him heartbroken when his brother and wife arrived dead in a container, suffocated, with their dead children in their arms. Tahir would never get over it, he'd told Cal, who could understand that but could see that his friend was a volcano waiting to erupt. As long as he kept busy and focused on his work with the Caseys he'd be fine. The pair had been used on driving jobs and drops and picking up money from firms attached to the Caseys. And one time with Jack they accompanied him and two others on a beating for a thug who'd terrorised a young family. But they had no idea why they'd been summoned today.

'What will we say if it's about that shit in the pub with the Saracen team?' Cal asked his friend.

'We tell the truth. Tell him what the guy said. And my girlfriend has told me that a lot of the girls up there are used as prostitutes, Cal. It is organised by these pricks at the flats. They're more or less selling the girls.' Tahir looked at Cal. 'This is not over yet. Maybe we should ask Jack if they can help.'

'I dunno, mate. It's not really what the Caseys do.'

Tahir shrugged. 'Well, it's not over. These girls are just innocent. Some are not even sixteen. They are using kids. They'll pay for this. Even if I have to do it myself and it takes time.'

The office door opened and Jack appeared, glancing from one to the other.

'Who'll pay for what?' he asked.

The boys glanced at each other and said nothing. Jack took a long look at both of them.

'In you come, lads. I want to talk to you.'

They followed him in, and he motioned them to sit down opposite his desk.

'I've a job for the two of you.'

Cal felt relief flood through him, and from the corner of his eye he could see Tahir relax a little.

'Now,' Jack said, 'this is a big job. Not like the stuff we've been doing for a few weeks, where you did well in a more minor way. It's going to involve you being armed, and ready to use a weapon. You got that?'

Cal felt a little nudge of excitement in his gut. He liked the feel of a gun in his hand. It gave him a certain power and made him feel safe. But Jack had warned them repeatedly that you do not pull a gun on somebody unless you are prepared to use it and prepared for the consequences. He'd stressed to them that if they started being little hard-men then he'd kick their arses all over Glasgow and they'd be back in the car wash dodging bullets from all the bastards who were after them. So they were well aware of what they were doing, and Cal did not want to upset Jack. He'd become like a father figure to him, and seemed to understand his situation, with his father missing and his mother trying to cope on her own. Even though things were a lot different for them these days since Kerry Casey took them under her wing, and he was living a very different life as a young gun for the Caseys, he still looked out for his ma.

'Sure,' Cal said. He looked at Tahir. 'We're up for that, all right, Jack. Anything you ask.'

'Right,' Jack said. 'I'm going to tell you something now, and if you breathe a word of it outside of this room . . .' He paused for a couple of beats, his eyebrows knitted. 'Well, you really don't want to think what could happen.'

They both nodded.

'Of course, Jack,' Cal said. 'We never talk about our work to anyone. Absolutely never.'

'I know that. You're good lads. And you'll do well. But this is a life-or-death situation, and it's the most important thing you might ever do in your life. So you need to understand the seriousness of it.'

Cal glanced at Tahir, both of them hanging onto Jack's every word. They waited for him to go on.

'You know the little boy Finbar? Marty Kane's grandson who's been kidnapped? I'm sure you know all about it from the papers.'

'Yeah, I read it. Finbar. Saw it on the news.'

'Me too,' Tahir said. 'People who take someone's child should die. If it was my boy I would kill them. No doubt about it.'

Cal eyed Tahir and hoped he wasn't going to get boiled up. He gave him a look that said just shut your mouth and listen, and Tahir seemed to get the message.

'Quite right too, Tahir,' Jack said. 'Well the situation is the boy has been kidnapped by enemies of the Caseys. One particular bad bastard is trying to destroy us, and he has taken the boy to show us that he can do anything to hurt us. Marty Kane is in bits about this. Kerry is beside herself with rage and we will be doing anything to get this boy back.' He paused. 'Tomorrow morning you will meet with a man called Jake Cahill. You don't need to know anything about him, and he sure as shit won't tell you much, but you do exactly as he says. He's flying in from Spain tonight and he'll instruct you. But the bottom line is, tomorrow there is a deal being made and the boy is going to be handed over, but we know where he is so we're going to get him before the ransom is paid.'

Cal looked from Jack to Tahir. This was big stuff. Bigger than anything he ever thought he would be doing. He didn't know what to ask, but he felt he should be asking something.

'So, er, Jack. You mean we'll be with this Jake Cahill when he goes in to get the boy? I mean, the boy will be under a lot of protection, I suppose.'

Jack looked at him for a long moment.

'Yes. He will. And yes, you go in with him. You'll both be armed. You know how to use your guns, so you do exactly as Jake says. At the moment, we're not sure whether we're going to storm the place where the boy is, or wait until they bring him out to transfer him to be handed over. You'll know soon enough. Just do what you're told. You got that?'

They both nodded.

'Yeah,' Cal said. 'We got that.'

'Yes,' Tahir said. 'I understand.'

Jack stood up. 'Okay. The two of you be at Kerry's house for ten tomorrow morning. You'll meet Jake then and you'll get your guns.' He paused for a moment, looking from one to the other. 'Now off you go. Don't do anything stupid tonight that will keep you up, as I need you to have your wits about you tomorrow.'

'Okay,' Cal said.

The boys stood up and turned towards the door.

'Christ, man!' Cal said when they got into the street. 'This is a big job. How do you feel, mate?'

Tahir seemed relaxed but had a steely look in his eye.

'I hope they let us kill the bastards. That's how I feel.'

Cal shook his head and puffed.

'Christ! The important thing is you do what you're told tomorrow, Tahir. All right? Whoever this Jake Cahill is, he's been brought here from Spain to do this, so you don't want to get on the wrong side of him.'

They walked down the street leading to the city centre and were heading home when Tahir's mobile rang. Cal watched as his expression changed and he pressed the phone to his ear as though trying to concentrate. He was speaking in Kurdish so Cal couldn't understand, but he could tell from his tone that there was a problem. Tahir broke off speaking and turned to Cal.

'Is Elia. She has been attacked with her sister. Those bastards from the other night. They came to the flats and ransacked her house. Her mother is terrified.'

'Shit!' Cal said. He looked at his watch. It was already getting dark.

'Tahir, listen. There is nothing we can do about that tonight. You heard Jack. We've got a big job on tomorrow and we can't get ourselves involved in anything.'

Tahir gave him a frustrated look.

'But I have to go and see her.'

'No,' Cal said. 'Not tonight. Maybe it's a trap. They'll know she'll have told you and you'll come up there. They might be lying in wait for you. We can't risk it. Leave it, Tahir. We can get to her tomorrow.'

Tahir huffed and went back on the phone, and Cal listened as his voice seemed to be attempting to soothe and calm her down. Then he hung up.

'Bastards!' he said. 'They won't get away with this, Cal. Elia is really upset. They slapped her around and punched her little sister. We have to get these bastards for this.'

Cal put an arm around his friend's shoulder.

'We will, Tahir. Just not now. It's not the kind of thing you just dive into without thinking it through. The other night in the pub, anything could have happened. We could have got kicked to death. We've got to be better than that, Tahir. And we have to keep our noses clean if we want to keep in with the Caseys. You heard Jack. We can deal with these pricks up in the flats in our own time. I promise you.' He paused. 'Maybe we'll speak to Jack about it once things settle down tomorrow after the job. But right now that's what we've got to focus on.'

Tahir nodded in agreement, but his eyes were dark and full of fury.

'Okay. But I am going after them, Cal. No matter who is with me.'

'Come on. Let's get home. I'll be with you, mate. You know that.'

They walked the rest of the journey into the city in silence, and then went their separate ways. Tahir was sharing a flat in the East End with two Kurdish mates now that he had enough money to pay rent. Cal was still living with his mum, and though he wanted his own place, deep down he was glad to be going home to her.

CHAPTER FIFTEEN

Kerry could hear the activity downstairs as she began to wake up. She had tossed and turned all night, going over all the possible outcomes for today. What if it was a trap by the Colombian? These people were completely ruthless when it came to wiping out their enemies. What if they did something to little Finbar? The words of Vinny a few days ago had kept ringing in her ears as she tried to sleep – 'blood will be on your hands'. She would never be able to cope with the idea that she didn't do enough to save Finbar. Kerry's hand reached down to her stomach where a tiny life was growing inside her, a life that was hers to protect. Yet here she was, preparing to walk into a lion's den where she could be torn to pieces. No. That will not happen, she resolved. She vowed never to let anything or anybody harm this little life. She would fight off any bastard who came near her and tried to wreck what she had right here. Because this, more than anything, more than an empire, was worth fighting for.

She reached out and picked up her mobile, scrolling down the calls. She saw the unanswered call from Vinny, and a flick of guilt lashed across her. She wanted to see him so much, but things had changed now. What had happened between them was brief and exciting, and it had felt deep and meaningful too, because she had got the answers to why he had disappeared from her life all those years ago. But they were on opposite sides of the fence in the way they led their lives and a relationship would never work, even if they both wanted it. But this baby was his too, and deep down she knew that he had a right to know. She pushed the thought away. That was for another day. She wasn't far gone, and there was nothing for anyone to see that she was pregnant – except for Sharon who had spotted her constant throwing up.

But it was not for sharing at the moment. Not with her family and no, not even with Vinny. Things were going to change after today, when Pepe Rodriguez came to Glasgow to think he could trample over the Caseys. He would soon find out that he was very wrong to underestimate Kerry Casey.

Her bedside phone rang and it was the housekeeper to tell her that Danny and some others had arrived. She swung her legs out of bed, stood up and went to the shower. She stood under the hot water letting it cascade down her body and watched rivulets over her stomach. She pictured her mother and how shocked but excited she would have been to find that her daughter was pregnant. And her father, she could almost see his smiling face – how he would have loved to have had a grandchild to hold. The tears came and she bit them back. Tears were for another day. And under her breath she said a quiet prayer to her mother to please watch over her today.

Kerry was glad to see Jake Cahill in the study along with Jack and Danny. There were several other men too, some of them who she knew were bodyguards who had often stayed a discreet distance from her when she went anywhere. Young Cal and Tahir were also there, both looking a little pale, but standing around at the back of the room where everyone was being issued with bulletproof vests. She hoped it wasn't a game to these boys, being put in the firing line like this. She still had doubts about using them, but she had made her point to Jack, and she trusted his judgement.

'Good to see you, Jake,' she said, as she embraced him. 'Thanks for coming over at such short notice.'

'Good to see you too, Kerry. And no problem. I'm glad to be here. Anything I can do to help bring this poor kid back to Marty and his family.'

'I hope so,' Kerry said. She turned to Danny and Jack. 'So, let's sit down and talk.'

Jack motioned the men from the back of the room and each of them took a seat around the table and on chairs by the wall.

'Right, lads, here's the plan,' Danny said.

He pointed to three of the men at the end of the table, and turned to Kerry.

'Kerry. Tom, Paul and Matt down there will be working in the restaurant for the day. It's all arranged. We don't have to worry about that. The manager was visited last night. Tom and Matt will be waiters, Paul here will be the duty manager who will meet and greet customers. There will be a few more customers in the restaurant, but they will be our people sitting having lunch, so as not to attract any suspicion that the restaurant is closed to the public.'

'I take it he will have had his people casing the place over the last couple of days.'

'Of course. But they won't have seen anything untoward. We're not expecting him to turn up on his own. He'll have at least two people with him, maybe also two more in at least one car. So there will be numbers there. We've had to factor all that into our plans. We're well covered. We have people all over the place who will be watching and tracking his mob when they arrive anywhere near the place. It's a good road to be able to watch from a discreet distance, and we'll have someone in the car park too. But he'll expect that.'

'Good,' Kerry said.

'Now regarding the boy.' He nodded towards Cal and Tahir. 'Jake Cahill will take the lads Cal and Tahir with him, and a driver. There will be another car following them.' He looked at Kerry. 'This guy Sinc, who's not here at the moment for obvious reasons, will also be in the car as he is the contact. He's the one who's going to be getting the message when to move the boy. We haven't decided yet whether to go into the house where they are holding the kid at the moment, or wait until they get the call to move him to the farmhouse. I'm going to leave that to Jake's judgement on the hoof. But if we need to storm any of the houses, then we have plenty of hands to do it.' He glanced up at Cal and Tahir.

'Would it not be better to wait until the kid has been taken out of the house and is being driven to the farmhouse?' Kerry asked, trying to picture the scene. 'It might be an idea to move in then, while he's in transit.'

Danny looked at Jack and Jake.

'We'll see, Kerry. That's why I don't want to say hard and fast how it will be. It might be easier to hit them in transit. But we have to watch out for the kid, you know, if it gets messy.' He paused. 'It might turn out that Sinc gets word to move the kid and bring him to the restaurant. So we have to be ready for that too. There's a lot of uncertainties because Rodriguez hasn't said specifically that he will bring him to the restaurant while the papers are being signed. We don't know enough yet, so we'll have to wing it.'

Kerry hoped her face didn't show the worry she was feeling for little Finbar being caught in the crossfire.

'Okay. I think it's best, as you say, to play it by ear.' She paused, glanced around at everyone. 'The little boy is the most important thing of all in this operation. I know we're all placing ourselves in danger, but that's what we do when our backs are to the wall. But there's an innocent little boy in the middle of this who is all that matters. I want all of you to keep that at the forefront of your mind, no matter what decisions you make at every single stage.' She spread her hands a little. 'Look, I'm not preaching or anything, but I cannot emphasise this enough. We have to bring this boy back alive and well. This is our only chance.'

There was a long moment of silence in the room and Kerry hoped it was sinking in to every single person how important this operation was. Then Danny turned to her.

'Now, Kerry. In the restaurant it will be very much a play-it-by-ear situation as well. Rodriguez and his thugs may already be there when you arrive, so you go in, and no doubt you'll be searched. You just sit down, whatever, make the greeting and wait. It's all over to you then, how you deal with this bastard. I know you hate him with a vengeance, and that he has brought all this down upon us, but I'm sure you know how to handle him. Just take it easy. You are there under pressure, to hand over the rights to everything your family has ever owned to a complete bastard, so he'll not be expecting you to want to hug him.'

'I know,' Kerry said, feeling she should take over. 'I'll know what to say and what to do when I'm in the situation, Danny. I'll be fine. Businesslike and cooperative.'

'Good.' He turned to the boys at the end of the table. 'They'll give you a nod when the action will start. Probably once you sign the papers. But again, we have to wait and see what happens. We have to be prepared just in case this bastard has got other plans up his sleeve.'

For a moment, Kerry remembered the organisation of Knuckles Boyle and the drugs bust where he was caught red-handed, and how it was a little more comforting to know that there was a raft of armed policemen in the vicinity as well as her own men. It had niggled her from the start that perhaps she should have brought Vinny and the cops into this. But she was too afraid they would take over and it would be out of her hands. They were on their own on this, and the moment she stepped into that restaurant, even though she knew the barmen and the manager and the guests were probably armed to the teeth, she would still feel on her own.

'Okay,' Kerry said. 'And what about little Finbar? Once we get him, where are we going to take him? It's not as though we can turn up at Marty's house.'

'I know,' Jack said. 'We're working on that. But we'll transfer him to the car that's following the lads, and then we'll have to work out where to leave him so he will be found immediately. Obviously we can't just leave him in the street. We're looking at taking him to the supermarket up on Maryhill Road as a possibility. But it's going to depend on how it all unfolds at the time.'

'Fine,' Kerry said. 'I want to be phoned the moment he is safe, so I can call Marty.'

'Of course,' Jack said.

Danny looked around the table.

'All right everyone, any questions?'

Nobody spoke.

'Okay, then good luck, everyone. Look after each other.' He gestured to the back of the room where there were guns on the table, rifles and ammunition. 'Go along and talk to Danny who will tool everyone up. Make sure your weapon is ready to use when you need it. Be decisive and accurate. You might only get one shot.' He turned to Tahir and Cal. 'And you lads do everything Jake tells you to do. Be ready and be safe.' He stood up. 'Right. Off you go. There's breakfast for you in the kitchen. Everyone stay around here and get organised until it's time to go.'

CHAPTER SIXTEEN

Kerry sat in the back of the Merc as it cruised along Great Western Road and out of the city. Earlier she'd watched from her bedroom as the various cars left with men tooled and booted. It was like a small army going out on an operation, and she had never seen anything like this in the years when her father or Mickey ran the organisation. Perhaps there had been more of this with Mickey, but she had been away for so long, and she had never seen any evidence of it on her visits home. It was a comfort to know that so many of them were like family and all pulling in the one direction, but she was not under any illusion of how dangerous the next couple of hours of her life were going to be. She'd felt a little nauseated earlier and could only risk eating a couple of slices of toast. But now that she was in the car and on her way, she was beginning to feel stronger. She spotted the restaurant in the distance as the car slowed down, and she turned around to see their other car that was following them. When they turned into the restaurant car park, the other car also slowed down but drove on. She knew it would be nearby and primed.

In the car park there were three cars: two Mercedes and one Range Rover. Instinctively she looked over her shoulder and watched as Jack got out, his eyes sweeping the area. The cars had blacked-out windows, so they had no idea how many people were inside or what they were doing. She wondered how many guns were trained on her right now.

'Should we just go in?' she asked Jack, as she pulled her bag onto her shoulder.

'Yeah. I think that's best. He might already be in there. But we've got a couple of cars arriving shortly, so they'll just sit in the wings and wait.' He took a breath. 'Let's go, Kerry. You all right?'

'Yes,' she said, and meant it. 'I'm fine. I'm ready.'

'Okay. You'll be all right. Just keep calm and know that we're all around. Nothing's going to happen to you.'

'I wonder how it's going down at the house where they're holding the wee man.'

'Don't concern yourself with that just now. Just focus on reeling this fucker in. He has to believe you mean business here today.'

They walked towards the door where a burly minder in shades stood in their way. He moved to the side and opened the door. Kerry walked in first to the dimly lit restaurant, full of dark shadowy corners and empty tables. She glanced around quickly and clocked her boy Tom behind the bar, and then Paul coming up to greet her. At the far end of the restaurant, just beyond the bar, three men sat around a table. They had golf clubs stacked at the side as though they were either on their way or returning from a round. They didn't look up when she came in but continued chatting. She hoped they were her men, but she hadn't seen them before.

She glanced around to the other side of the restaurant and then she saw him. Pepe Rodriguez. The bastard was really here. He'd come all this way to take from her everything she had, everything her father had built up: the pubs, the taxis, the property. Yes, the drugs too, and that was part of who she was, the part she hated. But this thug had come here to take it all, and he had used a frightened little boy as a means of negotiation. She stared hard at him, but he kept his eyes front and didn't look up, even though she knew he would be aware of her arrival. A tall, skinny, sallow-skinned man came forward from the bar along with a squat little man. They both looked South American.

'Mees Casey. You permit if we search. Sorry. But is necessary,' the small guy said, putting his hand out for her bag. She handed it to him. Then the tall, skinny guy stepped forward. He raised his arms in a gesture that would mean he could search. She did the same and put her arms out. He briefly ran a hand beneath her coat, across her back and briefly down her legs. He didn't linger on her thighs or the waist of her trousers. But he still gave her the creeps. Then he turned and did the same to Jack who stood giving him the cold stare while he performed his search. Jack pulled up the stool at the bar, sat and ordered a drink.

'Follow me, please,' the squat man said.

She walked behind him, her heart picking up speed, and she took a long breath and held it for a few seconds to keep herself calm. Only when she was almost at the table did Rodriguez turn around to face her. Then he got to his feet, something resembling a smile breaking across his handsome face.

'Ah!' He stretched out a hand. 'The beautiful Kerry Casey. I have been waiting for this moment.' He smiled, flashing strong white teeth. 'You are just as I remember you. Beautiful, but with the fire in your eye.' He squeezed her hand. 'Come. Sit. We can talk.'

Kerry kept her eyes on him, locking his gaze as she sat down and, as planned, slipping her jacket off and putting it over the back of the chair. She didn't know what to say, but she felt she should say something, because this bastard was already acting like she was some member of fucking staff.

'I'm here, Pepe,' she said, lowering her voice, 'because you leave me with no option.' She glared at him, her hatred burning her gut. Then she tried to soften her expression. 'But yes. I hope we can talk.'

'Of course.' He leaned forward. 'And please understand, Kerry, that we do business a little differently in my country. If we want something, then we have to find a way to take it. That is all that has happened here.'

'Yeah. Sure.' She glanced over his shoulder at one of his minders sitting a few tables away, his eyes everywhere. 'Tell that to the family of little Finbar Kane who you've been keeping for several days now. A terrified little boy. It's a cruel way you do business in your country, Pepe.' She spread her hands. 'But that is where we are. So let's get on with it.'

He snapped his fingers and the waiter came over. He ordered a glass of red wine, while Kerry asked for mineral water.

'No wine to seal our partnership, then, Kerry?' He said it with a hint of a snarl.

'What partnership? I didn't realise we were partners, if you forgive me. You came here to steal my business.'

'But it doesn't have to be like that, my *cariño*. We can be partners.'

This was news to Kerry. Being partners with a scumbag like him was never on the table at any stage, apart from something Frankie had mentioned on the phone and she thought he was just trying to wind her up. She had papers in here to sign everything over to him, but hopefully if their plan worked out she wouldn't have to. 'Partners?'

'Yes, yes. I want to work with you,' he continued quickly.

'I think you are smart and intelligent as well as beautiful. We can build something together in our enterprise. We can give to each other – my organisation and money and yours too.' He leaned forward. 'I talked to Durkin. He's a smart enough man, even if he doesn't look it. But we have talked about everything about where the business could go. He knows Spain very well. He suggests we all work together. We can make an agreement here. I don't want to take your livelihood, all that your family built. I want to make it bigger, more successful. This hotel is only the start.'

She listened in disbelief. She had to think on her feet how to handle this.

'I had not been under any impression you seriously wanted to go into business with me. When your message boy Frankie mentioned it I assumed he was joking.'

'But I do. I want that very much. '

'So why prepare papers for me to hand everything over?'

'Because on paper I will own everything. But you will work with me.'

'You mean I will work *for* you.'

'Well,' he shrugged, 'if you want to put it like that, but I don't see it that way. You will make a lot of money. But I will be the person who is head of the business. The hotel will be in the name of my company – and you can operate it for me. I have much money to invest in this, and also in the property around Costa del Sol and even in the north of

Spain. Not forgetting my shipments, of course. I have big plans. We can make huge amounts of money if we all work together.'

The very sound of his voice was irritating her, and it was all that she could do to contain her simmering rage. The waiter came across with the menus and stood reeling off the specials, and then there was a sudden noise as something crashed on the stone floor at the other side of the room. She turned automatically in the direction of the noise, as did Pepe, and while they were distracted, the waiter slipped something into her pocket. She kept her eyes on the source of the noise.

'Golfers,' she said. 'I think they are having a day out.' She forced a smile.

'See how beautiful you look when you relax, Kerry. I am very much looking forward to many times like this with you.' He picked up the menu. 'So, let's choose something to eat.'

She picked up the menu and the waiter came across from the bar and they both ordered.

'So do you have the papers with you?' Rodriguez asked.

'Yes. I had my lawyer prepare them. I understand you have papers too?'

'Yes, and they are translated.' He clicked his fingers and one of his flunkies came across with a folder with ribbon around it. He handed it to Rodriguez who then gave it over to Kerry. She glanced through it, but didn't get much further than the part where it said, 'I, Kerry Casey, hereby sign everything . . .' She flicked to the next page and the following pages, reading quickly.

'Where is the boy?' She placed the papers on the table and looked directly at him.

'The boy is fine.'

'Where is he? When will I see him?'

'In good time. Of course. We eat. We have lunch and then I will have him brought to you.'

'What, here? You'll bring him here?'

Kerry said it loud enough so that Jack could hear, and she hoped he would take action. The last place they wanted the boy to be brought was here, where it could all kick off and he could be caught in the crossfire. She saw him slip out his mobile. Kerry began to feel a little sweat stinging her back. She took a gulp of water.

'Are you all right?'

'Yes. I'm fine. I just want to see the boy. I have been so worried about him.' She took a breath. 'Can you show me a picture of him? All I've had so far are calls from Frankie Martin, and nothing solid to show me that Finbar is alive. You must have something.'

Rodriguez looked at her with his black eyes, then raised a hand and clicked his fingers. One of his flunkies came up to the table, and he spoke softly to him in Spanish. Kerry could understand that he was asking for him to get the photo up on his mobile. She watched, her mouth dry.

Then the flunkey brought up a photo and thrust it in front of her. She felt her heart stop. She hadn't met Finbar, but had seen pictures of him in the newspapers, and photos that Marty had shown her of a sunny, happy little boy. This was definitely his image, and that was today's newspaper next to him. But it was the face of a little boy with big watery eyes, frightened, his little mouth turned down as though he was about to burst into tears. Kerry swallowed her emotion and her chest ached. She nodded. The flunkey closed the picture and went back to his table.

'Now you see him. Okay?'

'It will never be okay, Pepe.' She glared at him.

He shrugged. 'But trust me. He will be here. So all you have to do is sign the papers and I make the call.'

Kerry got to the last page and took her pen from her bag. Then she glanced up at Jack at the bar who made the tiniest gesture with his hands that she took to mean stall things a little. Maybe he was waiting on word from the guys about Finbar. Fine. She steeled herself. She'd have to improvise. She flicked through the pages again, conscious that Rodriguez was watching her, and she pushed her hair back with one hand and massaged her neck, giving the Colombian a look that she knew he would think was a slight come-on.

'Look, Pepe,' she said, glancing at the papers. 'Before I sign this, I have to say that it's a surprise to me you suddenly saying you want to be working with me. I don't see how that's going to work if I don't have a stake on paper.' She shrugged and held out her hands. 'What you're doing here, Pepe, is taking my business, and asking me to work with you. For you, in effect. So can we not talk about a little wriggle room here?'

'Wriggle room? What is this? I don't understand.'

'Wriggle room,' she repeated. 'It means a bit of room for manoeuvre, for movement. Surely we can come to some kind of arrangement?' Kerry moistened her lips a little and knew she had his full attention. But Christ. She didn't know how long she could keep this up.

CHAPTER SEVENTEEN

Cal and Tahir sat in the back seat of the blacked-out Merc as they drove towards the house in Maryhill Road. Jake Cahill had told them on the way that the guy they were going to pick up was Sinc, another piece of shit who had been used by the kidnappers to move Finbar around. Sinc sat between them now, clutching his mobile phone as though it were a lifeline, and Cal could almost smell the fear coming off him. They had only met him moments before as he was brought out of the Portakabin at the scrapyard where he was being held, and marched to the Merc by two of the guys Cal had seen from time to time working security for the Caseys. They were hard-looking bastards, and Cal was surprised that Sinc didn't have a mark on him, but his face was deathly pale. Cal knew there was another car behind them as backup, and right now he didn't even know what the plan was. Sinc's mobile suddenly pinged with a text, and Cal could feel him go rigid. He eyed the line. Then he listened as Sinc read it out to Jake.

'That's them,' he said. 'The text says, "We'll be ready. Ten minutes. Ring the bell twice. One of us will go with you to the next address."'

'Fine,' Jake said. He nudged the driver to slow down a little. Then he took out his mobile and made a call. 'Lads.' His voice was soft, gentle, in control. 'They're ready. I want you to drive past the house a couple of times and tell me what you see.' Then he hung up.

A few minutes later, as they continued towards Maryhill Road, Jake's mobile rang and he answered it.

'Okay. Fine. I see.'

He turned around so he was facing the back seat. 'Right, boys. Before we get there, we're going to stop up the road and I'm going to get out of this car and go with the car behind us. Okay?' He looked at Cal. 'You, son, will stay in the car with Sinc, so it's only the two of you who go to the door. You got that?' He looked at Tahir. 'You will come with me. You understand?'

Tahir nodded, and shot a sidewards glance at Cal. Jake went on.

'You, Cal, bring the kid out, and whoever else they are bringing, and you get the kid safely in the car, then you take your instructions from them. Do you understand?'

Sinc and Cal both nodded.

'Don't worry about whatever fucker they bring with

them. We'll deal with him in due course. You just drive to the address as instructed. You're okay with that, Sinc.' It was more of a statement than a question and Sinc looked as though he knew better than to say no.

Cal could feel the tension in his gut as he glanced at Tahir.

'So will they just hand the boy over to Sinc and me? Just like that?'

'Should do. That's what they've done so far, is that right, Sinc?'

'Aye,' he sniffed, nervous. 'Except last time at the Paki warehouse I had to go in the back door and carry the wean out. What if they ask me in?'

Jake was silent for a few moments.

'Then you go in. There's nothing we can do about that. You go in, and you keep your fucking face straight and you do everything just as you've done before. You don't talk to them, you don't even fucking look at them. You just take the boy and get out and into the car and you do as they say. Forget about us, forget about everything – just do what you've been doing for the past two drops.' He narrowed his eyes and looked at Sinc. 'You make sure you don't make any stupid mistakes here that arouse suspicion. If you do that, then it's fucking the end of the story. You got that?'

Sinc nodded but didn't reply.

'And don't look as though you're shitting your pants, for fuck's sake. Everything depends on you carrying this off.'

'I'm all right,' Sinc said, but his voice had a worrying croak to it.

A few minutes later they pulled the car into the roadside and Jake turned to Cal.

'Be careful, son. You'll be fine. We'll not be far away.'

He told Sinc to climb into the front passenger seat, which he did. Cal sat in the back watching as Tahir and Jake got into the back of the big Range Rover. Cal felt his heart beating under the bulletproof vest. As they drove off, he put his hand in his jacket pocket and ran his fingers over the Glock pistol. He knew how to use it, and it gave him a little jag of adrenalin just touching it.

When they got to the address, the car stopped and for a moment they sat in tense silence. Cal saw the driver glance at him in his rear-view mirror and make a gesture for him to get a move on. Cal swallowed. He nudged Sinc on the shoulder, firm enough to let him know that as of this moment, he was in charge.

'C'mon, let's go,' Cal said.

Sinc hesitated for a few seconds then opened the car door and got out. Cal got out of the back and they both walked up to the door, saying nothing. It crossed Cal's mind that Sinc might just blurt it all out when the door opened, and he'd have to be ready. He glanced over his shoulder hoping he could spot the Range Rover close by, but it was nowhere. He felt his mouth dry as Sinc rang the bell twice. They stood, barely breathing, as a curtain twitched upstairs and someone glanced out. Then they heard footsteps on the stairs and muffled voices. The door opened just a little on the chain and Cal could make out the skinny, unshaven face of a man with dishevelled hair and dark circles under his eyes.

'Where's your mate?'

The question seemed to throw Sinc and he looked a little bewildered, then he caught on.

'Aw, Lenny? He's fucked with food poisoning. Shitting all over the place.'

The man's eyes darted from Sinc to Cal and he kept his face deadpan.

'Who's this cunt?'

'He works for me,' Sinc said, squaring his shoulders. 'He does drops for me. He's all right. He's sound, man.' He paused for a second. 'Where's the wean? I don't want to fucking hang around on the step in case anyone notices.'

The sound of bolts being slid, and the door opened further.

'Come in.'

Shit! Cal said to himself, his heart suddenly taking a jolt. He didn't even dare to look at Sinc as they stepped over the threshold and into the damp, cold hallway. As soon as they did, they heard the sound of a child sobbing. Jesus! Cal was so overwhelmed by the sound that it was like someone punching him in the chest. He fought to keep control.

'Will be glad to see the fucking back of the wee bastard. Been greetin' for two solid fucking days. Follow me.'

They walked behind him along the hall which stank of dirty clothing and stale fried food. Then the sounds got louder as they approached a door. The guy pushed the door open and Cal stepped back, hoping his face didn't show the shock that was surging through him. Sitting on the couch was a little boy, his face tearstained and flushed, snot in his nose and sweating from crying. His wails sounded as though his throat was sore and he lay propped up on a cushion weeping. He looked up when they came in.

'Wh-Where's my mummy? I want my mummy.' Then he sobbed, burying his face into the grimy cushion.

Cal glanced around the room, where another man sat in the corner and didn't even look round at the visitors. He held the TV remote control in his hand and kept flicking channels. Eventually, he turned.

'Thank fuck!' he said. 'Pissed off listening to the wee shite greetin'. No matter what you give him.' He gestured to the toy truck and colouring books on the floor.

'Let's get moving,' Sinc said. 'Who's coming with me?'

The skinny-faced guy pulled on his jacket and ran a hand under his nose. Cal shot a glance around the room and saw a couple of used wraps that he'd bet had been coke.

'Come on, then,' Sinc said, turning to Cal. 'Get the boy lifted and let's get the fuck out of here and get this job done.'

Cal went forward to the boy and reached out his hand,

but the boy shrank back. Cal glanced around at the guy with the remote control, and it crossed his mind that he might have been terrorising the kid. He made a mental picture of his face and vowed he would pay when this was all over. Cal sat down on the couch and stroked the boy's hair.

'Come on, wee man,' he said gently, putting his arms around him. 'You're all right, pal. Come on.'

Cal lifted him into his arms and stood up, feeling choked with emotion as the little boy buried his face in his shoulder and sobbed.

'Let's go,' Sinc said, as they moved towards the door, back down the hall and opened the front door. 'Get him in the car, into the back seat.' He handed him a jacket. 'Here. Cover his head with this in case any fucking busybodies are watching.'

Cal did as he said, and walked quickly to the car and into the back seat. As soon as he did, he caught sight of the driver hitting a button on his mobile. And over the brow of the hill, he saw the Range Rover in the distance. He breathed a sigh of relief. But this was not over yet.

'Right,' Sinc said, once they were into the car. 'Next address. You all ready?'

'Aye,' the skinny man said. 'You'll drop me back here once we get rid of the wean, won't you?'

'Aye,' Sinc said. They drove away from the address and Cal could feel the boy's heartbeat as he held him close, caressing his face. He could feel his chest heave with sobs, even though the boy was beginning to drift off to sleep, his big blue eyes flickering and looking up to this stranger who was holding him. And as the kid gripped his hand tight, Cal made another vow that every single person who was involved in taking this wee boy would pay with their lives.

They drove out of the city and down the road until the buzz of the traffic was gone and the roads and landscape changed. The boy was fast asleep but his body jerked in fitful little sobs now and again. Cal kept his eyes straight ahead as they drove in silence, the skinny-faced guy next to him, staring out of the window and his face twitching with nerves. Cal clocked the driver glance in his wing mirror and from the corner of his eye, he could see the Range Rover coming up behind them. Then it happened. Suddenly the Range Rover engine roared and it just raced ahead of them, then stopped abruptly, swerving into the side and clipping their wing, almost pushing them into the ditch. The driver screeched to a halt.

'What the fuck, man!' The skinny-faced guy jolted forward, then quickly reached below his sweatshirt and pulled out a gun. 'What the fuck is this?' He pushed the gun into Sinc's head. 'You playing fucking games here, ya wee cunt? I'll blow your fucking brains out. What the fuck's going on!'

Cal squeezed Finbar tight as he began to wake up with

the noise and whimpered. Then the skinny-faced guy switched the gun to point at the child's head, and Cal felt his stomach drop.

'What the fuck's going on?' the skinny man barked.

His words were barely out when out they saw the Range Rover doors open. Jake Cahill and Tahir rushed, guns ready, towards the car.

'Who the fuck are you?' the skinny man screamed. 'Get fucking back right now or the kid gets it right in the fucking head. I'm telling you.'

The rear passenger seat window was rolled down by the driver, and Jake and Tahir stood with the guns aimed at the skinny man.

'Listen, son. The game's up. Now don't be doing anything silly here. It's over. Just put down the gun and come out of the car.'

'No fucking way! That'll be fucking right. The boys will be down from the house any minute. They're expecting us to arrive right now.'

'Just calm down now. Come on. Come out of the car and nobody gets hurt.'

'Aye, and I'm going to believe that shite?' He pushed the gun into Finbar's head and the boy cried out in pain. 'I'm telling you, the kid is getting it. Get out of my fucking way.'

'Listen,' Jake said, 'there's no way out of this for you now. You have to come with us before the boys come down and all hell breaks loose. You'll be a dead man then because they'll think you're part of the betrayal. Now wise up before it's too late.'

Suddenly there was the roar of an engine and from the front window, Cal could see a car racing towards them with its headlights blaring.

Jake kept the gun on the skinny man, who kept the gun on the boy.

'Make your mind up time, son,' Jake said.

Jake nudged Tahir, who immediately swivelled around and fired off two shots through the windscreen of the oncoming car. The car swerved into the ditch, and in that moment Cal threw open the car door and dived onto the ground on top of Finbar, staying low and covering him. Then the mayhem. There were shots pinging off the car, the wheels and the windscreen shattering. He daren't look up. The boy was silent and Cal held his little warm body close, telling him his mummy was coming soon. Eventually there was an eerie silence.

'You're all right now, Cal. You can come up. Quick. Get the boy into the Range Rover.'

Cal scrambled to his feet with the boy in his arms and climbed into the back of the Range Rover. As he did, he looked out of the windscreen to see Jake Cahill dragging the skinny-faced man out of the Merc and forcing him to kneel on the ground. Then, without even flinching, Tahir came up behind him and put a bullet in the back of his head. Cal closed his eyes tightly and clutched the boy to his chest. But he had seen the blood spurt like a fountain from the skinny man's head as he fell face down, and in that single moment, he knew he would never again feel a sense of justice like this.

CHAPTER EIGHTEEN

Kerry kept an eye over Rodriguez's shoulder to where Jack was sitting at the bar. They must have been in the restaurant twenty-five minutes by now, and she was thinking they should have heard from Jake and the boys. But nothing. She was finding it hard to concentrate on anything else, but she had to. It wouldn't be much longer now, she told herself. She clocked the guys with the golf clubs at the other side of the restaurant who were getting noisier the more drink they were downing. Kerry picked at the salad she'd ordered while Rodriguez ate heartily as though they were an ordinary couple enjoying lunch. She watched as he poured olive oil onto a side plate and mopped it up with bread, washing it down with red wine. She felt the urge to lift the bottle and smash it all over the smug bastard's head. But she knew she couldn't.

'So,' he said, between mouthfuls of food, 'tell me how you see our arrangement working if you own part of the business on paper.' He raised his eyebrows, waiting for an answer. 'I'm interested in what you think. I really am.'

Kerry picked up the contract from the table.

'Pepe, everything that is in here, is mine. My family built it. My father. All I ask is to be named as a partner in the business. I agree we can work together and make our organisation grow. But I will work with more determination, if I can see it is mine also.'

He sat back for a moment and dabbed his mouth with his napkin. He let out a sigh.

'But, my *cariño*, it cannot work that way. I can promise to you that you will see the profits, that you will benefit, and that in some ways nothing will change in your organisation and family. But it *has* to belong to me. For future investments I make, I need to be seen as the sole owner of the business. In order to raise money, I have to show people that I have already major assets.' He gave her an emphatic look. 'Don't worry. I will look after everything you have made and grown. But you, *cariño*, will belong to me.'

Rage coursed through her and she could feel a flush coming to her neck. Stay calm, she told herself. Listen. Swallow it. Wait. It can't be long now.

'And, Kerry. You are forgetting that today I come here to see you. To do this business. But remember. From where you are sitting, you do not have a choice. *Entiendes?*'

Kerry picked up the pen and went to the back page. She looked up from the papers.

'I want to see the boy. Can you please bring him now? Before I sign?'

He shook his head slowly. 'When you sign.'

She swallowed back her anger. Then suddenly, from the corner of her eye, she saw Jack move to get off the bar stool. As he did, one of Rodriguez's henchmen took out his mobile, read something, then got up from the table where he sat a few feet away from them. He walked towards them and leaned down, whispering something in his boss's ear. Another two men at a table, clearly Rodriguez's, also got up. Jack got off his stool and pulled out his gun. Kerry just had time to see Rodriguez's expression change to rage as he glared at her. But before he could do anything there was an almighty smash at the end of the bar where the golfers sat, and glasses were being thrown. Both of them glanced up, and now the golfers were on their feet as the door burst open and three armed men came rushing in, firing shots all over the place. The golfers fired back. Rodriguez moved to get up, as his henchmen fired into the room and rushed forward to grab him. Jack fired and one of them dropped to the floor, then the golfers fired again as two more men came bursting in the door. As the henchmen pulled at Rodriguez he stumbled, and as he got up, Kerry reached into her pocket for her gun. It was now or never. She had to do this. She took aim and fired, watching as he fell down, but she'd only hit him in the leg. Before she could fire again two more guys came in firing across the room and she had to dive to the floor, Jack on top of her while the shooting went on. She looked up to see them shooting back and for a single second she saw the look of evil on the face of Pepe Rodriguez as he caught her eye. One of his henchmen fired back, chipping a lump out of the table, but Jack kept her covered. Then, suddenly, the shooting stopped. The place fell ghostly silent. Jack eased himself up and she sat up. Jack was hit in the shoulder, and there were bodies everywhere – three of them were the Rodriguez men. Paul behind the bar was hit and blood seeped through his shirt. She could hear cars roar outside. Rodriguez was gone. She got to her feet as Jack stood up.

'We've got Finbar,' he said. 'He's in a car with Jake and Cal.'

Kerry put her hand to her mouth to stop the tears of shock and relief.

'Oh God, Jack. Is he all right?'

He nodded, trying to stem the flow of blood from his shoulder.

'He's shook up, but they've got him. That's all that matters.' Seeing her tears he stepped forward and held her close. 'And we're still here. The Caseys are still here, and that fucking Colombian was dragged out of here like a wounded dog. I hope the cunt bleeds to death.'

'Sorry my shot was crap. It was all happening so fast, Jack.'

He eased her away from him.

'Come on. We'd best get out of here. I've got a team

coming in to clean up. Let's get ourselves sorted – a couple of the boys were injured.' He glanced at the back where the golfers were examining each other.

She smiled. 'You didn't tell me they'd be looking like that.'

'I thought the less distractions you had the better. They were a good decoy though, eh?'

'Definitely. Well done. Let's go. Can you get Jake on the phone?'

Jack punched in a number and spoke.

'Jake. I've got Kerry here. Thank Christ you got the boy safe.'

He seemed to be listening to Jake speak.

'Yeah, it was a bit messy right enough here too, but we're all sound. Rodriguez is gone. Dragged out by one of his boys. But Kerry shot him.' He smiled and handed Kerry the phone.

'Jake. You got Finbar. Thanks. How is he?'

'He's a wee pathetic soul, Kerry. Poor wee kid has been scared to death, but he's cuddling into Cal here in the back seat. He'll be all right when he gets his mammy. What do you want us to do?'

'Hold on a moment, Jake. I'll put you on loudspeaker.'

She turned to Jack. 'We can't take him to his home, obviously, so we're going to have to leave him somewhere and call the cops, and call Marty.'

'Aye,' Jack said. 'But we've got to be nowhere near it when it happens. Why not get Jake to take him to the Tesco up in

Maryhill Road? Cal can walk right in with him, but call the cops and Marty so they arrive a minute later. Cal can bail out and the wee boy will be too excited to see his ma to wonder what's happening.'

'How does that sound, Jake?'

'That's fine. We're not too far from there, so call everyone in the next five minutes. Give Cal a chance to get in and settle the boy, so he's waiting for his mum.'

'Great,' Jack said. 'But we won't call anyone till you're at the supermarket in case you turn up and there are routine cops there bagging a shoplifter or something, and you have to about-turn. Just call us when you get there. What about CCTV though?'

'It's fine. Cal will pull his hood up.'

'Great.

Kerry hung up. Within five minutes, Jake phoned back to say they were at the supermarket and the coast was clear. She took out her mobile and punched in Marty's number. He answered straight away.

'Marty. We've got Finbar. He's safe. He's well. We're about to call the cops as we can't be anywhere near it. We're taking him to the Tesco on Maryhill Road and leaving him there, but don't worry. One of our boys will be watching over him till the cops and you arrive.'

'Oh, Kerry! Is he all right? Are you sure?'

She could hear the quiver of emotion in his voice.

'He's fine. I don't know how you'll explain all this if the

cops start asking questions, but don't worry about that just now. Just go and get your grandson.'

Jake Cahill pulled into the Tesco car park which was reasonably busy with shoppers, cars and taxis, people moving with trolleys. Cal was glad to see that little Finbar had calmed down and though he was still clinging to him, he was looking out of the window and pointing to the supermarket.

'My mummy and daddy take me here. We going to see them now?'

'Yes,' Cal said. 'Your mummy and daddy's coming soon, Finbar. You just be a good boy with me now and we'll go inside and wait.'

'I like you,' the boy said putting his arms around Cal's neck.

'You've got a wee pal there, Cal,' Jake said. 'You've been good with him, son, I'll say that for you.'

'He was in a right state when we saw him, Jake. That house. Stinking. And that bastard sitting there. He needs wasting. And he needs it soon.'

'Aye. You're right about that.' He looked out of the window and at his watch. 'Okay. I'd say they'll all be here pronto, so why don't you go inside. Don't go too far in, just through the entrance and the main area, and take him over to the newspapers, where he can stand and look at comics or something. Then take a step back, so you can keep an eye in case some perverts sees him on his own.

Then you can just walk away when I phone. His ma will be there before he even notices you're gone. Got that?'

'Yeah,' Cal said, opening the door. 'I'm cool.' He got out and lifted the boy into his arms, then pulled up his hood so it covered a lot of his face. 'Come on, wee man. Let's get your mum.'

'Where is she?' the boy said, looking around him.

'She'll be here in a minute. We have to go in here now. You be a good boy, won't you?'

'I'm a good boy. I'm a big boy,' Finbar said.

Cal carried him as they made the short walk through the automatic doors and into the entrance. He stood for a moment, then put Finbar down, who stood clinging to his thigh. He hoped he didn't make this difficult and draw attention to himself. Then Cal took the boy's hand and crossed over to the newspapers and magazines shelves. Finbar was immediately engrossed and began looking at superhero magazines on the stand. Cal took a few steps back but close enough so he could still see the doors. His mobile rang.

'Right. Get yourself out now. They've just arrived, bells and whistles, three cop cars too. And another car with them which will be Marty and his family. Count to ten and then disappear.'

'Will do.'

Cal bent down and ruffled the little boy's hair.

'You're a good boy now, Finbar, aren't you? Listen to me.

I want you to stand here and watch those big doors and in a couple of minutes your mummy and daddy will come through there to you.'

Finbar looked at him, a little worried

'You stay with me?'

'Yes. I'll stay. But if you just watch the big doors, I'll be back in a second.'

He didn't look back at the boy as he saw the doors open and the cops come in, four or five in uniform and behind them a young couple. Their eyes lit up when they saw Finbar.

'Mummy! Daddy!' Cal could hear Finbar shouting as he walked out.

'Finbar!'

Cal glanced over his shoulder to see the boy's mother and father drop to their knees and envelop the boy. All three of them were crying and there were police all over the place. He quickened his step. Then just outside he saw Marty Kane standing by the path. He caught his eye and could see the clever, confident man who had picked him up from a Manchester police cell only a few weeks ago. Now he looked like a shadow of himself, tired and old. Marty glanced at Cal and gave a slight nod of recognition. Then Cal walked briskly towards the waiting car and jumped inside.

'Let's go,' Jake said. 'We have unfinished business at that house.'

CHAPTER NINETEEN

Marty Kane turned into the large driveway of his son's house, his heart in a turmoil of joy, and dread of what lay ahead. He had remained in the supermarket car park at a discreet distance while his son and his wife rushed into the store along with several police officers. He'd wanted Finbar's mum and dad to have their reunion by themselves. His chest almost burst with emotion the moment he saw his son emerge from the store, little Finbar clinging to his neck, his mother ruffling the boy's hair and chatting animatedly to him. The picture of delight and sheer relief on the faces of all three would live with him for ever. When he got back to his car, Marty let the tears come as he watched them drive off under police escort.

Marty's wife opened the door when he rang the bell and he stepped inside. Her face was flushed with tears and exhaustion. For a second they just looked at each other, then she fell into his arms.

'It's all right, darling. It's over.' Marty caressed her hair as he held her. 'He's safe. Thank God he's safe.'

'Did you see him?' she sniffed on his shoulder. 'Does he look all right? Oh Jesus, did they hurt him, Marty?'

'Sssh,' he consoled her. 'He looks great. None the worse for wear and he was chatting to his mum and hanging onto his daddy.'

She eased herself out of his arms.

'Joe phoned. They were taking him to hospital just for a check. They'll be here shortly.'

'That's okay. That's just routine to make sure he's all right. They won't keep him there as they'll want to get him back into his routine immediately. But honestly, he looked fine.'

Marty looked down as little Johnny came into the hall.

'Where's Fin? Is he here, Grandpa?' He rushed forward.

'No. Not yet, son. But your mum and dad will be bringing him home any moment.' He knelt down and touched his grandson's face. 'Let's go and see if we can find some of his toys for when he arrives. He'll be desperate to play with them.'

'Oh yeah. Let's get his Superman toys from the playroom.'

The boy took Marty's hand and as he glanced over his shoulder Marty saw his wife standing, beaming and wiping her tears with the back of her hand.

'I'll put the kettle on,' she said, and disappeared into the kitchen.

Marty knew he still had to face the questions from his wife and from his son. When Kerry had phoned him to tell him they'd got Finbar, he'd had to conceal his joy. He had to wait until the call came from the police to tell his son the kidnappers had dropped the boy at a supermarket. He hated himself for the betrayal, and as his son was leaving the house, he gave Marty a look of distrust that cut him to the quick. Marty had insisted on coming with them, but said he would wait outside the place in case they needed him. As they'd walked back to their car, they didn't even look in his direction. They didn't need him. He felt shut out. And maybe he should be.

Marty sat drinking a mug of tea and looking on as Johnny knelt up on the sofa, staring out of the window, watching every car that passed. Then he spotted his dad's Jag swing into the driveway, and leaped off the sofa.

'They're here, Grandpa! Look! Fin's here.'

Without another word he scrambled out of the room and raced to the front door. Marty heard the car doors close and he put down his mug and stood up. He watched as Finbar's mum unbuckled him from his car seat and lifted him from the car, the little boy's arms draped around her.

'Look who's here!' she called out to Johnny, who was bouncing up and down on the doorstep.

Finbar turned around and his little face was a picture of happiness. Marty went out into the hall as they came through the front door.

'Granny! Granny!' Finbar yelped as he wriggled free. He ran into his grandmother's arms.

Then he saw Marty.

'Grandad! Grandad! I was looking for you! I was waiting for you, but you didn't come!'

Marty felt like a knife had sliced through him. Guilt, shame and relief all flooded through him as the boy ran into his arms. He scooped him up and cuddled him tight, stroking the back of his head and kissing his cheek.

'I know, son. I know, sweetheart. I was looking for you too. But listen. It's okay now. You're home. Come on. Johnny got your toys in the playroom.'

Finbar turned around to his parents and stood for a second, then he ran towards them and hugged them hard. Then without a backward glance he raced with his brother to the playroom as though he'd never been away.

Marty shook his head and smiled.

'He'll be fine.'

All four of them stood in the hall in a long moment of silence, then Joe's wife, Alice, turned to her husband and fell into his arms.

'Oh, Joe! Oh Christ, Joe!'

'Come on now, sweetheart. Don't let him see you crying. It's okay now. Everything is going to be okay.'

'I'm sorry,' she sniffed. 'I'm just . . . I'm just so happy. I kept thinking of what our lives would be like if we never saw Fin again. I . . . I . . . He's back, and I'll never let him out of my sight again.'

'Come on,' Elizabeth said. 'Don't think that way now. It's over.'

They'd sat in the kitchen drinking tea and there was an almost euphoric atmosphere as Finbar had kept running back into the kitchen as though to make sure everyone was still there.

Joe had talked about his conversation with the police and how they were sending specially qualified officers later to have a gentle word with Finbar to make sure he was coping and not suffering from any discernible trauma, and also to see if they could glean any information from him. They cautioned his parents to keep an eye on him because any emotional damage might not appear immediately and it could be weeks before it showed up in his behaviour. Alice kept saying no matter what showed up they would make it better, that everything was going to be fine. Marty had sensed a bit of a distance in his son's demeanour and he wondered if it was all beginning to hit him and take its toll. He found that Joe didn't look him in the eye much, and it worried him. As they began to relax and Marty and Elizabeth talked about getting ready to go home to their own house and leave them alone, Joe walked Marty into the big living room and closed the door.

Marty stood by the fireplace, bracing himself. He'd been dreading this moment.

'Dad,' Joe began. Now he did look him in the eye. 'There's no easy way to say this, so I'm just going to say it.' He looked a little nervous. 'I know you lied to me.'

The words hung in the air for a moment and Marty kept his face straight but didn't answer.

'Dad. Look. I know you lied. I know Finbar's kidnapping was something to do with the Caseys, so please, don't insult me by lying to me again.'

'Son–' Marty said.

Joe put his hand up to silence his father.

'Please. Hear me out. I don't know what this was all about, and I don't even know if it's over, but I know you have been aware since the very start that Finbar's kidnapping was to do with the Caseys and whatever shit they're involved in. I'm not talking about all the stuff in the papers and rumours. I'm just taking an educated guess here. I know you, Dad, I've watched you all my life. And I can see in your face when you're lying to me. I know you must have been going through hell, and I'm sorry you had to do that by yourself. But you should have told me.'

Marty said nothing for a moment, working out how to handle this. This was his son he'd lied to from day one.

'Dad, I need you to tell me what happened. I know how the Caseys work and it won't go any further. It was them who had something to do with getting Finbar back, wasn't it?'

Again, Marty said nothing.

'It had to be. Kidnappers don't just pitch up to the supermarket and dump a kid they've been holding. I mean, maybe they thought the cops were about to rumble them or something, but I don't believe that. Tell me. Please.' He paused for a moment. 'Please, Dad. Our whole relationship depends on this.'

Marty looked at his son and his heart burst with love for him, for the pain he had been through, pain he would not have had to endure if Marty Kane had not been the lawyer of the Caseys all these years. He didn't have to do that. He'd made a fortune from being the most successful and sought-after criminal lawyer in the business, yet he was embedded with thugs and drug dealers who shored up the Casey empire. It suddenly dawned on him that if he didn't tell his son the truth right now, then he would lose him, and he would lose his grandchildren and maybe even Elizabeth.

Marty sighed. 'Joe. I had to, son. I couldn't tell you the truth. I wanted to. I wanted to just let the police get on with the whole investigation, but it was too dangerous. The people who took Finbar are evil and unscrupulous, and they have tentacles everywhere. I was so scared to get the police involved in case it would get botched up, as these things sometimes do, and I was afraid we wouldn't see Fin again. I couldn't afford to do that.' Marty swallowed. 'It's my fault, son. It's my fault he was taken. My fault because of my association with the Caseys. But never in my nightmares did I ever think this was possible.'

'Why couldn't you tell the cops all this?

'As I told you. It was too risky.'

'So who got Finbar?'

Silence.

Then Marty spoke.

'Please. You cannot ever speak about this to your wife or to your mother. This is just between us because it has to be. Are you able to do that?'

'Dad, I have my son back. I can handle anything.'

'Kerry Casey's men got Finbar back. The ransom demand was that she give up everything the family and organisation has built up. Millions. She was prepared to do that. But . . . But she didn't.'

'What do you mean?'

'The Caseys are a powerful organisation and they have worked on this for the past few days. Of course they considered the police, but everyone was so afraid of it falling apart and anything happening to Finbar.'

'But how could they guarantee it wouldn't by what they were doing?'

'She was making the deal. She was stringing the kidnappers along, telling them she'd pay the ransom demand, would sign over everything to them – all the family business interests. And at the same time, because of the background work her men had done, she established where Finbar was being held. And they went in and took him.'

'What? They just barged into the kidnappers' house and took him?'

'No. Not like that. Finbar was being moved to the place where he was going to be handed over as part of the ransom.'

'Jesus Christ, Dad! And you knew all this?'

'No, I promise you, son, I did not know this part at all. They told me nothing of the operation. Nothing at all. Just the other day I was about to ask Kerry to share information with the police because I couldn't take the agony of what was happening to us. But then this all happened so fast.'

'So what happened?'

'I don't know exactly and I don't care. All I know is that as Finbar was being moved, the Casey men moved in and took him. I don't know how or where.'

'But there will be bodies somewhere.'

Marty said nothing.

'And what about the ransom? Did Kerry pay it?'

'No.'

'What happened?'

'I don't know the details, and that's the truth.'

'So there will be bodies wherever the handover was meant to be, too. Jesus!'

Again, Marty didn't answer.

'I don't know what to say, Dad. Christ almighty! I get some kind of twisted sense that I'm supposed to thank Kerry Casey, but right now I hate her whole stinking lifestyle and the bunch of gangsters that caused my son to be stolen from me. And you know what? He was stolen because of you.' His voice shook with emotion. 'Yes. Because of you, Dad, and part of me hates that you are so fucking rooted with these gangsters that you even stood back and lied to me, to my wife, Christ, to your own wife, my mother. You lied to all of us while God knows what could have happened to my little boy. Because of your association.' He shook his head. 'It's . . . It's just sick. It's just not fair.'

Marty stood helpless as suddenly his son broke down in tears. All of the tension, the worry, the anger burst the dam and he stood with tears running down his face. Marty stepped forward and put his arms around him, unsure if he would push him away. But he didn't. He felt his son's arms go around him and he sobbed into his chest, like the heartbroken little boy he'd been thirty years ago when Marty had to break the news to him that his brother, their only other child, had been knocked down and killed by a car on the way home from school. That was the last time his son had cried in his arms. And now this. Marty couldn't find the words to comfort him. So he just held him until he stopped. When he eased himself out of his arms, they looked at each other.

'I need time to process this. All of it,' Joe said. 'I need to know how I can work my way through this, and I also need to work out how I'm going to lie to my family now. Just like you. I don't know how to do that, Dad.'

Marty touched his shoulder. 'Son . . . Just concentrate on your family. That's all you do. Your mum and me will go home now and leave you be.' He looked into his eyes. 'I'm sorry.'

Marty turned away from his son, because there was nothing more he could say. Nothing more he could do. But he prayed that he had not lost him.

CHAPTER TWENTY

Sharon began to stir in the coolness of the late-afternoon breeze drifting in from the terrace. She opened one eye and took in the muscular chest of Vic Paterson, as he lay beside her, breathing softly in a deep, contented sleep. This was not supposed to happen, but it had, and the truth was she had loved every frenzied, mind-blowing moment of it.

The small tattoo on his shoulder of a lion up on its hind legs moved with him as he slept. She hadn't remembered seeing that during their brief fling many years ago. And when he'd stripped off earlier today, Sharon had been so swept up in the moment of passion that she barely took time to notice his body. The rush she had felt through her from just having the feel and strength of a man to pull her into his arms and devour her the way Vic did had almost knocked her off her feet. Nobody had ever made love to her like that – never Knuckles Boyle – and not even Vic, when they had their secret trysts all those years ago. They were either improving with age, or just so yearning for the touch of each other that they couldn't get enough. Finally, they'd collapsed, spent, exhausted, and fallen asleep. Now, as she was fully awake, she expected a feeling of guilt. But there wasn't one. Sure it was reckless, but it had happened so quickly after Vic had insisted on walking her to her door in case there were any problems. They'd kissed on the doorstep, and by the time they'd got down the hallway, their clothes were strewn everywhere. Sharon couldn't even remember the last time she'd behaved so recklessly. But the very last thing she felt right now was guilt. She was old and wise enough to know what this was, and smart enough not to worry if it didn't go any further.

Vic had made a proposition to help the Caseys and that was why she had been seeing him, and this shouldn't have been on the cards. But true to his word, he'd been helping and dropping crucial information in the past few days to Sharon since their meeting in Fuengirola, and had been bang on in everything he'd told them about the Colombian, being able to say how many bodies were coming with him to Glasgow, so Kerry could get her operation organised. She trusted him. That much she was sure of. And he was being well paid for his trust and work as Kerry had already agreed. He was on their payroll now too. It was a perilous path Vic had taken, because if he was rumbled by the Colombians or the Irish mob or that weasel Frankie Martin, he wouldn't see daylight again. Vic knew that. But he was fearless. And smart. Sharon ran her finger across the lion tattoo and he woke up. He turned to her and pulled her on top of him and she could feel how quickly he was stirred. They stayed that way, him moving his body and pulling her to him and she could feel his breath begin to quicken.

'Sharon. You are one very sexy lady.'

She smiled and kissed his neck. Then she leaned over and picked up her phone. It was almost four thirty. Shit! She had to pick up her son from school, so there was no time for this caper. Reluctantly, she eased herself off him.

'You're just a bit sexy yourself – you with your lion tattoo. What's that all about?'

He smiled, touched it.

'It was one of the lags in the nick. He was into all this spiritual, symbolism shit and he said that was mine – strength and power he said, was stamped all over me. Aye, cheers, mate, I told him. That's why I'm doing nine in the slammer. Not much power in there. '

'You've plenty of power.' She stood up from the bed. 'But you're going to have to take it elsewhere, darling, because I have to pick up my Tony. So you need to make yourself scarce.'

He reached out and grabbed her gently.

'You're making me feel like a cheap whore – throwing me out after you've had your way with me.'

She kissed him. 'Come on. You know how it is. We must promise ourselves not to bloody do this again.'

'Yeah.' He kissed her back. 'Not for a few days anyway.' He gave her a playful slap on the backside as she stood up.

As she crossed the room towards the shower, Vic's mobile rang on the bedside table and he answered it.

'What? Fuck me, Frankie. Sure. No problem, mate. I'll head to Málaga airport now.'

Sharon turned around as he leaped out of bed.

'What's happening?'

'Fuckin' hell, Shaz! That was Frankie. The Glasgow business went tits up. Rodriguez got shot, and the Caseys dropped two of their men, for fuck's sake – Colombians. Christ! Kerry Casey really knows how to ruffle the fuckin' feathers, don't she?'

Sharon smiled to herself. 'He didn't say anything about the kidnapped boy?'

'Yeah. They only fuckin' weighed in and stole the kid back! Christ!' He pulled his polo shirt over his head and shoved his legs into his jeans. 'Tell you what, Shaz. The shit is going to hit the fan all over the shop now. You'd better get onto your mate and let her know. I've got to go and pick up Rodriguez at the airport and we've got to get him fixed up by docs. But he'll be fucking foaming at the mouth, the cunt.'

'Good,' Sharon said. 'Serves the bastard right for stealing a little boy. Fuck him!'

But despite her bravado she knew there would be hell to pay for this. She would phone Kerry on the way to pick up Tony, but she would bring one of the guards with her for protection. As she came out of the shower, wrapped in a towel, Vic was ready to leave. He put his arms around her and held her close, kissing her on the lips, then he looked her in the eye.

'Sharon Potty-mouth. You are some woman, and I'm not giving you up easily this time. You do know that, don't you?'

She kissed him back. 'Vic. We are living very dangerously. You do know *that*, don't you?'

'I wouldn't have it any other way. But seriously. I don't want this to be a one-off.'

She smiled. 'Go on. You've got work to do. Try not to crash your car with that Colombian bastard in it!'

He grinned and walked to the door.

'I'll let you know how the land is lying. Just you be careful out there, sweetheart. You sure you can trust all your men, those guards around here?'

'Yep. I'm sure. They're Kerry's men. They'll be fine. I'm okay.'

And with that he was gone, and she stood looking at herself in the mirror knowing that whatever the rest of the day brought, it would not be pleasant.

On the way to school with a guard in the front seat, she phoned Kerry. She answered immediately.

'Sharon,' Kerry said. 'I was about to call you. That Colombian bastard got his comeuppance today, courtesy of the Caseys.'

'I've just heard about five minutes ago. Vic told me. I was with him. That bastard Frankie Martin phoned, said Rodriguez got shot and two of his men got dropped as well.'

'Three I think was the final count. Two of his Colombian mob and one from Glasgow or Dublin or wherever. Rodriguez is not happy.'

'You do know that this will get a lot worse now.'

'I know, Sharon. That's why I was calling you. We need to get a few more people out there. And I want everyone on high alert. Rodriguez's mob will hit us pronto. That much I'm sure of. What does Vic know?'

'He's on his way to the airport to pick up Rodriguez and the others and then he'll be told. When he knows, I'll know. And I'll call you immediately.'

'Good. But you're going to have to dig in over there with our bars and, especially, the hotel site. Is the site all locked down?'

'Yes. We have armed security there. There isn't much more we can do. The work has started and there's a lot of heavy plant there.'

'Okay. We'll have to tee them up. And the bars too. Just tell everyone to be on their guard. I'll get some more people out tomorrow. Just bodies in case we need numbers. But we're preparing for some kind of hit back here too. Durkin will probably take care of that since he's in bed with Rodriguez. He was part of all this shit, Sharon. I haven't spoken to him since that first day, but he must have been part of the kidnapping too, and in my book he's history.'

'Mine too. But we have to just be very careful how we play it. Danny and Jack will see you all right. What about Jake Cahill?'

'He's still here. It was him and young Cal and Tahir who stormed the kidnappers. Proper operation it was. I haven't seen them since, but Jake said they are taking care of some unfinished business. I didn't ask.'

'What about Marty? He must be so relieved to get Finbar back. The family must be so happy.'

'I'm seeing him later, so we'll see how he is. But he'll be glad it's over. I'd be surprised if we don't get a bit of heat from the cops in the next day. There was already something in the news about a shoot-out in the restaurant. Once it leaks out that the boy is back, they'll be hammering a few doors – probably mine first.'

'Okay, Kerry. I'm at the school now, so I'll talk to you later.' She hung up.

The Colombian looked to Frankie like he was trying hard not to explode. They were sitting on the terrace of the sumptuous villa-cum-fortress where Pepe Rodriguez was holed up along with his most trusted henchmen. It was only the second time Frankie had been to the villa, and he clocked that there were even more armed bodies lining the road up to the house than he remembered the first time. His new boss was definitely feeling under threat. Frankie couldn't help but gloat a little inside that the Caseys had fucked him over in spectacular fashion. This prick had come to the Casey turf and tried to rip their heart out, and had been sent back with his big-shot fucking tail between his legs. Yes. Frankie was glad, and there was no doubt that he did feel a little gutted that he wasn't a part of it. That surprised him a little, but in some twisted way he admired the way the Caseys had come lashing back. But there was no point in even spending a breath brooding over what was past. Frankie had chosen his path and now he had to stick with it. It wasn't as though he had a lot of choices anyway. Once he had gone over to the other side by betraying the Caseys, there was no going back. The people who had been his friends and associates, men he'd stood with when their backs were to the wall in turf wars in Glasgow, would now be glad to cut his throat. Well, fuck them. That was never going to happen. It was all about survival. And he was with the Colombians and the Irish mob now. He'd well and truly burned his bridges back in Scotland, but he knew there was a place for him here with this bunch of fuckers. Rodriguez liked him – he could tell that, and he had trusted him to be the go-between with Kerry, trying to get the ransom demand sorted. But now that it had gone tits up, he hoped Rodriguez wouldn't suspect that he had dropped

Kerry Casey the gypsy warning that had enabled them to be so primed and ready for Rodriguez.

Frankie sat on the sofa next to Vic Paterson, who had picked Rodriguez and his cohorts up from the airport and brought them to the house, where the doctor had treated the Colombian's wound. His thigh was a bit of a mess, but the doctor patched him up, telling him to keep his leg raised and the weight off it for at least a week until it healed. Various flunkies fussed around Rodriguez and he waved them away or beckoned them when necessary. There were three other men in the room – two of them Colombian killers who Frankie had met before, and Pat Durkin, who sat fidgeting with his cup of coffee and looked well edgy. Frankie was wondering if Durkin was beginning to feel that he'd got in too deep with this mob, but if he was, it was too late now. That pleased Frankie too, that Durkin was slightly squirming. He sensed his fear of the Colombian, but Frankie – even though he knew Rodriguez was one ruthless bastard – did not fear him. And from the body language of Vic Paterson since he met him, he got the impression that he didn't fear him either. Everyone else in the room was more or less shitting their pants in case Rodriguez pointed the finger. Frankie braced himself as he turned to him.

'So, Frankie,' Rodriguez said. 'Your Kerry Casey was not so easy to destroy this time. Why do you think that was?'

Frankie didn't quite know how to answer that, but just by the tone of this fucker there was something sinister in the way he said it.

'What do you mean, Pepe? Did you not expect her to fight you? You've met her very briefly, and I remember you said that you thought she was a tough bitch – or she tried to be with you.'

He made a face, his mouth downward.

'No, no. I thought the bitch was a bit of a tiger, but this is not the way I expected it to turn out. We rip the heart from her family by taking the little boy. I did not expect her to take a big risk with that.'

Frankie waited for a moment, then he answered. 'Well, Pepe, with all due respect, then perhaps you should have made Kerry come to you instead of you going to her.' He paused, knowing all eyes were on him. 'Look. I did say to you that if you could bring her to you, here to Spain, then you would be better protected. But you wanted to go there. I honestly thought that might be risky. There is no real protection for you in Glasgow.'

'That's not true, Frankie,' Durkin chipped in, a little petulant. 'I had my boys there. We cased the place and checked it over and we were tooled up.'

Frankie risked a shrug but tried not to look nonchalant.

'Yes, Pat. You were tooled up. But as it happens, the Caseys were more tooled up. And that's what happens if you go onto their turf.'

Rodriguez turned to Durkin. 'I expected better protection from your people, Pat.'

Durkin's face fell, and right at that moment he looked as though the writing was on the wall for him. Frankie glanced at Vic whose face showed nothing. The air was crackling with tension. Beads of sweat formed on Durkin's head as the room became silent.

'Pepe, my men were ready. We had plenty of people. There was nothing much more we could have done. You have to believe me on that.'

Durkin glanced anxiously at Frankie as though he was hoping he would help him out here. Frankie stared straight at Rodriguez, his face like flint. Silence for a long moment. Then Rodriguez took a deep breath and his nostrils flared. He made a gesture at his raised leg.

'This bitch shot me. She could have killed me if she wasn't such a bad shot. Where did her gun come from, Pat? Your men frisked her when she arrived, yes?'

'Yes, yes, of course, Pepe.' Durkin nodded furiously, squirming in his seat. 'She was clean when she came in. I've spoken to my boys and they searched her. But . . . but . . .'

Rodriguez raised his eyebrows as though toying with Durkin. 'But . . . but . . .' Rodriguez repeated. 'But someone on the inside of the restaurant was able to slip her a gun. Right in front of all of us. So how did this happen? Who of your men checked this place out? They didn't check it out well enough.'

Durkin nodded.

'I know. I've spoken to them, Pepe.'

'They failed. Your people failed. And because of that three of my men are dead and I have this.' He pointed to his leg. He waved a finger and shook his head. 'There is no room for failures in my organisation.'

Durkin nodded vigorously, his face flushed. Nobody spoke. Then Rodriguez snapped his fingers. From the other side of the terrace, one of his men stood up and walked across, making for the open patio doors as though he was going inside. But Frankie watched as he didn't go in. Instead, he pulled a pistol from his shoulder holster, and in one seamless movement stuck it into the nape of Durkin's neck and fired. The shot echoed around the hills in the distance, and Frankie tried to keep his poker face on as Durkin for a single second looked like a fish gasping for breath, then keeled over onto the floor. Frankie glanced at Vic and they watched straight-faced as the blood seeped out of Durkin's head and a crimson pool formed across the white marble tiles.

The silence was deafening. Without even looking at Durkin's body, Rodriguez turned to Frankie and the others.

'Now, we must be ready to hit back at Kerry Casey for her foolish actions. You understand me? Everybody? This time we do not fail.'

'Of course.' Frankie was the only one who answered. The others all nodded but said nothing. He wished he could be a fly on the wall when Kerry Casey got this latest news.

CHAPTER TWENTY-ONE

'He did what?' Kerry shouldn't have been shocked at hearing how Durkin was shot like a dog, but she was. 'Christ almighty! This changes things. The Irish mob won't take this lying down. The Durkins were big shots for a generation. They've executed the head of a big organised clan.'

'I know,' Sharon said. 'But that's what Durkin deserves for getting into bed with the bloody Colombians in the first place. It's all about greed, Kerry. Pure greed. A fat lot of good it did the little bastard, because now his organisation will be in chaos.'

Kerry's own words, 'executed the head of a big organised clan', rang in her ears, because it sounded a little close to home. Rodriguez had already shown how unscrupulous he was when he kidnapped a three-year-old boy. But assassinating the head of a powerful gang who he'd just hooked up with was either reckless, or sending a message to everyone that this was what happened if you messed with him.

Kerry was beginning to wonder if Rodriguez was really thinking things through, or if he was a bit out of control. And if he was, then the cracks would start to show.

'What's your thinking, Kerry?' Sharon asked.

'Well. Just shocked really. But also thinking how much of a mess that leaves for the Irish mob, and how we could benefit from it. I think I need to talk to Billy Hill, back in London. He was more in cahoots with Durkin's crowd over the years, and in recent months, so he might have a bit of intelligence on who will be jostling for position.'

'They'll all be cutting each other's throats in Dublin to take over,' Sharon said. 'But they have a good chunk of manpower over in Spain, and they are currently with Rodriguez. Once they get wind of Durkin's execution, they'll either shit it and do a runner, or pledge allegiance to the Colombians.'

'That still leaves a big hole in the Irish family though. The Durkins were a dynasty out of Dublin, and a lot of people will want to hit back. I'm going to get Danny and Jack in and we'll have a talk about it. See if there's someone we can talk to there. And Billy Hill – he's a bit of an outcast now because he didn't join with the Colombians. In fact, he might be feeling the heat, thinking he might be next. So what do you think about talking to him? Do you agree?'

'Sure. Hill isn't the worst of them. He always struck me as a bit of an old gent. I'm sure that's why he couldn't go with the Colombians. He doesn't have the stomach for the way they do business.'

'But he must be feeling he needs some handers around him too. I mean he's a big organisation, and well established in Spain, but I'd say he's still a worried man when he hears this.'

'Yes,' Sharon said. 'But in our own backyard, I think we have to tighten a lot of stuff up now. Rodriguez will be coming after us, big time.'

'I know. I'll get the lads in and we'll have a talk. Are you okay over there?'

'Yes. Vic is keeping me informed. He called me as soon as he was out of Rodriguez's villa. He said some flunkies just moved in and started cleaning up around them with Durkin lying dead on the floor. Says they put him in a sheet and carted him off. So his corpse will no doubt turn up somewhere pronto.'

'Don't you think you should come back?'

'No. Unless you want me to. I think I should be here because we have a lot of bodies now, and I don't think I should just walk away. We've just started work on building a hotel. We need to make sure every area is covered.'

'We've got people to do that though if you don't want to be there. I'm thinking of your safety, and Tony as well.'

'I'm okay. I've got guards everywhere and Tony is well protected too. I'll hang fire for the next few days to see where this goes.'

'Fair enough. Talk later.' Kerry hung up.

She went across to the window and stood watching the cars arrive with more men to beef up security around the various businesses the Caseys ran in Glasgow. She felt a shiver run through her. This was different than it had been before, when she was going after the individuals who had murdered her family. Battling the Colombians was like taking on an empire, and though she had the manpower and firepower to do it, she hoped she'd also have the guts for it. She heard her mobile ring at the other side of the room and went across to see Vinny's name on the screen. Before she could stop herself she picked it up.

'Vinny.'

'Kerry. How you doing?'

She almost smiled at the question. How was she doing? The truth was, she didn't know if she was coming or going.

'I'm all right, Vinny. Sorry I didn't call you back. I . . . I'm just in the middle of such a lot of things right now.'

'Yeah. I guess you are,' he said.

She knew she was meant to take the full meaning of that and she did. There was a long moment of silence and she pictured his handsome face.

'How's Marty and his family?'

'I haven't spoken to him today, but they will be so relieved. Everyone is. It was the worst time ever.'

'Kerry, I need to talk to you. Informally. Can I come and see you?'

'What about?'

'You know what it's about. The whole kidnapping thing. Nobody believes for a moment that the kidnappers just handed the boy back. I think you know that didn't happen.'

Kerry didn't answer. Whatever else Vinny was to her, he was a cop, and she didn't want to say anything on the phone that could be incriminating. She chided herself for the suspicion that he might be taping her and trying to reel her in. Vinny wouldn't do that, she told herself, or would he?

'Vinny. Look. I don't know what to say to you here.'

'Just let me come and see you. I have things to tell you that might interest you.'

The irony wasn't lost on her. *He* had things to tell her that might interest *her*? That was nothing to what *she* had that might interest *him*. If it wasn't so serious it would be laughable.

'Okay. I'll see you at my house.'

'When?'

'Tomorrow. In the morning. But just you, Vinny. Nobody else.'

'Okay. I'll be there. Just me.'

The line went dead.

CHAPTER TWENTY-TWO

Cal sipped from a mug of tea as he sat in the city centre café waiting for Tahir. He hadn't gone home after Jake had dropped him, because he didn't feel ready. He hadn't really come down to earth, and he didn't want to go home to the house where his mum would be able to sense from him that something had happened. She knew he worked for the Caseys now, and she accepted that this was what he wanted. Even though she worked for them, lived in a flat she could not have afforded if it hadn't been for the generosity of Kerry Casey, he was pretty sure she wasn't involved in anything criminal. She wanted the best for her son, and Jen, who was doing well in rehab. But for Cal, the talk of university and studying had long gone; he'd told her he was earning good money now, and that this was his future. He was sixteen and he had made up his mind. He could see from the look on her face that she worried about him, that one day something bad would happen to him because of what he was involved in. If she'd known what he'd done this afternoon, she would have died of shock, and that's why he didn't want to be going home, having to look her in the eye right now. He was sure he had done the right thing, putting a bullet in that bastard's head. The only thing that haunted him a little was that it was very much in cold blood – not the way it had been earlier when he and Jake and Tahir had hijacked the kidnappers' car and they were shooting at people who were firing back.

When Jake had told him after they had seen Finbar back to his parents that they had unfinished business at the house, Cal knew what he meant. The weasel-faced guy who had sat looking at the TV when he'd gone into the house with Sinc had to be dealt with. He was scum of the earth. Jake told him that Sinc had already been taken back to the scrapyard where they were holding him, and he'd be dealt with later. He told Cal this bastard at the house was his. When they'd gone up to the door, they'd battered it in, and run through the hall, finding him in a cupboard. Jake had dragged him out by the hair as the guy was screaming that he was only doing what he was told. He was shouting that he never harmed the boy. But Cal knew by the frightened look on Finbar's face that the kid hadn't been well treated by this piece of shit. So, when Jake gave him the nod, Cal took his gun out of his waistband and shot him. Right there and then, as he looked straight back at him with wild, terrified eyes. Cal still didn't know what he'd felt at that moment. There had been anger and a sense of justice, but he did not feel guilty, not then and not now. He wondered if he should. But it was done now and that was it over. He looked up from his mug of tea and saw Tahir come into the café, his eyes darting around. He looked nervous.

'You all right, mate?' Cal said as he slid into the booth.

Tahir nodded. 'Yes. I'm good.' He picked up the menu. 'I'm hungry.'

The waitress came up and they both ordered burgers and Coke, then they sat for what seemed like an age and didn't speak. Eventually Cal broke the silence.

'That Jake Cahill is some guy, is he not?'

Tahir nodded. 'He's cool. A little bit scary too. Don't you think?'

'Yeah. The way he just dropped those guys. Glad I'm on his side.'

Tahir nodded, but Cal felt uncomfortable with the small talk. Tahir didn't know that he had gone back to the house with Jake as he hadn't told him on the phone. But somehow he felt they should be talking about this, about what they'd done today.

'The way Jake just told you to put a bullet in that guy when he knelt down,' Cal said. 'How did you feel about that?'

Tahir gave him a long look, and shrugged. 'It was like a war. Like a battle. I had already shot at least two people, and Jake had too. So this was one more.'

'But it was different. The way you did it.' Cal was trying to pick his words. 'I . . . I was wondering what was going through your mind. You didn't hesitate.'

Tahir shook his head and stared past Cal.

'No. I was thinking that this guy was part of what happened to the boy – to Finbar. He was part of it, and in my book he should die. It's like my family. My brother would be here now if people didn't want to make money from him. He would still be in the refugee camp in Turkey. But he died because people like that guy today are making money.' He took a breath and sighed. 'I don't know, Cal. Maybe that is all I know. I did it because it was right.' He looked at him. 'What about you? Where did you go?'

'I took the wee man to the supermarket where we dropped him off and his family came. It was great to see. He's a great wee kid – was cuddling me and everything. But earlier, when I went in with Sinc to get him from the house, the kid was terrified. He was just a wee thing lying sobbing on the couch. It choked me, man, it really did.'

'Bastards.'

'So, after we dropped the boy, Jake says to me we have unfinished business.'

Tahir looked up as the waitress came with their order and placed down the plates. He waited until she went away then looked at Cal for an answer.

'Yeah,' Cal said. 'We drove to the house and battered the door down. And then we found the guy in a cupboard. Jake dragged him out kicking and screaming. Then he nods to me – same as he did to you – and I shot him. Right there.' He made a little gesture with his finger as a gun.

'Wow! Just like that?'

'Yeah. He was facing me though. I could see his eyes.'

'You are freaked by that?'

Cal sighed, as he picked up his burger.

'A little bit. But it will go away. Like the others, they got what they deserved.'

Tahir took a bite of his burger and spoke with his mouth full.

'So, my friend, we are killers now. We must be careful. People will want to kill us.'

'I know,' Cal said. 'But I think we did good.' He went into his zipped jacket pocket and took out a wedge of cash. 'Here. This is what Jack gave me when I went back to the house. A grand for each of us.'

'Fuck! Really?'

'Yes. He said we did well. That this was a big moment for us today in difficult circumstances, he said, but we earned our stripes.' He smiled. 'He actually said that – we earned our stripes.'

Tahir smiled, stuffed a chip into his mouth.

'We did, my friend. We earned our stripes today.' He took a swig of his Coke. 'Now we deal with the bastards who are selling the girls up at the high flats.'

Cal let it hang for a moment, because there was something

about his friend's demeanour that made him think he was enjoying this killing a little too much.

'We have to be careful, Tahir,' Cal said. 'I think we should tell Jack Reilly about it and see what he thinks. We should watch how we do this, because *we* don't want to be the guys who are staring down the barrel of a gun, like the bastards today. Just let's calm it a bit.'

'We'll see,' Tahir said. 'But I promised my girl I would fix this. And I will.'

'And we will. Okay?' Cal stabbed a couple of chips with a fork. 'Come on. Let's eat, then we can go for a game of pool.'

Kerry was glad to be sitting around the table with the people she could stake her life on. Danny, Jack, Jake Cahill and Eddie the chauffeur. Even Auntie Pat was there, sat alongside Marty Kane, who looked gaunt and tired. A couple of other men who were involved in the day's earlier proceedings also joined them and they tucked in to some kind of Spanish rice dish prepared by Elsa. Kerry looked around at them as they ate. They were family and today had been a good day. It had been bloody, more bloody than she ever imagined she could ever be a part of, but it had been a good day. Little Finbar Kane had been returned to his family, and Pepe Rodriguez had been sent packing, with a bullet in him. She'd been surprised at the little sting of regret she felt that she hadn't killed him. But his tail was far from between his legs, and everyone around here knew he would be back with a vengeance. The Caseys hadn't even lost one man – three were injured but were patched up, and the operation all in all was a success. But this meeting wasn't only about celebration, it was about what next.

'So, Danny,' Kerry turned towards her uncle, sitting on her right, 'do you agree we should talk to Billy Hill? I only met him that time he came up and he seemed to be in with Durkin and Rodriguez, so I'm not up to speed on what's been going on with him over the past weeks.'

'I can tell you that he's been frozen out big time and he's having to work hard to keep his supplier in Spain onside with him. You see, Rodriguez will be pushing everyone out in Spain and trying to get a bigger slice of everything. And because he and Hill didn't see eye to eye, he'll have him on his hit list. No doubt about it. And Billy will know that. I've known him a long time – used to meet him many years ago with your old man, Kerry. He's all right, but a bit slippery. But right now, I think he'd be glad to come on board with us.'

'Good, so can I leave that to you to make the contact, Danny?'

'Sure. I'll talk to him in the morning.'

Kerry turned to Jack. 'What do you think will happen next in Glasgow?'

Jack swirled the wine in his glass and placed it on the table.

'I think the people who were working with Rodriguez on the kidnapping of wee Finbar will try to hit us in some way, so we are on our guard for that. They lost a few bodies today, so they'll be sore. But some of these people today might also have been part of Durkin's mob over from Dublin to help out, so right now we don't really know who we're looking for.'

'What about this Sinc character? He must be able to tell us who he was working for,' Kerry said.

'He did,' Jack said. 'Jimmy Pearson, his name is. We're looking for him, but he's nowhere to be seen. He's a prick and he owns that night club and restaurant up off Sauchiehall Street. An arsehole who spends a lot of time in Spain and he launders money but we don't know who for. He's never really featured on our radar before, because he keeps a lower profile. But we're thinking he's mixed up with a lot of people over on the Costa del Sol. He might actually have disappeared over there in the last day or so. But we'll find him. Problem is he might already have set some irons in the fire here, so that's why we're watching.'

'So where are Sinc and this Lenny character now?'

Jack looked at Danny and the two men at the end of the table dropped their eyes to their plates.

Jack reached across for garlic bread and tore a piece in half.

'Oh them? They're history.'

There was a brief moment where nobody spoke, and Kerry glanced at Jake Cahill, his face impassive, then at Auntie Pat, who raised her eyebrows a little.

Then Marty Kane cleared his throat.

'Chaps,' he said, 'I know you can imagine how difficult these past few days have been for my family. I just want to say thanks. From my heart.'

Everyone stopped and turned to him, expecting him to say more, but Marty looked choked as he swallowed, then raised his glass.

'To everyone here. You brought me back my grandson today. My life. Not everyone in my family would like to know that it was you who gave us our boy back, and if they did, they might not like it. But I will always be in your debt.'

Silence. Then Auntie Pat chipped in. 'How is the wee guy settling back in, Marty?'

Marty smiled for the first time since he had arrived. 'He's fine, Pat. He's good. Thanks.'

Marty had spoken with humility as he sat among criminals. And Kerry felt humbled, in turn, by his loyalty. Marty had to keep secrets from his own family. And so too did Kerry, as she sat among her family carrying her own little secret inside her.

CHAPTER TWENTY-THREE

Kerry awoke with a feeling of excitement, the first thought to come to her that she would be meeting Vinny this morning. She lay with her eyes closed, images of their final lunch together flooding her mind. That afternoon, as they'd sat opposite each other in her favourite Italian restaurant, La Lanterna, she'd been clear and even a little cool with him as they both knew that the relationship as it was really had nowhere to go. She probably shouldn't even have been having lunch with him, far less the brief nights of passion they'd shared. But it was what it was, she'd decided at the time, and even though Vinny had looked a bit dejected, he would know in himself that this was how it had to be. But they'd parted as friends, both of them trying to play down any feelings they had about each other. And for Kerry's part, her mind was made up anyway. There was no room for Vinny in her life. That was before she discovered she was pregnant with his child. Yet even now, as she lay, the palm of her hand resting on her navel, trying to imagine the little life inside her, she was still sure there was no future for her and Vinny, so there was no point in even fantasising – despite the feelings that stirred in her.

Kerry had learned to build walls like that from early on, when her mum had sent her away as a teenager to live in Spain. There was no point in weeping for ever for things that you couldn't change, things you could not have. It had stood her in good stead all of her life – except when she suffered the miscarriage a year ago which had taken the heart from her and left her paralysed with grief. But she was getting over all of that now. A new heart beat inside her, and soon she would go to the doctor and organise a scan so that she could see the baby for real, and love it even more, if that was possible. She stretched her hands behind her head and lay listening to the activity outside, cars coming and going, voices of the security guards. The place had been buzzing with people in the last twenty-four hours, but up here in her bedroom and study on the first floor, she was solitary. She could indulge herself in these reveries like this, allowing herself to think of what her life would be if she was just an ordinary woman expecting a baby and waiting for the father to come and see her.

She sighed and picked up the remote control and clicked on the television where the news was blaring. She peered at the image of a large building ablaze somewhere in the city. Then she heard the reporter describe an Asian warehouse on the Clydeside that had been burned to the ground last night, which the police were treating as an arson attack. Then a video panned to the owner, in tears, telling the reporter he didn't want to talk about it or speculate, that he was too devastated. The warehouse had been in his family for two generations and his own father had built it up when he came here from Pakistan, a penniless immigrant in the 1960s. Kerry felt sorry for the poor man and his family. She'd almost forgotten that Jack had told her at the time that he wanted to torch the place, but she'd told him no, that they were better than that. Jack wouldn't have ordered it to be done behind her back, so someone else must have done it – maybe connected to the thugs who had forced him to keep the boy. Perhaps they suspected he'd double-crossed them. She threw back the duvet and got out of bed, and as she turned towards the bathroom, another news report pricked up her ears. 'The bodies of three men have been found in Glasgow with gunshot wounds to the back of their heads,' the reporter said. 'They were found in a lock-up garage in the East End of the city. That puts the body count to six in the past twenty-four hours in what now looks like a vicious gangland turf war.' Police were investigating rival gangs and finding who was responsible following the shoot-out yesterday near the farmhouse on the outskirts of Glasgow, and also probing if it was connected with the kidnapping of top criminal lawyer Marty Kane's grandson Finbar. Kerry listened to the speculation in the reporter's story. It was all sources and rumours, and police saying nothing. Because the police didn't actually know anything, she thought. She padded into the shower, hoping that Vinny wasn't going to burst her head quizzing her about this all morning.

Kerry checked herself in the mirror as she looked at her watch, and heard the front doorbell ring. She was dressed in a navy cashmere V-neck sweater that showed her curves, and faded jeans that hugged her long, slender legs, and a pair of tan Chelsea boots. She wore very little make-up as she didn't want to look like she was going on a date. Because this definitely wasn't a date. There was a knock on her bedroom door and Elsa called to her that Detective Inspector Vincent Burns was here to see her. Kerry told her to send him up to the study and to bring some tea up for them, and she quickly went out of the bedroom and down the hall to wait.

Kerry was standing by the window when there was a soft knock on the door of the study, and she called come in. And there he was. Vinny stood in the doorway, in jeans and a black polo shirt that was tight enough for her to imagine his fit body underneath. She immediately batted the thought away.

'Vinny,' she said, trying to conceal her excitement. 'Come on. Sit down. Elsa is bringing up some tea.' She ushered him to the easy chair by the fire and walked across the room with him. Then she met his eyes and smiled. 'Good to see you,' she said softly. 'I mean that.'

They stood face to face and she automatically stepped into his arms. He hugged her close and she felt the warmth of his body, and a little shiver ran through her as he eased himself away, then kissed her gently on the lips. It was fleeting, but the softness of his lips on hers brought a blush to her cheeks, and Vinny noticed.

'Jeez, Vinny,' she laughed. 'You've got my blood up there. That wasn't supposed to happen. You're not supposed to kiss me.'

He was still holding her and studying her face.

'I know,' he said, touching her hair. 'I'm sorry, Kerry. What can I say? It just felt so natural.' He eased himself away. 'But that's it. No more of that.' He grinned and moved towards the easy chair. 'I'll sit here and you can be over there and I won't even look at you. I'll pretend to myself that we are more or less strangers, and that those beautiful nights in my flat were just a figment of my imagination. I'll pretend that I never had any feelings for you in the first place. Even when I was fourteen.'

Kerry was taken aback by the way he was talking and stood there watching him, wondering what was happening. Surely this was not why he had come here, to see if there was a way back, because there wasn't.

'Vinny,' she said. 'Come on. Stop your carry-on.'

'Sorry. Probably too much coffee,' he smiled. 'Seriously,

Kerry. I mean everything I said there, but I know the score, so I didn't come here to bleat about what has come and gone for us. Really, I didn't.' He paused for a beat and she made sure her face was straight. 'I came here to talk about everything that's gone on in recent days. Informally. Of course. And I think I have some information you might be interested in.'

'Okay.' Kerry looked at the door as it opened and Elsa came in with a tray and teapot. 'Let me get you some tea then we can chat.' She went to the table and poured out two mugs of tea, and brought a plate of croissants, and another with jam and butter, and sat them on the coffee table. 'Come on. We can eat and talk at the same time – we were brought up in Maryhill!'

They both smiled, and there was a little pang in her gut at how lovely it was to see him, be with him like this, even if the meeting was not about them. Kerry tried not to watch as he opened the croissant, prepared it, then took a bite of half of it, and a gulp of tea.

'Sorry. But I'm starved. Had to go to the office straight away with all this shit overnight, so I haven't had breakfast.' He held up what was left of the croissant. 'Good shout with the croissants, by the way. Very posh for a couple of kids from the schemes.'

'You bet,' Kerry said, joining him in a croissant and tea.

'Have you seen the news? Bodies all over the place.'

'I just saw a bit of it when I woke up.'

'And a Pakistani warehouse got torched.'

'Yeah,' Kerry said, as disinterested as she could manage. 'I saw that too.'

'We think it's all connected.'

'How do you mean?'

'All linked to the kidnapping of Marty Kane's grandson. That's what we're looking at.'

'You got evidence pointing to that? Or just speculation?'

'Put it this way. We have a couple of leads.'

'That's what the cops always say when they don't have anything.'

'I know. But in this case we do.' He paused. 'And it's leading me here.'

Kerry rolled her eyes to the ceiling, trying her best to look incredulous.

'Christ, Vinny! Come on! There's got to be half a dozen hard men in this city who can wreak havoc on any given night. Why come here?'

'The stiffs that were found this morning.'

'What stiffs?'

'Billy Sinclair, Lenny Wilson and Rab Bolton.'

Kerry shrugged her shoulders and made a don't-know-what-you're-on-about face.

'We have information that they were part of, or in some way involved in the kidnapping. They're not big players, by any shot. But we believe they were involved in moving the boy from place to place.'

Kerry kept impassive. 'How do you even know he was moved from place to place?'

'We've had specially trained officers teasing some small bits of information out of the boy, Finbar. Obviously it has to be softly-softly, but so far they've gleaned that big boys came and took him somewhere. Then another place in a car, then somewhere else.' He sipped his tea, watched her. 'Some things look as though they are adding up.'

'Then why don't you track down the *places* you say he was taken to and talk to the people there? Put some pressure on them?'

He put his mug down. 'Because, spookily enough, they're all dead. All of them. One guy found yesterday afternoon with a bullet in his head – and the house where he was shot has been searched and we may have DNA traces of Finbar. And the warehouse. I mean, who torches a warehouse for no reason? Nothing to suggest that it's a racist attack. So we think maybe the boy was even there.'

'How can you think that?'

He waited for a long moment. 'Because someone came forward to the police.'

Kerry knew he was watching her closely and she made sure she didn't show a flicker of anything. She thought of Donna. They had paid her five grand to get out of town and keep her trap shut. Surely the little bitch hadn't gone to the cops. She'd been in the car when Jack and his boys had roughed up Rab Bolton and she was savvy enough to know that he was having information beaten out of him. Would she really go to the cops?

'What do you mean, came forward? Who? Someone in the kidnap gang?'

He shook his head. 'I can't say. But no. Not someone in the gang. But someone who saw something. That's all I can say.'

Kerry let it hang for two beats, then she shrugged. 'Oh, well. I'd say you've got it pretty much wrapped up then, Inspector Morse.' She knew her tone was sarcastic, and that Vinny would take it as such. 'So why are you here?'

Silence. He looked hurt. And Kerry hated herself for treating him like this, but really, he had no right to feel hurt. What the hell did he expect? Vinny looked down at the back of his hands for a long moment as though he was studying them, searching for words. He finally looked up, and their eyes locked.

'I'm sorry, Vinny. I didn't mean it to sound like that – like "why are you here", as if we've got no history. But you know what I mean, don't you?'

His look was beginning to disarm her, and she couldn't allow that to happen. Eventually he sighed, sat back and stretched out his long legs, steepled his hands over his chest.

'Kerry. I'll tell you what I think.' He paused for effect. 'I think the Caseys are in trouble. I think you took on too much when you upset the Colombians – that Pepe Rodriguez scumbucket.'

Kerry sat back, folded her arms, closing shop, showing no response. Vinny continued.

'I think Marty Kane's boy was kidnapped by them to get at you, and I think that your . . .' He hesitated. 'Well, for want of a better word, your foot soldiers stormed in the other day and took the boy back, leaving behind a trail of bodies. And I also think your boys torched that warehouse on the river, and also put a bullet in the head of the three stiffs who turned up dead today. By the way, that's three extra stiffs from the ones killed during the shoot-out where we believe the kid was rescued.' He stopped, raised his eyebrows. 'How right am I so far?'

Kerry gave him as dubious a look as she could muster, while wondering how the hell he could be so well informed.

'Yeah, sure, Vinny. I don't think I've seen that movie you're describing. But it sounds like a belter.' She sat forward, picked up her mug and gulped from it, looking straight at him.

He never took his eyes off her, and eventually she was forced to look away.

'Look, just listen to me for a moment. Hear me out.'

'I'm all ears, Inspector.'

'Pepe Rodriguez is spearheading a major coup from the Costa del Sol to Amsterdam to the UK, and our boys in the Drug Enforcement Agency have been tracking his movements for months. He's got the purest cocaine and he's planning to flood our streets with it, the crack market, the lot. There are a few other big shots over there on the Costa del Sol who don't like the way he's muscling in. But he seems to have the manpower and the clout, and he's making inroads – and he has the best of coke. I mean, no cocaine is ever a hundred per cent pure, but his stuff is ninety-six per cent. So that's top dollar shit.'

Kerry processed this for a moment, then answered. 'So if you've been tracking him for months, why can't you stop him? There must be some way you can get what you need to nail him. I thought the DEA were all over Europe working together?'

'We are. We do. And we share all our information. But we need more.'

'So why come to me? What am I supposed to do, Vinny? You're losing me here.'

He looked at her, and she knew he was trying to read her.

'You could get inside his organisation. You could work with him.'

'What?' She almost laughed.

'I'm serious. Isn't that why he was coming after you? For your big hotel complex you're planning out on the Costa del Sol? He wanted that, didn't he?' He waited a second, but put his hand up as though trying to stop her from speaking, even though she hadn't been going to say anything. 'In fact, he was going to take that off you. And you'd have been working for him.'

'Look, Vinny. I–'

'I know what you're going to say. Where am I getting all this information? Trust me, Kerry. We have snitches on the periphery of a lot of the action from here to Colombia that pass us information.'

For a moment, Kerry was trying to work out if someone in her organisation was passing information. She couldn't think of a single person, but would talk to Danny and Jack as soon as Vinny was gone.

'But you sound so well informed, Vinny. What's stopping you from taking that a bit further? Nailing him. Big time. You must be able to do that. Christ! Sure, they nailed Al Capone on tax dodging! Surely to Christ you can work out something that he must be doing so you can take him down.'

'It's not as easy as that. We don't want to get him on parking tickets or some shite, because he'll just come back bigger. We need to strangle him completely. Strangle his supply.'

'What about the Irish?' she said. 'He works with them – they went over to him.'

'They're history. Pat Durkin is dead.' He hesitated. 'Shot dead in Spain. But I'm sure you already knew that, Kerry.'

She said nothing, and they sat in silence.

'Kerry. Will you think about what I've said?'

She was feeling exhausted by all this, by the information he had, by his proposition, and just the fact that he was here and she had to hold back from touching him, from talking to him, from telling the truth about what was going on in her body.

'Vinny, I have to go and talk to some people. I've got a lot on my plate right now.'

She stood up, and he sat for a second watching her, then he got up. He took a step towards her and she felt she should take a step back but she couldn't. He reached out and touched her hair, then brushed the back of his fingers on her cheek.

'Kerry. I . . . I . . .' He seemed lost for words for the first time since he walked in the door. 'I can't get you out of my mind.'

'Vinny. Come on. We've done this. We talked about this. Come on. Don't do this. Not now.'

'I can't help it, Kerry. I want you to know that.' He stood there, the electricity crackling between them. 'I don't think I've ever stopped loving you. I don't know if I ever can.'

He took a step closer, and before she could stop herself, she was in his arms and he was kissing her on the lips that way he did when they ended up in bed together in his house. But this was different. This was *her* house. He was a cop sent to see if he could get her onside, and now he was throwing all this emotional stuff in. And all the time, she was standing there, choking that the biggest betrayal of all was that she had his child inside her. But she pushed him away and they stopped kissing, stood breathless, feeling the heat of their bodies. She stepped back.

'Vinny. Please.' She felt her chest tighten. 'Don't do this to me right now. I can't take it.'

He let her go and touched his lips with his finger.

'I'm sorry. Honestly, Kerry. That was so not meant to happen. Please believe me.'

She half smiled and shook her head to take the heat out of the situation.

'You're something else, Inspector, you really are.' She ushered him to the door. 'Now go on. I've got a lot to do.' She touched his arm. 'But really. I'm so glad to see you.'

'Will you think about what I said?'

'About what?'

'About working with us? Helping destroy Rodriguez. I know I can get you the protection you need over in Spain with the cops there. We have specialists. People your people could work with.'

She put her hand up. 'Vinny. Please. Let me digest everything you've said. Okay?' She walked him to the door. 'Now get the hell out of here and let me get back to work.'

He smiled as he backed out of the door, and when she closed it behind him, she stood for a moment in the silence of the room, suddenly feeling as lonely as she'd felt in a very long time.

CHAPTER TWENTY-FOUR

Before she even picked up her mobile from the bedside table, Sharon knew it could only be bad news. She opened one eye and could see the orange glow of the Costa sun begin to push itself out of the sea. She looked at her phone. It was six a.m., and Enrico, the security boss on the hotel site, was calling. Christ! She sat up, pressed the answer key and cleared her throat. Before she could even speak, Enrico's breathless throaty voice was already ranting.

'Sharon! Sharon! Fackeeng beeg problem at the hotel! Is like a bomb site! Really! Like someone drop a fackeeng bomb! You need to come!' He paused, and she could hear people talking. 'Oh sheet! An now my boys tell me we have two men dead. Fak!'

'Okay, okay, Rico. I'll be there as soon as I can. But listen. Just calm down. Tell me what you know. As much as you can. Just take your time. Are you okay?'

'Yes. I'm fine. I just got here. The workers just arrive and they call me straight away. Blood everywhere. What they do to my boys. Fak, Sharon! You don't do that to a pig what they did.'

He sounded as though he was somewhere between tears and rage, and she tried to bring him back so she could listen.

She leaped out of bed, pulled back the blinds and opened the terrace door. Then she stepped out into the chilly morning air, and stood in the stillness, trying to take in what Enrico was saying, once she calmed him down.

As was normal, he told her, his deputy had visited the site after ten last night to check that the two nightshift guards were all right and the place was secure. Even before Rodriguez had been shot in Glasgow, the hotel site had been like a fortress with security and a high perimeter fence around the five acres of ground. The foundations were only a third the way up, and although there was a mammoth building task ahead, it was clear that the building was going to be a massive complex, covering a lot of ground. There were a couple of site cabins at the main entrance and in the middle of the site, and they were always manned, with armed guards in radio and phone contact at all times. There was even a panic button so they could contact Enrico if there were any problems and he would have men on the site in minutes. But whatever happened last night, nobody even made it to the panic button. His deputy had spoken to them and left after twenty minutes and then the workers turned up this morning to see the devastation. Demolition vehicles had been brought into the site – it must have been at first light or some time in the middle of the night – and torn down every piece of brickwork that had already been done, and cement poured into the foundations. All the plant they had been paying a fortune for was wrecked and set on fire.

Enrico had been called when the workers came in the morning to see the fire in the distance. They had called fire-fighters who were on the site now, and also the Guardia Civil. The workers had found the bodies, eyes burned out, hands chopped off. One of the dead guards was a father of a seven-year-old girl who was taking her first holy communion in a few days. When he was telling her this part, Enrico's voice choked with emotion. Sharon listened to as much as she could, while walking to the shower, and then she told him she would be there in twenty minutes. As she was about to go into the shower, she hit the button to call Vic, but there was no answer. How could he not have known about this? She chided herself for being suspicious. Maybe they hadn't told him. And if they hadn't did that mean they didn't trust him and had rumbled that he was a spy for the Caseys? Suddenly she felt under threat. Christ! She had a quick shower and wrapped in a towel came out and phoned Kerry. She sounded groggy woken from a sleep an hour early.

'Kerry. It's me. The payback has already started.'

'Christ, Sharon! What happened? You all right?'

'Yeah, I'm fine. I've just been woken by big Rico. Someone has wrecked the hotel. And I mean wrecked. I'll be on my way there shortly. But we have two security men butchered by these fuckers.'

'Jesus! What else can you tell me?'

'Only what Rico has said.'

She relayed the information he had given her.

'Who's the deputy?' Kerry asked. 'Could he have been got at or something? Maybe he disconnected the alarms or something?'

'That's my first thought. He's disappeared. Rico can't get him, so something's fucking well dodgy about that.'

'Did you meet the deputy? Who is he?'

'I didn't see much of him. I deal with Rico all the time. He seemed to be surrounded by a lot of reliable guys. I'm pretty sure he is. Until this. But the place was like Fort Knox. I don't know how they got all this stuff up and in there as quick as this.'

'Someone must be in on it,' Kerry said. 'But that's not our problem right now. We can look at that. Are cops there?'

'Yeah. Rico says the place is swarming. And fire brigade.'

'They're going to be asking some questions.'

'Don't worry. I can handle that. But the problem with these cops is that sometimes you don't know whose side they are on. Might be a couple of them on the take. Who knows. That's what we're up against.'

'What about anything else? Any other stuff going on? I'm sure this won't be an isolated attack.'

'Well it's just after six in the morning, so whatever has happened anywhere else in the night hasn't got to me yet. But no doubt, it will.'

'This is bad, Sharon. But we knew they would hit us, and hit us hard. The hotel is vulnerable, being out in the open like that. And at least it's not built yet.'

'Yeah. But it shouldn't have been vulnerable. It was well secured. It really was.'

'Okay. Best you go out there and see what's going on. But make sure you take a couple of guys with you, because they might be trying to lure you into something.'

Sharon was suddenly wondering if she could trust anyone around her. She seldom left anywhere without a couple of guards within sight of her, but if something was rotten among them then nobody was safe. She thought of Tony, sound asleep in his room. He'd be getting up for school in the next hour, and she didn't want to leave him. But she had to. She pushed the key for the main guard and heard him yawning. She told him to get two more people to stay at the house and three to take her to the site. Then she unwrapped her towel, patted her face with moisturiser and threw on some clothes. It was going to be a long day.

As she was heading in her phone went again.

'Sharon? It's me.'

She recognised the voice of Nick Oswald, who was in charge of the three bars the Caseys owned along the coast towards Marbella. Her stomach lurched.

'Talk to me, Nick.'

'Sharon. All sorts of shit happened last night. One of our bars was firebombed, and two guys were hit in a drive-by shooting. One of them is dead.'

'Fuck! When? Why am I only hearing about this now? Why wasn't I called last night?'

The two beats of silence from him were enough to make her suspicious. He should be more upset than this. The Costa could be rough, given the number of hoodlums who were down there, but someone firebombing your bars and shooting your people all in one night was definitely not par for the course.

'Oh, I tried calling you.'

'My phone was on all night, Nick. It always is. What the fuck is going on?'

Another pause. It filled her with fear. If she couldn't trust people like Nick, who could she trust? Nick was a Liverpudlian wise-guy who had been given the job of managing the three bars through someone who knew Mickey Casey. It was a mistake to still have him in the job, she suddenly thought, and this should have been dealt with earlier, but had been overlooked. But in the brief meetings she'd had with him he'd seemed sound enough. She was now thinking different.

'Sharon. Look. I'm sorry.' She could almost hear him swallow. 'I . . . I wasn't there last night. I've been AWOL for a couple of days.'

'What? What the fuck, Nick! What do you mean you've been AWOL? You're not fucking paid to go AWOL. Where the Christ were you?'

'I met this bird. I took a couple of days. It was stupid, I know. But I thought it's only a couple of days, and everything will be fine.'

Sharon decided to say no more to this bastard over the phone. Either he was so monumentally inept that he hadn't understood her briefing that they were all under threat, or he had been got at by Rodriguez. Either way, he had to go. And maybe permanently.

'Look, Nick, I don't want to talk about this right now. I've already got a huge problem down at the hotel site. So you get back to the bars and see what damage is done and give me a phone. We'll meet later.'

'Sure. Sorry, Sharon.'

She ignored the sorry part.

'And keep your phone fucking on.'

She hung up.

Frankie Martin climbed into his silver Mercedes convertible, pulled on his Ray-Ban sunglasses, then checked his image in the rear-view mirror. He took a second to admire his suntanned face and ran his fingers down his freshly shaved chin. Sitting back into the leather driving seat, he stuck the key in the ignition and pushed the start button, savouring the moment when the car purred to life. He took one last second to check his navy and white striped shirt was crisp and perfect and his light blue trousers and tan leather loafers, to finish off his effortlessly stylish look. Everything about him reeked of success and money, right down to his gold Rolex watch on his wrist. He was beginning to enjoy this life on the Costa del Sol, he decided, as he eased the car out of the parking space and onto the road, heading out towards Marbella and Puerto Banus, the warm breeze on his face.

The eight a.m. call from Rodriguez's right-hand man Pablo had been short and to the point.

'Pepe wants to see you. Alone. Midday, Puerto Banus. Café De Santos. Don't be late.'

Frankie had been a little irritated by this Pablo fucker talking to him as though he were the help, but he knew there was nothing he could do about it – not right now anyway. He'd been just as curt back to the Colombian, retorting, 'I'm never late. Ever.'

So now he was headed to the bar in the port after a morning run on the beach and a hot then freezing shower to get his blood up, and ready for what lay ahead. Given what happened to Pat Durkin yesterday, it had crossed Frankie's mind that he might be next on Rodriguez's hit list. But he'd consoled himself by the fact that the Colombian knew that

Durkin had been totally in charge of the mission to meet with Kerry in Glasgow that went tits up. Frankie had been told he was not required, so he'd taken a back seat, and that's why he was delighted that it ended in an almighty fuck-up. After the cold way Rodriguez had had Durkin assassinated, Frankie and Vic had left later and gone for a drink in a café off the motorway. They hadn't become buddies in the short time they'd been acquainted, but Frankie had got the measure of the big man and he guessed it was better to have him inside the tent pissing out than the other way around. So he'd had a few drinks with him and they'd swapped stories of stuff and faces from old days, and how things had changed. The big man didn't give much away, though, and that told Frankie that he had to keep an eye on him, and play his cards close to his chest. When you were playing in the kind of shitty field they were all in right now, you had to watch your back at all times. There was no such thing as a team player, no matter how much some cunt swore their allegiance to your crew. Deep down it was every bastard for themselves, and nobody knew that more than Frankie. As he took the slip road for the port, he allowed himself a little thought on what Rodriguez would want to see him about, because he did say that he wanted to see him alone. The café was in the middle of the port and a well-known public place for posh fuckers, from the owners of the million-pound yachts to the rich ladies out lunching with younger men. So it was unlikely that

Rodriguez was intending to have him shot. Too public for that caper. No, Frankie decided. With Durkin out of the way, Rodriguez was maybe going to give him a bigger role. That's what he craved. That's what he'd always craved. When he parked his car and strolled towards the café, he could see the Colombian was already seated, in jeans and brown loafers and a polo shirt, looking a million dollars. No scars on him to mark him out a gangster, Frankie thought. This fucker looks like a rich lawyer or businessman out to play. But that was far from the truth. Frankie squared his shoulders and strutted purposefully towards the table. He clocked big Pablo at a nearby table by himself, and two other henchmen at the back, just sitting sipping water, watching.

'Frankie.' Rodriguez put down the glass of water he was holding. He motioned him to a seat opposite. 'Sit.'

Frankie stood just for a second longer, long enough to look him square enough in an expression that said, I'm not a fucking pet collie, you cunt. But he smiled through it, and sat down, crossing his legs. He kept his Ray-Bans on and turned his head to the water's edge where the floating mansions nudged each other, the tinkling sounds of the masts in the breeze sounding like a fanfare announcing your arrival in a rich privileged world.

'Beautiful here, Pepe, isn't it amazing?' Frankie said in the way of small talk, as much to show he wasn't afraid of him as to break the ice.

'Is magnificent. It has everything here. Everything a man could want. Food, wine . . .' he gestured towards a table of women who Frankie knew were watching them, 'and of course women when we need them.' He took a breath and then lit a cigarette from his packet, then said, 'Not like where I come from. Not like Medellín with the smoke and the buildings. Beautiful country, but when you live in the city, it's shit.'

'Sure. Every city is the same.' Frankie couldn't believe he was coming out with this shite. He hadn't come down here to talk about the meaning of life, so get to the fucking point, Rodriguez.

The waiter came and Frankie ordered a coffee.

'I have no time for lunch, Frankie. We do that another day. I just wanted to talk to you. In private.'

'Sure. I'm good with that, Pepe.'

Rodriguez took a long drag of his cigarette and held it in for a second, his full lips opening a fraction to let out a stream of smoke.

'This business,' he said, waving his hand in a dismissive way, 'with Durkin.' He looked directly at Frankie. 'He had to go. You know that, don't you.'

It was more of a statement than a question, and Frankie knew he wasn't expected to disagree. He nodded but didn't reply.

Rodriguez looked away from him.

'Durkin failed me. I cannot have failures in my business.

Not ever. I believed him when he said he had the bodies and the people to make things happen. But is not true.' He sighed as though bored. 'So. Now he is gone. But we are not advancing, you know what I mean?'

'Yes,' Frankie said. 'I understand. Some things take a little time.'

The Colombian looked at him and his eyes darkened a little. He waved a finger. 'No, my friend. Time, we do not have.'

Christ, Frankie thought, what the fuck am I supposed to say to this psycho? For a moment they didn't speak. Then Rodriguez leaned forward.

'Last night,' he said, 'or, I mean in the middle of the night, we hit the hotel. We demolished it. Or as much as we could. We took out two of their fucking guards too.'

Frankie raised his eyebrows, surprised. He hadn't expected this. When he and Vic had left yesterday, nothing was said about the next big hit. He wondered what this meant for him, if he wasn't getting briefed. His stomach did a little flip.

'Really?' he enthused. 'Well that's good news. I can only imagine how that is going down back in Glasgow. Good.'

Rodriguez nodded, and raised his finger to make another point.

'And,' he said, 'we also hit one of their bars on the coast. Burned out. And we shot two of their boys there.' He shrugged. 'Just a message to go back to Kerry Casey, to say this is only the beginning.'

Frankie nodded slowly, wondering what he was going to say next.

'So,' Rodriguez said. 'We can do some damage here, we can fuck things up in their property and bars, but we have not hit the target. Not completely. We have to finish the Caseys. Take them apart. Piece by piece. We have to take them and their business for us. We have to be in charge – not Kerry Casey.'

'No,' Frankie said. 'And to be honest, they will have taken a bit of strength from what happened in Glasgow. They will feel they gave you a good kicking. But they will also be watching their backs, Pepe.'

'Fine,' he said. 'Sure. They did well in Glasgow.' He rubbed the thigh that Kerry had put a bullet in. 'But they weren't watching their backs enough last night.'

'No. True. It was a good hit.'

'But is not over. Much more to do.'

'Of course.'

'And that, *amigo*, is where you come in.'

Frankie took off his Ray-Bans and held the Colombian's gaze as he looked into his eyes as though searching for any signs of betrayal. He waited.

'You will go to Glasgow, Frankie. And you will finish this off. Kerry Casey is your target. You kill her, you kill the empire, and then, they come over to us.'

Frankie hoped his face didn't show the shock that was registering right now from his head to his bowels. Go back to Glasgow? Bump off Kerry Casey? Fuck me! If I show my face back in Glasgow someone will blow my head off and they'll place it on Kerry Casey's dinner table for cunts like Danny and Jack to smirk at. But he couldn't show any of that right now. So he swallowed and took a breath.

'Go to Glasgow?' he said. 'Pepe, you know I'm a dead man in Glasgow. There is a price on my head. I got the call from a mate a few days after I disappeared, and I was told the Caseys are offering a million for me. There are people who will queue up to bump me off.' He paused, noticing how Rodriguez looked unimpressed. 'Look, I'm not saying it's a bad idea. But we need to think about it.'

'Then that is up to you, Frankie. You think about it, you plan it. I give you everything you need – money, guns, whatever you need. You can find some people in Glasgow or Manchester or Dublin who will come over to you. Then you go to war with the Caseys. On their ground. I can make sure you win. If you offer enough money to people they will come with you. Is human nature.'

Frankie said nothing, listened, as Rodriguez went on. 'And when it is over, you will have the big prize. You and me. We will be partners. You will be my partner in the business here, and in Amsterdam, and in everywhere I have the control. You will be with me. You will have more money and power than you ever dreamed of, because now you will be playing with the big boys. Because as you know, my friend, the Colombian cartels run the whole show. The Russians and Albanians, they think they can take us on, but they cannot. We let them have their turf, but we can cut their heads off any time we want. This is the big game. This is what you are now.'

For a moment, Frankie wondered if this fucker was on something, if he had been snorting his own purest Colombian marching powder. He did look a bit wild-eyed, like some revolutionary raving about taking over the world. But fucking hell. This was a lot of shit to put on someone's shoulders. He tried to get his head around it. In theory, given a shedload of money, he could get some people on board. He'd have to take a long look at it, get some people back in Glasgow and Dublin and Manchester, people who liked him before all this became so fucked up. People who were loyal to him, not trying to shaft him. They were all bastards at the end of the day, but Rodriguez was right: if you gave enough money to people, they would do anything. He could make this work. He had the balls for it, that much he knew. And in the end the biggest prize of all, the Casey empire. He could wipe out Kerry Casey and the top tier, and the rest would fall. He'd always wanted to be powerful, but he just hadn't thought it would come to this. But then again, he had betrayed his best friend and partner in crime, Mickey Casey, and if he could do that, then getting rid of that smart bitch sister and the clan of sycophants around her would be a breeze. At least, right now, he had to convince himself of that. Because opposite him was one dangerous, ruthless fucker, and if he dared to show any flicker of fear or disagreement, then he knew he'd be lucky to make it back to his car without a bullet in his back.

CHAPTER TWENTY-FIVE

Kerry listened as Billy Hill bleated about how he couldn't do business with the Colombians any more. But she made sure she showed little reaction. She didn't have a lot of sympathy for him. And she wasn't about to welcome him into the fold with open arms. Because Hill, along with Pat Durkin, had been part of the cabal who had brought the bastard Pepe Rodriguez into their lives in the first place. She wanted to tell him that her memory wasn't short lived. And she wanted to ask him if he could remember the last time they met – when he stood side by side with Rodriguez and Durkin, and the message to Kerry and the Casey organisation was that they were muscling in on her empire. To be fair, Hill had been the least menacing and slimy of the three of them that day they'd met in the Glasgow hotel, but Kerry had been in no doubt whose camp Hill was in. But now, he was coming here to her, offering his help. She was grateful for that, because right now, with the shit hitting the fan all over the place, she needed all the bodies she could get, and having the Hills and his mob in London onside with her, she just might be able to take the Colombians on. But she wasn't about to let him off the hook that easy. They were having lunch with Danny and Jack in La Rotunda restaurant on the ground floor of a famous Glasgow landmark on the banks of the River Clyde. The circular red-brick restaurant, which had once covered a deep tunnel across the river, had been a favourite of Kerry's during visits to Glasgow from Spain as a teenager when her mother and Auntie Pat would take her dinner. She tried not to think of those cherished times now, as she concentrated on what Hill was saying. She watched as he spoke rapidly in his Cockney twang, laying it all out on the table for her.

'So, the bottom line is, Kerry,' he said, pushing back his shock of lush silver hair. 'I'm out. I'm finished with those Colombian fuckers. I mean, after the way they took Pat out. That's a fucking liberty, that is. Pat could be a bit of a cunt at times, but he didn't deserve that.'

'It's how they do business, Billy,' Kerry said, giving a little shrug. 'I don't know why you're surprised about that. What did you expect from Rodriguez?' She paused, seeing his face fall a little. He looked like he'd been expecting her to be more onside with him. She let it hang for a moment as Hill's eyes darted from Danny to Jack. Kerry leaned forward. 'For a start. Did you see what they did to John O'Driscoll? Did you know about that? They gouged his eyes out. Chopped him up like a piece of meat, for Christ's sake. What did you say about that?'

Hill immediately put up his hands.

'Absolutely fucking not. No way. On my grandson's life, I knew fuck all about that. I promise you, Kerry. That's the whole problem I had with them. I got the feeling from the first week that somehow I didn't feature in Rodriguez's grand plans for the future. To tell you the truth, I was suspicious that Durkin was double-crossing me, because I know he was capable of that. But before I get the chance to really pursue it, suddenly he's history.'

Hill looked from one to the other around the table, his face flushed, and Kerry detected the whiff of desperation in his demeanour. This was one of London's most hardened criminals, well used to bodies piling up, punishment beatings and executions. He'd been running drugs, guns and women from Europe for years and was powerful and feared in London and Spain. Yet here he was, a worried man, ready to throw in his lot with the Glasgow mobsters who he'd been told were out of their depth.

'You didn't know about O'Driscoll? Nothing at all? What about Marty Kane's boy being kidnapped?' She studied his face for lies.

'Fuck all, Kerry! I promise you! All I was told by Durkin was that they were going to hit you hard. When I asked what was going on, I was told it was a kidnapping. The last thing I expected was for it to be a little kid. That's just bang out of order.'

'So why was the Colombian freezing you out?' she said. 'I'm curious. Seriously. I need you to tell me everything, Billy.'

He took a gulp of his wine and seemed to relax a little, his shoulders dropping as he sat back.

'As far as I can see, and based on what I hear from my boys and connections over in Spain, Rodriguez and his gang are basically just muscling in on everyone. There are plenty of players on the Costa who are small potatoes when it comes to cocaine trafficking. They either work for the big boys, or they have their own smaller operations. Rodriguez is hoovering them all up. I hear he's offering big bucks to people he's picked out to join forces with him. Don't get me wrong, the Colombians are already big in Spain and across Europe – of course. But with the Russians and Albanians putting themselves about a lot more these days, they need to make sure they hang onto their turf, and the end game is about being top dog so that everyone from London, Manchester to Dublin to here in Scotland buys from them. The middlemen are all theirs. I'm told he wants to take charge of the women, the gun running – the fucking lot. It's me who's taken the risk bringing in the guns over the years and I've got it down to a fine art – same with my cocaine importing. Sure, I'd have been up for buying some coke from him, but not exclusively. I'm not a fucking

Commie where we all have to deal with some single regime running the show. I'm my own man. When your Mickey was alive, him and Frankie worked with us, with Knuckles Boyle, and we all traded with Durkin's mob. I have contacts across Europe and so did they to an extent. But I have the most. I'm not about to chuck all that in the fire to team up with some cunt who kidnaps little kids to prove a point. No way.'

Kerry glanced at Danny and Jack who had been silent during Hill's rant. He sounded to Kerry like a defence counsel trying to convince the jury that his client was a good guy, despite the pile of evidence to the contrary. But she was satisfied that he was rattled enough to have come to them, and sounded indignant and sincere enough in what he was saying. She hoped to Christ she wasn't being taken in. But people like Danny had known him years ago, and though he was a slippery bastard in his day, Hill was older now. He had grandchildren, and he was rich. He wanted to keep it that way, maintain his lifestyle, and avoid having his eyes gouged out.

'Okay,' Kerry finally said, looking at Jack and Danny. 'I think we can do business together, Billy. For the moment anyway. As a self-preservation move. Let's call it that. Rodriguez is going to come after us. He was coming after me anyway, after what happened to him here. But once he gets wind that you've come over to our side, then we can expect an avalanche. So we have to be prepared for that.'

She looked at Danny, expecting him to come up with the logistics.

'Yeah,' Danny said. 'We need to be able to trust each other, Billy. I told you that when we spoke the other day. I mean a hundred per cent. But we also need to know that your boys are on our side. Completely. You need to be sure who you are bringing to this fight, and the last thing we need is someone who can be got at. So you be clear about that.' He glanced at Jack. 'It won't end well for any spies in the camp who betray us. You make sure they know that.'

Hill narrowed his eyes. 'I'm bringing my best men. I've already beefed up my security on my businesses down the road, so I've freed up the very top guys to come on board if Rodriguez brings the fight to us.'

'Oh I don't think there is any "if" Rodriguez brings the fight to us, Billy,' Danny said. 'It's a case of how, and when.'

Jack nodded slowly, and they sat for a long moment saying nothing. Kerry looked at all three of the men in front of her, and a little shiver ran through her that – apart from Sharon in Spain – these were the only people she could trust her life with at the moment. She thought of Vinny, and his proposal for them to help the cops bring Rodriguez down. That conversation was for another day.

Cal and Tahir were playing pool in the public bar of the Norseman up on Maryhill Road, which allowed them in despite them being under eighteen. The pub was owned by the Caseys, but big Paddy O'Hare ran it for them, and it wasn't the kind of bar the cops would routinely pop into for an age check on the clientele. It was a rough shop, and most of the customers were either connected to the Casey organisation – working for the various businesses they ran as a front to launder dirty money – or just locals who didn't want to wander all the way down to the town for a drink. And it was unlikely that any of the shiny, upwardly mobile punters from the city would drop in for a cocktail. Neither would enemies of the Caseys venture in if they had any sense. The beer cellar at the back of the Norseman had been the scene of a few punishment beatings over the years, and one fatal shooting, for people who had grassed to the cops. Much as Cal and Tahir liked to go out on the town if they had a weekend off, this was the place they hung out during the week. It was close to the tenement flat Tahir shared with a couple of other immigrants. Plus, they felt a bit safer there, because the shit they'd been involved in in getting the Kane boy away from the kidnappers had made them feel a bit exposed. But tonight they were both a little restless, because they had stepped out of line when Jack had expressly told them not to.

Cal chalked the tip of his cue as Tahir leaned over the table to take the shot. Then, quick as a flash, he stuck the black ball in the pocket and raised his head, a smug look on his face.

'Game over, my friend.'

Cal looked at his watch. He'd been a bit jumpy all day after he and Tahir had gone up to the flats last night where Tahir's girlfriend, Elia, lived with her family. After Elia had told Tahir about the thugs using the young girls for sex and selling them in the blocks of flats to men, they had told Jack about it, and he said they had to wait until things died down after the last few days, and they would do something about it. But the previous night, when they'd gone up to see if Elia was all right, they'd seen her getting out of a car driven by a man. When Tahir confronted her, she broke down in tears, and told him the thugs had been around again and they'd threatened to firebomb their houses if they didn't play the game. Tahir dragged the driver out of the car and started beating the shit out of him. Cal was waiting for a mob to appear at any moment but they didn't. It was then that Tahir pulled out his gun and shot the guy in both kneecaps, leaving him screeching in agony. Elia, hysterical, ran off towards her house, and Cal dragged Tahir away and they ran like hell back to the main road and jumped into a black hackney cab, then headed to the city.

'What the fuck did you do that for?' Cal rasped to him when they got into the car. 'There will be all sorts of shit flying now. Fucking hell, Tahir. Jack told us to hang fire.'

Tahir's face was white with rage, but he kept his voice low. 'Did you not hear what she said? They are selling the little girls to every pervert who comes around. I told you. I have to stop it.'

'But Jack said–'

'I couldn't wait for Jack, Cal. Not when I heard her. Not when I see she gets out of the car with some . . . with some bastard who has touched her. Raped her.'

Cal had watched as his friend shook his head and stared out of the side window, tears of anger in his eyes.

They hadn't told Jack what happened, and hoped it would go away. But Cal knew deep down there would be consequences. As they were pulling on their jackets to leave the Norseman, Tahir's mobile rang and he pushed it to his ear. Cal knew by the look on his face that it was trouble.

'Wait!' Tahir was saying. 'Slow down. Just tell me, Elia. What happened? Who is there now? What?'

Then his phone seemed to go dead and he looked at Cal, his face a mix of rage and panic.

'It is Elia. These bastards have her. They said to come and get her. They said they want to talk to me. Fuck, Cal!'

'Hold on, Tahir,' Cal said. 'We can't just go up there. They'll fucking shoot us! We can't!'

'We have to, Cal! They have taken her. They will harm her. Maybe they will be raping her – all of them.'

His voice was raised and Cal glanced over his shoulder to where big Paddy behind the bar was watching them intently. A couple of other punters at the bar looked at them, then at Paddy.

'You all right, lads? Is there a problem?'

'No,' Cal said. 'It's all right, man.'

But by the time he turned around, Tahir was already out of the door. He glanced again at Paddy, then ran after him.

As he got outside, he saw Tahir opening the rear door of a taxi that had just let someone out.

'Wait for me,' Cal said, as he jumped in beside him. 'Fucking hell, Tahir! This is crazy!'

Tahir didn't answer. He stared straight ahead, and Cal could see the driver give them a look in the rear-view mirror.

'Keppochill Road, mate,' Tahir said. 'Can you hurry?'

Cal felt his mouth go dry with fear. The last time he'd been this scared was in the middle of the shoot-out to get little Finbar Kane away. But he had had Jake Cahill covering his back then, and he was also armed. He'd felt safe and secure with a gun in his hand. This time he had nothing in his pocket but a few quid and his mobile. He wanted to phone Jack, but he knew if he did there would be serious consequences for disobeying an order. From the corner of his eye, he could see Tahir lift up his fleece, and the glint of the pistol in his waistband. This was not going to end well, whatever happened. The taxi pulled up close to the flats, and Tahir handed the driver a tenner. They didn't even wait for the change as they jumped out.

'So what now, Tahir? We don't even know where they are.'

Tahir was already bringing up Elia's number into the mobile.

'We call her. Maybe they'll answer.'

'Then what? They tell us to come and meet them? Jesus! What do you think is going to happen then, Tahir?'

Tahir glared at him. 'Someone is going to die tonight. But it won't be us.'

'Christ almighty!' Cal said.

Then he heard Tahir speak. 'Is okay, is okay,' his voice consoling. 'I'm coming. Let me speak to the prick.'

Tahir glanced at Cal whose bowels were churning. Jesus! He didn't even have a knife. He glanced around him, waiting for some mob to jump out of the shadows and batter them to death. He couldn't even see a brick or a bottle he could pick up for protection.

'I am here. Tell me where you are. What you want? Let her go. I give you what you want. Is it money? I have money.'

Cal stood close to him and he could hear the voice on the other side of the phone mocking him.

'You have money, you wee cunt? You got fifty grand? Then bring it now.'

'I haven't got the money now,' Tahir said. 'But I can get it.'

Cal's eyes widened and his mouth dropped open. He spread his hands and mouthed, 'What the fuck!'

He glanced over Tahir's shoulder, and in the darkness of the dimly lit street saw a row of lock-up garages, one of which had its door pulled up. Out of it piled at least half a dozen thugs, armed with baseball bats and sticks. And they were striding towards them. He looked at Tahir whose face was chalk white, but eyes wild with rage.

'Shit, Tahir!'

'Let her go,' Tahir said again into the phone. 'I'll get the money for you.'

But there was no voice at the other end. Just the sound of people running towards them, roaring, tribal. And Cal stood frozen with fear. Then he saw Tahir take out his gun. Christ! He thought of his mum. Then a shot rang out and one of the men heading towards them fell to the ground. But it didn't stop the others rampaging towards them. Tahir fired again, and another was hit, but by this time they were upon them, and Cal braced himself as two burly thugs came at him with a baseball bat. He felt the wind go out of him as one of them hit him in the stomach, then as he bent over, he could feel the force of two bats on his back.

'Tahir! Oh fuck!'

He was losing consciousness, as boots and bats laid into him on the ground. But as he opened one eye, he saw Tahir being dragged away, and one of the thugs had his gun. He curled into a ball, pretending to be unconscious or dead, as the boots rained on him, and then they stopped. He watched, barely conscious, and through blood and blurred vision he saw the naked figure of Elia being thrown out of the garage. As she stumbled and fell to the ground, one of the thugs poured petrol from a can over her. Tahir was being dragged, his face bloody and beaten, towards her. They were going to die tonight. All three of them, Cal thought.

'I'm so sorry, Mum,' he whispered as he lay, tears in his eyes, waiting for the onslaught.

Then, suddenly, there came the screech of tyres. Cal eased himself up on his elbow, and he saw two four-by-fours scream to a halt and four guys jump out of each of them. Then the shots started. What the fuck! Some kind of assassination squad, he thought. Then he saw one, two, three of the thugs fall as they were hit by gunfire. Then another. Then the rest of them scamper for cover. He crawled over and got onto all fours, then tried to get to his feet. But the pain was agony and he spat blood. Then he saw one of the guys coming towards him. It was Archie, one of the Casey crew. Was it Archie? He wasn't sure and thought he was going to pass out. He felt his arm on him.

'You all right, Cal? Can you stand up? The cavalry's here.' He grinned.

Cal got up on shaky legs. He looked at Archie, bewildered.

'Big Paddy phoned Jack.' He shook his head. 'If you think this is trouble, wait till big Jack gets his fucking hands on you.' He put his arm around him and supported him as Cal staggered alongside him.

He could see Tahir on his feet, blood pouring from his face. He'd been slashed at his ear and one of the guys was trying to stem the blood flow. Another of the guys put his jacket around the naked girl and helped her into a car. Tahir went along with them.

'This is some shit going on up here,' Archie said to Cal.

'But it ends tonight. Come on. Let's get you down the road and get fixed up. The lads will sort these cunts out.'

As Cal was helped into the car, he saw three bodies lying in pools of blood. He had survived tonight. But he was not looking forward to seeing big Jack.

CHAPTER TWENTY-SIX

Sharon was on her way to meet Nick Oswald, but not at the site of the firebombed bar, or in the other café he had suggested close to Fuengirola. She wasn't that daft. Before they were due to meet, she'd sent two of her boys to the bar just to sit having a beer like any other punter on the pavement café. They waited. But it was no surprise to Sharon that the bastard didn't turn up. Two other faces did though, and Sharon's boys recognised one of them as part of Durkin's Irish mob on the Costa del Sol. So it had to be presumed that Nick was now working for Rodriguez. And it looked like they were lying in wait for Sharon to turn up. The boys had left twenty minutes after Nick failed to show, and called her to report what they thought. She instructed them to find him. And to her surprise, within about two hours, they did. Through their contacts, Nick had been clocked in the departures car park at Málaga airport. No luggage. Just a worried look that grew more desperate when he'd felt the gun in his back and was marched into the waiting car. Right now he was being held in the back room of a timeshare agent's office tucked into the edge of an urbanisation off the Marbella road. Sharon hadn't even known the timeshare office existed, but she was learning fast how widespread the Casey empire was, dotted along the Costa coast.

As her driver pulled the car into the street outside the office, Sharon was feeling a little queasy. It wasn't that she didn't have the stomach for a fight. She'd shown that, all right, not two months ago when Knuckles Boyle had waved her off the morning she left their house, to be driven to Manchester airport by the thugs he'd sent to assassinate her. She'd promptly gunned down the two of them and left them to die in the mud as she'd made her escape. That was what had brought her to Kerry Casey in the first place. She'd lived then because she was determined she'd survive Knuckles' attempt to execute her. But this was different. She was about to witness how the truth was extracted from people who betrayed you. This had been something that Knuckles would have done routinely but she'd never been part of that. Now she was. She braced herself as she opened the passenger door of the Mercedes and stepped out. She noted the guards in the back get out swiftly, their eyes sweeping the street and buildings, watching for trouble. She followed them into the office, and past the receptionist, all blonde and busty and glowing with a

Spanish tan. She glanced at them, smiled, then her eyes went back to her computer screen. For a fleeting moment, Sharon wondered if she knew what was going on.

Nick Oswald sat in the back room, located down a corridor and a flight of stairs to what looked like an underground car park. He was tied to a chair and his face was bloodied. Sharon looked at the two bulky shaven-headed hard men standing over him, tattooed freak shows, then at the older man in the brown leather bomber jacket, who she knew as Johnny Duncan, who ran a string of estate agents the Caseys used to launder money. Johnny took a few steps away from where Nick sat sniffing, and jerked his head for Sharon to walk with him. They went and he spoke softly.

'As you can see,' Johnny said, 'Nick has been a bit slow in getting the idea here.'

Sharon nodded. 'What's he saying?'

'Well. Nothing, at the start. Hence the little slap he's had. But he's a bit more forthcoming now.'

'Did they get to him?'

'So he says. But he's not admitting much, other than he was told to disappear for an overnight. Won't say who by though.'

'Has he got a name?'

'Oh, I'm sure he's got a name all right. All he has to do is give it to us. We need to know who it was. I mean it doesn't take a fucking detective to work out that it was Rodriguez or Durkin's mob who put him up to it. But we want to know for sure. We need more than he's saying.'

Sharon nodded. 'Maybe he'll tell me,' she said. 'Let's just lay off with the slapping till I talk to him.'

Johnny shrugged. 'Sure. All yours.' He gestured towards Nick.

Sharon had avoided looking Nick in the face when she'd come into the room, as the fear in him was palpable. Shit! She actually felt sorry for him. Because she knew that no matter what he told her now, he wasn't getting out of this alive. It crossed her mind to wonder if he had a family, here or back home. She glanced down and could see his legs shaking with fear. She motioned for the others to move away, then pulled up a plastic tubular chair and sat down opposite him, not really knowing what she was going to say to him.

'Nick,' she said blowing out a sigh. 'Christ, Nick! Why do this?'

His face began to crumple and close up and she could see the bruising and the weeping cut below his eye. Below the blood staining his light blue T-shirt showed a smiley sun and the message 'Have A Nice Day'. The cruellest of ironies as he sat there, his face a mask of fear.

'I didn't do anything, Sharon. I didn't know they were going to fucking torch the places.' He sniffed. 'I was just told not to be there for one night.' He shook his head. 'I'm sorry. I'm so sorry.'

Sharon didn't speak for a few beats; she could feel Johnny's eyes on her, and the other two heavies whose answer to everything was to beat the shit out of someone. And maybe it was. But so far it hadn't worked.

'Look, Nick. Okay. You didn't know. I accept that.' She clasped her hands together. 'But come on. You're not stupid, man. You should have at least guessed they were planning something bad. All you had to do was make one phone call to me. A text even. I'd have got you covered. I'd have taken you out of the situation. You must have known that.'

He sniffed but said nothing, his head dropped to his chest.

'Did they pay you, Nick?'

Silence, just sniffing. She glanced over her shoulder at the deadpan faces staring back. Eventually, Nick nodded.

'Okay. Tell me,' she said.

He wiped his nose. 'I've got a habit. I hide it well. I didn't mean it to get out of hand, but it has. I owe a lot of money.'

'You owe money? Who do you owe money to? You go to someone outside of us to get your coke?'

'I had to. I couldn't let anyone know I was using this much.'

Sharon nodded. Stupid question she'd asked. Of course, if he was a coke-head, he wasn't going to be buying it from any of the Caseys' suppliers. He'd have been bounced out of his job if he did that.

'How much do you owe?'

'Nearly twenty grand. It shouldn't have been that. I didn't owe anything like that. I never even bought that amount of coke. But they've just fucking plucked this figure out of the air and told me I owe it.'

'So why didn't you come to me?'

'I was scared. Of what would happen if I came to you.'

'Christ, Nick.' She shook her head. 'Well for one thing, you wouldn't be sitting in this level of shit. You'd be out of a job, but that would be it. How bloody stupid can you be?'

He broke down, sobbing. 'They said they would get my ma shot back home. They even knew her address. How the fuck did they know that, Sharon? I haven't been home in two years. Nobody even knows where I come from. My ma's an old woman. She lives by herself. Fuck! They said they'd throw her under a bus.'

They sat in silence, just the sound of Nick's sobs, then Sharon spoke.

'Nick. Listen to me. I'll get someone to make sure your ma is all right. I promise you.' She paused. 'But you need to tell me who you spoke to. You need to say who you met. I need names. And I need them now, Nick. Because you need to understand that I can't spend any more time on this. Just give me what I need to know.'

Sharon sat, her stomach churning, looking at him. She knew when she walked out of the room it was over for Nick, not matter what he told her.

Eventually he said, 'It was Terry Dawson. He's Irish. One

of Durkin's mob. But I didn't know him. He got in touch with me a couple of days ago. Said my coke debt was paid. He gave me money and told me to get out of town for the night.' He paused. 'He was with some other guy. Spanish or maybe South American. I don't know. He put a gun to my head at one point. And it was then Dawson told me they would get my ma if I opened my mouth.' He sniffed. 'That's why I ran. I just wanted to go home. I knew as soon as I talked to you that you'd be suspicious. I wasn't even going to call you. I was actually on my way to the airport when you phoned.'

'Well, you know I didn't go to the place we were supposed to meet. I'm not daft. But there were two pricks there. Waiting for me, I suppose.' She looked directly at as much of Nick's eyes as were visible beneath the puffiness that was now coming up. He was silent. 'Nick. Did you set me up?'

She already knew the answer before Nick nodded, tears streaming down his face. Sharon stood up. Allowing them to firebomb the pub was bad enough. But by setting her up to be murdered, Nick had signed his death warrant. There was nothing more to be said, and by the look on Nick's face he knew that. Sharon turned to the others and made a face that said, he's all yours. Then as she walked towards the door, she heard Nick speak through sobs.

'Sharon. Will you make sure my ma's all right? I'm sorry.'

She didn't answer. She opened the door and went

outside into the corridor, then walked out of the building past the receptionist who didn't even look up at her. She got into the passenger seat of the car and closed the door.

'Not pleasant,' she said as the guards got in. She turned to the driver. 'Let's go.'

As the car drove out into the main road, Sharon's mobile rang. It was Rico.

'They found my deputy. In his apartment. Fackeeng smothered with a plastic bag on his head.'

'Thanks for telling me, Rico. Talk later.'

She hung up. It wasn't even midday and the shit was piling up.

Frankie Martin came out of the arrivals hall at Dublin airport and merged with the crowd, his eyes everywhere, just in case. Nobody but he knew when he was leaving Málaga, which flight he was on, or even where he was going. Rodriguez had told him it was up to him how he played the game now. He told him he trusted him. He gave him a bank card with access to any amount of money he needed, because war is an expensive business. And Rodriguez's parting words were that the rewards would be huge if he came back the victor. Christ, Frankie thought. The cunt had even embraced him.

CHAPTER TWENTY-SEVEN

Kerry had decided to let Jack deal with Cal and Tahir after their vigilante antics the other night. But she was furious with the pair of them, especially Cal, because now she had Maria in her kitchen in tears. Kerry placed a cup of coffee onto the table and looked at her oldest friend as she wiped tears from her blotchy face.

'I mean, it's not that I'm not grateful for everything you have done for me, Kerry, for us, for our Jen and Cal. You've given us not just a roof over our heads, but a home, and a feeling of family that we haven't had for years.' She sniffed, sipped her tea. 'I know I'll be indebted to you for the rest of my life. The moment I asked for your help, I knew this, and I never hesitated, because I was desperate. But I just don't know if we can go on like this.'

Kerry sat impassive, knowing everything she was saying was right. When she had seen Maria at her mother's funeral, she'd been shocked at the pale, haunted figure she'd become, in hock to moneylenders and waiting for the midnight knock from police to say that her heroin-addict daughter had been found dead. Kerry had welcomed her into the fold with open arms. Maria knew what that meant and so did Kerry. She had given Maria a job and a lifestyle she would never have been able to afford. There would always be a price to pay, and they both knew that. Kerry should send her packing. That's what more ruthless bosses would do in her line of work. But watching Maria wipe her nose with a crumpled tissue, Kerry couldn't help but feel for her. Maria's son was only sixteen, but already he had killed on behalf of the Casey empire. Jack had said he and Tahir had earned their stripes early, just as he had at that age, and he had high hopes for the boys. But Maria knew nothing of this. Sure, she knew her boy worked for them, and she wasn't stupid. She knew they'd be collecting money, working with the more experienced men as enforcers, but she did not know he was already a killer. And she wasn't about to hear about it at this table. Kerry had told Jack and Danny that she wasn't happy that Cal and Tahir, but especially Cal, had been put in the frontline so young. Yes, they had acquitted themselves at the shoot-out to get Finbar back, but Kerry had hoped that the future for these boys would be in the legitimate Casey empire, not as killers or hired guns. But Jack and Danny had explained to her that although the boys were young, they were ready, and they were good hands. And they were keen to be involved. She would let it go for the moment, she'd decided. But she hoped she would never have to break it to Maria that her son had been killed fighting battles for the Caseys.

'Look, Maria. You have to get it into perspective. What Cal and Tahir did the other night was well out of order, and believe me they know that. Jack is with them now, and I'm going to speak to them shortly.' She tried to pick her words. 'But remember, these are just young boys. They're maybe feeling a bit puffed up because they're working for us now, part of something big, and they got a bit big for their boots. But they'll know better the next time.'

'Cal has two broken ribs, and his face is battered stupid. His body is covered in boot marks.' Maria shook her head. 'And Tahir's got a slash right down his cheek. Marked for life – poor laddie.'

'I haven't seen them,' Kerry said, 'but I know. They're very lucky our lads got a call and rescued them. But they know they shouldn't have acted on their own.'

Kerry looked at her watch. She waited, wondering what Maria was going to say next.

'Kerry,' she began, nervous, 'maybe it's time for me to find another job. And for me to find another way to live. As I said, I'm so grateful. But I can't give up my son for this.'

She looked at Kerry and her pleading eyes filled with tears again. Kerry reached across and put her hand over hers. She thought of her own child inside her, how it would turn out, how she would feel if the son or daughter she had grew up to break her heart. And she resolved that when this war was over, she would find a path for Cal where he could grow as a person, not as a killer.

'Come on, Maria. Take some time to think about it. You know how tough it is out there. You know what can happen – the sharks and the shitbags preying on people. You've left that behind you. Your life is good now. Of course, working for an organisation like this, there will be some problems along the way. But believe me, things are going to change. What we do just now isn't how I see the future. I told you, I have big plans for the Caseys. Big plans. And I want you to feature in them too. We have property, businesses you can get involved in. You can be valuable to us, and you can live a good life without waiting for some bastard to knock your door.'

Kerry didn't want to lose Maria, because she was working well and with her organisational skills Kerry could see how she could fit in as they grew in the new direction she wanted to take them in. She didn't want to see her friend return to what her life had been. Because that was what would happen. It wasn't fair. But there was little opportunity for people out there, grafting away, and they never really got out of the mire. Only the few did, through education or crime. Kerry knew from her early childhood in poverty that her father dragged them from that to wealth through crime. In truth, everything she had, including her expensive education and law degree, was facilitated by the proceeds of crime. She had never regretted it. She knew what her family was – she just hadn't expected to be sitting here trying to sell her criminal empire to her oldest friend. But that's how it was.

Maria pushed her fringe back from her forehead and rubbed at her eyes.

'I know,' she said. 'I never want to go back to what my life was. I admit that.' She swallowed hard. 'But I don't know how I can live with the fear that I might lose my Cal. He's only sixteen. He never tells me anything of what he does.'

Kerry sighed and stood up. Maria knew the meeting was over.

'Cal's a young man now, Maria. He's not going to tell you everything. You know that.' Kerry paused. 'But he will be all right. He'll have learned from what happened, and he knows that he's got a lot more to learn. He'll be fine.'

Maria dropped her gaze to the floor for a second and Kerry's heart sank a little. She knew that Maria was well aware that she had nowhere else to go. She stepped close to her friend and they hugged tight before Maria turned and went out of the door without another word.

Kerry left the kitchen and headed down the hallway towards her study. She opened the door to see the bruised and swollen faces of Cal and Tahir.

In the fading afternoon light, they looked like battered children from some kind of conflict you would see on television. She quelled her shock and strode across to them, where they looked at her, sheepish through swollen eyes. Kerry stood over them, hands on hips, as Jack gave her a look. She could tell by the body language that he had been laying into them.

'You're in some nick, lads,' Kerry said, glancing from one to the other. 'What in Christ's name possessed you to go on some kind of suicide mission to Springburn?' She kept her voice soft but firm. 'Just who do you think you are? You think this is some kind of movie you're in?'

The two of them sat statue still, looking at the floor.

'Look at me!' Kerry's voice went up a little. 'I'm seriously considering letting the pair of you go. Completely. Out. You know what I mean? Do you understand that?'

They nodded. Kerry folded her arms.

'I don't hear you.'

'Yes,' Cal and Tahir muttered in unison.

'Is that what you want? Because there are plenty of other half-arsed thugs out there who'd be glad of a couple of idiots they can use as cannon fodder. You might make a few quid and have a bit of a swagger about you, but they will eat you up and spit you out. Is that what you want? Because you are free to walk out of that door right now and never come back here.'

Both of them shifted in their seats.

'No,' Cal said.

'No,' Tahir said shaking his head.

'We're sorry,' Cal said.

'It's my fault,' Tahir said. 'I shouldn't have led Cal into the danger. It was me. I was trying to help my friend . . . she–'

Kerry interrupted.

'I know what you were trying to do, Tahir. Jack has already told me everything. But that doesn't matter a damn. You work for me, you do what I tell you, or you disappear right now.' She paused, feeling sorry for the two of them, for Tahir with his handsome young face now bearing a scar that would identify him for the rest of his life. 'I have plans for this organisation. Good things that will happen, and I only want to have people around me who will listen to and learn from the trusted men who have been with me for years. I don't need young boys to make my plans any better. So far you've done very well and Jack told me you'd been shaping up. Earning your stripes.'

'It won't happen again,' Cal said.

Tahir shook his head in agreement. 'Never,' he said. 'We are sorry.'

Kerry stepped back. She'd had enough of this for the day. She couldn't be wet-nursing teenagers who were stepping out of line. If it hadn't been for Cal being Maria's son, she would have told Jack to send them packing. But she couldn't do that. And right now, she needed all the hands she could get. Even young boys like them had a role. They'd already proved their worth on the ground, they were plucky and smart. But not smart enough to know when they were walking into an ambush. Perhaps it was time to take them out of the game and let them do menial tasks. She'd speak to Jack and Danny about it later. She looked at Jack and signalled that the meeting was over.

'Right. Let's go, boys. I've got work for you,' Jack said.

Kerry was preparing to go over to Danny's house to have dinner with him and Auntie Pat. The occasional meals she had there made her feel the presence of her mother, who was there in Pat's actions and smile, and she loved to sit and talk of the old days. It was like therapy, to get away from everything that was blowing up all around them. She was showered and dressed and downstairs, having phoned the driver to meet her in the yard. It had crossed her mind that she would want to confide in Pat that she was pregnant, but she swiftly batted the idea away. Where would she even begin with that story? Once it was told, it put an entirely different complexion on everything, and she knew that Danny, much as he would support her all the way, would be concerned that she was in this predicament. Mingling with the cops was one thing, he'd told her, when she'd had to reveal that she'd had a fling with Vinny Burns – even a fling wasn't the end of the world, though he'd urged caution – but actually having a baby with a cop who was on the other side of everything that they were doing right now would cause an explosion. He'd perhaps think that being pregnant by Vinny might cloud her judgement. Throwing it into the mix wouldn't be a good idea. She was about to get her jacket from the hall cupboard when she spotted Danny, Jack and Mick coming out of a car that had just pulled into the yard. Their faces were grey with concern. It could only be bad news.

She stood in the kitchen as the door opened and Danny came in, his eyes on fire with rage.

'What's up?' Kerry asked, dreading the answer.

'Jimmy McConnell. Bastards shot him. Point-blank. In the middle of the fucking street.'

'Oh, Christ! Not Jimmy!'

Kerry's knees felt a little wobbly. Jimmy was only twenty-five and one of the young guns who had been with the family for the past few years. He was whip smart and a lovely, loyal tough guy who would have done anything for Kerry. His wife had just given birth to twins.

'Is he . . .?'

Danny nodded.

'Oh aye. Fuckers got him right in the back of the head.'

He ran his hand through his hair, and Kerry noticed they were shaking. Danny was sixty-two now. He shouldn't be picking up dead bodies.

'What happened?'

Jack spoke. 'He was coming out of the bookies going to the bank and somebody must have followed him. He wasn't carrying any money, so he might have been on a private errand or something. But on the way back they got him. As he crossed the road and got close to the bookies, the car pulled up. Apparently one guy got out, door still open. Went right up, put a bullet in and jumped back into the moving car.'

'Christ!' Kerry said. 'Where is he?'

'The ambulance came. But he was already dead. He'll be in the hospital mortuary.'

'Jesus. Does his wife know?'

Danny shook his head. 'I need to go there now. Before it comes on the evening news.'

'You want me to come?'

'No,' Danny said. 'I'll do it. Jimmy was my boy. I trained him up. Had high hopes for him. Jimmy wasn't just a guy with a gun, he was smart. He was the kind of lad you could have moved up in the game. Anywhere. Maybe even Spain.' He sighed angrily. 'Fucking bastards. They'll pay for this.'

'Any ideas? What's the word?'

'Don't know. It's a hit. A planned hit. So Rodriguez has still got somebody on his side over here. Not that we didn't expect him to hit back here as well as Spain. But we'll find who he's working with here, all right.'

CHAPTER TWENTY-EIGHT

Frankie Martin stood across from O'Donoghue's bar in Dublin. He'd crossed from his hotel through St Stephen's Green, stopping at one point to sit on a bench and listen to a busker strumming his guitar to some old ballad. For a ridiculous moment he'd even felt like any other tourist enjoying the softness of the morning. But Frankie was far from that. The last time he'd been here was two years ago, with Mickey Casey, for a meet with Pat Durkin to set up the deal that would let them be bigger players in the game. Now, as he sparked up a cigarette and took a long drag, it wasn't lost on him that he was the last man standing of the trio. It wasn't something he'd be putting on his CV as an asset. But then again, the guys he was about to meet wouldn't see it like that. The fact that Mickey and Durkin were dead and he wasn't would tell them that he was a survivor. But it might also tell them that he was a treacherous bastard, which was closer to the truth. Either way,

Frankie wasn't about to start stressing over what they might think of him. Because when it came down to the bare bones, every fucker could be bought. Even though the boys he was about to meet were loyal soldiers of Pat Durkin, he knew they'd soon dry their tears if there was a whiff of greenbacks. He took one last puff of his cigarette and tossed it away as he crossed the street and pushed through the swing doors of the pub. The bar was busy with lunchtime punters, hung-over stag party lads topping up with a hair of the dog, and tourists taking the weight off weary feet. Frankie took a couple of steps into the throng at the bar, his eyes scanning the room for a face he recognised. Then a voice behind him in his ear.

'All right, Frankie?'

Frankie turned around slowly, because deep down you never really knew who was breathing in your ear like this. He was met by the roguish grin of big Dessie O'Brien.

'Howya, you handsome fucker?' The big man's blue eyes twinkled in his granite face.

'All the better for seeing you, big stuff.'

Frankie smiled back at him, even though he wasn't actually glad to be seeing Dessie's face at this stage of the game. He thought he was here to see Joe Boy O'Leary and Felix Riordan, two of Durkin's closest associates who ran the Dublin coke trade for him. O'Brien was obviously here for the muscle, and who could blame Joe Boy and Felix these days if they never crossed the door without serious protection. Nobody would make a move on you if Big Dessie was there. A settled traveller, but fighting gypsy at heart, Dessie could pull an attacker's arms off and stuff them up their arse if the need arose. Frankie had seen him take out three men in a fistfight one night, tossing them into the River Liffey like a discarded chip bag.

'The lads are up the back. Come on.'

Frankie felt the grip of Dessie's giant hand on his upper arm as he ushered him through the packed pub.

The crowd thinned out the further along the bar they went, until there was a table at the far corner, where Joe Boy and Felix sat with pints of just poured Guinness. They looked up at him as he approached, but their expressions were not glad-to-see-you-mate. Frankie knew they'd be looking for a post-mortem into Durkin's demise, so he'd have to put on his best funereal face.

Joe Boy got up first and stretched out his hand.

'Frankie. Good to see you.'

'You too, man,' Frankie said shaking his hand warmly.

As Felix stood up, Frankie reached out to shake his hand. Felix's eyes narrowed a little, and he seemed to hang back for two beats, but eventually he took Frankie's hand.

'What in fuck's name happened out there with Pat? Brutal, man! Fucking brutal!' Felix said, looking Frankie in the eye.

'Totally,' Frankie replied. 'And so fucking unexpected.' He sat down. 'We were just sitting there and the Colombian was banging on about how there was a failure in Glasgow with the operation to get Kerry Casey. Then out of fucking nowhere, one of his boys pulled a gun and stuck it right into Pat's head. Fucking awful to see.' Frankie shook his head as if it had actually bothered him.

'What did *you* do?' Felix asked.

'What did *I* do? Are you fucking kidding me, Felix? Pat's lying on the deck with blood seeping out of his head, and Rodriguez is sitting there calm as fuck. I did absolutely nothing. I'm not stupid.' He paused. He wasn't afraid of these two dicks by any means, but they were entitled to an explanation. Frankie leaned forward. 'But the thing is, as you know, it went tits up in Glasgow. I was nowhere near that. I wanted to be, or at least to be able to advise Pat about anything that would help with the landscape, but he fucking froze me a bit on it. I don't know why that was. He said he had his own men, and some of the Irish boys in Glasgow, and he said it was sorted. I wasn't required. So I was never involved in it. Look, I'm not saying it would have been different if I had. But I know the Caseys. Fuck, man! I grew up with them. I know how they operate. If Pat had brought me in I could at least have marked his card.'

The pair said nothing for a few moments, but Frankie knew they would be aware of some of what happened with the Glasgow operation, and they would have to admit to themselves that it had been a failure.

'Drink, Frankie?' Joe Boy asked. 'Then we'll get talking.'

'Aye,' Frankie said. 'I'll have a large vodka and fresh orange.' He half smiled. 'I'm on a health kick.'

Joe Boy looked up to where Dessie was hovering with a pint in his hand, and told him to go and get the drink. Frankie breathed a little sigh of relief. He had business to do with these boys today, and he needed them onside. He knew it was risky coming to Dublin after Durkin had been executed in front of his nose in this new set-up they were all involved in. But he thought it was worth the risk. He'd told Rodriguez there would be repercussions from the Durkin clan over what happened, and it was in his interests to quell any trouble before it started. That's why he was here. To keep them in the fold. And to get them to help him in the fight ahead in Glasgow. They were all on the same shitty ship here. There were no lifebelts if you jumped over the side. All of them were chasing money and power. Frankie had to convince them that he could bring that to their doorstep.

Dessie returned and placed Frankie's drink on the table, then he retreated to the bar to watch the football match on TV, as well as keeping an eye for any trouble coming in the door. Frankie took a good swig of his drink. He had the feeling he might need it to get through whatever lay ahead here.

'So,' Joe Boy sat forward, folding his arms on the table, 'this Colombian fucker. What's he like?' He rubbed the back of his hand across his nose and sniffed. 'I think we can safely say he's a bit of a ruthless cunt, given what happened with Pat. But tell me, Frankie, because you're right in there now. Why should me and the rest of the posse here throw in everything with him? We're pretty much top dogs here. Sure, we've got the fucking ongoing turf shit with the Monaghans, but that's just the way it works. We're getting the better of them though. No doubt about that.'

'Sure,' Frankie said. 'But you could make it happen quicker, if you had more heavy-duty help.'

'Meaning what?' Joe Boy asked as Felix also sat forward.

Frankie took another swig of his drink, holding the moment as he sensed they took the bait.

'Rodriguez will throw anything you need at it. Money, guns, bodies – anything you need to stamp all over the Monaghans, wipe them out. Once they're bleeding, the smart ones will either come over to you or fuck off out of the game.'

Frankie watched as Joe Boy glanced at Felix as they both processed the information. They were no rocket scientists, this pair, but it wasn't rocket science to know how to wipe out your enemies. You just pummelled them into the ground, picked them off until every one of them was shit scared to step out of the door, and they didn't even feel safe in their own homes. Any turf wars Frankie and Mickey had sorted in Glasgow were small scale though, among no-mark toerags who had got too big for their boots. They were easy to beat, but there was always the next dipshit, fresh out of jail and feeling like Al Capone, who thought they could take on the Caseys. Frankie and Mickey had always relished the challenge. But the Dublin drug wars were bigger than anything he'd ever done. Two gangland families had been going at it for years and there was blood all over the walls. Even the cops couldn't get to grips with it. But Frankie hadn't come here to sell the idea that the Colombians would throw in handers with Durkin's boys. He'd come to make sure he could get them onside to take on the Caseys and help trample their empire. That was the brief from Rodriguez, but it was up to Frankie how he worked it. If it meant pitching in with them to get rid of their own enemies, that wasn't a problem.

Joe Boy looked at Felix and they both finally nodded.

'That's good to know, Frankie. I like that.' He paused. 'But we've also got a big operation here. I mean, our coke market alone is massive. You know that. We've got our own people we deal with in Spain and Amsterdam. We don't have a problem with supply and shit, so why do we need to do business with Rodriguez? I know Pat talked it up to us before he left. He convinced us that by pitching in with the Colombian, we'd have access to some big fuck-off hotel complex and much more property than we already have. But then he bumps Durkin off. I mean, where does that leave us?' He lowered his voice. 'I'll tell you the problem we have at the moment. I've had the accountants looking at our investments and money and where everything is, but it's looking like Pat moved a substantial amount to Spain. The accountant said he was investing in new business. But where the fuck is this new business? That's what I want to know. Has Pat invested our money with this Colombian cunt?'

Frankie had never been that close to the conversations between Durkin and Rodriguez, so he couldn't say if the Irish mob's money was now already in Rodriguez's grasp. But he suspected it was.

'I can't tell you the answer to that, guys. But all I know is that Pat was thick as thieves with Rodriguez. He was heavily into their operation, and it was him and Billy Hill who were selling the Colombian to the Caseys at that meeting with Kerry Casey a few weeks ago. But it was a frosty meeting and she didn't get on with Rodriguez, so that's why there was a bit of trouble there in the past couple of weeks.'

'I know about that,' Felix said. 'What the fuck was that all about? O'Driscoll? Cut his fucking head off? That's bad craic, man. Bad craic. O'Driscoll was all right. He was over here a few months ago and was a sound man.'

'He was,' Frankie said, recalling how he and O'Driscoll had grown up with the Caseys. 'It was a bad business, and I pointed that out to Pat and to Rodriguez after it happened.'

'What did Pat say?'

'To tell you the truth, he wasn't that arsed about it at all. He was . . . How can I put this without being insulting? He was kind of carried away by the Colombian and the way he did business. Like he was infatuated by the power he seemed to have,' Frankie exaggerated.

'Fuck's sake,' Felix said. 'What the fuck happened to Pat!'

'Who knows,' Frankie said. 'But that's over now. All you can do is move forward. Keep going. Look, you can only work with what you've got in front of you. And you need to look and see what your best opportunities are.'

They sat for a long moment in silence, and Frankie swirled the ice at the bottom of his glass, then signalled to Dessie for another. The big man came over to the table and the other two ordered two more pints.

'So,' Frankie said. 'Another situation I want to talk to you about.' He paused. 'Kerry Casey.'

'Mickey's sister,' Joe Boy said. 'She sounds ballsy enough all right.'

'She is that,' Frankie said. 'But she'll come a cropper.'

'Tell that to your Colombian mate who got a fucking bullet in his leg when he tried to take her on in her own turf,' Felix grinned. 'That was a fucking belter, by the way.'

Frankie nodded, half smiling. 'Yeah. It was that. But it shouldn't have happened. The operation wasn't handled properly. She should have been there for the taking. She *is* there for the taking.'

'What do you mean?'

'Rodriguez is taking everything from her. Everything. The hotel in Spain. The property investments along the coasts, the bars and restaurants in Glasgow. He's taking the lot. By doing what you need to do to your enemies here in Dublin. By wiping the Caseys out.' Frankie paused. 'That's where he wants your help.'

Joe Boy and Felix shot each other a glance and sat back. They said nothing.

'There's a big prize here, if we all pitch in together. You take the Monaghans and the Caseys out of the game, and you throw in with the Colombians in Spain, everything opens up to you.' He spread his hands. 'And by the way, Rodriguez's mob is closing down everything in distribution in Spain. Anyone you dealt with in the past might not be dealing with you in the future. Or, if you deal with them, you'll find it's Rodriguez's guys at the other end of the phone. He's cleaning up over there, I'm telling you. Why do you think I'm there?'

'I thought you were there because the Caseys will shoot the fuck out of you if you ever set foot back in Glasgow,' Felix said, his voice laced with sarcasm.

'Aye, right,' Frankie said. 'I'm in Spain because I can see the big picture, and I can see who's going to be in that picture. And the Caseys are not in it. They'll be history by the time this is finished.'

'And what about us? Can you see us in this big picture?'

'Of course,' Frankie said. 'If we work together. We can run the whole fucking show from here to London to Spain. We can be bigger than ever.'

Joe Boy nodded slowly. Frankie knew he had laid it out on the table for them. At the end of the day, it wasn't really negotiable. Joe Boy and Felix knew the Colombians were bigger than any of them, or all of them put together. Only stupid people like Kerry Casey thought she could take them on and win. But the Irish weren't that daft. They knew that the man who had come to see them today was making them an offer they couldn't really refuse.

CHAPTER TWENTY-NINE

Kerry wasn't sure if she was doing the right thing, but the thought had been niggling away at her for the past few days, so she'd decided she wanted to run it past Danny and Jack. The way things were going in Spain with the fire-bombing of the bars and near-demolition of the hotel site – the cost of the damage running to hundreds of thousands of pounds – had made her wonder if her dreams were just that – dreams. The Caseys were criminals. Even if she didn't want to remember her beloved father as a criminal, she knew that's what he was. She'd always known, growing up – nobody else in the housing scheme where she grew up was living like they were. But being sent away and living abroad, she'd always felt detached enough from it, and even though she'd been educated and lived off the wealth her father created as his criminal empire grew, it had been easy for her to not think about it. But all that had been a very long time ago. And if she was ever in any doubt that the Caseys were deep in the criminal underworld, it was never more clear to her than at the bloodbath at Mickey's funeral. It had only been weeks ago, but it seemed longer somehow, and so much had happened so fast. Acquiring the hotel site and having Sharon on board had seemed like they were headed in a direction where she really could do just one last bit of business and then look to buying property and a legitimate future for the Caseys. Danny and Jack were happy to go in whatever direction the Casey family went. They'd been there most of their lives, and they knew Kerry was carrying on her father's dream of being a legit business empire. But it was slipping from her grasp now. She'd been thinking of Vinny's proposal that they should work with them and the criminal intelligence force and bring down the Colombians. Of course she knew he was right, but was that really who she was? Deep down, she knew she had it in her to deal with the cops – which in most criminals' eyes would make her a grass. But she didn't see it like that. She saw it as a means to an end. She did have the fight in her to take the Colombians all the way, but at what cost? Could she really stomach it if the bodies seriously started piling up, and she was the head of the family who was sending people to their death on a daily basis? Her niggling conscience wasn't how criminals thought, she told herself, and even though she continually pushed those thoughts away, they kept creeping up on her. She knew they would never be forgiven in the criminal world for working with the cops, and nobody would ever trust a Casey again. But what if all that was left after the war with the Colombians was over was the house she was standing in? In order to be honest with herself, she'd decided just to sound out Danny and Jack, to share her thoughts with them and see how they would react. Now she heard the door of the study and their voices outside, then the door opened and she beckoned them in.

'Danny, Jack,' Kerry said as they entered the room. 'How's it going? You know, I'm almost afraid to ask these days.' She managed a half smile and they both nodded in agreement.

'Aye,' Danny said. 'It's beginning to look like World War fucking Three. Especially over in Spain. We've been beefing things up there, but these Colombian bastards have got a lot of bodies on the ground, Kerry. They're everywhere. And what we're hearing is this Rodriguez bastard is bringing other players into his mob – other dealers and traffickers who've been working for years with various gangs from here to London and Dublin, are now moving over to him.'

'But what's going on? How come they're just buckling like that? There must be some hard bastards over there who have been years getting themselves established. Why are they rolling over?'

Jack sighed. 'The way I hear it, they're being offered big deals, better distribution than they already have, so it's cheaper to bring their stuff into the UK. And also, the Colombian is promising them the purest coke, so it can be cut up more, giving them more profit. That's what the talk is anyway.'

'But they're giving up their independence. Selling out.'

Danny shrugged. 'Maybe a question of not selling out, but more a matter of no option. The word is well out on how they dealt with O'Driscoll, and the cold execution of Pat Durkin. That will send messages across the board that anyone is fair game. Durkin and his mob have been massive in Spain for a generation, then just like that, bang, he's out of the game. I've heard that Durkin's extended crew are raging, but I also heard something else, last night.' He paused, looked at Kerry and Jack. 'I didn't want to phone you about it, Kerry, because I wanted to verify it first. And I have. About an hour ago.'

'What?' Kerry asked.

'That fucker Frankie. He's over in Dublin, tapping up Durkin's boys to come over to his side.'

'Christ!' Kerry said. 'Will that happen?'

Danny nodded. 'Oh, aye. It'll happen. There's a lot of bad feeling about Durkin among his boys and closest associates. He was a big player with a lot of people in his organisation. But they won't *all* want to take on the Colombians. If Frankie is offering them a deal to join up with them, then I'll be surprised if they don't.'

'And what about the other family in Dublin?' Kerry asked. 'The Monaghans. What happens with them?'

'Well,' Danny said, 'if Durkin's mob join with Frankie

and the Colombians, then the Monaghans will be history before too long.'

Kerry shook her head. 'So what do we do about that?' She looked at both of them. 'Can we get the Monaghans to join with us?' She felt seriously out of her depth.

They sat for a moment, then Jack spoke. 'Too early to approach them, I'd say. But we might have to look at that. We've never had any bad blood with the Monaghans. In old man Durkin's day it was accepted that people dealt with whoever they wanted, and we *chose* to work with them and not the Monaghans. But it was amicable. We never did them any harm and they never bothered us. They did their business and we did ours – kind of mutual respect.'

'Okay,' Kerry said. 'Worth thinking about.' She took a long breath and they sat for a moment as she worked out how to pick her words.

'I wanted to speak to you, Danny and Jack, to run some thoughts past you.'

They looked at her, interested, but said nothing.

'It's about Vinny. He came to me recently – I told you, during the kidnap. And he seemed to be well informed about the Colombians' every step and assumed I knew what was going on. Of course I said nothing to him, and we resolved the kidnapping by ourselves. But he was planting the seed about us coming in with the cops – I mean the whole criminal intelligence mob across Europe and the DEA – and working with them. He was making all sorts of promises that we would be allowed to operate after it was over, but that we could bring down the Colombians. He said that once we got Rodriguez out of the way, we would be allowed to carry on until our goal of going legit. He even said we would be protected by their people over in Spain.'

Danny and Jack looked at each other, eyebrows raised.

'Sounds like a right bag of shite to be wading into though – then you can't get back out. I mean how the fuck can we trust cops?' Danny puffed. 'And apart from that, who the fuck would ever trust us again after that if it came out that we were working with cops? '

Kerry shrugged a little. 'Well we did trust the cops before – with Knuckles. And we got through it, lived to tell the tale.'

'But this is different,' Danny said. 'This is the Colombians, who might well get the whole of the crews across Spain and Dublin in with them, and we're the only ones they're fighting. Except we're with cops. That would get out, Kerry. We'd get lynched one by one.'

'I know,' Kerry conceded. 'That's one of the things I'd be afraid of. One of many . . .'

'Too true,' Jack said.

'It's just a thought I wanted to put to you. What do you think? Would it be worth even having a further talk with Vinny? All three of us? Nothing guaranteed, by any means. Just a talk? We don't give anything away. Though, to be honest, I sometimes think he knows more about what we're doing than I do.'

Jack and Danny looked at each other, then after a few beats, Danny spread his hands.

'Nothing wrong with having a chat with the cops. Or with Vinny. But just him. I quite liked the guy, and he was good as his word the last time. But this is a much bigger deal. We're not talking about taking out a dick like Knuckles Boyle. This is the Colombians. But there's nothing to be lost by just having a chat with him.'

'Okay,' Kerry said. She didn't know if she was pleased about it or terrified. 'I'll give him a call. See if we can have a meet. In here, so we can be private.'

After they left, Kerry stood at the window, watching them talking to a couple of the security men, as though they were issuing instructions or getting information. Then they got into their cars and drove out of the steel gates. She crossed the room and picked up her mobile and held it in her hand for a moment, staring at the screen. It was over a week since Vinny had spoken to her, and deep down, she thought he would have been back in touch, not to ask about a deal, but on a personal level. She chided herself for feeling that, because what they'd had was over, and she'd been convincing herself of that every day. Or trying to. She steeled herself for the call. She would be friendly and to the point. She'd tell him she wanted to meet him for a chat along with a couple of her most trusted men. No doubt he'd be over like a shot. She'd never really got the impression that Vinny was ambitious in his career. If he had been, he would probably have risen higher up the ranks by now, in London or wherever he wanted to be. He probably could have gone right to the top. But he'd told her he was driven to do the right thing, to get his hands dirty, because of some of the things he'd seen done to innocent people through drugs, especially when he worked in Colombia. Part of her was afraid to get involved with him because of his passion to bring down the cartels. The Caseys would be getting used by the police, and they would want their pound of flesh. How did she know they could even trust the cops not to throw her people to the wolves in their own quest to destroy the cartels? She didn't want her people to be cannon fodder. But she had to test the water. She scrolled down and hit the key for Vinny's mobile. It didn't ring. Just what sounded like a network voice saying, 'This number is no longer in use.' She tried it again. Same voice. That's strange, she thought. People like Vinny never changed their mobile number. Too many people you knew had your number for you to start again with a new one. Her gut told her there was something odd about it. Before she could stop herself, she had looked up the number for Glasgow Police HQ, and asked to be put through to the specialist squad where she knew he worked. The phone rang a few times, then a male voice answered.

'Crime Intelligence.'

She felt a little flustered, but quickly calmed herself.

'Hello. Er. Sorry to bother you. I'm looking for DI Burns. DI Vincent Burns. Is he available at the moment?'

Silence. Kerry held her breath.

'Hello?' she said.

'Hold on a moment please. Who is this calling?'

'My name is Kerry Casey.' She knew he would recognise the name.

'Hold on please.'

Something wasn't right. She stood, the phone pressed to her ear, listening for any noise she could hear in the background. Then a different male voice came on the line.

'Hello. Can I help you?'

'Hello. I'm looking for DI Vincent Burns. Is he available?'

'Who's this please?'

Kerry was getting irritated.

'It's Kerry Casey. I just told your colleague. I wanted to speak to DI Burns.'

'Can I help you at all, Miss Casey? DI Burns is not here.'

'Do you know when he'll be back? I tried his mobile. We spoke recently, and I had his mobile number, but it's saying it's no longer in use.'

Silence. Kerry waited but there was no response.

'Could you possibly give me his new mobile?'

'No. Sorry. I don't have that.'

'Could you get a message to him? Ask him to give me a call when he has a moment.'

'Can I help you at all?'

'Christ!' Kerry said under her breath. 'No. You can't. I wanted to speak to DI Burns. Will he be back in later?'

Silence.

'No, Miss Casey. DI Burns won't be back. He doesn't work here any more.'

Kerry felt as though someone had punched her in the stomach. Had Vinny just completely gone? Had he disappeared, decided for his own good it would be better if they got out of each other's lives? There was no sign the last time they spoke that he was going to leave Glasgow. But maybe he had decided there was nothing more to stay for.

'Okay, thanks,' Kerry said. 'Has he gone back down to the Met? I know you can't tell me that, but if he has, perhaps you could get in touch with him and ask him to call me some time. There's a business matter I wanted to discuss.'

Silence.

'I don't know where he works now. I'm sorry, I can't help you. But if you have something to discuss with the police, I'm happy to get someone to come along and see you.'

'No, thanks. It's all right. That's fine. Thanks for your help.'

She hoped whoever was on the phone didn't catch the tremor in her voice. She was more shocked and devastated than she would have believed possible. Vinny was gone. Just like that. He'd walked into her life, then walked straight back out. Just as he'd done all those years ago.

CHAPTER THIRTY

Sharon was on her way to a crisis meeting with the four closest associates of the Casey family on the Costa del Sol. Two more bars had been torched last night, and an estate agents' office they operated down near Estepona was ransacked, with computer files and disks stolen. The attack on the estate agent could be hugely damaging. Although she was told that everything they'd stolen was backed up on files centrally, the fact that they'd been in there and got hold of files and clients' accounts, maybe even bank accounts, could cause all sorts of chaos, even sabotage potential deals that were in the making. The bars would be refurbished, and customers would filter back, but all this shit was bringing more and more police scrutiny on the Costa and that was the last thing they needed at the moment.

She'd called Kerry this morning to tell her the bad news, and thought she'd sounded more down than she had been in recent days. Probably the hormones, she thought. But when Kerry told her that Vinny seemed to have disappeared, Sharon guessed that was the root of the problem. Kerry always gave the impression that whatever she'd had with Vinny was dead and buried – despite being pregnant with his child – but that didn't fool Sharon.

But Vinny was gone now, and with everything falling down around them, the only thing to do was fight on. Kerry had told her of her meeting with Danny and Jack where they'd discussed Vinny's proposal to come onside with the cops. She told Kerry that if she'd been at the meeting, she'd have suggested they think seriously about getting into bed with the cops. Sure, it went against everything she'd done, and the life of crime she'd lived with Knuckles Boyle, but this was now about survival. And the way it was looking, they were being pummelled from every angle. Especially now, with that spineless bastard Frankie Martin pitching in with Durkin's mob in Dublin. That could only mean trouble for Kerry wherever she operated. But with Vinny Burns going off the radar, throwing in with the cops might well be off the table as an option now. Vinny she trusted, but she couldn't be sure of anyone else. They were all just going to have to dig in and fight their way out of this.

Sharon's driver took the slip road off the motorway and into the small town of San Pedro, where the meet had been arranged. The former fishing village had grown and spread out over the years and was a favourite haunt for ex-pats who wanted to stay away from places like Fuengirola and Torremolinos where there were hordes of tourists all year round. The four-by-fours pulled up outside the small restaurant, and two of Sharon's bodyguards got out first and did a quick scan of the area before one of them opened the car door for her. She got out and walked into the restaurant and headed for the back of the room where she could see four of the Caseys' men already sitting. Big Phil McCann, whom she'd met when she first got down here, was first on his feet to welcome her. He was from Glasgow but had been based down here for the past eight years looking after several bars and expanding the Caseys' property empire. With his cropped salt-and-pepper hair and smart clothes he looked like a well-heeled executive, but Danny had told her Phil had made his reputation by the age of fifteen in Glasgow when he walked into a bar and shot dead the two hardened criminals who had murdered his big brother in cold blood in front of his wife and family. By the time he was twenty Phil had a few other scalps under his belt, and his path in life was well and truly settled. Now in his forties, he was wealthy, being allowed by the Caseys to run his own show over on the Costa on what was considered their turf but with a huge pay-off for himself and his organisation.

'Sharon,' he said. 'Aren't these some bastard days we're in.'

'They sure are, Phil.' She glanced around the others who all kind of grimaced back, then sat down.

'So,' Sharon said. 'Any more bad news on top of the bad news? What about the files from the estate agent? I'm worried about that and so is Kerry. Have we any intelligence at all that we can use to track them down?'

'We have.' Alex Murray, a dark-haired suntanned squat guy in his forties nodded. 'We're on it. I've got info on who the actual fuckers were who carried out the robbery. So it's a start. I've got someone picking them up today, so we'll get something out of them. Let's hope it's not too late.'

'I was talking to Pete at the estate agent,' Sharon said, 'and he's already emailing everyone on their client list and letting them know there's been a robbery and to respond to nothing unless it is directly from a member of staff. The office will be up and running again in the next twenty-four hours.'

'Good,' Phil said. He turned to a tall, lean man with a scar down his left cheek and a shaved head. 'What about the pubs, Matt. Any intel?'

Matt was the go-to guy who had friends all over the Costa, and if someone needed finding, he could track them down. He was a handsome, blue-eyed charmer, who moved in all sorts of social circles, but anyone who double-crossed him never lived to brag about it.

'We pulled in a guy this morning – wee scally from Liverpool who's on the run down here. Somebody from across the street said they saw him hanging around late last night at one of the bars, so I think he must be up to something.

He's being questioned as we speak.' Matt drew his lips back a little in a sarcastic smile.

Just at that moment, Sharon's mobile rang and she was about to let it ring out when she looked and saw Vic's number.

'Excuse me a second, guys, I have to take this.' She pushed the phone to her ear and waited for a voice.

'Sharon. Get out of there now! Hurry! There's a crew on its way to blast everyone. I've only just heard. They'll be there any minute. Hurry!'

Sharon felt her legs go weak. She turned to look at everyone and they obviously saw the colour drain from her face.

'We need to go. Quick. A fucking Rodriguez hit squad is on its way.'

Nobody said a word. Everyone got up, pulled guns out. Suddenly there came the sound of a car screeching to a halt, and they all looked at each other, then around for an exit.

'Fuck!' Phil said. 'Sharon. Come with me.' He pushed her down to a crouching position as the sound of gunfire cracked outside.

When Sharon looked up, none of the others was there, the place was in silence, and she assumed they must be hiding. Then two masked gunmen burst inside with machine guns and peppered the whole place, one of them jumping behind the bar and firing. There were groans and shouts. Others were shooting back and one of the masked men went down. Phil shot another in the leg. He was hit on the shoulder. But he pulled Sharon over to the back door where they slithered out and into the car park. There was the sound of police sirens. Then Tom came staggering out, bloodstained.

'The fuckers got Billy. He's in a bad way. Losing a lot of blood.'

'Cops will be here any minute, Tom. Go back in and see what you can find on those two cunts on the ground. See who they are.'

Tom ran in without questioning. Sharon looked up as one of her bodyguards came skulking round the corner, gun in hand. Then Tom reappeared.

'They got Donny, Sharon. He's dead. You all right? We best get out of here.'

'Christ!' Sharon said.

Donny was in his early thirties, had been in Spain five years and was married to a Spanish girl, who was now pregnant. He was brought along as an extra hand as well as Billy, who'd only arrived from the UK three weeks ago after a three-year stretch for armed robbery, and was working for the Caseys.

Sharon didn't have time to think. Phil helped her to her feet and Tom rushed her to the car, as Phil jumped into his Merc and sped off.

'I need to talk to Dave,' Sharon said as she got into the passenger seat of the car. She looked at her watch. 'He should be picking up Tony around this time. Let's go there too. Just to make sure he's all right.'

Sharon pressed the speed dial for Dave, the big bodyguard who picked up Tony from school every day and brought him back to the house. But the phone was going straight to messages.

'He's not answering.' She glanced nervously at her watch again. 'That worries me, after what just happened.' She pushed out a sigh. 'Christ! What just happened in there, Tom? How the hell did these bastards know where we were when we only made the arrangement this morning?'

Tom shook his head. He'd been Sharon's main bodyguard since she arrived in Spain. The big, serious Glaswegian was a convicted armed robber, used for his brains and brawn. He was now forty, and moved over to the Costa to work with the Caseys eighteen months ago. He ran their illegal gambling shops from bars along the coast and was close to Donny.

'I don't know, Sharon. But we need to find out. They were on top of us in no time. As soon as we saw the car coming screeching down the street, we had our guns out. But they came out guns blazing and Donny got it straight away. Christ! His brains were on the fucking pavement. How am I going to tell his wife? Poor kid.'

'I know,' Sharon replied, her eyes scanning the landscape now that they were approaching the back road towards the school. She could see streams of cars coming towards her and passing.

'School must be out. Those will be parents' cars. Dave should have picked up by now. Why the hell isn't he answering his mobile?'

She rang it again, but nothing. She rang Tony's mobile, but it went straight to voicemail. She could feel her heart begin to beat faster.

By the time they got to the school there was only a handful of cars parked and most of the kids had filtered out. Sharon was opening the door even before the car pulled to a stop. She jumped out.

'Wait here. I'll check to see if he's out yet.'

But she knew even before she rushed up the steps to the school entrance that Tony was already gone. A middle-aged woman who she knew was the guidance teacher approached her with a slightly bewildered look.

'Sorry, Mrs . . .' Sharon was flustered and couldn't remember her name.

The woman gave her an understanding smile.

'Temple,' she said. 'Margaret Temple. How are you, Sharon? Is something the matter? You look a little harassed.'

Sharon swallowed and tried to compose herself.

'Sorry, Margaret. I'm looking for my Tony. The driver picks him up, but I can't get an answer from his mobile, or Tony's. I was passing and got a bit worried.' She paused, afraid to ask. 'Is he . . . I mean, are all the kids gone?'

The teacher cocked her head to the side.

'Yes. Only the ones with games – you know rugby – are

down in the fields, but the rest of them are gone. Tony doesn't play, so he must have been picked up.'

Sharon felt physically sick. She put her hand to her mouth.

'Are you sure?'

The teacher glanced around her and spread her hands.

'They're all out here like lightning at the end of the day. But wait and I'll just check with the office. One of the girls might have seen him go.'

She disappeared into the glass office and returned a few seconds later, looking as though she was trying hard not to frown.

'Yes, Tony's gone,' she said. 'He left in a car, as he usually does. One of the girls was out in the yard at the time, and he got into a car and was driven away.'

'Did she see who was in the car?'

'I don't think she would know who it is that picks him up. I don't think she paid particular attention, to be honest. Quite a few of the parents send their drivers for their kids.'

'Please,' Sharon said. 'I'm sorry. But can you please ask again, was there anyone else in the car?'

The teacher grimaced a little then turned back into the office. She returned again a second later.

'Two people in the car. The man who met him at the gate and another man in the back seat.'

Sharon steadied herself against the wall.

'Are you all right, Sharon? Can I get you a glass of water?'

'No,' Sharon managed to croak. 'Thanks. I'll try his number again.'

Sharon turned and ran out to the car and jumped inside.

'Jesus, Tom! Something's happened. Tony was picked up all right – but there were two people in the car.'

He looked confused.

'Two? It's always Dave. Only Dave. He loves the kid and they have banter all the way home.'

Sharon bit back her tears and tried to breathe, but she could see Tom from the corner of her eye.

'They've taken him, Tom. I know it. Oh please God, don't let anything happen to him.'

'Come on, Sharon! It's probably all right,' Tom said, unconvincingly. 'Maybe he'll be at the house by the time we get there.' He put his foot down and they roared through the country roads and back onto the motorway.

Sharon sniffed as she looked out of the windscreen, trying her best not to break down. Everything she had ever done was for Tony. He was her heart and soul. If anything happened to him and she was to lose him, her life would be over, finished. She clutched her mobile tight, then composed herself as she phoned Kerry.

'Kerry. All hell broke out here earlier. Someone got wind of our meeting, and a mob from Rodriguez came in and shot the place up. We lost two men.'

'Jesus Christ!' Kerry said. 'Are you okay?'

'Yeah. Big Phil took care of me, but they got him in the

shoulder, and we lost one of our bodyguards outside. Our boys got two of theirs too.'

'Shit. How in the name of Christ did they know where the meet was? It was only this morning we arranged it after last night.'

'I don't know. But we're finding out. But, Kerry. Our Tony's gone.' She could hear her voice quiver and she swallowed a sob.

'What? How?'

'He gets picked up from school every day by Dave, one of the guards. Today there was no answer from either of their phones, and so I went to the school straight from the shit earlier, because I was worried. But he's not there. Someone at the school said he got picked up. But there were two people in the car. Two people, Kerry.'

'Jesus,' Kerry murmured. 'Look. Try not to panic. It might be all right. Where are you now?'

'On my way back to the house.'

'Okay, phone me when you get there. But just stay calm. We'll sort this.'

'Kerry,' Sharon tried to speak. 'If anything happens to Tony . . . Oh, Kerry!'

'Sharon!' Kerry said. 'Don't worry. Just go to the house. Call me when you get there.'

When they got to the house and the steel gates opened automatically, a quick glance showed that Dave's car wasn't there and the place was eerily quiet. It was always that way in the afternoon, but now it looked threatening. She glanced across the yard to the main door of the house. The guard in the security cabin at the front gave her a wave. Sharon opened the door and got out of the car, and had to steady herself as her legs felt weak. She rushed across to the security.

'Has Dave been back yet with Tony?'

He shook his head. 'No. Not since he left to pick him up an hour ago.'

Sharon turned to Tom, who strode towards her and ushered her into the house.

Tom went into the kitchen and as Sharon slumped onto the sofa she clutched her mobile, willing it to ring. But it didn't. She sat, sipping the cold sugary drink Tom had made for her to help her shock, and staring at the fireplace, suddenly feeling that her entire life was falling apart. Then her mobile rang. But it wasn't Tony, or Dave. It was Phil.

'Sharon. It's me. We just got a call. These cunts picked up Tony and Dave.'

'Who? Who's the call from?'

'I don't know. Some faceless, nameless cunt, saying he's phoning on behalf of Rodriguez.'

'Christ, Phil. What are they saying? Where's Tony?'

'They said they're dropping both of them off at a café on the boulevard of shops near Marbella.'

'What the fuck? Are they okay?'

'I think so. I've got people heading there now. All they

said was they just wanted you to know that they can do anything they want to anybody they want and, the fucking words were, "You have no power."' He paused. 'If I get my hands on the cunt that made that call, I'll wring his neck myself.'

Sharon didn't know what to think, what to say. Her mind was a blur of what might happen if Phil's boys turned up at the restaurant. Were they being lured into a trap that would be another bloodbath, with her Tony caught in the crossfire?

'Christ, Phil. I want to go there too.'

'No. Sharon. Please. You shouldn't. Just sit tight. We'll get your Tony back. Stay where you are. Honestly. It's the only thing to do.'

Sharon thought about it, and said nothing, then eventually, 'Okay. But please, call me straight away, as soon as anything happens.'

'Don't worry. We will.'

She hung up, looked up at Tom, then stood, but staggered. He held her tight and patted her hair. She loosened her grasp. This was no time for her to go to pieces. She made a vow to herself that when Tony came back here and she was sure he was safe, she would make it her mission to find each and every one involved in snatching him. This was no longer business, as these bastards were fond of saying. It wasn't business when Knuckles Boyle arranged for her to be executed by his associates. It was personal. And taking Tony was as personal as it could get. They would pay for this. Rodriguez would pay personally, and she would make sure of it herself.

She called Kerry to relay the news, then went to her bedroom, lay on the bed and wept.

It was only an hour later that Sharon heard a car on the gravel and she jumped off the bed and went to the window. The car pulled in and she stood, her heart thumping in her chest, as the back door opened. Then Tony got out, looking a little pale but carrying his school rucksack. She took one glimpse then bolted out of the room and downstairs, flung open the front door and raced into the yard.

'Tony! Christ, darling! Are you all right?'

She ran towards him and threw her arms around him, holding him tight. Tony glanced around at the men who'd got out of the car, and for a second he looked a little embarrassed, then he buried his head in his mother's shoulder.

'Oh, Mum! I was scared. But I'm all right. Honest. I'm fine. They didn't hurt me.'

She eased him away, and looked at his face, pushed back the fringe flopping over his eyes.

'Oh, Tony! I was so worried about you.'

'I didn't know what happened. I just went into the car and the guy was there in the back seat. Dave said they'd stopped the car on the way here and told him to come in and get me as normal, and if I moved a muscle, then they'd come out and shoot both of us,' he said, breathless. 'Who are they, Mum? I heard you talking about Colombians or something. Is that who they were? How come they let me live?'

Sharon looked around as Dave stood on the sidelines, giving her a sheepish look.

'I'm sorry, Sharon. There was nothing I could do. I felt so helpless. I'm sorry.'

'Sssh,' Sharon said. 'We'll talk later, Dave. Don't worry. You're all safe now. Go into the house and have a drink and relax a bit.'

'I'm starving,' Tony said.

'Of course you are. Always,' Sharon said smiling, delighted to hear the words she feared she would never hear again.

Sharon was on the flight from Málaga to Glasgow with Tony on the seat next to her before she even had time to think things through. Still reeling from the shock of her son being snatched, she'd talked to Kerry the night before as she was bundling Tony's clothes into a case, determined to get him out of the country pronto. Glasgow may be under siege, but on the Costa del Sol she'd felt suddenly exposed. If she was alone she could cope with hoodlums taking pot shots at her, but worrying twenty-four seven over Tony was killing her. They'd taken him once, they could take him again. Kerry had been understanding and told her they would look after him at the house for a couple of weeks till this heat died down. She'd said she'd even make enquiries about getting some private tutor for him so that he wouldn't miss lessons. And the Casey house was like a fortress, so no matter what was going on outside, Tony would be safe.

Sharon ruffled Tony's hair as the flight took off, but he was eyes down into his book. He hadn't seemed annoyed about leaving his school friends, because the fact was, in recent weeks, he'd hardly seen them due to the tight security. He loved Spain though, and she had to promise him it was only for a few weeks, then he could come back to swimming in the pool and everything else the sunshine had to offer. As the plane took off, a wave of exhaustion swept over Sharon, and she rested her head back and tried to catch some shut-eye on the early afternoon flight.

From her bedroom window, Kerry was glad to see the Merc drive into the yard, and the rear door open. Sharon stepped her long legs out, all Ray-Ban aviator shades and perfect lush blonde hair swirling in the breeze. Kerry felt her face smile a little with the sheer admiration for this woman who she'd grown so close to recently. Their life stories couldn't have been more different, yet here they were, calling the shots in a criminal empire, fighting a war on several fronts, and so far they were still standing. Kerry knew how valuable Danny and Jack and the trusted closest associates had been to her from the start, guiding her through storm after storm. She could not have managed this far without them. But Sharon had also played a major part in her confidence and belief in herself. Sharon was living proof that you get back up when you've been trampled down, and you win. And she was tougher and more ruthless than Kerry when it came to the killer instinct. When she'd called last night to say she wanted to get Tony out of Spain, Kerry didn't hesitate to tell her to bring him to Glasgow. She'd put Tony up in the house. The Caseys would protect him, she promised. And they would.

Kerry went downstairs to the kitchen to greet them.

'Sharon,' she smiled, 'great to see you. And I have to say looking fabulous – considering the shit that's flying around.'

Sharon lowered her shades to reveal dark shadows under her eyes, and Kerry had to concede that sunglasses covered a multitude. But her eyes were clear and full of the usual fire and determination.

'Don't know about that, love,' she said, her voice a little husky. 'I'm bloody knackered, actually. But when the going gets tough . . .' She smiled. 'Well, you just pray it doesn't get much tougher.' She pushed back her hair with her glasses. 'And to think that years ago when the going got tough, I just racked up my credit card. Changed bloody days, I'll tell you.'

Kerry smiled at her bravado.

'You want coffee? We're having dinner here later.'

'Coffee? No thanks, pet. I could do with a stiff drink though.'

Kerry turned to Tony, who was standing silent, and looking a bit shy.

'Hey, Tony. Will be great to have you around the house. Come on. Let's all go upstairs and I'll show you where you'll be staying.' She ushered them to the door. 'Don't worry about your bags, we'll get them brought up.'

While Tony was settling into his new quarters, complete with a massive flat-screen TV, Kerry watched as Sharon swiftly downed a gin and tonic.

'Christ. That hardly touched the sides,' Sharon said.

'Another? We'll be having dinner shortly. I'm sure you can manage one before that.'

'Very small one.'

She sipped her second drink, moving across the room and sitting on the sofa. Kerry sat on the armchair by the fire with a glass of mineral water.

'So, how are you after all the drama of the last few days?' Sharon asked.

'Getting through it. And I like to think we're winning. But the panic and stress with Marty's boy was off the scale. Marty was broken. And now with your Tony being snatched . . .' She shook her head. 'Rodriguez is such a bastard. We really have to get him. We will.'

'If I could get my bloody hands on him . . .'

'I know,' Kerry said. 'But I had Jake Cahill in yesterday

and sent him back to Spain. I told him to concentrate only on taking Rodriguez out.'

'Oh,' Sharon said. 'I didn't know.'

Kerry thought she looked a little deflated, but dismissed it as tiredness.

'That's how Jake works,' she assured. 'When he's given a job, nobody knows what he's doing, but he never fails. And he'll get Rodriguez – that much we can be sure of.'

There was a moment's silence.

'Yeah. I can see how Jake is the man for the job, Kerry.' She pushed out a sigh, sipped her drink. 'But really. I want to ask you something. Something that would mean a lot to me. After our Tony.' There was a catch in her voice. 'You know, in that very moment at the school when my gut dropped, as I realised he'd been taken, I'll never feel terror like that again. Ever.' She swallowed and composed herself. 'I mean, even when Knuckles was about to have me murdered, and I sat in the back of the car that day, I felt cold fear, but nothing like the sheer terror of that moment when I thought maybe I'd never see Tony again. I'll honestly never get over that. And when he came back, much as I was overjoyed and still am every time I look at his face, the need for revenge is eating away at me.' She paused again, took a breath. 'I want to be the one to take Rodriguez out.'

Kerry looked at her, trying to comprehend the depth of her feelings.

'You want to kill Rodriguez? Sure. We all do. But he'll get his day all right. Jake will wipe him out.'

'But, Kerry, the one thing I want to do more than anything in the world is to look him in the eye and tell him that he took my son, my heart and soul, and I want to see the fear in his eyes, when I kill him.'

Kerry was a little taken aback at the intensity in Sharon's voice, the slight flush rising in her cheeks as she went on.

'I'm not an emotional wreck or anything. Not by any means. I'm not going tonto. But look. I want to do this if the opportunity is presented. That's what I'm saying. Can I work with Jake Cahill?'

'No, Sharon. Jake doesn't work with anyone.'

There was no easy way to say it. Kerry knew Jake wouldn't have anyone working with him, or even knowing when or where he was doing a hit. She wouldn't even ask him. Yet she had never seen such anger or desperation in Sharon's demeanour.

They sat quietly for what seemed like a long time. Then Kerry spoke.

'Sharon. Listen. Please believe me when I say that I understand how angry you are, and I know you would gladly pull the trigger on Rodriguez. I felt that same sense of burning rage when I held my dying mother. It was like the heart had been ripped out of me and I didn't think I would ever rid myself of that rage until I had taken everyone responsible out. And in the end, I did. But I gave the job to a professional, to someone who I knew and trusted and who would go about the business clinically, without emotion getting in the way. That's Jake Cahill. He executed the men who came to Mickey's funeral and shot the place up, but he did it cleanly. If I had done it, I'm not sure it would have been like that. And apart from anything else, I could have been killed.' Kerry paused, hoping that her speech was getting through to Sharon. 'I can't take a risk like that with you. I can't do that. You have become so crucial to our survival here and in Spain, and you're part of our family now, and I don't want to lose you.' She glanced at the door. 'And that boy in the bedroom along the hall? I mean, what would Tony do if something happened to you, Sharon? Come on. Think this through. You have to think of the future, the long game here.'

The silence hung for a few moments, and Sharon nodded her head slowly.

'I hear what you're saying. And I have thought about nothing else. Kerry, if it hadn't been for you and for your family, I honestly don't know where I'd be. Apart from people taking shots at me in recent days, even with all the shit around, it's the happiest, most vital I've felt in years. Even meeting Vic again – but that's another story.' She half smiled. 'I'll respect your decision. But all I'm saying is please consider that if Jake Cahill is in a situation where he can take Rodriguez out cleanly, well, maybe he could think about allowing me in. Could you even ask him? Is that ridiculous?'

Kerry sighed. 'Yes, it is a bit ridiculous. But okay. I'll mention it to him. But I'm not going to push it. It's up to him what he does and how he does it. I just want the news that Rodriguez is history. We all do.'

The subject was closed.

CHAPTER THIRTY-ONE

Frankie Martin handed the woman the wad of notes and jerked his head in the direction of the hotel bedroom door. If she was impressed that he'd paid her two hundred quid for an hour's work, her surly expression didn't show it. These Eastern European birds were like that. You never knew what they were thinking, their faces always with that glum look bordering on catatonic. For all he knew, maybe it was the hookers who were sneering at the punters, at the pathetic specimens they must encounter in a day's work. Maybe they said nothing, because they looked down their noses at the men who felt powerful because they were paying them. Maybe secretly the women felt *they* had the power, because they could take the money and be free of these bastards in as long as it took them to get their rocks off. But Frankie didn't care about that. Pound for pound, he never had a better shag than a Russian or Ukrainian bird, their legs up to their waist and a knowledge and dedication to the task that went beyond any hooker he'd ever shacked up with. The woman said nothing, stuffed the money in her handbag, then went to the door. It surprised him a little that she glanced over her shoulder for one last look as he lay there naked on the bed. She didn't smile or say goodbye. She just left.

Frankie lit a cigarette and lay back on the pillows, inhaling deeply, satisfied at how things were going so far. He was holed up in a Glasgow hotel at the edge of the city centre where he would be well away from any of the faces he might have bumped into in the town. Since he left Dublin two days ago, he'd been here, making sure Joe Boy and Felix had sent some bodies who they'd set up in a couple of flats along the riverside. It hadn't taken them long before they'd sent their first message to Kerry Casey. Two bookies were firebombed last night and two of the Caseys' men were bumped off in drive-by shootings. Frankie had been having dinner in his hotel room when he heard the scream of sirens across the city, and he looked at his watch thinking, job done. Kerry Casey would have had a sleepless night, and must by now be wondering what the hell she'd taken on. He'd relayed the news to Rodriguez who'd told him to keep it up until they were trampled into the ground. The Colombian hadn't even flinched when he told him he had to part with two hundred grand to organise the troops over from Dublin and set them up in the city. It was all a means to an end.

Frankie's mobile rang and shuddered on the bedside table, and he picked it up. He automatically pulled himself up to a sitting position when he saw the name on the screen. Rodriguez. He wasn't expecting a call from him, so whatever this was, he knew he had to be on the ball with answers.

'Frankie, *que tal, coño*?'

'I'm good, Pepe.' Frankie found himself almost smile at the Spanish way of using the word '*coño*' which meant 'cunt', as it wasn't normally used as a term of endearment in English. But he knew Rodriguez was using it in a friendly way. '*Que pasa?*' Frankie added, throwing in a bit of Spanish and hoping to fuck the Colombian didn't come back to him in Spanish.

'Excellent,' Rodriguez said. 'We must talk about a couple of things. You know this bitch, the English bitch, Sharon. The one who is Kerry Casey's partner in Spain.'

'Yes, of course.'

'Of course you know her. She's the woman who hit you on the head, isn't she?'

Frankie felt a little flush of shame rise on his neck, and he wanted to tell Rodriguez to fuck right off with his sarcasm, but he knew he couldn't. So he didn't reply and let the silence hang for two beats until Rodriguez spoke.

'We had a problem with her yesterday.'

'Yeah?' Frankie asked.

'*Si*. We had planned to take her out in a meeting she was

having with some other of Casey's big shots. But I'm afraid it failed.'

Frankie thought someone might have phoned him from Spain to tell him this, but he hadn't heard a thing about it. Another failed attempt by Rodriguez to make his mark. It was beginning to look like he wasn't living up to his reputation – give or take a few dismembered corpses that were lying around in recent weeks. The operation in Glasgow had failed, and now this. It wasn't looking good.

'What happened?'

'We lost two men, they lost two bodyguards. But we didn't do well enough.'

Frankie wondered what he was supposed to say here.

'Well. What can I say, Pepe. I didn't even know about the operation, of course. I'm over here, but maybe if you'd told me, I might have been able to organise it a bit better. After Durkin's crowd failed in Glasgow, you can't really be going into things like this and failing a second time. Know what I mean? It sends the wrong message. The word will be getting around that maybe we're not that well organised, and some of these bastards who want to take us down will smell blood.' He paused, waiting for Pepe to interrupt him, but he didn't. 'So all I'm saying, is maybe you could bring me in on shit like this. I've been around the course a few times, *amigo*, and I know what I'm doing. Whoever you sent on that job didn't. Simple as that.'

Rodriguez said nothing, and Frankie hoped he hadn't gone too far.

'Okay, we will talk about this. But also, we took this Sharon's boy for a little while.'

'You took her boy? Her son?' Frankie was shocked. 'Why?' He knew how much Sharon doted on the lad.

'Just to show her that we can do anything. We didn't harm him. We just took him from school and his driver, then let them both go. We were going to kill the driver, but we decided not to. He's a lucky man.'

Frankie thought this was a completely pointless exercise, but he knew better than to say that. So he said nothing, waited for Rodriguez to speak.

'Anyway. We will get Sharon in time. I think we have to, soon, because she is significant over here in the Casey business, and she has to be taken out.'

'I see,' Frankie said, not knowing what else to say.

The silence lasted longer than he expected and Frankie wondered what the Christ was going on.

'Okay. Frankie. Here is the next thing. For you, as you are over there. I want you to take charge of a shipment that is coming over to the UK. This is the best, the purest cocaine that the UK will ever have seen. It is coming from my country. It is uncut, so it will make much money for the people you make the deals with. Every person who gets his cocaine for cutting will make more than three times the money they have before – ten times more if they want to cut it more. That is why so many people are coming over to be with me, and leaving the shitty dealers they have here. Because I can provide better, no, the best cocaine in the world.'

Frankie already knew the plan behind this, and the pure cocaine was the carrot Rodriguez had been dangling to bring everyone over to his mob. But he assumed Rodriguez would already have people organised to sort it out and distribute it when it came to the UK. This was not what he did. He wasn't some flunkey who worked in distribution. There was an awkward silence and he didn't know what to say.

'You understand, Frankie?'

'Yes,' he said hesitantly. 'I know the background, but what do you want me to do here in the UK? I'm not sure what you mean?'

'I want you to make sure it arrives safely and make sure it is put somewhere and stored until you can have it distributed in the coming days. You have to organise this. You have to choose the dealers. You must know these people who can pay top dollar for this. We are looking at eight tonnes of cocaine, my friend.'

Frankie felt flustered. What the fuck was this all about? He'd been sent to Scotland to grind the Caseys into the ground, and now he was being told to follow a container of coke? Eight fuckin' tonnes? He didn't even know what that amount of coke looked like.

'But, Pepe, are you forgetting that I am here to bring the Durkin boys onside and work with me to bring Kerry Casey and her family down in Glasgow? That is what I'm doing. We already started – two bookies were firebombed last night, and I know they are reeling from that. We are making strides here. I can do this for you.'

'Of course you will do it, Frankie. That is why I chose you. Because you are capable of doing so. But this cocaine shipment. I cannot trust it to anyone lower down. This is big business and I cannot let some person do this for me who may fuck it up. If I lose this cocaine, the prospects are not good for me. And if they are not good for me, then they are not good for anyone who works with me. Do you understand? We have to get this right. That is why I am giving the job to you.'

Frankie was still a bit bewildered but he knew he was being told in no uncertain terms that there was a job in front of him and he couldn't get out of it. Not that it was anything he hadn't done or overseen before. Bringing in shipments of cocaine and heroin was how he and Mickey had earned their spurs in the game, so he knew what to do. But not on this scale. And on principle, he still didn't like it. He'd gone beyond distributing coke. He was a bigger player now.

'Fine,' he said eventually. 'Just tell me where and when. I'll sort it, Pepe. How is it coming in? Where is it coming into?'

'Okay. That is good. I will call you later. But it will be I think Portsmouth or Southampton. And it is in an industrial-type container. Metal tubes.'

Frankie was already thinking ahead, wondering where he could get this shit stashed, and who he could really trust in this new regime. And who the fuck he was going to offload this to. Because if anyone got wind there was a load of uncut coke coming into the country, some of the fuckers he dealt with would sell their own children to get a piece.

'Fine. When you're ready, you can tell me the details. Meantime, I will carry on what we are doing.'

Rodriguez hung up without saying goodbye, and Frankie looked at the mobile and spat, 'Dago cunt!' then tossed it onto the bed. He walked across to the window and peered through the net screening at the afternoon traffic snaking its way along the city centre and up towards the motorway. Pictures of himself over the years came to flooding to his mind. And somewhere inside him, there was a little pang of homesickness that he could never come back here, that this city for him was dead.

Kerry picked at her fingernails as Danny and Jack sat opposite her in her study and relayed the damage from the previous night. The worst news was that they'd lost two of her men, and she felt even worse that they were people she had never even met. People who worked for her organisation, and who were cut down because of that. This was a shitty way for lives to be led, and in darker moments like this, Kerry sometimes wished she could run a million miles away from it. And she would, in time. But before she could do that she had to fight back, to use everything she had to survive and to destroy the bastards who had dragged her back into this black hole.

She shook her head as Jack told her that he'd been to see the guys' families and told them they'd be looked after.

'You know what I hate more than anything?' Kerry said. 'I hate that I don't even know these men. I never even met them, and they are lying in the mortuary because they worked for me.'

Danny glanced at Jack, then leaned forward.

'Don't beat yourself up about it, Kerry. Believe me, Tonzo and Jim would have been working for some other crew if it wasn't the Caseys. Don't be thinking they are just innocent wee lads. They were tough guys, hard asses who served time in jail, and they weren't any strangers to violence in all shapes and forms. Sure it's unfortunate, as they were good enough men, and reliable, and we can be sorry for their families, but we'll see them all right. But we're in the middle of a battle here, and we've a long way to go. So we can't worry about every single casualty.'

Kerry nodded slowly, thinking that Danny was talking like some old military man, as though lives were just collateral damage. But the truth was, in this game, as in conventional war, they were. He was right. She had to stop over-thinking it and get on with the fight.

'Anyway,' Jack said, 'we have to gear ourselves up for even more trouble. I'm hearing that Durkin's mob, or what's left of them in Dublin, have gone over to the Colombians. And that they have people here in Glasgow to get us.' He clasped his hands on the table and looked at Kerry. 'A couple of guys called Joe Boy and Felix are running it for the Irish here, backed up by their IRA mates on the south side of the city – Shawlands mostly. So they're up for a fight. We need to be ready for more of the same from last night. But the thing is, we don't have any businesses they own to knock out, and we don't have enough bodies to go to Dublin and do damage to their businesses there. The Monaghans will do that for us – but we'll need to put a lot of money their way. When it comes to here, we have to rely on intelligence here to see where these bastards are holed up. I've got people working on it, who'll do anything for money, so if they find out where they are, then they'll tell me, no matter whose side they're on. Money talks. Always has. So we'll find out where the fuckers are, then we'll hit them.'

CHAPTER THIRTY-TWO

Sharon stood looking out from the terrace as the Costa sun burned away the clouds. She'd only come back yesterday from Glasgow, but it already seemed like ages since she'd seen Tony. The way he'd hugged her so tight as she left for the airport brought a lump to her throat as she remembered him trying to fight back tears. She swallowed hard. Soon this would be over, she told herself, and things would be different.

Sharon was finding the extra security suffocating at times, but she knew there was no option. After that Colombian lowlife's stunt, kidnapping Tony just to show that he could, nothing was being left to chance. There were extra guards around the house and also posted on the twisting road up to where the house stood in the secluded spot overlooking the sweeping landscape far enough away from Marbella, but close enough to the motorway if they had to move fast. She'd only left the house to visit the architects and builders on the site of the hotel as they began to clear the debris and work out how long the firebombing of the complex would put them behind schedule. It had all looked so promising just a few short weeks ago. Now she felt like a prisoner, holed up with only the staff at the house and the guards for company. It couldn't go on like this, she promised herself. She had to find a way to hit back at Rodriguez. But the one man who could help her hadn't been in touch since Tony was returned. Sharon had been desperate to ask Vic if he'd known of Rodriguez's stunt, but she was sure if he had he would have tipped her off. At least she hoped he would have. He'd already saved her life at the meet in San Pedro with his phone call to say Rodriguez's men were on their way. She hadn't even yet been able to thank him and had expected him to get in touch later that night, but nothing. She wondered if maybe Rodriguez was doing a post-mortem of the operation and trying to find out who tipped her off that they were coming. The longer she didn't hear from him, the more she worried that Rodriguez had found out it was Vic who was the traitor inside his organisation. If he had, then for sure Vic would be dead by now.

In her more paranoid moments, she worried that maybe Rodriguez knew what Vic was doing but was letting him carry on, watching him closely, having him followed in the hope Vic would unwittingly serve her up to him on a plate. But deep down she knew Vic would be wise to that. He was smart and cunning, and surely he'd be one step ahead of the rest of them. And she consoled herself by the fact that so far, two of Rodriguez's operations had already failed – one in Glasgow to get Kerry Casey, and the other in Spain, to destroy Sharon and the rest of the organisation. In her conversations with Kerry they'd agreed that Rodriguez might be a ruthless, brutal bastard, firebombing the hotel site and taking out a few bars on the Costa, but he had failed to hit his main targets. There was weakness in his armour, and Sharon just had to find it. If only she knew where he moved, any place that he would be, she could work on it, but she needed Vic for that kind of insider knowledge. And as she lay in bed this morning, watching the darkness lift and light spread across the sky, she realised she needed Vic for more than that. Their encounters had been brief, but she was surprised at the sense of longing she felt for him, for his touch, his strength and power alongside her as they'd made love. Two lonely souls who could recall a lifetime ago when they trod on dangerous ground, among killers and robbers and drug dealers – but nothing as perilous as they faced now.

Sharon's mobile shuddered on her bedside table. She checked the time. Six thirty. Then she recognised the number and she pulled herself up on the bed. It was Vic's mobile. She picked it up – would it really be him on the line? What if this was Rodriguez or one of his sidekicks with Vic's phone, because Vic was already dead? She pushed the answer key and put the phone to her ear.

'Sharon.'

She recognised Vic's voice. He was alive. She was surprised at how relieved and glad she was. She waited two beats.

'Sharon? You there? It's me.'

'Vic,' she said. 'Christ, man. I was so worried about you! I thought you were . . .'

For a second he didn't answer, then he spoke.

'Dead? Me? Come on, Shaz. It'll take more than any of these fuckers to bring the Vickster down.'

She smiled, picturing his mischievous grin, all bravado and flair, the stuff that had drawn her to him all those years ago. Christ! She should have left Knuckles then, taken the consequences, but at least she would have been with someone she was pretty sure would never plan her execution. But that was water under the bridge. This was now, and Vic was here, and alive.

'What's happening? I didn't hear from you, then that bastard took our Ton–'

Vic interrupted. 'I know, Sharon. What an absolute cunt that Rodriguez is. When I heard he'd taken your lad, I felt like cutting the fucker's throat. But I didn't know anything about it until it was already done. I was away – dropping Frankie Martin at Málaga airport. When I got back, he told me about it. Cunt was laughing. And I knew you'd be in bits. I don't know how I stopped myself from ripping his lungs out.'

Sharon swallowed, touched by his concern.

'It was the worst two hours of my fucking life, Vic. If anything had happened to our Tony, I'd just chuck it, honestly I would.' She paused. 'But I promise you this – it's not finished. It will only be finished when I put a bullet in that bastard's head.'

'I know, sweetheart. Believe me. I know how you feel. But you have to be careful. You mustn't let your anger cloud your judgement. You'll get him back. When the time is right.'

'Will I, Vic? I mean, will I ever be able to get out of this bloody house, get back to what me and Kerry were planning to do, and build ourselves a legit business here? I feel as though I'm being bombarded from every angle, and all I'm doing is fighting back but not winning. Kerry feels the same way too. It's all going shit crazy back in Glasgow – bodies everywhere.'

'Yeah. I heard,' Vic said. 'Frankie is doing a good job over there, from Rodriguez's point of view, and he's throwing plenty of money at it. So Kerry Casey's boys have a fight on their hands.'

'She's up for the fight, Vic. We all are. But it's like dodging bullets all the time, and when it comes to collateral and money, the Colombian will have more resources.'

'Yeah. But there's more than one way to skin the cat, Shaz. You just have to be canny. Listen. We need to meet. I've got some stuff to tell you.'

'What. What stuff?'

'I don't want to say on the phone. But I know there is a way to really hit this bastard so hard he might not get back up again.'

'You do? Seriously?'

'Yep. But it's going to take some balls. And some organisation.'

'What is it? Talk to me.'

'Not now. Look. Can you get out of the house and meet me for lunch this afternoon? In the Doña Lola hotel outside Marbella.'

'Every time I go out of the house I have at least two bodyguards. I feel I'm being followed all the time.'

'But if you can get to the hotel, you're safe. Nobody will be following me, so once you're in, we'll be on our own. Don't worry. He can't have eyes everywhere. He's not that powerful. Can you do it?'

Sharon was already out of bed and walking towards the terrace doors. She could do it. She wanted to. She had to.

'Okay. Can you meet me there at two?'

'Great. I'll call you to say exactly where I'll be. I have use of a suite there, but nobody knows about it. And I mean nobody, apart from one of my old muckers who rents it long term.'

'Okay. Call me when you're on the way.'

'Will do, sweetheart. It's been too long.'

He hung up before she had a chance to reply, and she

held onto the phone for a moment, as eager to see him as she was to find out what information he had.

Before she left the villa, Sharon had called Kerry to tell her what Vic had said. Kerry had been a little sceptical, even though she said she trusted Sharon's judgement. What if it was a trap? Sharon assured her that all of her instincts told her that Vic would never do this. He'd already saved her life, and if he'd wanted to take a step back then he would. But the way he was talking, she told Kerry, he seemed as keen to get the Colombian as they were. She related what he said about Frankie Martin, and Kerry was intrigued and told her to find out as much as she could on Frankie and the mob he'd surrounded himself with in Glasgow. The word on the street there was that various crews in the city were coming together to work against the Caseys, so they were running out of allies.

As Sharon's blacked-out silver Merc swept into the car park of the Doña Lola hotel, she told Larry, her bodyguard, that he could go for lunch in the hotel and relax for a while until she called him. Larry was a man of few words, and whatever he was thinking you couldn't see it in his stony face as he nodded slowly, keeping his eyes front. She knew he would probably assume that it was more than a business meeting that had brought Sharon out of the villa and down here, but it wasn't his place to pry. The bodyguards and security that now surrounded Sharon at the villa and in most of their businesses along the Costa were handpicked by Danny to do what they were told and ask no questions. A couple of them had come from Scotland and some from Belfast and Dublin. Sharon had already seen how they did business when Rodriguez had sent his men to wipe her out at the café that day, so she felt she was in good hands.

She got out of the car as her mobile rang and Vic's voice told her to come straight up to his suite on the second floor. She walked briskly through the automatic glass doors of the hotel and across the foyer to the lift, a quick glance around the place where the well-heeled came for lunch or for business, or for secret, discreet assignations. As she stepped into the empty lift and pushed the button for the second floor, she felt a little stir of nerves in her gut. When it pinged and the doors opened, she got out and walked along the quiet corridor, her heart beating a little faster, she couldn't stop thinking that if this were a trap and she'd been lured here, then there really was no way out. She pushed the thought away as she gently knocked on Room 203. The door opened, and Vic stood there, a smile spreading across his suntanned face, his eyes bluer than ever in the sun streaming in the window onto him. For a couple of seconds they didn't speak, then he stepped back and made a mock bow to beckon her in. As she did, her eyes took in the splendour of the room, white sofas and furnishings, lavish paintings on the wall. Then she turned and looked at Vic.

'They couldn't get you an upgrade then?'

They both smiled, and for a short, almost awkward moment it was as though they didn't know what to say. Then Vic stepped closer and brushed her cheek with the back of his fingers. He drew her into his arms and kissed her softly on the lips, brief and tender, then lingering. She could feel him against her and had to fight the urge to let herself go. She eased away, feeling a little breathless. He took a step back.

'Jesus, Vic. I could get all hot and bothered here, but we've got things to discuss.'

He smiled and took her hand and led her across the room to where a table was laden with food and silver domes.

'We have,' he said, turning to her. 'But tell you what, Sharon. I've missed you. No messing or nothing like that. I just missed seeing you, holding you like that.'

'Me too,' Sharon said and she meant it.

They sat and poured glasses of chilled white wine and she surveyed the table of fresh fish and salad as they clinked glasses.

'To the future, Sharon,' he said.

'Yeah,' she said. 'I hope so. Most days I can't get beyond the next day, never mind the bloody future. But sure, here's to it.'

'Right. Okay. Let me get down to it now and tell you what's going to happen and see how you and the Caseys can get a way in to this Colombian bastard and his gang of dickheads.'

'I'm all ears,' Sharon said.

'Okay. Frankie Martin. You know he's in Glasgow, don't you?'

'Yeah. We do.'

'Rodriguez sent him to Dublin to get Durkin's boys onside with him, or as many of them as he could. It wouldn't have been easy because a lot of them will never forgive him for the way he executed their boss – even if Durkin *was* a little prick. But Frankie has pulled it off, and got a lot of them with him – paying them plenty – and they're in Glasgow.'

'This much I know,' Sharon said, wishing he would get to the point. 'He's already started doing some damage.'

'I know. But I also know that he's got an even bigger job on hand. And this is how you may be able to get to him.'

'Really? What kind of job?'

'Frankie has to handle a shipment of coke when it arrives in the UK. He's to handle the deals and distribution.'

'Frankie Martin doing distribution? He'll not be pleased about that. He doesn't like to get his hands dirty like that.'

'I know. He's well pissed off. But this isn't just any old shipment of coke.' He paused, knowing by the look on her face that Sharon was intrigued.

'Well go on then, for Christ's sake! Don't keep me guessing.'

He made a gesture with his thumb and forefinger.

'This is the best, the purest Colombian marching powder the UK will ever have seen, Sharon. Uncut. Pure. Straight from the coke factories in Medellín. Eight fucking tonnes. We're talking forty-four million quid here as soon as it hits the UK, and ten times more on the street once it's cut.'

'Eight tonnes?' Sharon's mouth dropped open. 'You have to be kidding me. Nobody shifts that amount of coke into the UK in one go.'

Vic nodded and raised a finger.

'Oh yes they do, if you're Pepe Rodriguez, with the powerful Colombians and their money behind you. Pepe is using the pure coke to pull every major dealer from Glasgow to London and everywhere in between into his web, because once they cut this shit, they will make so much more than anything they've ever bought before. It's only going to top dogs, big shots who run their own show, and who have agreed to buy into his mob on the promise that they will make millions faster than they could ever imagine by dealing with anyone else.'

'Christ! They'll be flocking to him like flies around shit.' She picked up her glass and swirled the wine around. 'And he's put Frankie in charge of it, I suppose, because he thinks he's the only one who can make sure it all goes down successfully.' She glanced at Vic. 'He's putting a lot of trust in a double-crossing bastard who might just take the lot and disappear.'

Vic shrugged. 'Sure. But then where would he go to? He'd be hunted down and Rodriguez would be hanging slices of his liver all over the place as a lesson to others.'

'Yeah. Suppose so. But Frankie will still be raging that he has to be actually physically involved.'

'Yeah. But he knows if he passes this test, then he'll become Rodriguez's right-hand man in Spain, and that makes him a millionaire with a lot of power. In that position, Frankie could really wipe out the Caseys once and for all. At the end of the day, even dealers and crews who are faithful to Kerry and the Caseys for the old man's sake, well, they'll see pound signs and a chance to be top dogs, to be part of a Colombian cartel. Christ, some of these witless fuckers would dine out on that alone. They'll all be vying for position, and Frankie will be the guy dangling the carrot in front of them.'

Sharon nodded. 'Yep. He's such a cunning bastard, he might just be able to do that.'

Vic sat back and stretched out his long legs, and Sharon couldn't help but admire how fit he looked in his white linen shirt, sleeves rolled up to reveal muscular, suntanned forearms.

'But he's got to get the stuff to the point where he can actually distribute it first. He'll have people lined up to buy and part with a shedload of money for it. And that's where he can run into trouble.'

'Meaning what?' Sharon said. Her mind was working on

how Knuckles used to get his drugs delivered to the warehouse and the cutting and processing that went on from there. But this was different.

Vic leaned forward.

'Meaning he could get ambushed.' Vic gestured with his hands as though he was holding an assault rifle. 'Bang, bang, bang. Bye-bye, Frankie.' A smile spread across his face.

Sharon also smiled because she could see the picture.

'And I take it you mean ambushed by the Caseys?'

'Who else? If you want to hit this Colombian fucker hard, then that's how it's done.'

Sharon thought for a moment before she answered. 'Of course, you don't think the rest of the dealers he's handpicked for the prize coke will also be planning the same ambush?'

'Of course. But you just have to be ahead of the game.'

'Oh aye. And Frankie's going to be stupid enough to let us know where this is all going down. It'll be watertight, Vic. Frankie won't put a foot wrong in the planning of this, because he knows he can't afford to.'

'Yeah. You're right. I'm sure the dealers won't be told where and when until hours before the meet.'

'Exactly.'

He smiled again and touched her hand.

'And that, sweetheart, is where Vic comes in.'

She shook her head at his mischievous grin.

'And how's that?'

'Because I'm riding shotgun with the driver who's bringing the shipment in. Driving from Spain right to Portsmouth, then on to wherever Frankie tells us. I'll be with it all the way. And so will your guys.'

He looked so pleased with himself that Sharon couldn't help but smile. He really meant this. He was really going to put himself on the line for her. She was a little taken aback. The way he was talking and building the story up, she was half thinking she'd maybe get a call from him giving her some intel on where the shipment was going. But this was a big deal.

'Jesus, Vic. You could end up dead for even thinking this. If Rodriguez ever had an inkling–'

He interrupted her. 'That cunt thinks the sun shines out of my arse, he does. He's been so all over me like a cheap suit since Frankie left that I half expected he was a faggot – inviting me to dinner, going on to some club in Marbella and drinking till the small hours, telling me about his life back home in that Colombian shithole. I can't get the measure of this fucker when it comes to exactly who he is. I only know that he's an evil bastard, but a flawed one, because two of his operations so far have gone tits up. But last night, he invites me to dinner and it was then I was telling him about how I used to drive containers with cannabis over in the old days for a few of the lads. So he knows that I'm reliable and I know my shit. Then he told me about the plan and what Frankie would be doing, and he asked me to ride shotgun. He said there will be a hundred grand in my account the day I leave, two hundred grand in my account if I can get the shipment safely to Frankie. And he said after that I can do what I want. I can come on board with him, or I can fuck off and do my own thing.'

Sharon raised her eyebrows. She couldn't wait to tell Kerry this news.

'Are you sure you haven't let him shag you?'

He burst out laughing, then stood up, and eased her onto her feet.

'Absolutely. He's not even a good kisser. Too much tongue straight away. I hate that in a man.' He chuckled, pulling her towards him, running his hands down her back and pushing her buttocks against his groin. 'C'mere, you mad woman. I've been thinking about this every day.'

He kissed her hungrily, pushing himself hard against her, and she felt a little weak at the knees as he caressed her thighs and pulled her dress up, then ran his hands across her pants, gently fondling her as she groaned with pleasure at his touch.

CHAPTER THIRTY-THREE

Kerry had been awake half the night, her head buzzing with figures and calculations. And also guilt. Sharon's early-evening call had blown her mind. Eight tonnes of uncut cocaine worth forty-four million pounds was heading to the UK. Eight tonnes. Christ almighty! She didn't even know what eight tonnes of cocaine looked like. But she knew that forty-four million pounds could help build her hotel, set the Caseys up with strings of property in Spain and the UK. It could make them a legitimate business, one that was proud to sit at the top table with any other enterprise raking in a profit. The killings, and the hits, and the swimming in the sewers with the rats that went with the territory of running a criminal empire, would end. The Caseys would be kingpins, respected for their financial worth, not feared, the way they'd been under Mickey Casey and Frankie – and to an extent her father in the old days. What had surprised Kerry was how swiftly she took to the prospect of getting her hands on that cocaine. She hadn't baulked at the idea, nor had she flinched at the dangers that lay ahead. She was taking this cocaine. It would be hers to sell. Never mind the delicious humiliation of Rodriguez and Frankie Martin that stealing their massive haul from under their noses would bring. All Kerry could think about was the means to an end. This would be the biggest deal of her life, and she was going to win it.

But that was only half the story of her night tossing and turning in her bed. The guilt came in waves as she lay in bed working out the logistics. She was actually thinking like a gangland kingpin. Was that really who she was, carrying a longed-for baby inside her, even though she had no idea what the future of being a single mother would hold? Should the baby not be her one and only priority? Again and again the guilt came, but each time she pushed it away. She was doing this *for* her baby, for *their* future, and to fulfil the dream of the father and mother she'd adored. Nothing would stop her. Nothing. And now, as she watched Danny and Jack come into the yard, she squared her shoulders and shook off the guilt and the misgivings that had plagued her. She couldn't wait to tell them what lay ahead.

Kerry had come downstairs to greet Danny and Jack in the kitchen where the housekeeper had prepared a breakfast of toast and scrambled eggs for them, before being told to take a couple of hours off.

'Oh, good stuff, Kerry,' Danny said as he saw the table. 'I'm starving. I didn't take time to eat, as you sounded desperate to talk.' He turned to her. 'Is there a problem? It was quiet in the city last night, thank Christ. So the Irish must have been out getting pished.'

'No problem,' Kerry assured, motioning to them to sit down. She looked from one to the other as they took their seats. 'Not a problem. But a major opportunity has come our way. One that I think we have to grab with everything we've got.'

Jack looked at Danny, then to Kerry as she poured coffee from a cafetière into mugs.

'You look well buoyed up, Kerry. I hope this is good news for a change.'

Kerry sat down and pulled her chair in.

'Okay,' she said. 'I'll cut to the chase. Sharon called me last night. Wait till you hear this! Rodriguez is about to ship eight tonnes of pure, uncut coke to the UK.' She paused and smiled as Jack spluttered his coffee. 'Yes,' she said. 'That's what I did too when I heard, Jack.'

'Eight tonnes of uncut coke?' Danny said. 'Fuck me, Kerry! That's about forty million fucking quid. Nobody does that.'

Kerry raised a finger. 'Forty-four, actually, according to recent markets. Forty-four million pounds, guys. Can you believe it? I know. Hard to take in. But it's coming our way, and guess who's in charge of the shipment, who's going to be in charge of distributing it here to all of our enemies?'

Jack looked at Danny and sat back and grinned.

'Please tell me it's that scheming prick Frankie.'

'Got it in one.'

'For fuck's sake,' Danny said. 'Frankie? I mean he talks a good game, and he's a right treacherous bastard when it comes down to it, but I know for a fact he's never handled that amount of coke. Never. Even when he and your Mickey were running things here, they were never there for the big distribution. They bought from the big dealers, from the guys whose minions got their hands dirty. Sure, they might have run a few trucks of cannabis in back in the very old days. But cocaine? In eye-watering amounts like that? Christ! I don't know anyone in the country who'd handle that amount.'

'From what I gather from Sharon, Frankie will be drawing all the big shots from here to London and Dublin who will pay top dollar for a piece of this. The lure of making massive amounts of money from the uncut coke will be pulling them in.'

'That's for sure. Everyone will want that. And I mean everyone. Frankie will be shitting himself that he's been given this to handle. He could get seriously ambushed by every fucking dealer he picks to buy the stuff.' Danny rubbed his chin. 'So this is coming from Sharon? What's the story?'

'Okay,' Kerry said. 'I'll tell you. But here's the best part.' She waited two beats. 'Sharon was with Vic yesterday. You know he's on our side, and he's dropping intel to her all the time – that's what saved her life last week when Rodriguez sent the hit squad to wipe her and the rest of our boys out in that bar on the Costa.'

They both nodded, as Kerry took a breath and a swig of her coffee. She was excited just talking about it.

'Well, Vic told her that Rodriguez has asked him to ride shotgun in the truck that's transporting the shipment. So for us, that's as good as a tracker from the moment it leaves Spain until it docks in the UK at Portsmouth. Then it will be going to wherever Frankie has organised. So whatever his plan, we'll have an inside track on what's going on.'

Danny shook his head and smiled at Jack.

'Fuck me, man. That's unbelievable! That's like handing us this on a fucking plate!'

Jack puffed and sat back with his hands clasped behind the back of his head.

'Aye. But is it too good to be true? Once the word gets out that a shipment like this is on its way, all the fucking bandits from here to Bombay will be coming out of the woodwork.'

'I know,' Kerry said. 'But Vic said that he expects Frankie won't give his prospective buyers any details at all until a few hours before the meet.' She spread her hands. 'To be honest, we're not even sure of the logistics, as they'll probably be in Frankie's head at the moment. But he's got to part with some of the details to the guys who're driving the stuff, and that includes Vic. So anything he gets, we'll get pronto. It puts us right in the front line.'

'I'll say it does,' Danny said. 'And the firing line.' He ripped off a piece of toast and stuffed it in his mouth, then washed it down with a gulp of coffee. 'But if we can ambush this fucker, get there first and get our hands on this stuff, then we can make a fucking fortune.'

Kerry nodded. 'Exactly. Enough to help build our hotel, add to our properties, and turn us into a major player.'

Danny shook his head wistfully and smiled.

'You know your da always said he was an entrepreneur, Kerry. He always looked at the long game. Even when we were robbing and doing our stuff back in the days, your da used to make me chuckle when he'd say he was an entrepreneur. Christ! He'd love this.'

Kerry smiled at the thought, but this wasn't some small-time gig to pull in big money in one fell swoop, and escape unscathed and with all men left standing. This was as big as it got. This would take balls, and planning, and orchestrating with everything they had. Given the state the Caseys were in at the moment, with their enemies circling them and bodies piling up, this might be their last roll of the dice.

'So,' Kerry sat back and folded her arms. 'Let's do this.'

Frankie Martin was feeling frazzled. It was a long time since he'd had to wine and dine and press the flesh like this with cunts that he always had to watch his back with. When he and Mickey were running the show, they'd source their drugs from Knuckles Boyle and the Hills in London.

But there were other dealers out there who were operating at that level, and most of the time they stayed out of each other's way. As long as you didn't stray onto someone else's turf you were safe. But they all knew each other, they were all aware of each other's capabilities and that there was never really any limit to what they would do to get what they wanted. But since Rodriguez dropped this job on him, Frankie had had to be up and down the country putting a deal together with the big shots who he knew would bite his hand off to get a piece of the action now. And some of them had a few Neanderthals in their outfit who would actually physically just bite your finger off anyway for the sheer hell of it or to make a point. So he had to have his wits about him twenty-four seven, as he swanned around in secret locations putting his cards on the table.

There was a Turkish prick, called Mete, who ran a string of used-car dealerships in north London as a cover for the shedloads of heroin and cannabis he'd been importing for years. He looked like a sack of shit in a shiny worn-out suit and grubby shirt, but Mete was a multimillionaire with massive connections from the UK to Morocco to Spain. Frankie had only met him twice before, a couple of years ago along with Mickey, and Mete had then been floating the idea that maybe they should look to partnering up in the future. This was his big chance, Frankie had flannelled him, and by the time they'd finished lunch in some pretty decent Turkish restaurant in Watford, Mete told him he was good for five million quid's worth of the uncut cocaine. Cash on delivery. No fucking funny business, he told Frankie. Aye fine, Frankie had agreed, promising it was a straight-up deal and to stand by for more information on where and when the deal would be done.

There were another three dealers – one of them Tommy Fitz, from Liverpool, a thickset scally, who looked like he was the first in his family to walk upright, but actually had a brain as sharp as the flick knife he'd produced from his pocket at one point to roll expertly over each finger with the dexterity of a surgeon. Frankie had watched his brain tick over as he finally came up with the deal for six million for his cut of the coke. But as he rolled the flick knife over his fingers he told Frankie that if anything went wrong, such as the bizzies being on his tail after he picked up his cut, then it would be on Frankie's head. Frankie didn't protest, as they shook on the deal.

The other hood was Billy Morton from Manchester, who'd been a sworn enemy of Knuckles Boyle and whom Frankie knew and didn't like. But he had the money and he told Frankie the past didn't matter a fuck if he could get his mitts on uncut coke.

There were another couple of dealers across the country who were in for smaller amounts, so things were moving at a pace. Of course it was no surprise to him that all of them were more than happy to be invited to the party. Some of the thicker but deadly bastards were flattered that they were even being considered top dog enough for such a big deal. And all of them said they'd be happy to part with the millions that Frankie was asking for their cut of the shipment. Each of them knew that by the time it hit the streets, they'd get their money back tenfold and more. Even the dumb-looking bastards could count like traders on a city floor when it came to cutting and selling coke.

But the biggest dealer of them all was Jumbo Keane, fresh out of Strangeways Prison last week after a ten-year stretch for his part in the brutal murder of a jockey who'd been discovered in the boot of a car on the M6. The jockey had made the fatal mistake of double-crossing Jumbo by throwing a race in favour of one of Jumbo's biggest race-horse rivals and losing him a small fortune in the process. Jumbo didn't forgive easily, as the protesting jockey had found out to his cost. But ten years was nothing to a man like him, whose criminal empire ran smoothly while he was inside thanks to his faithful crew, who'd also made sure that his years in jail were comfortable, having greased a few palms of the prison staff. He was out now, and Frankie knew that the prospect of getting his hands on a haul of uncut coke would stick him top of the heap all over the Midlands.

Frankie had found him a silent and distant customer, a man of few words who didn't brag or tell stories, but also with a menace in his dead grey eyes that gave him the creeps. Jumbo wasn't a man to throw his arms around you and be glad for the opportunity. Frankie had taken him to dinner in a restaurant of Jumbo's choice where he noticed that every flunkey fawned over him, then at Jumbo's suggestion, to a club where the women were gorgeous and pricey, and it was there they'd parted company. Jumbo had told him in the dark corner where they'd sat that he hoped they could do business together in the future. Frankie kept things close to his chest, telling him that he'd be given details of the meet only a few hours before it was due, and that he'd be expected to part with a lot of money. Jumbo was stony-faced and agreed, told him he was in for twenty million. Frankie had to keep his face straight at the eye-watering amount, but they shook on it. Jumbo didn't ask any more questions, and that was niggling Frankie even now, as every other dealer he'd spoken to had wanted to know a bit more about when it was arriving. But Frankie was wise to them, and there was no way he was going to be parting with anything that would let these fuckers ambush him. Big Jumbo, even though he was a bit creepy, knew how to do business. He had the money and he told Frankie he'd be ready and waiting for his call. Then Frankie had watched him disappear with a Russian girl half his age through a tacky velvet curtain and into the darkness of a back room, no doubt to make up for lost time he'd spent at Her Majesty's pleasure.

CHAPTER THIRTY-FOUR

Sharon punched in Jan's phone number on her mobile. It seemed like a lifetime ago that she'd been talking to the big Dutch truck driver who had regularly transported drugs for Knuckles Boyle from Amsterdam to Manchester. They'd got to know each other over the years as Sharon had opened the warehouse in Amsterdam for Knuckles where his shipments would be stored while in transit. It had been such a smooth operation, and Jan had asked no questions, only followed instructions, and picked up his money from his bank account once he delivered. On the few occasions that they'd spent some time having a drink or a bite to eat in Amsterdam if she was over inspecting the warehouse, he'd told her that one day he'd give all this up, move to the Caribbean or somewhere and open a beach bar, then live out the rest of his life in the sun. Given that he was driving drugs for criminals, he was lucky to have survived this far. Now Sharon was about to make him the offer of a lifetime.

'Jan?'

'Who is this?' His tone was flat. But his voice brought back a surge of memories.

'I like to think of myself as one of your good friends, Jan.'

A couple of beats, then she heard Jan give a little chortle.

'Ah, Sharon. Of course. My very good friend indeed. How are you? I think about you and wonder where you are these days . . . after everything.'

'Well, I'm alive, Jan, and very much kicking.'

'I bet you are. I'm very happy to hear your voice. Where are you?'

'I'm in Spain. Doing some business here.'

'Ah, I see.'

Discreet as ever, Sharon thought. She'd hoped he'd be. When she'd spoken to Kerry, Danny and Jack last night on a conference video call on her laptop, she'd told them that she knew she could trust Jan. It was her suggestion that they bring him in on the plan. All she had to do now was convince him.

'So, Jan. Are you busy these days? Much work?'

'Some,' he said. 'Now and again. Not as regularly as with you. But I make a living.'

'Not retired yet to the dream life on the sunkissed beach then, knocking up cocktails for rich ex-pats?'

He laughed. 'Not yet. But one day.'

Sharon waited a couple of seconds, knowing that he'd be intrigued by her call. Then she broke the silence.

'Jan. Listen. I've got this plan that might just make that dream of yours a reality.'

'Ha! You have? And will I live to tell the story?'

She knew she couldn't lie to him.

'Well, sure there's a risk with everything, as we all know. But you've lived all your life with risks, haven't you?'

'I have. I'm not afraid of risks.'

'That's what I want to hear.' She paused and listened to him breathing for a moment. 'I've got a job for you if you want it. Only you though. It would bring you a fortune – enough to disappear and build your own dream in a far-off land if that's what you want. Enough to secure the rest of your life, so that the only risk you take is how long to stay out in the sunshine. What do you think of that?'

'Oh, I like that. Do I have to kill someone? Because it's not really my thing.'

She knew he was toying with her and she laughed.

'Ha! No. Not unless it's absolutely necessary. But then that's always the way. I want you to drive from a location – I'm not quite sure where at the moment but it will be in Spain, I believe – to the UK.'

'And what is my cargo?'

'Nothing.'

'Nothing?'

'Yep. Nothing. All you have to do is follow a truck that I

will give you details of, in due course. You just follow it at a discreet distance, for as long as it goes, wherever it goes. It will be going from Spain, probably to Portsmouth.'

'And I just follow this truck?'

'Yes. Then later you pick up a few troops, and they go in the back of your lorry. So you'd have to make sure it's comfortable and able to accommodate them as they might be there for a few hours at least.' She paused. 'And there will be some weapons on board for the operation ahead.'

There was a long moment of silence, and Sharon was picturing Jan's big impassive face as he processed the information, no doubt assessing correctly that this could be a bloody shitstorm. Anything he'd done before had been to transport the goods and walk away. This was different.

'Hmmmn. I see, Sharon. It seems risky.'

'Yeah. That's why you get paid the big bucks, Jan. And I mean big bucks.'

Again the silence as he assessed the risk.

'And how much?' he asked.

'Two million. In your bank account. Half when you start driving, the rest when you get to Portsmouth and shadow the truck until it stops.'

'Then I walk away.'

'Yep. Then you walk away. You disappear. Take a flight somewhere and the world is your oyster.'

'It sounds very, very tempting. But also dangerous.'

'It's all of that. But it's a once in a lifetime chance, Jan.' She waited. 'Are you in? You are the only man I would trust with this operation.'

The silence seemed to go on so long that Sharon's heart sank. A risk too far maybe for Jan, the man who'd been happily driving truckloads of drugs for fifteen years. Then he spoke.

'I'm in. Let me know the details when you can.'

Sharon let out a little sigh of relief.

'Thank you. I knew I could count on you. We'll talk later.'

He hung up without answering.

Frankie Martin ordered another Jack Daniel's and Coke from the bar of his hotel. As the barman slid the drink across to him, Frankie eased himself off the bar stool and picked up his drink. He could see that the bar in the swish city centre hotel was beginning to get busy with people heading for pre-dinner drinks or on their way to a function. It wasn't the kind of hotel where Frankie would have expected to bump into anyone who may recognise him, but just on the off chance, he decided to head to his penthouse suite. As he came out of the lift and walked along the long corridor to his room, he felt his shoulders sag a little, and he tried to shake off the gloom that was rising in him. This would be his last drink for the night, he promised himself, as he was beginning to feel morose. He'd noticed that any time he'd come back to Glasgow in recent weeks he'd felt this sense of loss. Even though he didn't want to live here, and he knew the old life he'd had was dead and gone, somehow just being back in the city, with its smells and its noise and its greyness, made him feel something akin to grief. He couldn't quite understand it, but he had to shake out of it right now. In a darker moment in bed last night, he'd even been stupid enough to mull over the ridiculous scenario that he could contact Kerry Casey and push a deal towards her that would bring him back into the fold. What the Christ was he thinking about? Where did that come from? He'd well and truly burned his boats when he set up Mickey's execution, and then the funeral debacle. There was no way back for him, and even if there ever had been, he couldn't work under Kerry. No way. But his ego kept niggling away at him. Deep down he felt that if Kerry was out of the picture, then the boys would come over to him if the money and the deal was right. Money bought loyalty. Always did. Maybe not with Danny and Jack and some of the older guys, but there was young blood in the Casey crew, and with the right deal, maybe, just maybe, he could win them over. It was a ridiculous notion, wasn't it? he asked himself.

But still he kept thinking about it. What if he duped the whole fucking lot of them? What if he double-crossed Rodriguez and stole the whole lot of the coke for himself? Of all the arseholes he'd met with over the last couple of days, Frankie wondered if he could do serious business with

Jumbo Keane, if they were to work together. With forty-plus million pounds of coke, and with the muscle of Jumbo behind them, Frankie could just about take on all comers. Sure it was a crazy plan, he told himself, but it kept coming back. He had to push it away and concentrate on the business at hand. The reality was that he had a job to do in the next few days that was literally a matter of life or death to him. If he failed, he was dead. He had nowhere to run to. He couldn't come back to Glasgow, and he couldn't go to Spain where he would be hunted down no matter how long it took. And right now, as he stood watching the lights across the city, his mobile ringing on the bed shook him back to reality.

Frankie knew it was Rodriguez but he wasn't going to give the fucker the satisfaction of thinking he was jumping to attention. He let it go for three more rings. 'Hello.'

'Frankie, *hombre*. You are good, yes?'

'Yep. All good, Pepe. Things getting sorted.'

'So you have set up the deals with people? Are you organised?'

'Of course. I'm good. Been meeting with people all over the shop the last few days. I'm ready when you are.'

'And these people, Frankie . . . You can trust them?'

Frankie thought for a moment before he responded.

'Well, you can trust them as much as you can trust a lion when you walk into the fucking cage with a fillet steak in your hand. You get in, and get out very fast.'

He heard Rodriguez let out a little laugh, and pictured the handsome bastard's scheming face.

'I see what you mean. Is to be expected, of course. Because you will be torn to pieces if you hang around the lion's cage too long.'

'Yeah. Long enough to get the money,' Frankie said. 'Then get the fuck out.'

'You have your plans for the meetings and exchange?'

Frankie was growing impatient. What was with the fucking questions? But he knew he couldn't say that.

'Pepe. I'm sorted. I'm waiting for you to tell me what next.'

'Okay. Well you don't have to wait any longer, *amigo*. Because tomorrow the shipment is leaving Spain.'

'Tomorrow?'

'Yes. The plan is for it to be in Portsmouth in two days. I am sending Vic with the driver as backup. He's done this kind of thing, and he's good muscle, in case you need it. Nothing can go wrong.'

Frankie thought about Vic for a second. He liked the big guy, but there was something about him that he couldn't put his finger on. Maybe it was because he didn't fawn over Frankie or give him any notion that he would take orders from him. He was a hard-looking bastard, but they'd had a few laughs and beers together. A good man to have on your side, he decided.

'Okay. Might be useful. As long as he knows I'm in charge.'

'Frankie. This is your show. You know that.'

'Aye.'

'Okay. The shipment is coming in a truck carrying steel rollers. You know what I mean? The kind that are used in industry for conveyors, like in packaging or in shipping. They will be different sizes. The rollers are like cylinders, hollow inside, but once the cocaine is in there, then they are secured at each side with more steel screwed in to keep everything in place. I've seen the shipment. It looks good.'

Frankie pictured how the rollers would look and concluded it was a pretty good way to stash a lot of coke.

'Yeah. That sounds good to me.'

'So all you have to do is make sure everything goes well once it arrives in the UK, and is brought to wherever you have organised it to go.'

Frankie had organised a warehouse in Trafford Park industrial estate on the outskirts of Manchester, where the coke would be stashed for the hours before the dealers arrived. An old mate, Benny Evans, who he'd known from the Costa del Sol, owned it, and for fifty grand in his hand, Benny told him he could stash his haul there as long as it was gone by morning. Benny said he didn't want any filth sniffing around his doorstep as he'd been smuggling cannabis freely and unnoticed for more than a decade. So he'd better be sure that the cops weren't following his truck. Frankie assured him it was watertight, and over a few stiff drinks, Benny knew he couldn't knock back fifty big ones without even having to lift a finger. Frankie'd arrange for each of the dealers to come separately to pick up their cut and part with their cash. He had thought of meeting each dealer individually on the way up from Portsmouth. But it was too risky. Better to have the gear in a place where he could have several armed troops stationed around and watching. The obvious risk was an ambush on the way up the road, but it was going to be hard to eliminate that because once you were on a motorway, you never knew who was going to drive up your arse.

'It's all sorted, Pepe. Once I know what ferry it is on, I'll make sure I've got people looking after it. I've got that all organised. Just give me times and stuff.'

'Okay. We will talk tomorrow. You are happy, yes?'

Frankie was silent. What kind of fucking question was that, for Christ's sake? Happy? How in the name of fuck could he be happy overseeing the smuggling of eight tonnes of cocaine into the country, and trying to dodge all the vicious bastards planning to rob him?

'Yeah, Pepe,' he said sarcastically. 'I'm as happy as a pig in shite, me.'

Rodriguez laughed. 'Good man! Keep smiling, Frankie. Even when the guns are pointing at your head, *amigo*.'

The line went dead.

'Keep smiling? Keep fucking smiling?' Frankie said aloud. 'Aye right, you dago prick. I'd be smiling if I was looking at your bastard cold grey corpse.'

CHAPTER THIRTY-FIVE

'It's on the move.'

Sharon's voice in the early-morning call had woken Kerry from a vicious nightmare where she was back under the table at her brother's funeral with her mother's screams as someone was dragging her away, but her body was so heavy that she was paralysed as she tried to move. She was glad when the phone rang.

'Did I wake you, Kerry? Sorry.' Sharon sounded bright and cheery.

'Yeah,' Kerry said. 'But I'm glad you did. Was having one of those dreadful nightmares where you're powerless to move and all hell is breaking loose around you. Weird.'

'It's stress, pet. I've had a few of those black nightmares, more so in the days after Knuckles' sidekicks tried to top me. They'll pass though.'

'I know. I'm fine. So tell me. What's happening? The truck is moving?'

'Sure is. I got a call from Vic this morning to say they're well up the road to Santander. Looks like they'll be on the boat tomorrow. It takes around twenty hours, so they'll not be in Portsmouth until day after tomorrow – early doors. Vic will call me to say exactly which ferry he's on.'

'Should I have a couple of bodies on the ferry, do you think? Just to be around watching?'

'Not sure that would be a good idea in case it arouses any suspicion. Anyway we'll have big Jan there, and I'll have him well briefed on what Vic looks like so he can keep an eye on him. He'll hopefully be travelling not far behind Vic at the moment, as he's been in Spain since yesterday but he hasn't called me yet. I'm not expecting him to phone until he's getting on the boat, so he can give me an update. Have you got people sorted at the other end to meet Jan in Portsmouth?'

'I have. Jack has handpicked a few and they'll be on their way there tonight.'

'Good. All sorted then. What can possibly go wrong!' Sharon joked.

'Oh, yeah, sure,' Kerry said. 'If only it was as easy as it sounds.'

Sharon's ballsy outlook made Kerry feel a little more confident, but they had a long way to go.

'I've been trying to second-guess who Frankie will be punting the coke to back here. I don't suppose you have any ideas?' Kerry asked.

'Hmm. Could be anyone really. But it will only be people in the top tier who have the kind of money he'll be looking for. Uncut coke is like gold to anyone who can get their hands on it, but the price will be mega.'

'You don't know who they could be?'

'Nah. And to be honest, it wouldn't matter a damn if I did. If they've got that kind of money, they'll be rich and they'll be powerful – well tooled up if they're picking up that kind of stash and parting with a shedload of money. So they'll be well protected. We'll just have to be the same.'

'We will be. I'm going to talk to Danny and Jack this morning, because we need a plan in place for where and when we hit the truck.'

'Okay. You talk to them from your end, so that when Vic phones me tonight or in the morning I can let him know. He might have a couple of ideas to throw in by then. I don't think he'll know where Frankie is meeting him until he gets into the UK. But I don't suppose Frankie will be waiting on the docks waving a flag. I'd be surprised if they don't get onto the motorway and head north straight away.'

'You think they'll come to Glasgow with a haul like that?'

'Unlikely. Nobody in Glasgow or Scotland has the kind of money to take a good whack of this much coke. But if Frankie's smart, he'll have lined up a few dealers – not a lot – but a few who will be able to afford it. I think he might have a plan to offload it somewhere in the Midlands. Hard to say really. But we'll know more when Vic calls.'

'Great,' Kerry said. 'It's so valuable having Vic on the inside. But I can't help think that he's really putting himself in the firing line.'

There was a pause before Sharon answered.

'I know. I'm worried about him. I like him a lot, Kerry. We're good together. I'm not saying anything will ever come of it, but having him back in my life has been lovely. Even if he wasn't sticking his neck out for us in this, he saved my life, remember. But hey, I'm not daft. I think we both know how fickle these things can be.'

'That's for sure,' Kerry said, thinking of how Vinny had just walked out of her life.

'Okay,' Sharon said. 'By the way, Jake Cahill's still here, isn't he? I know you said he's stalking Pepe Rodriguez, but I haven't heard from him at all.'

'Yeah. You won't hear from Jake, Sharon. That's not how he works. He's like a shadow. I'll only hear from him when the job is done. Then we can celebrate. But let's get these next couple of days out of the way first.'

'Sure. Talk later.'

The line went dead, and Kerry lay back on the pillows, thinking of what Sharon had said about how fickle relationships were. She'd been fickle enough in her own relationships most of her life, and even when she was with Tom, deep down she'd never expected it to last for ever. So when she suffered the miscarriage, it spelled the end for them. But then Vinny came along and knocked her for six.

She hadn't expected that. She ran her hand over the warmth of her stomach and thought of the little life beating inside her. She'd be going in a couple of weeks to get the scan to make sure everything was good with the baby. She wished she could have told Vinny, but it would have been pointless, and anyway, wherever he was, he could at least have told her he was moving away. Maybe one day in the far-off future she would tell him he was a father. But right now, the only relationship that mattered to her was the one with the little baby she was carrying.

Jumbo Keane was loving being back in the thick of the game. It had been fine in the nick as he did his time, knowing that the bank accounts were stacking up and it would be business as usual by the time he got out. If anything, the books were looking even better when he'd got around the table with the main players in his crew. Moving the money around so that he could have at least twenty million in cash was a bit more tricky. Luckily, over the years, his organisation had always kept massive piles of cash. He had so much raw cash it would have made the cops' eyes water. Keeping that amount of money safe and accessible, yet far enough away so that nobody could get a sniff of it, had taken some serious ingenuity. But it worked. There were piles of as much as three million quid stored under the floor of a wine cellar in a farmhouse he'd built just before he was sent down for murder. It was in several special heavy-duty steel caskets he'd got knocked up by a blacksmith he'd grown up with. There were also two- and three- and single-million blocks in various locations across Manchester. And in an ironic twist, several millions were buried in oil drums under the floor of the car dealership that Manchester cops used to buy and repair their fleet of squad cars. Jumbo was particularly tickled by that, and it helped him sleep at night when he was in jail, knowing that he'd fucked the cops over so many times he should be given some kind of medal of dishonour. But the past couple of days his boys had had to work flat out to get a lot of the millions out and available. And this afternoon there was a container with fully twenty million on its way to a builders' yard he owned. It would be kept there until the call came in from Frankie to say where and when the meet was.

The biggest stroke of luck this morning had been the call from one of Benny Evans' boys. He and Benny went back a long way, and they'd done a lot of business together back in the days when they only smuggled cannabis. But it had all gone tits up a few years ago when a mule of Benny's who was driving a van load of hash across Europe heading for the UK got stopped in the north of France by a routine police patrol. His man sang like a canary and stuck everyone in to the cops. So when one of Benny's men called to say he had information on a big stash of uncut coke coming from Spain to Benny's yard, Jumbo felt he had actually won the lottery. He'd been planning to ambush that fucker

Frankie Martin anyway, but the big problem he had was finding out where he was bringing the stuff to, as Frankie said he'd only be told a couple of hours before the meet. This was like handing it to him on a plate. Sure there might be a few bodies to take out in the process, but the payoff would send Jumbo Keane into folklore. He looked out of the office window in his builders' yard as his boys pulled up in their SUVs and Mercs. He watched them coming out and across the yard – all top men, reliable, men you could trust with your life if you were going into battle. Which they were. He took a puff of his cigar and nodded his head in acknowledgement as they headed towards him.

Once they were all seated around the long table in his office, Jumbo stood up and walked slowly around them, knowing they were following his every move.

'We're about to make history, boys,' he said, puffing his cigar. 'That's why I've had you busting a gut to get all the readies prepared and handy. I take it you've got all the cash accessible?'

They all nodded. He could see they were a little edgy, but that was how he kept his boys sharp. Even those closest to him could never really tell what Jumbo was thinking. Even if he occasionally got drunk with those closest to him, Jumbo would never impart his innermost thoughts or feelings. They'd talk business or old stories of robbing and fighting their way up to the top table, but nothing else. He would never want to show weakness. Because when you showed weakness to guys like this, there was always one who would use it against you one day. It was cold, and it was hard, and these boys had seen him commit brutal crimes over the years, enough to make them shit scared of him, but each of them was rich beyond their dreams. And now he was about to make them even richer.

'We've all made our money over the years, boys, all of us through hard graft.' He smiled a little. 'Might not be working shifts or clocking in, right enough, and we had to slap a few faces along the way . . .' He waited as the chuckle around the table seemed to relax the men a bit. 'But that was our line of business. We wasn't born with a silver spoon, or had any of the privileges of the kind of cunts who would look on people like us as scum. And half of them are fucking criminals anyway – especially the politicians and the bankers. No. We did it our way, and we did well.' He paused, took a long draw of his cigar and let the smoke out swirling in a cloud in front of him. 'But like all businesses, we have to keep building. And now we have the opportunity to go beyond anything we would have thought possible.' He waited, as they all gazed up at him in anticipation. 'Pure, uncut cocaine. Eight fucking tonnes.' He glanced around and could see them looking at each other, their faces shining with excitement. 'I'm talking the finest marching powder the Colombians produce. It's coming our way, lads. And by the time we cut it and sell it on, well . . . you can do the fucking maths on that.'

'Christ!' Tommo Grant let out a whistle. 'That's fucking

mega, Jumbo. Eight fucking tonne. We're talking two hundred million maybe. Who knows!'

'Yep. So. All we have to do is get it.'

He waited for someone to ask a question but could see they were afraid to ask.

'I've made a deal for twenty million's worth of it. But now I've discovered that actually we can take the fucking lot. If we do this properly, it's all ours.'

'I take it there will be an army protecting this, Jumbo?' Davey Crossan asked, then quickly added, 'I mean, not that it won't be anything we can't handle.'

Jumbo nodded. 'They'll be well protected. But we've got the element of surprise on our side. We've arranged a meet with them, and they are only going to tell us where the meet is, a couple of hours before it happens – obviously in case we ambush them, which of course we would.'

A few grins and sniggers went round the table.

'But as luck would have it, we already know where the location is.'

'Fuck me,' Davey grinned. 'Belter!'

'So when they arrive, after their long journey overland from Spain and the ferry and all that shit, we'll be the reception party waiting for them.'

'Fucking dancer!' Brian Harty piped up. 'We haven't done anything like this in ages.'

'We haven't done anything as big as this in our lives, Brian,' Jumbo said. 'At least not with a payola as big as this.

But anyway, we can gloat about it once we've got it all in our possession. I'm expecting they will all be tooled up to their teeth, but they'll be no match for us.' He strode to the top of the table, stubbed out his cigar, and sat down. 'So. Are we all up for this?'

'You fucking bet! Bring it on,' came the cries from all around.

'Great. So pick out your most reliable troops, and get everyone tooled up. I want to be into this place, find a way to hide out and be ready long before these fuckers get there.' He turned to Tommo. 'Guys. You all liaise with Tommo as the day goes on, tell him who you've got in manpower, arms and stuff, and Tommo will get back to me today, so we can work out a plan. But we're looking to move in by early morning.' He spread his hands. 'We all clear?'

Everyone nodded. Jumbo stood up.

'Okay. We'll talk later. Just keep your eye on the main game here. I don't need to mention loose talk, of course. And make sure you don't bring anyone with you who isn't top fucking drawer. Because this could get a bit messy.'

Nobody answered, but they all stood up and shuffled out of the room, looking buoyed up for the battle.

CHAPTER THIRTY-SIX

Cal and Tahir exchanged glances as they listened intently while Jack issued his instructions to the small team that he'd assembled for the job. The two of them had been called into Jack's office yesterday to be told they'd be part of a handpicked crew that was about to embark on a job that would put them up there among the big boys in the Casey gang. They weren't told the details but were informed it was a life-or-death job. If the team failed, it was likely that none of them would survive – including himself, Jack said gravely. Cal and Tahir had been buzzing when they left the office, feeling honoured to have been chosen. The last time they had been on any frontline operation was to grab Marty Kane's grandson from the kidnappers, but because of their antics afterwards up in Springburn, both of them had been put back on normal work, collecting money and well away from anything that involved violence. Now this was it. They'd been told they'd be away for a couple of days, and to pack light, and keep their mouths shut even to their loved ones. Cal had told his mum he was being sent to meet some people in Edinburgh, to keep her from worrying. He hadn't looked back when he left the house this morning after a long hug from her, but he knew she was watching him all the way out of the house and down the road where he was picked up in a car. It had occurred to him that he might not see her again, but it was only a fleeting thought. That would never happen, he told himself. Now Cal sat with his arms folded, his face impassive as Jack spoke. The other six men who were in the room were familiar faces to Cal, and he knew they were at least ten and more years older than him and Tahir. And he knew their reps as hard men. He was thrilled to be sitting among them, to be considered good enough to be one of the top crew.

'So,' Jack said. 'We are doing something tomorrow that, if it's successful – and it has to be – people will be talking about us for years to come.' He paused, glanced at the faces. 'If you come out of it alive, the rewards will be big time. Because you will be part of the gang who humped the Colombian cartel right up the arse.'

Cal glanced around the table and saw that the other guys were smiling a little, because Jack had a bit of a smile on himself. So he looked at Tahir and both raised their eyebrows, not quite knowing what else to do. They listened as Jack went on.

'The Colombians – that Pepe Rodriguez cunt who butchered O'Driscoll and who stole Marty Kane's wee boy – are going to get robbed. They're bringing in a massive shipment of coke, and we' – he took a long moment to look all of them in the eye – 'we are going to take it right out of their fucking hands. Just like that. And the real bonus is, not only do we get to fuck the Colombians, we get to fuck Frankie Martin, that traitor who betrayed us all. Because as you know, Frankie is in bed with that murdering mob of cunts now and he's trying to bring us all down. But this is the fight back he will never expect. None of them will expect us to take them on like this. This shipment lands at Portsmouth, but you won't move in there. It's all arranged. We have an inside track – that's all you need to know about that. But what Frankie and the Colombians don't know is that we are ahead of the game. We have a truck that is already following the shipment that gets to Portsmouth. So once it comes up the road to Manchester, that's when you lads will move into the back of it, and it will follow the truck to its destination. When it gets there, that's when we go into action.' He stopped for a moment and walked a few steps around the table. 'I won't be in the truck with you, but I'll be behind you in one of our cars. I'll have your backs. But I want you to have each other's backs at all times.' He looked at Cal and Tahir, then to the most senior of the squad. 'I brought Cal and Tahir in because they've proved beyond doubt that they are capable, after the way they handled the job on Marty's boy. But remember, they are young, and they take orders from you, Pete. Everyone in this room does. You are in charge. Cal, Tahir, you'll be with me in the car following.' He took a breath. 'Are we all clear here? Anyone want to ask questions?' Cal glanced at Tahir, then around the room, where everyone was silent. 'Okay. The cars are waiting outside to take you down south. You'll stay in a hotel tonight, so no fucking around. Get to bed and be sharp and ready by six in the morning. Got that?'

Everyone nodded and as Pete stood up, they got to their feet and filed after him out of the room.

Once they were well out of earshot of everyone else, Cal turned to Tahir.

'Shit just got real, man.'

'Yeah,' Tahir replied.

'You scared?' Cal asked.

'No.' Tahir shook his head, and looked back, his dark eyes a little expressionless. 'I have nothing to lose, man. I already lost everything I had.'

Cal slung his small rucksack over his shoulder as they headed for the waiting four-by-four.

'Don't talk like that, mate. You've got me. And your girl. Don't talk like that.'

'Yeah. You're right. C'mon. Let's go.' He looked Cal in the eye, then he walked ahead of him to the car.

*

Frankie Martin had wrestled half the night with the notion that had started to plague him so much, he'd decided to give it serious consideration. What if there was a way back to the Caseys? The answer was almost a hundred per cent no in his mind. But what if there was just the slightest snowball in hell's chance that he could get back in, if he brought this shipment of coke to Kerry Casey's table? Would she really knock back forty million quid's worth of coke because of the past? The answer that kept coming back to him was yes she would, and she'd hang his balls from the rafters just for asking to get back, after his treachery. Frankie, deep down, had never seen it as treachery though. To him, by setting up Mickey's execution he had done the Caseys a favour, and he knew that there were plenty in the organisation who would agree with him on that, but they would never utter it out loud. Mickey had become a liability with his big mouth and noising up all the big boys. Truth is, he'd been holding them back, and only Frankie could take them to where they should be. If it hadn't been for the complete tits up bloodbath at Mickey's funeral, Frankie would be riding high right now. And Rodriguez, even if he was in the picture, would not get the better of him. If only he could make Kerry see that. If only he could get her to see beyond losing her mother. Because if you were truly the head of a gangland family who lived the way the Caseys had lived, then you had to take hits like that – even though her mother's death had been extreme.

She'd have to get over it if she wanted to take the Caseys onto the great things she kept banging on about. Of course, he had to keep all these thoughts to himself, because if Rodriguez could read his mind he'd have been a dead man by now. But Frankie was here, in Glasgow, far from Rodriguez's eyes. This was his operation. And he could decide how to pull it. The other thought that had been gnawing away at him was the possibility of luring Kerry to him, with the promise of giving her everything, then bumping her off. He knew he was more than capable of doing that in cold fucking blood. That would get rid of her once and for all, and for the right money, everyone would eventually see that he was right; that he did the right thing for the family. For business. Everyone would benefit if they saw it that way and came over to his side. It had been nagging at him so much now, that his gut instinct was to act on it. Why not just phone the bitch?

CHAPTER THIRTY-SEVEN

Kerry and Danny had spent most of the morning talking to Billy Hill who had made the trip from London. Over the past couple of weeks, she and Danny felt they could put more trust in Billy, because he'd been backing them with bodies and security in the wake of the recent attacks. They'd decided to bring him in on the cocaine shipment, as there was no doubt that from London he would have access to bigger players who would be into buying big chunks of pure cocaine. One of the problems Kerry had noted since she took over was that they felt a little out of the loop on the buying front, because all of that side of the business had mostly been done by Mickey and Frankie. Now both of them were gone, she had to rely on Danny's limited contacts and also what Jack knew. But she'd never been in the same room with major dealers before, buying or selling. Billy Hill had, so it was good to have him onside.

When Billy arrived, the first thing he'd told them was that

he had heard that a massive shipment was heading to the UK. This meant someone, somewhere was talking. Danny assured Kerry that it was none of their crew but said that really anyone who Frankie had pulled in over the past few weeks from Dublin to Manchester could have been running off at the mouth. The way Frankie had been hauling in the numbers from Durkin's mob had to be risky, Danny insisted. He would be working with people now that he really couldn't be sure of, and when you did that you could never be certain that everyone around you was keeping their traps shut. There were bragging rights to be had by any toerag who could boast that he was part of something big that was about to happen, and that's how stuff like this leaked out. Billy said he'd heard from two different sources in London that the coke was coming in over the next few days. But nobody had any details.

'So,' Billy had said as they sat in the study, 'there is gossip, and that's not good. The best thing to do is to shift this shit as quick as possible.'

Kerry looked at him, a little bemused. 'And you don't think we've already thought about that, Billy?' She couldn't resist the dig, just in case it had slipped his mind that she was actually running the show here.

She quite liked Hill, because he'd never rubbed her up the wrong way, or given her the creeps the way Pat Durkin had when she'd encountered the pair of them that first time. Billy was old school and had known her dad, but that didn't mean he wasn't as slippery as they came. He hadn't become a multimillionaire with property in London and Spain, as well as a yacht sitting in Puerto Banus, without doing a few people over in his day. She knew all that, but still she felt they could do business. Since all the trouble started with Rodriguez, Billy had been frozen out, so he'd an axe to grind. But all of that aside, he wanted to do old-fashioned business with the Caseys, because he felt he could trust them.

'Well. You know what I mean, Kerry. When people on the ground are talking about a shipment coming in, then anything can happen. You never know whose palms are getting greased to give information out.'

'Well, we don't even know when or where it's coming into for sure,' Kerry lied a little. 'But we'll be on it, Billy, and we do really appreciate everything you've done for us recently.' Kerry wanted to dig at him again that he should remember that it was he and Durkin who had brought Pepe Rodriguez into their lives, and this was why they were all in this mess, but it would have been pointless. They had to work together now. 'We've been bombarded from all sides for the past few weeks here, and we need to fight back and hit hard. This shipment is perfect for us, if we can make it happen.'

'Great. I'll back you up on that, Kerry, all the way. Everything you need. But with that amount of cocaine, as I said, you need to move it fast. I've got three major players who will take that off your hands for big money. Cash money. No fucking ambushes or any of that shit. Because the boys I'm talking about know they will make a mint from pure coke.'

Kerry nodded and glanced at Danny.

'So what are you saying to us, Billy?' Danny chipped in. 'Because we're seriously not looking to scrap over this. But when we get it, and believe me we will get it, you're right. All we want to do is offload it for the right price. No fucking funny business. Because if that happens there will be blood all over the walls, and most of it won't be ours.'

Billy rubbed his chin then spread his hands. He looked from Danny to Kerry.

'Look. I can promise you this. I never felt good about what happened in the past with the Colombian, the way Durkin just went right over to his side. I didn't know when I met you that Rodriguez and the Durkin mob were going to come at you like this. I was never anywhere near that. I told you. The bastards froze me out, and I'm glad they did. But now, I'm here to make this happen. I'll throw as many people at this as you need, so that if it comes down to a fight, then your boys walk out of it on top. With the coke, and ultimately with the readies.'

Over lunch, Hill told them the names of the dealers he would shift the coke to. One was a Moroccan crook who had been in the UK for thirty years and was now the apparently respectable multimillionaire owner of a string of restaurants and property, but his organisation still dealt in heroin and cocaine, mostly smuggled in by mules. He was up for a third of the total, and would pay it on the day when it was handed over to him. The other two were big London dealers who had been buying coke from their own sources in Amsterdam and Spain over the years, but were prepared to pay top dollar for the purest of stuff. The money was there, he assured them. All she had to do was say yes, so that everything was ready to roll when the coke arrived. It all sounded good, but Danny looked a little uneasy. He sat forward, elbows on the table, and steepled his hands.

'So, Billy. Why are you suddenly prepared to push the boat right out and throw everything in to help the Caseys?' He paused for a moment, glanced at Kerry, then at Billy, who looked a little flushed. 'I'm only asking, mate, because I've always been a suspicious fucker all my life, as you well know. So, if you've got anything to say, then let's hear it now.'

The taut silence seemed to go on for ever, and Kerry saw Hill squirm a little. He picked up his glass of water, took a mouthful, then put it back down and leaned forward.

'Okay,' he said, spreading his hands. 'I'm going to be a hundred per cent honest with you guys.' He flicked a glance at Kerry. 'Your big hotel plans on the Costa del Sol. I really want a piece of the action there.'

'That's not on the table, Billy,' Kerry snapped.

Hill put his hands up.

'Hold on, Kerry. Hear me out. Please. Just for a moment. Look. I want to invest a good whack of my own dosh into your hotel. I mean it sounds, and from the plans looks, like such a massive, fantastic complex, it's something I really want to be a part of. The kudos of being involved in something like that. Know what I mean? It's right up my strasse.' He paused and took a breath. 'And I wouldn't just be investing money. I'd bring security, more bodies than you can come up with.' He turned to Danny. 'Mate. You know I'm respected in London and in Spain. You know all the faces who know me, and straight up, I can bring all that behind your crew. So if you ever needed additional muscle, it's there for you – anytime, anywhere. That's what I bring to the table – as well as money.'

For a long moment they sat saying nothing. Kerry could see by the look on Danny's face that Hill was talking a lot of sense. But she wasn't about to buckle to any agreements right now, in the middle of a major operation. She took a long breath and pushed out a sigh. Then she looked Hill in the eye.

'Okay, Billy. I'm not going to agree to anything right here and now. But I can promise you that we can talk about this. All right? That's as much as I'm saying. Once this is all over, we can get around the table and look at some facts and figures. Okay?'

Hill nodded eagerly. 'That'll do me, sweetheart.'

Kerry let the 'sweetheart' line go, because there were more important things on her mind right now. But she almost smiled to herself at his chutzpah.

By the time Hill and Danny left, Kerry felt exhausted, and at last, alone in her study, she put her feet up and her head back on the cushion and closed her eyes. She was drifting into a deep sleep when her mobile rang on the table beside her.

CHAPTER THIRTY-EIGHT

Kerry picked up her mobile with one eye open, but there was no number on the screen. She pressed it to her ear, eyes still closed.

'Hello?' she said, a little sleepy.

'Kerry. It's Frankie.'

Her eyes snapped open and she sat bolt upright on the chair.

'What the fuck!' she spat, standing up, feeling a rush of adrenalin.

'Kerry,' Frankie broke in. 'Look. I . . . I don't want to fight.'

'You don't want to fight?' Kerry heard her voice go up an octave. '*You* don't want to fight! Well that's good coming from a fucking traitor who betrayed the very people who gave you a home, a life, the family who gave you everything, you useless, lowlife bastard. *You* started this, you prick. *Your* thugs butchered John O'Driscoll – someone who had been a loyal friend to you and this family all his life. You took Marty Kane's grandson away. Marty Kane! And you and your scumbag mobsters have murdered the very people in this family who'd have stuck their necks out for you.' Kerry took a breath for a moment, because she could feel her voice shaking. Calm down. Think for a moment, she told herself. But just hearing Frankie's voice lit such a fuse of rage that if he stood in front of her right now, she could put a bullet in his chest. Calm down, she told herself again. You are in charge here. Frankie said nothing, and the silence seemed to go on for ever as Kerry choked back her anger. Then he spoke.

'I'm sorry, Kerry. What else can I say?'

Kerry let it hang for a moment. She was calmer now. She had to be. Because if this bastard was phoning her, it could only mean there was more treachery coming her way.

'What the fuck do you want?' Kerry's voice was softer, but firm.

Again, the long silence, and Kerry could feel her heartbeat.

'I want to come back.'

Kerry couldn't believe her ears. Frankie Martin wanted to come back. Christ almighty!

'Back where? What the Christ do you mean?'

'Back to the family, Kerry. I want to make amends. I *can* make amends. For everything.'

Kerry's voice was calm. 'You've either lost your mind, or you're out of your nut on drugs. Because let me tell you something, you piece of murdering shit. There is no way back for you. Not now. Not ever. Not anywhere in Glasgow, and never in this family. And if you ever set foot in this city and I hear about it, you will be a dead man before nightfall. You got that? Now I'm hanging up. Don't even think of ever approaching me like this again. Because if you do, I'll find you.' She paused. 'You're a dead man walking, Frankie. You have nowhere to run. There is no way back.'

'Kerry, please. Don't hang up. Listen. I can put forty million quid of pure Colombian cocaine on your table. For the Caseys. For them to sell. For your hotel and all the dreams you have. I can make that happen.'

Again, Kerry had to wait a few seconds to process this. There was no way in a million years a devious bastard like Frankie would make any kind of deal like this. It had to be some kind of con to lure her into a trap. Little did he know that he was about to be robbed of his forty million coke haul as soon as it hit the UK.

'Don't talk bullshit. You've got forty mil of coke? Yeah, in your dreams, you egomaniac. Nobody in their right mind would entrust you with forty *grand* of coke, never mind forty million. You know your problem? You've run out of places to go. And you're running out of time. You're like a cornered rat, desperately trying to free itself from the trap by gnawing its leg off. Too late. It's too late for you.'

'Kerry! Listen. It's on a ferry to the UK tonight. I promise you. I've been given it to sell for Rodriguez. He's put me in charge of the shipment. Pure cocaine. I've got buyers set up when it arrives. I'm ready to ditch everyone and let you have it. Free. It's yours.' He paused for a moment. 'It's going up to Manchester to a place I've arranged to offload it. But only you will know where that is if you agree to see me.'

This was as weird as it came. What the hell was he playing at? If Kerry didn't know that there *was* in fact a shipment of coke on its way here, she would have hung up, but the fact that she knew he was telling the truth meant she had to listen. She said nothing, and eventually he spoke.

'Kerry. I want to talk to you. Just you and me. Come down to Manchester. Then I'll hand over the cocaine to you. If you want to put a bullet in me, then you're free to do that. At least I'll know that I've done something for the Caseys to make up for everything I'm responsible for.' He paused. 'Or you can let me back in, and I'll do anything. Take a back seat. Run any kind of shit for you, anywhere you want.'

Kerry didn't know how to answer this. Whatever he was playing at, her gut told her it was a trap. But she needed to buy a little time. She had to tell Danny and Jack about it.

'Look. I need to go. I can't talk to you any more. You make me feel physically sick.'

'I understand that. I'll call you later tonight. You won't have much time. Once it's in the UK, it's gone before the day's over. And the Caseys will lose out on the biggest deal of their lives. Don't be the head of the family who loses a deal like this.'

Kerry allowed herself a slight smile as the line went dead. She noticed that her hands were trembling as she brought up Danny's number.

Jake Cahill had been surprised at the holes in Pepe Rodriguez's security. He'd been on his tail day and night for several days and the clown didn't know it. What Jake had seen though was that one of his main bodyguards was a major coke-head. He'd watched the fat little Colombian snort the stuff enough to convince him that he needed it to function. That meant he was wide open, there for the taking. What was it with these guys that they didn't get that? Now, he could see him bark out orders to the foot soldiers in the grounds surrounding the villa where Rodriguez and his henchmen were holed up. The house was a big ridiculously ornate job, with turrets and peaks and looked like something out of a Disney movie rather than the ancient castle it was trying to resemble. Tacky as hell, it sprawled across the barren hillside with nearby outhouses that, again to Jake's surprise, none of these idiots ever checked out. The dirt track led to a slightly bigger road in the direction of the motorway at the edge of Marbella. From where Jake sat on a hillside more than three hundred yards away, he was able to look through the telescopic sight on his high-powered rifle and see almost everything that went on in the house. He could watch Rodriguez swimming in the pool or relaxing on a sun lounger, and one afternoon he witnessed some kind of meeting or celebration, with various cars pulling up and half a dozen guys who looked Colombian piling out. They'd done all that Latino manly back-slapping and cheek-kissing stuff, and Jake had smiled to himself knowing that they'd stick a knife in each other's backs at the drop of a hat. They'd all sat around the table eating from a barbecue and drinking wine, then whisky. Later in the afternoon as the sun was going down, they were joined by five women who arrived in a limo to get the party started. Jake noticed that Rodriguez didn't seem to take part in any of the frolics with the women, and it was clear that the Colombian associates were invited for the afternoon as a privilege or treat. He did notice, however, that on some evenings a succession of skinny youths that just had to be rent boys had been brought in to the house, and then he watched them leave a couple of hours later. So Rodriguez liked boys, it seemed. Not that it would matter a damn to Jake, but bringing in rent boys left you wide open for all sorts of problems. You'd have to assume that they had been handpicked and well paid. But that wouldn't stop them from passing on information or details to any of Rodriguez's enemies, if the price was right. So Jake had just watched and let it all soak in, because the time was coming when he would do his job and move on. He was waiting for word from Danny that the shipment headed to the UK was in the hands of the Caseys. Only when that was done, would he strike. In truth, he could have put a bullet in Rodriguez at least three times a day right from where he was sitting with this assault rifle he'd bought for jobs like this. He got it from an ex-SAS sniper who'd taken out several Taliban soldiers from nearly three thousand yards away. When everything was weighed up, Jake had decided the best place for the execution was right here, where Rodriguez thought he was untouchable. But he was a patient man, and he was happy to bide his time.

Sharon listened to Kerry as she relayed the conversation she'd had with Frankie Martin. Like Kerry, she could scarcely believe her ears.

'It's a trap, Kerry. Pure and simple,' Sharon said. 'The minute you show your face, you'll be history. You know that, don't you?' She waited as Kerry didn't answer. 'You're not thinking of going, are you? Don't. You'll get killed.'

'I know what you're saying, Sharon,' Kerry said. 'I've had long discussions with Danny and Jack and we're pretty sure he's trying to lure me to my death. But Frankie of all people must know how risky that is. He must know that if I turned up to meet him, I'll have more security than the Queen ready to pounce. I just can't figure what he's playing at.'

Sharon couldn't figure it either. But she was one hundred

per cent sure that Frankie wasn't trying to buy his way back into the family. He had to know that as a traitor there was only one fate for him. And he would know that Kerry had plenty of old heads around her who would be advising her exactly that. So what was he playing at?

'I mean he's getting robbed anyway, Kerry. He's not daft. He'll know that if anyone has opened their mouth about the coke coming in, then there will be a posse in every possible stopping point to move in. He'll have considered that. Maybe he's thinking it's all too dangerous, and he's getting killed anyway, so his only hope is to buy himself back into your favour. But you and I both know that even if you did take him on, your boys would be queuing up to take a pop at him. He must know that too. I'd say the best thing to do is to hit Frankie while he's being robbed. It gets the bastard out of the way once and for all. And, by the way, if you need a hand with that, then I'm up for coming over.'

'I know you would be, Sharon. And I might even do it myself.'

'What? You're not going to meet him, are you?'

'Well. We've discussed it, and we might do it. At least we're going to listen to what his proposal is, where a meet would take place. Then we can have it well covered so that if I did turn up – just him and me as he is asking – I wouldn't be alone.'

'Kerry, it's well dodgy. Especially you going,' Sharon said, choosing her words carefully. 'I'm not saying you're not capable of it, because I know you are. But, well, things happen in situations like that. I mean, anything can happen. And . . . And . . . You're pregnant, Kerry. It's risky. Too risky, if you ask me.'

'I know. But I'm just saying it's on the table at the moment. That's all. And the plan would be that if I do meet him with his proposal then it's us who'll be ready for him. We can get rid of Frankie once and for all. But, Sharon, the thing with this operation is everything hinges on your man Vic keeping us informed. We've got troops down there ready to get into Jan's truck, but until we get a location where the drugs are being offloaded, then we can't do anything.'

'Yeah. We should hear tonight. They'll be on the boat. As soon as Vic phones, you'll know.'

'I hope he's all right. Did you expect him to call by now?'

'Well . . .' Sharon bit the inside of her cheek. She'd hoped he'd have called by now, and deep down she was beginning to get worried. 'I did, but I'm sure he will. Maybe he's waiting until he's got all the information he needs. I'll call you as soon as I hear.'

It was only a few minutes after she said goodbye to Kerry that Sharon's mobile rang again and she was surprised at how it made her jump. The last few weeks were taking their toll and she hadn't slept much over the past two nights. This was no way to live, and somewhere deep down there was a part of her that wished she could run a million miles away. But this was where she was now, and she would have the fight to get through it. She picked up the phone and a little jolt went through her gut when she heard Vic's voice.

'You all right, girl?' Vic's voice was soft.

'I am now,' Sharon said. 'I was worried.'

'Don't. It's okay. Listen. I haven't got long. Once we're off this boat, we're heading north. Place called Trafford Park industrial estate. Old yard. It's a warehouse. That's all I know at the moment. I'll text more when I can. The driver, Bobby, is as thick as pig shit, so he just does what he's told.'

'Great. I'll let Kerry know and we'll get on it.'

There was a silence and for a moment Sharon thought he'd hung up. Then he spoke.

'Sharon. Look. When this is all over, I want to talk about you and me.'

Sharon didn't know what to say. She hadn't even begun to consider if there was a future with Vic, given the way they led their lives. But she knew she had feelings for him, real feelings. Now was not the time to even talk about it though.

'Vic, let's put these next few days out of the way first. Honestly. That's all I want to think about.' She paused. 'But please be safe. I miss you.'

The line went dead.

CHAPTER THIRTY-NINE

By the time they were on the outskirts of Manchester, Kerry felt as though most of her life had been unfolding in front of her. There had been little conversation during the four-hour journey as the Range Rover swept them down the motorway. Most of the talking and planning had been done last night as Danny, Jack and she finally made the decision that she should take Frankie up on his offer of a meet. Like her, they felt it was a set-up, but if it was arranged and planned to the letter, they assured her she would be well covered. They knew that Frankie would know that too, so they doubted he'd just come walking in all guns blazing. This was an opportunity to take Frankie out in one go. What swung their decision was the call from Sharon to say that Vic had given her an exact location as to where the truck was coming with the cocaine. When Frankie had called Kerry again last night and she'd agreed to meet him, he'd told her the location. It matched the one

Vic gave, so they knew they were in business. What they had to do was to make sure there were plenty of bodies on hand nearby and if possible inside the warehouse by the time the shipment came. In theory, it sounded achievable. The locations matched. Frankie would be there, and so would the shipment. The Casey boys were following the shipment in their own transport, so by the time it was in the warehouse, Danny was sure their own troops would outnumber and outgun anything that Frankie could come up with. But it was still risky, Danny said. Very risky for Kerry to put herself on the frontline like this. He told her she had nothing to prove. She'd already put herself on the firing line the day Pepe Rodriguez came to kill her at the restaurant in Glasgow, and Danny told her that the story about how the Caseys foiled the attack from the Colombian cartel would enter into gangland folklore, as would she. Now, as Kerry sat in the back of the car, Danny's words 'gangland folklore' rang in her ears. She'd come such a long way from the high-powered lawyer who pitched up for her brother's funeral. And it had been an even longer way from the teary-eyed teenager who left Glasgow to go and live in Spain, feeling she'd been banished for something she hadn't done. Now she'd come full circle: she was back in Glasgow among the hoods and the killers, the blood of her enemies on her hands. But she didn't feel ashamed by it, or by the reality that she and her gang of criminals were about to rob a massive haul of pure cocaine and sell it for their own profit. And for some reason she couldn't even explain to herself, she wasn't afraid to walk into the meeting with Frankie, even though there was a chance she would not come out alive. She was calm and collected. This was her time.

The Range Rover pulled into the motorway café a few miles from the city where Danny had arranged to meet some of the other troops he'd sent down overnight. Kerry saw a couple of her boys from Glasgow standing around smoking next to three cars that were parked alongside each other. Big Pete got out of one of them when Kerry's car pulled up, and came across to greet them. Danny suggested they go inside for a coffee and the three of them, along with one of Pete's men, followed. Once they were sat down at a table far away from the other customers, Pete gave them the low-down on the warehouse. He pulled a piece of A4 paper and a pen from his top pocket and placed what looked like a plan on the table. Danny cocked his head to the side trying to look at it.

'I see you wanted to be an architect at school, Pete,' he chuckled. 'What happened? Did your pencil break?'

Pete laughed. 'Aye, very good, Danny. I'm drawing what I see here, and I think this is quite good.' He grinned. 'I'm a great believer in putting things down on paper so we can see where we are.'

'It's good,' Kerry said, smiling. 'So is there much going on around it? I mean in the industrial estate? Is it busy?'

'Well. It was nearly four in the morning when we got to the place to have a look, but not much to see. As we were leaving there were a few cars going in and out, but all down at the other end.' He marked it on the paper, with an arrow pointing away from the building he'd drawn. 'Down here is the entrance to the estate. It looks like a lot of the units are either shut down or just storage places. I mean, there's no big working warehouses with trucks going in and out, probably the way it was a few years ago. And the warehouse where we're going looks more for storage than anything. It was locked and shuttered. But of course we got in, had a good look around, and then put everything back in its place.' He stopped, took a breath, then looked from Kerry to Danny. 'But I did leave a couple of our best shooters in there. Don't worry, they're well hidden, and they're used to sitting on their arses for hours on end waiting for a target. Ex-army sniper boys. They know how to do this stuff. They'll only come out when the shit hits the fan. Is that all right?'

Danny pursed his lips a little.

'Great. But are you absolutely sure your boys are nowhere to be seen? Because Frankie will have a team getting in there just about now. In fact I'm surprised there was nobody down there last night to keep a watch on the place. That's a big fuck-up on his part. He knows this shipment is coming in there today, so it would have been smart to have the place watertight to make sure people like us or anyone else isn't already there as a reception party when it arrives. What the hell was he thinking about?'

Kerry looked at Danny.

'Maybe he's just saying this is the place, and he's about to phone and change it at the last minute. Maybe he's trying to second-guess that we would get our own people in the place and ready.'

Pete shook his head. 'Kerry, I've worked with Frankie. He's a slick bastard when it comes to a lot of stuff. I mean, he looks the part and talks a good game, but he's not as clever as he thinks he is. Never has been. If it hadn't been for your Mickey, Frankie would not have got as big as he is.'

Kerry wasn't so sure about that, but she didn't want to get into a discussion. All they could do was deal with what was in front of them. And unless Frankie phoned to change the venue, then this was it.

Danny looked down at the paper again.

'Right. So on the main drag here. We can be close enough to get in there smartish once the truck is in?'

'Yep.' Pete looked at Kerry. 'But there's another truck, isn't there, with our boys in it. It's going to be coming into the estate looking as though it's going to some other building, isn't it?'

'Yeah,' Kerry said, looking at Danny. 'Are we well covered then?'

Danny nodded slowly. 'As much as we can be without getting noticed.' He looked at Kerry. 'Are you okay?'

'I'm fine,' Kerry said. 'I just want to get it done.'

For a moment nobody spoke, then Pete got up.

'I'll go and get ourselves sorted then.' He turned to Kerry. 'You'll be all right, Kerry. The boys I've got in there are top hands. Don't worry.'

'I'm not worried,' Kerry said, and she meant it.

Jumbo Keane had listened quietly, his face impassive as his boys relayed to him what they'd seen at the warehouse last night. The place had been recced a couple of days ago and there was never any movement around it, and since Evans said he wasn't going to be there, Jumbo had expected it to be quiet. But two of his boys had seen some movement there in the early hours of this morning. There had been a couple of cars parked in one of the neighbouring buildings, and they'd seen at least three men on the prowl. That was as much as they could say, as there was no sign that anyone had broken into the building the last time they looked. They hadn't been in there themselves, as Jumbo decided not to do that in case they aroused suspicion. But the fact that there had been some activity around the place disturbed him. It could mean that Frankie was double-crossing him, that he was planning to ambush him knowing he would be carrying a huge stash of cash on him in the suitcases that were now locked and secured in the boot of his Mercedes outside, with two men standing guard. Frankie was sly enough to try that caper, Jumbo thought, but was he really brave enough, or stupid enough? Jumbo's men would hunt him down if he double-crossed them. But it could also mean that some other bastard could be planning to ambush the shipment. Someone who knew through the grapevine that pure cocaine was coming into this warehouse, and was hard enough to try, could set up their own ambush. Jumbo was only in for twenty million of this coke, so other dealers must have been primed by Frankie, but it would be stupid to have them all coming to the one place, like some kind of fucking fire sale. No. The activity meant danger, so he was gearing his men up for a fight.

Cal had been awake since six in the morning with only a few hours' sleep, but he was buzzing. He sat in the back of the Mercedes along with Tahir and listened as Jack spoke to Danny on his mobile. Along with the other eight men who had travelled down to Manchester last night, they'd stayed in a hotel. He'd been thrilled to be sitting at the same table with guys he knew were considered among the most feared hard men in Glasgow. They had all been given their weapons and ammunition this morning, and now the gun inside his jacket pocket made him feel powerful and part of something big. From what he could gather as Jack spoke, there were already people inside the building waiting. But he'd watched early this morning as the big truck that had been following the shipment pulled into a transport café off the motorway and their boys got into the back of it. Cal had been outside smoking a cigarette with Tahir and he'd exchanged glances with Tahir at that point, and knew they were both thinking the same thing – that Tahir's family had perished in the back of a truck just like that. They didn't say anything, but Cal just gave his arm a friendly squeeze as he stubbed out his fag end on the ground and suggested they go back inside and join Jack. The truck with the cocaine in it was parked at the other side of the car park, so when it left, the truck carrying their boys would go too. And Cal, Tahir and Jack's car would follow at a discreet distance.

Frankie Martin got out of the car he was being driven in as it pulled to a halt outside the warehouse. Two of his men in the car behind got out first and he saw them do a quick scan of the area before he approached the building. Frankie tossed one of the guys the key to the padlock, and he watched as the shutters noisily went up. He let the guards go inside first and hit the lights, then after a few moments they came out and told him it was clear. Frankie looked at his watch. His last conversation with Kerry Casey had been short and to the point. He told her the shipment would be here in twenty minutes, and he wanted to talk to her before it arrived. She told him she was on her way. This was the biggest gamble of his life. There was no way that Kerry Casey was coming here to do business with the man who had her brother killed and who was responsible for the carnage that killed her mother. Kerry was coming here to kill him. It came down to that. It was him or her. He had plenty of bodies standing by, and he could hear the engines of a couple more cars arriving. It would be like Fort Knox by the time Kerry arrived.

CHAPTER FORTY

'Looks like Frankie hasn't come to the party alone,' Danny said as they drove into the industrial estate and saw the fleet of cars in the distance. 'If that's the place at the end there, then he's mob-handed.'

'So are we,' Kerry said, her voice betraying the little tweak of angst lashing across her gut. 'Where will our boys be, Danny?'

'Nearby. They'll have clocked this lot by now. They'll be prepared.' Danny turned around to face her. 'Are you all right, Kerry? Seriously?'

Kerry looked him in the eye.

'I'm all right, Danny. I'm ready.'

She slipped her hand into the pocket of her jacket and touched the small pistol. It was the same gun Jack had given her the day she went to meet Pepe Rodriguez. She had used it then, and she would use it today. She just hoped her shot was more accurate this time.

As the car pulled up, one of the security guards looked at her, then went inside.

'Do you think they'll frisk me?'

'Don't know,' Danny said. 'Normally they would. But the way Frankie's been talking to you, he said you'd be free to put a bullet in him. So he might show some faith and not frisk you if he thinks there is any chance you're going to invite him back in. He's that fucking naive.'

'What if they do frisk me?'

'Then you hand it over, and say what the fuck did they expect? A bunch of red roses?' Danny smiled. 'You'll be fine. Our boys will be watching you every step of the way, and the rest of them will be here shortly.' He glanced at the driver. 'When you get out, we'll turn the car around and drive twenty yards down the road, then turn back to face here. So they'll think we're just waiting for you.'

Kerry pushed back her hair and opened the rear door. She stepped outside and stood up, squared her shoulders. She glanced one last time at Danny and gave him a tight smile. She took a few steps away from the car, as Frankie Martin appeared from the darkness into the huge doorway. He stood tall, the way he always did, well dressed, his hair slicked back like a businessman about to do a deal. Or, Kerry thought, it was a smart suit to get buried in. He didn't smile and his face gave away no impression of what was going on in his head. He stepped forward.

'Kerry,' he said as they were only a couple of steps away from each other. 'Good to see you.'

Kerry didn't answer. She looked him in the eye, a cold rage inside. This was the man who had changed her life for ever.

For a long moment they said nothing, and the bodyguard who had come in with her turned and left. As they stood in the silence, Kerry couldn't help her eyes quickly scanning the length and breadth of the warehouse. She wondered where Pete's guys were. Hopefully not lying somewhere with their throats cut. She could see Frankie's lean jaw twitch a little.

'Just you and me, Kerry.'

Kerry nodded. 'Yeah. You and me, Frankie.'

'It shouldn't have come to this. It really shouldn't have.'

Kerry pushed out a sigh, but she felt calm.

'Don't you think it's a little late to be raking up the ashes? Look. You know what you did. You can't change the past any more than I can.' She paused, looked him in the eye. 'What's donc is done.'

There was a flicker of surprise in Frankie's eyes. He hadn't been expecting her to be this agreeable. For a moment he said nothing. Then he managed to pull an expression that looked hurt and tormented.

'I'm so sorry for everything, Kerry. I loved your Mickey like a brother, and I worshipped your mother. I'll never forgive myself for what happened to her. I hope that one day you'll understand that anything I did, I did for the good of the Caseys. For the future. So that we could have everything.'

'With you running the show,' Kerry said. She felt she had to put at least a dig in or he wouldn't believe her act.

'Yes. That's right. With me in charge of the family. I know what's good for the Caseys and I know how to make them bigger than anything they ever dreamed of. More than your father's dreams, and more than yours.'

Kerry nodded and sighed. 'Yeah. With Pepe Rodriguez and the Colombian cartel pulling all your strings, Frankie.'

His eyes narrowed.

'For the moment it seems that way. But in time, we can take Rodriguez down too. He's not untouchable.'

'I think we've already proved that, Frankie. He'll not be putting his last trip to Glasgow on TripAdvisor.' Kerry allowed herself a wry smile.

Frankie smiled and nodded.

'Aye. You're right about that. But that just proved that he can be beaten.' He paused, then put his hand in the pocket of his suit jacket. 'And I'm the man to do it, Kerry. For the Caseys.'

Kerry watched as he suddenly produced a gun from his pocket. He pointed it at her, and she felt her legs go a little weak. Then it felt like something snapped inside her head. She took a breath and looked him in the eye.

'You'll need to kill a lot more than me, Frankie. Are you

really that stupid?' She looked over Frankie's shoulder to see the two guards emerging from behind a pillar, rifles pointing at Frankie.

'Don't be a bigger dick than you already are,' one of them piped up.

As he turned around swiftly then back at her, she could see the red rising in his neck and his eyes blazing. He lurched forward and grabbed hold of her and put the gun to her head.

'You shoot, she gets it.'

Frankie dragged her backwards and Kerry felt powerless as she saw the two men still with the rifles pointed at him. But she knew they couldn't shoot or they might hit her, and the cold metal of Frankie's gun dug into her temple. Suddenly there came the sound of a truck outside, and rapid gunfire as though it was hitting something metal. Frankie turned and fired at the truck, but the gunmen sent back two bullets and he fell to the ground, his arm still around Kerry's neck. She could see blood pumping out of his thigh and also dripping from his hand. Kerry wriggled her free hand into her pocket and pulled out her gun, and in one movement she pressed it against his stomach and pulled the trigger.

'Fuck you, Frankie. Fuck you straight to hell,' Kerry spat.

She heard the dull thunk of power and Frankie went limp, his arms let her go, and she pulled herself free. She rolled over and got up on her elbow, still with the gun in her hand. She could see the blood pouring out of Frankie's stomach and seeping around him. And his face, wet with sweat and pale as the life drained out of him. And somewhere in that handsome face was the young man she'd known as she grew up. For a fleeting second she felt a little choked that it had come to this. But this was a war that Frankie had brought to her family. She had never wanted to be part of the bloodshed, but she had to fight back. He opened his mouth to speak but nothing came out, and she looked him in the eye and shook her head so it would be the last thing he saw before he died. Then Kerry slowly got up and carefully went outside.

It was chaos. There were people shooting at each other, and she crouched down behind the wheel of the truck to see shots flying everywhere, then car loads of more gunmen pull up. Who the hell were they? Not hers. She could see Danny shooting and someone, who by description might be Vic, coming out of the big truck with a rifle. He was shooting on their side so it must be Vic. She saw Cal, firing at guys who dropped, and Tahir too, both of them looking expert and determined . . . Then she heard a shout, 'Kerry! Over here!' It was the driver of her car. But as she crouched to run over, suddenly she felt something knock her off her feet. She caught her breath then put her hand to her abdomen. Blood. Oh Christ, no! Big Pete dived over, picked her up and rushed her into the car. Danny came racing over.

'Aw fuck, Kerry!' He bent over to touch her and saw the flow of blood. 'Fuck!'

'Danny. Please. Get me an ambulance. I . . . I'm pregnant.'

Danny's face was white with shock as he turned to Cal. 'Cal! Get an ambulance! Hurry!'

As Kerry was passing out, she heard Cal shouting in his phone that he was somewhere in Manchester in an industrial estate, trying to give instructions and directions. She lay bleeding, feeling no physical pain, only the pain of knowing that there was a baby in there and so much blood that it had to be dead.

CHAPTER FORTY-ONE

Sharon was on her way back from a meeting with the architects and project manager of the hotel complex. She'd wanted to cancel the meeting, as she was waiting by her phone for any word from Kerry, or Vic, or anyone to tell her what had happened. The last she'd spoken to Kerry was yesterday and she'd told her she was going to meet with Frankie at the warehouse. If Vic had called her, she'd have alerted him to watch out for her if there was a bloody battle. But he hadn't called. And as she saw on her watch it was almost one in the afternoon she assumed that whatever went down at the warehouse had to be over by now. Not hearing anything from anyone could only be a bad thing. But as she couldn't put the meeting off, she'd had to go, and now as she was on her way back to her villa, she could see the driver was weaving in and out of traffic.

'What's the matter?' Sharon asked.

'Some pricks in a Jeep behind me right up my arse. Every time I move lanes, they move.'

Sharon's bodyguard in the passenger seat adjusted the wing mirror so he could see better.

'It's a Spanish reg. Looks like a couple of workmen. But it could be anyone. I don't like this.' He turned to face Sharon. 'Let's take the next slip road, go through the towns instead of staying on the motorway.'

'You think it's a threat?' Sharon asked.

'I don't want to take any chances,' he replied. He took his pistol out of his holster and held it. 'Next slip road, Ernie.'

The driver nodded, and took the next cut-off. As he did, he checked his rear-view mirror.

'Bastards still behind us.'

'Then lose them, Ernie. Soon as we get to the main road.'

'I will.'

There were a few more vehicles taking the slip road together, so they had to slow down. Then, at the junction, as they were about to pull away, the car was suddenly thrown forward. It shuddered to a halt as it hit the high kerb.

'Fuck!' Ernie said. 'Cunts have rammed us.' He tried to turn the wheel and reverse, but the wheel was stuck on the kerb. 'Fuck. I can't get it moving.'

'Christ!' Sharon said, suddenly afraid.

There was the sound of an engine revving, and the jolt as they were rammed again.

'Fuckin' hell!' Ernie's face went white. He reached into his waist and pulled out a gun. 'They're coming at us. Cunts are armed.'

The bodyguard was out of his seatbelt and about to open the door.

'Get down, Sharon! Lie down on the seat. Ernie! Go out your door and I'll go out of mine. Just come out firing.'

Then came the sound of rapid gunfire. Sharon covered her head with her hands as the rear window shattered, showering her with shards of glass. She pulled her own gun out of her handbag and cocked it. From the corner of her eye she could see her bodyguard crouching against the door, firing off shots, diving to the ground. Ernie was also firing. But then the groan, as he fell to the ground.

'Shit. Ernie's been hit. Fuck! Stay there, Sharon.'

She lay motionless, terrified, as more shots peppered the car, and the men were obviously getting closer. There was only the bodyguard now, and her. She had to do something. She wriggled up and across the seat into the front, and slipped out. She landed on top of Ernie. He was still breathing, but with blood pouring from a shoulder wound. She lay on the ground almost under the car. Then she could hear voices in Spanish talking and laughing as they kept shooting. She crouched along the side of the car until she could see the three men coming towards them firing wildly. She aimed her gun, fired it, and one of them fell down, clutching his leg. She lay back down on the ground.

'Sharon? You all right? You should have stayed in the car.'

'No fucking way am I going to lie there and die.'

She heard the bodyguard fire off several more shots, but then rapid gunfire and he too was hit.

'Bill . . . You been hit?'

There was no answer. She crawled to the back of the car, but she could see nobody except the man she had hit. Then a voice behind her and her blood ran cold.

'Oi, señora! Que pasa?'

She turned her head slowly, her whole body trembling as she looked up to see the dishevelled skinny figure standing over her, a cigarette dangling from his lip, and the rifle pointed at her as though he had just found his prey. A second later, a fat little guy joined him with a smile on his face.

'Hola guapa!' He put his hand out for the gun. 'Don't be a stupid *coño*, lady.'

Sharon looked up at him, but still held the gun tightly, pointing it at them. If she fired at one of them she'd also be dead before they hit the ground. She thought of Tony. How would they tell him?

She held her hand out.

'Fuck you!'

The men looked at each other and sniggered. The skinny one jerked his head to the fat man, and he stepped forward and bent to pick her up. As he did, she managed to knee him in the groin, and he let out a gasp. Then she felt the sharp pain of a fist on her cheek.

'Don't fight, woman. You not win.'

She let herself go limp as he carried her across to the Jeep and bundled her into the boot, then tied her hands and feet. She lay on the smelly metal floor as they slammed the doors shut and locked them.

Jake Cahill had got the call he'd been waiting for. It was all over in Manchester. Kerry had been shot, and rushed to hospital. Two of their men were wounded, but they'd lost nobody. Frankie Martin was dead. There was some story about a shoot-out with a guy called Jumbo Keane, who Jake had heard of, but none of that was important right now. Because he had been given the green light to take Pepe Rodriguez out whenever he wanted. And now was as good as it was going to get.

Jake had set up his rifle on the tripod aimed down at the villa. He'd been watching with his binoculars as the Jeep sped up the main road then onto the dirt track sending up swirling clouds of dust. As it went through the gates of the villa, from his vantage point, he could see it pull up in the yard. Then from the patio door, Pepe Rodriguez emerged and strolled across to the car. Two of the bodyguards joined him. Jake watched as they opened the tailgate. Something was going on here. They were dragging a body out of the boot. Jake peered through the binoculars. It was a woman. He stood up. 'Fuck me,' he said aloud. It was Sharon. He could see her face, red and swollen, and she stood propped up by the fat bodyguard who he'd seen slapping people around. He watched as Pepe Rodriguez stood looking at her. Now, Jake thought, getting down on the ground. It had to be now. He crawled over to his rifle, and looked down the sight. He slowed down his breath and his heartbeat as he concentrated, making the adjustments, watching the scope as it centred on the target's chest. Rodriguez was smiling. He was saying something to Sharon who was standing there looking limp and defenceless. Jake breathed gently as his finger brushed on the trigger. He could see that Rodriguez was still laughing. Then he fired. It took three seconds for the bullet to arrive and wipe the smile off his face, then one second for him to fall down with the blood pumping out like a well. All the henchmen stood motionless, glancing around, terrified, waiting for the ambush. They dumped Sharon on the ground and ran. Jake watched as they piled into cars and four-by-fours and sped out of the gates of the villa then down the dirt track and disappeared in clouds of dust. Jake kept looking down the scope, and he saw Sharon turn over and crawl on her stomach the couple of yards across to where Rodriguez lay motionless. Then he watched as she quickly grabbed the pistol from his holster and got up onto her knees. Suddenly he saw Rodriguez's arm flinch a little and his head move. Bastard should be dead by now, Jake thought, as he raised the rifle and placed his finger over the trigger, ready to pull. Then he saw Sharon point the gun to the Colombian's head. She fired as Jake was about to pull the trigger. He watched as Rodriguez's head jerked with the force of the bullet at such close range. Job done. Jake picked up his gun and marched down the hill-side towards the villa, like a triumphant hunter who'd had a good day.

CHAPTER FORTY-TWO

In Kerry's dream she had been swimming with a little baby in her arms, splashes of water on the child's face, holding it close, the baby's arms tight around her neck. Then the water began to swirl and drag them under, and the baby's arms got tighter and tighter as the water dragged at it. Then the little child's hands let go and Kerry watched as she disappeared under the water, her big frightened eyes looking at her, her little chubby hand outstretched. Kerry could feel her chest bursting and then a warm hand on her cheek telling her everything was all right. She heard herself scream, 'My baby! My baby!'

'Sssh, now, Kerry,' the voice said.

Kerry was afraid to open her eyes. When she did, she could see a nurse in uniform, gentle, kind eyes.

'It's okay, Kerry. Your baby is fine.'

For a moment, Kerry thought she was still dreaming. She looked at the nurse and tried to speak, her mouth moving but no sound.

'Yes,' the nurse nodded. 'Your baby is fine. You're going to be all right now.'

The floodgates opened. Kerry felt warm tears spill out of her eyes and down her cheeks onto her neck as she sobbed. Everything came rushing back to her: the warehouse, Frankie, the chaos and mayhem of the shoot-out. Someone had shot her and she'd survived. Her baby had survived. Then she opened her eyes fully and thought she could see Vinny in the doorway, but she must have fallen into a dream again, for it couldn't be Vinny. Not here, wherever she was. She closed her eyes, and then opened them again, as the nurse turned around and smiled to him.

'Are you the father?' she said innocently.

'I . . . I . . .'

'Vinny,' Kerry said through tears. 'Oh, Vinny, I'm so sorry.'

Vinny stood for a long moment, his face shocked, broken, torn. Then the nurse realised she'd made a mistake to assume.

'Sorry,' she said. 'I'll leave you two alone.'

Vinny took a few steps towards the bed, his eyes locked on Kerry.

'Oh, Kerry! I'm so sorry!'

'You went away, Vinny. What was I to think?'

'I was working, Kerry. Undercover. I couldn't even tell you I was going.'

Kerry sniffed. They looked at each other and he reached

out and held her hand, then bent down to kiss her cheek and she felt the softness of his hair on her lips. She thought she could hear him sniff too, and he stayed like that for a long time. Then he broke away, his eyes moist.

'Is it my baby, Kerry? It has to be.'

Kerry couldn't speak. She nodded, sniffing.

'Oh Christ, Kerry!'

A doctor appeared at the doorway.

'You should be resting. I said no visitors, only close family.'

'I'm the father,' Vinny mumbled.

'Oh. I see. Well I'm glad to tell you that your baby is a fighter. Kerry lost a lot of blood yesterday and she's lucky to be alive, never mind baby too. So it's a battler too. But there's been a trauma and she needs complete rest to recover. We had to remove a bullet from Kerry's stomach.'

Vinny nodded, awkward, shifting on his feet. The doctor was looking at him as though he was some thug.

'When can I go home?' Kerry managed to mutter.

'If you're fit enough we can airlift you to Scotland tomorrow to a hospital there.'

'Thanks,' she murmured.

The doctor left, and she turned to Vinny. 'How did you get here?'

'I was following a villain called Jumbo Keane. We've been tracking his mob for months while he's been in jail. Then he got out and word came through that he was onto a big deal. Pure cocaine coming in from a Colombian cartel. We've been watching and tracking Pepe Rodriguez for weeks too, months actually, but more in recent weeks. We knew Frankie was in with that mob, but we lost his trail a few days ago. It was just one or two big mouths who told us this stuff was coming in. So we were a bit behind.'

Kerry said nothing. She hadn't spoken to anyone yet, but she guessed that since Vinny hadn't mentioned Danny or arrests to her, that perhaps they'd all got away before the cops came. She wondered about the cocaine and hated herself for even thinking that, when she should be lying here grateful that her baby was saved and that she was still alive.

'I take it you know what I'm talking about, Kerry.'

Kerry closed her eyes and shook her head.

'Jesus Christ, Vinny. Can you just not be a cop for one minute? I don't know what you're talking about.'

'We didn't get the coke anyway. But somebody did. So we don't know if it was Jumbo's mob, some other guys who ambushed it, or the Caseys.'

'I'm tired, Vinny. Can we talk tomorrow? Please. I might be getting home.'

Vinny smiled. 'I'm never going to win with you, Kerry, am I? But you're having my baby, so don't shut me out.'

Kerry didn't answer. She lay back on the pillow and closed her eyes.

'Later, Vinny. I need to sleep.'

Vinny kissed her again, then he left without another

word. She sank back relieved, his words, 'don't shut me out', ringing in her ears. She was so delighted to see him and so glad he didn't baulk that she was having his baby, even though she didn't know how they could go forward together. But somewhere in all those emotions, she was desperate to find out if the Caseys got the cocaine. The cops didn't seem to have it, so either it had been hijacked by some other crew, or the Caseys had it. She closed her eyes. That was for another day. Right now she was tired and safe, and overwhelmed with sheer love for the little baby inside her that had survived against the odds.

ACKNOWLEDGEMENTS

And finally, it's that time where I'm delighted to thank everyone who supports me, from my readers, to close friends and family.

My sister Sadie, is my constant friend and support in every step of each novel. Also her family: Matt, Katrina, Matthew and Christopher, who listen and often inspire my thoughts. Paul, who keeps my techno stuff and website up and running. My brother Des and his family. And Connor, who always eagerly awaits the next book!

My cousins, the Motherwell Smiths, and the Timmonses for their love and laughter, as well as Alice and Debbie and all their family in London for their hospitality.

My cousins Annmarie and Anne for great times and chats with the kids. And also, Helen and Irene.

I'm lucky to have such great friends in Mags, Eileen, Liz, Annie, Mary, Phil, and journalist friends: Simon, Lynn, Annie, Mark, Maureen, Keith, Ross, and Thomas in Australia.

Also, Helen and Bruce, Mairi, Barbara, Jan, Donna, Louise, Gordon and Janetta, Brian, Jimmy, Ian, David, Ronnie, Ramsay, and the eternal sailor Brian Steel.

In Ireland, I'm grateful to Mary and Paud, for their support.

And in La Cala, Yvonne, Mara, Wendy, Jean, Maggie, Sarah and Fran, Lillias and Natalie – all of them who help promote my books on the Costa del Sol.

Thanks also to my publisher Jane Wood for her wonderful support, and my editor Therese Keating for her fantastic, meticulous editing job. Also Olivia Mead in publicity, and all the top team at Quercus who are the best.

And of course, the growing army of readers I'm so privileged to have. If it wasn't for them, I wouldn't be writing this.